I0678037

WILDE STORIES

2018

Wilde Stories
2018

The Year's Best Gay Speculative Fiction

edited by Steve Berman

Lethe Press
Amherst, Massachusetts

Wilde Stories 2018: The Year's Best Gay Speculative Fiction
Copyright © 2018 Steve Berman. ALL RIGHTS RESERVED. No part of this work
may be reproduced or utilized in any form or by any means, electronic or
mechanical, including photocopying, microfilm, and recording, or by any
information storage and retrieval system, without permission in writing from
the publisher.

Published in 2018 by Lethe Press, Inc.
6 University Drive • Suite 206 / PMB #223
Amherst, MA 01002 USA
www.lethepressbooks.com • lethepress@aol.com
ISBN: 978-1-59021-319-3 / 1-59021-319-X

The stories in this volume are works of fiction. Names, characters, places, and
incidents are products of the authors' imaginations or are used fictiously. Any
resemblance to actual events or locales or persons, living or dead, is entirely
coincidental.

"Some Kind of Wonderland" copyright © 2017 Richard Bowes, first appeared in
Mad Hatters and March Hares (ed. by Ellen Datlow, Tor Books) / "The Library
of Lost Things" copyright © 2017 Matthew Bright, first appeared at Tor.com,
August 23, 2017 / "Salamander Six-Guns" copyright © 2017 Martin Cahill,
first appeared in *Shimmer* #38 / "Serving Fish" copyright © 2017 Christopher
Caldwell, first appeared in *People of Color Take over Fantastic Stories of the
Imagination* (ed. by Nisi Shawl, Positronic Publishing) / "Making the Magic
Lightning Strike Me" copyright © 2017 John Chu, first appeared in *Uncanny
Magazine* #16 / "A Bouquet of Wonder and Marvel" copyright © 2017 Sean
Eads, first appeared in *Georgetown Haunts and Mysteries* (ed. by Jeanne C. Stein
& Joshua Viola, Hex Publishers) / "Uncanny Valley" copyright © 2017 Greg
Egan, first appeared at Tor.com, August 9, 2017 / "Ghost Sex" copyright © 2017
Joseph Keckler, first appeared in *Dragon at the Edge of a Flat World* (Turtle Point
Press) / "The Summer Mask" copyright © 2017 Karin Lowachee, first appeared
in *Nightmare Magazine*, #62 / "Pan and Hook" copyright © 2017 Adam
McOmber, first appeared in *Vestiges:Mimesis*, Winter 2017 / "The Future of
Hunger in the Age of Programmable Matter" copyright © 2017 Sam J. Miller,
first appeared at Tor.com, October 18, 2017 / "The Secret of Flight" copyright
© 2017 A.C. Wise, first appeared in *Black Feather* (ed. by Ellen Datlow, Pegasus
Books) / "Love Pressed in Vinyl" copyright © 2017 Devon Wong, first appeared
in *Strange Horizons*, April 3, 2017 / "Cracks" copyright © 2017 Xen, first
appeared in *FIYAH Literary Magazine*, #3

Set in Garamond, Xan, Bodoni, and Trebuchet.
Interior design: Alex Jeffers.
Cover design: Inkspiral Design.

Contents

GHOST SEX 1
Joseph Keckler
SERVING FISH 7
Christopher Caldwell
SOME KIND OF WONDERLAND 23
Richard Bowes
PAN AND HOOK 41
Adam McOmber
THE SUMMER MASK...47
Karin Lowachee
THE LIBRARY OF LOST THINGS...61
Matthew Bright
MAKING THE MAGIC LIGHTNING STRIKE ME.............................79
John Chu
SALAMANDER SIX-GUNS 95
Martin Cahill
CRACKS 113
Xen
THE FUTURE OF HUNGER IN THE AGE
OF PROGRAMMABLE MATTER 155
Sam J. Miller
UNCANNY VALLEY 173
Greg Egan
LOVE PRESSED IN VINYL 209
Devon Wong
THERE USED TO BE OLIVE TREES...225
Rich Larson
THE SECRET OF FLIGHT...249
A.C. Wise
A BOUQUET OF WONDER AND MARVEL.....................................267
Sean Eads
AFTERWORD 285
Steve Berman

Ghost Sex

Joseph Keckler

I AM NOT SAYING I BELIEVE IN GHOSTS AT ALL, BUT I did have sex with one.

I never saw it but I did feel that cold feeling that you feel, supposedly, when a supernatural presence enters the room. I had only felt this cold feeling two other times in my life. Once when my friend Thain—who aspires to be a cult leader one day, by the way—took me to a séance in the Bronx and people were huddled into a side room at a botánica. One occult practitioner was waving some branches around and mumbling, trying to summon an otherworldly entity, and when I entered everyone looked at me and pointed and shouted *"Brujo! Brujo!"* announcing that I was a witch—even though I don't know the first thing about magic and what have you. But then, a few moments later: *whoosh*, a cold air overtook the room and the hairs on my forearm stood on end. Their spirit had apparently arrived.

The other time was when I'd been enlisted to portray the New York Dolls guitarist Johnny Thunders in the reading of a play. I began studying videos of him intently on YouTube, trying to imitate him and become him and then again, *whoosh*—my living room became alive with a chill and I was left to assume that the spirit of Johnny Thunders was suddenly near. I am not sure I did a good

1

job acting as Johnny in the presentation later that week, but I am inclined to suspect he was keeping tabs on me from the beyond.

Anyway, back to the story at hand. I was staying at an art colony that is famously haunted—if one believes in that sort of thing. Its lore involves fires, ailments, and the deaths of children whose graves are still scattered across the property. The place certainly gives off a gothic vibe. For instance, there's a Victorian mansion there where legend has it Truman Capote used to hold court from a strange velvet throne. Earlier that week I had been singing Schubert's "Litanei" in the music room of the mansion and a bat flew in and began circling me. I just kept singing: *and those who never smiled in the sun, but under the moon waited on thorns to see God, face to face in the pure light of heaven, all souls, rest in peace.* (In German, of course.) Round and round went the bat as the other artists snickered and cowered in the pews. I didn't even duck as it grazed my hair.

I sang in the mansion but I wasn't sleeping there. I had been put up in one of the satellite buildings, a partly subterranean apartment in a house. Dank but charming, it had linoleum floors and faced a distant wall of trees—it felt like the home of some old relative I'd visited in my childhood. A frazzled playwright warned me that he had once stayed in that room and a ghost threw a teacup at his head. But this man was terrified by the entire premises and would drive in his SUV from building to building—distances of twenty feet or so—for fear of hostile outdoor specters, and insisted that other residents accompany him to and from his car. He also had contended with spirits at other art colonies and in the town where he lived. So I assumed that he was just a universal ghost-magnet, irresistible to the unseen. And I didn't anticipate that I myself would have to dodge flying china in my cozy little abode.

Aside from hauntings, this art colony is known for being host to much cavorting; various twentieth-century masters of literary and musical form reputedly engaged in orgiastic escapades here. So when I received the acceptance letter, my friend Sheila implored me, in her Southern accent, with all the drama of a Tennessee Williams character, "Joe, *please* tell me you'll have an affair there! God, promise me you'll have one! *Don't you understand? It will make your relationship stronger!*" But I was determined to be on my best behavior because, as Sheila indicated, I had recently entered into a decidedly monogamous arrangement. In fact, I had just returned from a romantic trip to Italy, and I set up various postcards of Bellini, Masaccio, and Fra Angelico around my bed to remind me, at night, of my trip and my love.

But it was hard to go to sleep in my apartment. First off, it was very dark outside and I had to creep around a stone path in the black buzzing woods, to the back of the house, which spooked me a bit. Second, my apartment was attached to an old tool shed that you could get to from a passageway connected to the living room, through a filthy corridor that looked like the perfect terror-chamber for a serial killer to keep his victims chained up in. Third, every time I was on the verge of sleep I would see a white flash of light that would snap me back to the waking world and then there'd be a series of frantic footsteps emanating from the ceiling directly above my head.

I knew there was an eighty-something who once wrote for the macabre soap opera *Dark Shadows* somewhere in the building, working on a novel or something, and I figured he must have taken to doing midnight dashes across his room, perhaps as a form of physical fitness. Or maybe he was still asleep, and was simply being swept into spasms of somnambulant dancing. This explanation still wouldn't account for the white flashes, but I was willing to accept those as figments of my imagination.

One morning, after a particularly restless night, I inquired as to who was in the apartment above me. The lady behind the desk in the office replied, "Oh, no one's been up there for years. That's just used for storage. The only other active rooms are on the other side of the house."

This piece of information, which clearly supported the existence of the paranormal, both troubled and delighted me. I was unsure of what to do. Should I call my love, a self-avowed "materialist" who claims not to believe in anything that can't be observed? Yes, perhaps some skepticism would be of comfort. I picked up the phone, but instead found myself dialing my witch friend, Thain, an expert on supernatural codes of behavior and spectral etiquette. He had just awoken at four p.m. "So you want to banish a spirit?" he asked in his low, slow, South African drawl.

"Well I can't banish this ghost, because *it* lives there and *I* don't," I explained worriedly. "But is there some way I could make peace with it, so it would stop stomping around and disturbing my sleep?"

"Okay, calm down. I hear what you're saying. I do *hear* what you're *say*ing," he repeated, like a drunk therapist. "I'm hearing that you want to *commune* with a spirit."

"Yes, commune," I repeated. "I guess that would be it.... A friendly gesture. Is that possible?"

"It is possible," said Thain. "It is...possible. It's possible. What I can do is I can—what I can do.... What I can do is...is I can give you an *incantation*. Okay? An incantation, and a few instructions. Listen carefully. You're going to need a hand-dipped white candle and some whiskey."

"Scotch or bourb—"

"Bourbon," he said decisively, as though I were offering to hand him a glass of it right then.

That afternoon I made one trip to a new age-y store in town, and another over to the liquor store. I had no idea how a ghost could drink whiskey, but I hadn't made a fuss on the phone and chose not to overthink it now. After dinner that night, and the customary coffee hour that followed, I ventured back to my dwelling, and prepared everything just as Thain had instructed me.

I was to set out the whiskey on its own surface in a conspicuous location, as one would when leaving a glass of milk out for Santa Claus. So I dragged my nightstand to the center of the room and poured a generous amount of bourbon into a clean tumbler. Next to this, I lit the candle. I had scrawled the words to the incantation with purple Crayola marker on a sheet of paper torn from my giant desk pad.

I studied the words and tried to memorize them. Some phrases were in English, some polite way of expressing, "Spirit, let's get real, wouldn't you fancy popping in for a few glugs of bourbon?" And other phrases were in an unrecognizable language—I'd transcribed Thain's words phonetically, but had no clue what they meant.

Sitting cross-legged on the floor, I began repeating the invocation, the invitation. At first nothing happened. A distant creaking startled me. I arose for a moment, poured myself a glass of whiskey, took a sip, and set it aside. I closed my eyes again, regained my composure, and muttered the words again. Then I waited and repeated them again. I don't remember how many times I repeated these words but at a certain point: *whoosh.*

I was enveloped by a coldness, a coldness that did not, however, make me huddle or shiver. My arms lifted, as though they were preparing to wade in a pool. Then I was overtaken by a pleasant numbness. I felt that I no longer had control of my body, but I could feel it tingling everywhere. My arms moved very slowly up and down, and into different positions, twisting gently, as though guided by another presence. My spine shifted. It was like an erotic physical therapy session. And though Angela Lansbury's workout routine for the elderly, which Sheila had often described to me, sounded more aerobically vigorous, I suspect now that *this* strange yoga amounted to a more blissful experience.

My ghost was a body worker.

I was not sexually aroused in the traditional male sense, but every part of my body was erotically alive, the way I imagine people feel on certain drugs. If someone had been watching I guess they would have seen me sitting there in the candlelight, raising my arms again and again, like a lost raver, for perhaps an hour or more.

At some point I felt like I was being carried to my bed. For the first time in that room, I slept quite peacefully.

When I awoke that next morning, full of life, I found a puddle of white wax and two glasses of whiskey, both seemingly untouched. The footsteps ceased for the remainder of my stay, as did the flashes of light. We engaged in no further sessions. Although it was brief, and possibly imagined, I supposed that now I had an affair to tell Sheila about. But I would wait to tell my partner, who I knew would be upset that I believed in ghosts.

———————————

Serving Fish

Christopher Caldwell

ERIC RAN TOWARDS THE SHORE OF THE LAKE, STILL HALF made-up as Mahogany Eternique, heels in hand, gaffing tape undone, red taffeta train dragging behind in the mud. He sprinted until he reached the water's edge, picking up speed despite snagging his dress twice on branches that littered the shore, and fell to his knees. The cool water soaked through all four pairs of pantyhose as it lapped against his knees and calves. Panting, and clutching the side which ached from running a mile and a half in a corset, Eric tried to work up enough spit to speak without croaking. His nostrils flared wide. He breathed in the dank, algae smell of lake water. He licked his lips, glitter rough against his tongue, and pitched his voice as loud as he dared across the water. "Flounder, flounder in the sea, rise up from the depths for me…"

He stared across the surface of the lake for nearly a minute, watching the city lights reflect. Except for a few leaves washing up onto the shore, the water seemed untroubled. Eric called out over the water again, his voice cracking with expectation, "Flounder, flounder in the sea?"

But the lake's surface remained placid. He stared across the water for what felt like forever, not daring to blink. At last, Eric shuddered, and shut his eyes. A great spasm shook his body. Tears mixed with mascara clumped like oil droplets in his false eyelashes.

A rasping baritone rose above the sound of the cars behind and the water lapping against the shore ahead. "This is not, strictly speaking, a sea."

Eric's eyes snapped open. An enormous black shape lay just beneath the lake's surface. It's grown as big as an eighteen wheeler, Eric thought. The front end of an immense flatfish, scaly and covered in barnacles. broke the surface. Two jaundiced eyes the size of dinner plates on the same side of a misshapen head regarded him; a sideways mouth opened and closed, spiny teeth gnashing in the air. Eric straightened his back, his bodice sagging against his chest without the padding he used to fill it, and spread out his arms in supplication. "Though you may not care for my request, I've come to ask it, nonetheless."

The sideways mouth opened, and the voice echoed over the water. "I wondered when you would ask again. What is it this time?"

Eric's eyes glittered dangerously. "Revenge."

The yellow eyes seemed to wobble slightly. "You know the costs."

Eric smiled sadly. "I do."

The surface of the lake roiled, and a sudden salty wind sprang up from nowhere, stinging Eric's cheek and eyes.

The baritone voice cracked out up over the howling wind as the giant fish sank down into whatever depths it had come from.

"Granted."

WHEN ERIC WAS TEN, HIS PARENTS, DECIDING THAT HE needed to toughen up and be more of a man, sent him on a long crabbing and fishing trip with his grandparents. Nestled in the plush back seat of his grandmother's rust-colored Chevrolet Caprice, Eric read facts about Pacific marine life from the backs of collectible cards with glossy colored photos while his grandfather fumed about the traffic from Sacramento to Bodega Bay. "I don't know why these fools even get in cars if they can't drive."

Eric's grandmother sucked at her dental bridge; it gave her a sour look. "Roland, you pull over at the next stop and I'll drive the rest. Doctor said to mind your blood pressure."

"My blood pressure'll be fine. Wait'll we get to the boats. Sea air and a reel will fix us up. Maybe straighten the naps out of that boy's hair."

"Roland. Leave him alone."

"I just don't get why his mama let his hair get wild like that. He needs a military cut. Don't know where that nappy hair comes from, not my side."

Eric's grandmother sucked at her bridge again. "Quit pretending you had good hair before you lost it and drive if you're going to. I'm going to rest my eyes."

Eric read about the mating habits of the grunion. His grandfather turned up the radio and grunted in approval at the Stylistics. Eyelids heavy, lulled by the sounds of classic R&B, Eric fell asleep.

When he awoke, it was twilight and the Caprice was parked in front of a weathered motel that had seen better days. The seafoam green door to room seven was ajar, and his grandfather bustled in carrying luggage and a tackle box. His grandmother was still sitting in the front, and patted him on the cheek. "You hungry? I brought some red beans in Tupperware. I'll heat 'em up on the hotplate if you want something to eat."

Eric nodded and slid bonelessly out of the car, and trudged into room seven, wiping his feet on the mat and staring at the swirls on the carpet. They were the colors of pea soup and chocolate milk. The motel room smelled like the sea and old cigarettes. Eric lay down on the double bed closest to the window without taking off his Keds and stretched his arms out wide as if to fill as much space as possible. His grandmother poured a grey-brown mass of red beans and hamhocks into a little pot on the hot plate and hummed softly. Eric fell asleep to the sounds of the sea and his grandmother's wordless hymn.

The next morning, they went out on a mostly white fishing boat named "Aphrodite's Kiss" with a small group of retirees who seemed to regard the serious-faced, slight black boy with a mixture of amusement and wariness. One of them, an elderly man with an impressive mustache and wispy remnants of sideburns smiled at Eric with nicotine-stained teeth and asked, "Looking forward to a battle of nature on the high seas?"

Eric shook his head and fingered the pair of binoculars around his neck. "No sir. I hope we won't be fighting nature. I'm on nature's side."

The old man laughed and clapped Eric on the back. "This one's a regular John Muir."

After about a half hour, the boat found a still, quiet place on the ocean, and the crew cut the engines. Fishing reels came out. Eric's grandmother helped him bait his hooks with shrimp flies. "This one works especially well on sand dab, Baby Dumplin'."

Eric tried not to blush at the nickname and focused on attaching a two-pound sinker to his line. With his grandmother watching approvingly from over his shoulder, he cast off and waited. His grandmother leaned in close enough that he could smell her, a mixture of Oil of Olay, baby powder, and designer impostor perfume, over the salt smell of the sea. "Remember, sand dabs bite a bunch of times then stop. Don't pull 'em up the first time you get a bite. You gotta be patient."

Eric nodded, rested his chest against the railing, and felt the boat bob up and down on the waves. Overhead, seabirds whirled and screamed. The men sometimes punctuated the quiet with raucous laughter at jokes told at a volume too low for Eric to hear.

One by one the retirees reeled in their catch. Wriggling flat fish with eyes on the left sides of their heads flopped on the deck as they were brought up and pulled off hooks. The fish were tan and mottled like the backs of the retiree's hands. Eric kept his hand steady on his rod as he watched his grandfather drop six pancake-sized fish into a bucket. Minutes passed without so much as a tremble on his line from the rising ocean breeze.

Eric's grandmother patted his shoulder after stopping to pluck some fish from her own hook. "Not everyone is lucky all the time."

But then the end of his rod bowed down nearly an inch. His fingers tingled and itched, but remembering what his grandmother had told him, he waited. The line jerked seven times in rapid succession, then lay still. He began to reel in the line, eyes gleaming with triumph. He turned the handle, slowly at first, but faster as he felt the weight on the end of line. His grandfather squinted and peered over his shoulder, "Looks like you caught a nice dab or three, boy."

He turned the handle as smoothly as he could manage, although his arms ached from the effort. After what seemed an interminable period, a flatfish wider than Eric's head splashed through the surface wriggling on the end of his line. He whooped and brought it down on the deck with a fleshy thump. But when he leaned over to pull it from the hook, the world went quiet.

The air around him was still, and all the adults seemed taken by a spontaneous game of freeze tag. Eric blinked twice and rubbed his eyes. The fish was still wriggling. It opened its sideways mouth and spoke to him in a voice that was low and rasping. "Only you can hear me, boy. I slowed things down so we'd have a chance to talk."

"Fish don't talk." Eric set his jaw and glared suspiciously behind him. The adults were still motionless.

The fish flopped and made a rasping noise that might have been a laugh. "But yet I speak. Look, I wasn't always a fish. I'll spare you the details. I was once a man. If you throw me back in the sea, you'll have my gratitude. And my help if I can give it."

"What kind of help? Can you grant wishes?"

"Nothing so crude. But I can change things that are to things that are not, if you ask. Doing so will come with a cost, though."

The boy exhaled sharply. He had just read "The Monkey's Paw" in class. "What if I decide not to throw you back and forget about all this magic and stuff?"

The rasping sound again. "Then I get fried up, or eaten with butter and lemon, and you lose a chance to touch mystery."

"I'm going to throw you back, but not because I want magic or to be a detective or anything like that. But 'cause you can talk."

"Very well. But the offer stands if you change your mind. If you need my help, stand at the shore of the ocean and call, 'Flounder, flounder in the sea, come up from the depths for me,' and I will aid you as best as I can."

"Aren't you a sand dab?"

Rasp. Eric picked up the fish with both hands and threw it over the side. A thin red ribbon of blood trailed behind it through the water. Eric was so still that he did not notice that movement around him had resumed. His grandfather grumbled, "What you do a fool thing like letting that nice piece of fish go?"

"Roland, leave the boy alone," his grandmother said.

"Fine. But he don't get none of my fish. He can eat red beans again."

———————

DURING HIGH SCHOOL, ERIC FELL IN WITH A GROUP OF queer kids who played butch in front of their peers. He was adopted one day after yearbook class by Events Editor Phil, who eyed him and asked conversationally, "You like guys, don't you?"

Taken aback by the bluntness of the question, Eric could think to do nothing else but nod, and soon after found himself completing a trio that ran havoc on the seedy streets of Los Angeles.

Each of them adopted fake names for their clandestine lives; Phil called himself Lucky hoping that it would ring true, Nico chose the name Ram in a none-too-subtle advertisement of his sexual proclivities, and Eric's slight figure and beatific expression earned him the nickname Angel. Phil and Nico's parents relaxed whenever they saw Eric around; they were certain a good boy like that would keep their own wild children out of trouble.

On Friday nights, Eric would go with Lucky and Ram to The Study, a seedy gay bar in Hollywood that seldom checked ID. Ram liked rough trade, and there was a certain kind of thug that lingered over the too-strong drinks served up by the Korean bartender regulars called Chinese Andy. One Friday, just before the Spring term ended, Eric sat at the bar primly, hands in lap, sipping a throat-scorching Cuba Libre that had only the barest hint of Coca-Cola. Ram was in the back parking lot, probably pressed against the wall by some hard-living gangster who couldn't resist a bit of muscular teenage flesh. Andy kept an eye on Eric whenever Ram or Lucky wandered off, shooing anyone who got too close with a pestilential stare and pointed references about chicken not being on the menu.

This Friday wasn't especially busy, and Eric passed the time arguing with Andy about books they'd read. "I still think there's something deeply creepy about how Marq manipulates Rat Korga," Eric said, gesticulating a little with his right hand.

Andy shrugged and wiped down the counter with a rag, scrubbing at an ancient stain. "So you think it's really about a 'good' slave master? I just think it's hot."

The red padded front door slammed open as if to punctuate Andy's opinion. Eric whipped his head around to take in the figure filling the door: six-four in heels and sequins with towering wig and nails sharp as talons stood the biggest, baddest, blackest drag queen Eric had ever seen. For a moment the queen stood stock still, posed like an Old Hollywood Vamp and seemed to shimmer like the haze over the asphalt on the hottest summer day. Eric felt something new well up inside him. Not lust, covetousness. The drag queen seemed to evoke an unearthly, titanic beauty, like a Valkyrie covered in stardust and come to land in the pothole-filled parking lot of The Study. Then the spell was broken as the queen laughed and shouted out in basso profundo, "Chinese Andy! A girl can work up a thirst. Make mama a whisky sour."

———————————

IT WAS THAT SAME YEAR THAT RAM HAD THE BRILLIANT idea for the lot of them to rent a U-Haul truck and ride in the back to beach party in Malibu. Eric had misgivings. "I don't think it'll be safe."

Ram slapped him on the back. "It'll be fine! All six of us can't fit in Lucky's shitty Stanza. Think of it like a limo. Without windows."

"Don't think limousines use lawn chairs as seating." Lucky said, worrying a kiss curl into another position on his forehead.

Ram smirked. "Limos also don't let teenagers drink Ram's famous Malibu cocktails out of a gallon jug."

"Still sounds dangerous. No seatbelts," Eric said, peering into the gloomy interior of the truck.

Ram put his hand on his forehead mockingly. "Oh la, poor Angel is such a delicate china doll he would just break to pieces if we hit a bump in the road." Then, scowling, "Nigga, just because you high yella don't mean you ain't got warrior blood. You can see them African naps fightin' on your head."

Eric took a long swig from the jug of fruit punch and rum then clambered into the back of the truck with four others, muttering under his breath. Ram pulled the sliding door closed with a slam and darkness closed in on them. "The Elegance!" Eric shouted.

Except for being knocked around as the truck navigated turns and a moment of terror as Eric's lawn chair nearly collapsed under him, the half hour drive to Malibu was uneventful. When Ram pulled open the sliding door, the gallon of punch was more than half-finished between the four of them in the back, and they all blinked and squinted in the daylight.

Ram bowed with mock-gallantry, "My Ladies, your chariot has arrived."

Eric frowned. "I feel like I've been in a rock tumbler."

"You're no longer a diamond in the rough then," Lucky said.

Eric hopped out of the back of the truck, gathered what dignity he had left, and turned to take in the sights. The pale sands stretching beneath a stony promontory were covered with towels, pavilions, beach umbrellas, and folding chairs of a dizzying variety of candy colors. And the people! Black men, women, and drag queens of every size, shape, and shade from inky to ivory cavorted, posed, and preened by the shore. A towering coffee-and-cream colored drag queen in a feathered showgirl headdress was playing beach volleyball against a blue-black muscle-boy in speedos who couldn't have been more than five feet tall. A slender caramel-colored boy walked arm-in-arm with his dark chocolate boyfriend. Eric stood there trying to take it all in. Ram rumbled over his shoulder, "Girl, close your mouth before something flies in. We need to find a place to set down so haters can break their necks looking at us."

Ram strode towards the shore like a peacock, glaring at anyone who bothered to smile. Eric followed behind half-smiling, holding the half-empty container of punch. Lucky ululated in imitation of savages from bad movies and tromped puppyish over the sands, innocent of ugly looks and curses when he his passing scattered sand onto blankets and beach towels.

After they set up an umbrella and Ram lay out to drink up the sun in the sluttiest pose he could devise, Eric crept away from the group toward a narrow line of rock at the far edge of the shore. From there he could take in everything, the ocean, the dazzling people, the rich deep color of it all without worrying that he was too colorless by comparison.

From his perch on the rock, he saw the crowd part as if royalty was approaching. Standing nearly a head taller than everyone around her was Ebony Eternique, the drag queen he had first glimpsed months ago at The Study. She wore a rhinestone spangled gold bikini, a translucent cape and the highest Lucite heels Eric had ever seen. Her wig was arranged in a tower of gleaming curls dusted through with pearls and crystals. Despite her mass, she seemed to glide effortlessly. Her platform heels glittered in the sun and did not seem to sink in the sand. The wind blew her chiffon cape behind her and almost every eye was on her in admiration or envy. She was no mere queen anymore, but a Goddess, Venus in reverse come to wade inexorably into the sea.

Eric's heart beat fast, and his mouth tasted like chalk. Makeup, baubles, and poise had given Ebony power. This was magic. This was mystery. Mystery. The word struck a chord in his memory. He thought of a childhood trip to Bodega Bay, of a sand dab he'd caught and abandoned. With a sad, drunken smile, he turned his face away from the party and towards the sea spray. In little more than a whisper he called, "Flounder, flounder in the sea, come up from the depths for me…"

The world went still.

Seagulls froze in midflight. The water roiled and turned black. The sand dab surfaced. The flatfish had grown as big as a manhole cover. Much too large for that species of fish, Eric thought, remembering his animal cards.

It swiveled its froggy eyes towards him. The sideways mouth seemed to grin. "It's been a long time. Seven years? I thought you gave up on magic."

"I want to BE magic, like Ebony Eternique."

The fish wriggled. "You've been drinking."

Eric shrugged. "You said you could help me."

The fish made the rasping sound that might be a laugh. "I can give you the power to transfix men, to fascinate them with your gaze. I can give you the power to rule hearts. But it will cost."

"I don't have a lot of money."

The fish rasped. "Not that sort of cost. You will become a little more like me, and a little less like you. This is the cost."

Eric shrugged. "That doesn't sound so bad."

The flesh between his toes grew cold and began to itch. He felt skin pulled taut and stretch. He looked down in sudden horror as webbing knitted his toes together like a fin. The fish sank beneath the waves. Its baritone echoed out from behind Eric. "Granted."

The noise of the world returned again.

IT TOOK ERIC NEARLY A MONTH TO WORK UP THE NERVE to talk to Ebony Eternique about drag, and then almost another two after that to ask if Ebony could show him how to be a drag queen. Ebony had grabbed Eric's face with her strong, long fingers and stared at him for twenty seconds in the dim light of The Study before sucking her teeth, laughing and slapping Eric hard on the back. "I never had a drag baby, but there's something about you. Sure, I'll be your mama."

At first it seemed hopeless. Eric was terrible at doing his own makeup, awful at lip synching, and clumsy in heels. But Ebony didn't give up, and neither did Eric. And after she drilled him to the point where he could walk backwards down stairs in heels, do contour makeup in his sleep, and lip synch to songs in languages he couldn't speak, Ebony decided her protégé was ready.

Eric was set to make his debut at Diamond Catch, a notorious gay nightclub whose patrons were not at all shy about voicing their displeasure with substandard acts. He had run through a dress rehearsal earlier in the week, but that night was his first time in front of a crowd.

Three songs before he was scheduled to go on, he waited backstage with Ebony, who was going on just before him. Backstage was a cramped, crowded storeroom filled with musty costumes, cracked mirrors, and queens in various states of undress.

A skinny, pockmarked boy with frizzy hair and prominent front teeth was slathering on foundation furiously. Eric smiled tentatively. The boy put his hands on his hips. "I hope you don't bomb. I'm supposed to go on after you, and I'm still cooking. Buy me some time."

Eric adjusted his wig in the mirror. "I hope I don't either. I'm Eri—Mahogany."

"Eri-Mahogany? That's a bougie name. I am Sierra Sin. You may call me Mistress." Sierra turned to glance at Eric. "Well. You are most definitely a fishy queen. You look like a real girl. I bet you'll get all kinds of chasers."

"Chasers?"

Sierra snorted. "Don't you know nothing? 'Straight' boys who want to hit some of that ass you got padded."

Ebony called over her shoulder as she stomped toward the stage. "My baby ain't takin' up with no trash. And daylight is no queen's friend, so she'll be keeping that face in the night."

Eric looked at himself in the mirror again. His balls ached from being tucked out of sight, his feet were sore, the padding was hot, and his face was caked with makeup, but the illusion was startling. Mahogany was a goddess like Dorothy Dandridge or Lena Horne. Mahogany glided over to wait in the wings while Ebony performed her set.

All too soon, Ebony finished her lip synch, and gestured towards Mahogany. The basso profundo voice seemed to fill the world. "And I have a very special treat for y'all. My little baby is going to tear up the stage tonight for you, for the first time. Give it up for Mahogany Eternique!"

Mahogany prowled out onto the stage like a leopard, drinking up the spotlight that shimmered on her sequins. She could do this. Men were creatures for her to control. The music welled up behind her, and her lips took the shape of the words. Her eyes sought out a man and she thought, *want.* The sudden heat was palpable. She knew he'd do anything for her, and she reached out her hand and smiled contemptuously as he fumbled in his wallet to pass her a twenty dollar bill. One by one, she ensnared them with her smoldering gaze, making them feel her beauty. The crowd crushed against the stage trying to get close to her. She gave none of them a second glance until her gaze settled on someone who she didn't need to inflame. Andy. Eric's eyes lingered on his friend with a newfound understanding. Then the song ended, the lights came up, and he exited to thunderous applause.

FOUR YEARS AFTER THE BEACH PARTY, LUCKY HAD MOVED across country to go to college, Ram had found Jesus, gone back to being Nico, and turned into an enormous pain in the ass. But Eric kept in touch with Andy, who came to almost every one of his shows as Mahogany. Mahogany Eternique was doing three shows a week at two different clubs and making more than enough in tips and her cut of the door to pay the rent as well as foot the bill for wigs, makeup, accessories, and the fabric needed to create new and ever more outré costumes.

At least once a month he and Andy would make time to have dinner together. Eric would leave Mahogany behind in her world of wigs, makeup, and lip synch to talk to Andy about books someplace where no one paid any attention to him.

One month they went to Santa Monica Pier for dinner. Not any particular restaurant. Eric grabbed a corn dog, and Andy got fish and chips from a stand. They walked along the pier past the carnival games talking. Andy stuffed a ketchup-soggy fry into his mouth. "Hey, you want to try some of this? It's surprisingly good."

Eric shook his head. "I hate fish."

Andy smirked. "That's something I expect Mahogany to say. She wouldn't eat her own kind."

Eric shook his head. "Just because I serve fish realness three times a week doesn't mean I feel like being at the top of the food chain."

Andy stuffed a bit of fried cod into his mouth. "Your loss. Hey, wanna do that test your strength thing?"

"I'll win."

Seven carnival games and three stuffed animals later, the two of them sat in companionable silence on a bench overlooking the ocean. Darkness had settled in somewhere between the water-gun races and the darts. Andy put an arm around Eric. "It's weird. I hated that job at The Study, but meeting you came out of it, so being called Chinese for a year-and-a-half was worth it."

Eric smiled. "I'm glad you were there to keep me from being kidnapped by some OG with a thing for girly-boys."

Andy stirred. "I always loved this place. It reminds me of being a kid. Reminds of when I thought everything would work out all right, you know?" He slumped forward and his shoulders sagged.

"Hey? Something up?" Concern limned Eric's eyes.

Andy sighed. "Yeah. My mother. She's a tough old bird. But the cancer's come back, again. And each time the chemo's worse." His voice cracked. "I don't know if she can handle it again."

Eric turned to face Andy and squeezed his shoulder. "You got friends who love you. We're there for you."

Andy leaned in to kiss Eric. Eric kissed back, parting his lips, crushing them against Andy's teeth. The stubble on Andy's chin scraped against the smoothness of Eric's skin. Yes, Eric thought. He was hungry for this. Then, abruptly Eric pulled back.

Andy's eyes widened in confusion. His cheeks were still flushed and lips plump with arousal. "Is there something wrong?"

Eric smiled and covered Andy's hand with his own. "No everything's okay, I just need some air." He stood up and half-stumbled away from the bench.

Eric walked to the edge of the pier, a balloon tied to his left wrist, holding a teddy bear in his right hand. He looked over the railing at the black water below with the lights from the Ferris wheel and the carnival rides reflecting back like a parody of the night sky. He called out over the shrill music of the carousel and the popping of airguns, "Flounder, flounder in the sea, come up from the depths to me…"

The music cut mid-note. This time the sand dab loomed in the surf as big as a Volkswagen bug.

"Four years. Doing better than most. I imagine that little trick I taught you got some use?"

"What can you do about someone who's dying?" Eric shouted, although the world was still and quiet.

"I cannot resurrect the dead. But dying is another matter. I can cure someone who is ill. But there is always the cost."

"I need you to heal Andy's mother! Fuck the costs." Eric shouted. He felt an itching and a coldness down his left arm. Then pain in pinpricks. He rolled up the sleeve of his shirt in time to see iridescent scales push themselves through his skin to lie down flush like tiles along his arm.

The fish sank beneath the waves. "Granted."

ANDY MOVED TO DENVER ABOUT A YEAR AFTER HIS mother went into spontaneous remission. Eric and Andy kept in touch, although Mahogany's schedule remained full, and grew fuller as drag returned to mainstream attention via reality shows. Mahogany went on tour, and after a packed show before a Denver audience, Eric met with Andy for dinner at an all-night taco joint.

While nibbling on a carne asada taco with extra chile verde, Andy remarked, "I'm not used to seeing you all glamorous for dinner."

Eric, still made up as Mahogany, laughed. "I'm not crazy about it, but I went straight from the airport to the club where I did my makeup for three hours, and I'm famished." He illustrated this by cramming an entire carnitas taco into his mouth without smudging his lipstick.

Andy whistled. "If I knew you had such skills, I mighta hit that."

Eric slapped him playfully on the upper arm. "You had your chance."

After dinner they walked arm-in-arm together along the banks of the Platte River, laughing and remembering old times. Eric's eyes were luminous and sad. "Sometimes I feel like you're the only one I can be real with, Andy."

"Even dressed like this?" Andy squeezed one of Eric's birdseed breasts.

As they walked past stoner hill, a figure lurched out of the bushes. The sodium glare of the streetlights did him no good. He was fifty-ish and squat. He had a Fu Manchu style mustache that made his mouth look droopy and petulant. His greasy Jheri Curl hair reminded Eric of seaweed.

Eric clutched Andy's hand nervously; the strange man was carrying a crowbar in his right hand, and a car stereo in the left. The man's skin was pockmarked and his shoe-leather brown complexion had an ashy grey undertone to it.

"We don't want any trouble," Andy said, holding his hands out.

The man smiled. He held out the car stereo. "Y'all want to buy this? Like brand new. Only been used once."

Andy shook his head. "Naw, man. We don't want to buy stolen goods."

The man slurred, "Why you think it's stolen? You think you better than me?" His eyes narrowed at Andy. "You gooks always tryin' to steal good black women with your one-inch peckers."

Eric curled his hands into fists. "Not a woman, bruh. Leave us be."

The man's face contorted and he spat on the ground. "Faggot!"

He moved towards Eric with surprising swiftness. Panicking, Eric projected desire at the man. *Want.* The man's eyes widened for a moment and his jaw went slack. Then his face contorted again and he slammed his crowbar into Andy's face. The crunching sound was sickening, and as Andy slid to the ground, Eric fell to his knees in horror.

It was a precious few moments before Eric could compose himself enough to call 911.

AFTER AN AMBULANCE TOOK ANDY AWAY, AND THE POLICE had questioned Eric and promised an APB, Eric found himself in the blue-grey waiting room of the Trauma Unit at the nearest hospital. Half-dressed and all numb he stared at a cup of hot chocolate someone had brought him hours ago. It had gone cold and congealed. His lipstick was still perfect.

A tired-eyed doctor in faded orange scrubs hovered at Eric's shoulder. "You were Andrew Kim's friend?"

The "were" in that sentence slammed down in Eric's chest like a stone. He stood up, poised with his head held high, and walked towards the door. He did not wait to hear the doctor say, "I'm sorry."

Outside of the sliding doors to Emergency an EMT was taking a furtive smoke break. Eric walked near him and forced a smile. "Hey, what's the nearest body of water? Big body of water?"

"Sloan's Lake," the EMT pointed vaguely north, "That way a ways. But it's not safe at night. Especially dressed like that."

Eric broke out into a run.

AFTER THE FISH SANK INTO THE MURK OF SLOAN LAKE, Eric stood and felt tiny pinpricks all along his spine. Good, he thought. He sniffed the air particles wafting above: gasoline, sweat, cheap tacos from the down the road. He opened his mouth, ran a tongue over sharp barbed teeth that had sprouted just behind the set he had capped, cleaned, and straightened after adolescence. Without knowing how he knew, he knew where his prey was. Swifter than he would have thought possible, he darted along the shore and headed inexorably towards Federal Boulevard. He avoided cars and early morning pedestrians.

There. Across the street from him was a little yellow house. A Chevy Impala stood on blocks in the driveway. He knocked on the door forcefully three times. He heard stirring. The door creaked open on its chain. Fury rose up in Eric, its intensity driving all color from the world. The same piggy eyes. The Jheri Curl. The stupid Fu Manchu mustache. He forced his snarl into a smile and projected at the man. *Want.*

The man's face slid into a lazy smile. "So, you came here without your gook? You wanna play? I'll tap that ass if you can keep it on the downlow, baby."

Eric made his hips sway. He lowered his eyelids and parted his lips. "Oh, I got something that will sho' nuff set your world on fire."

The man rubbed his crotch. "Well hurry in baby, before someone sees you." He opened the door wide enough for Eric to slide in.

The door shut behind them with a slam. He grabbed Eric's ass and kneaded it. "I knew a bitch like you would want some of this."

"Yes," Eric said into his ear, feeling his new teeth lengthen. "What do I call you, Daddy?"

"Mm. Daddy. Yeah. Big Daddy is just right. Big Daddy got something for that ass." He slid his hand up from Eric's ass to reach for the zipper on his dress. Spines soundlessly ripped through the taffeta, and dripping with fluid, rose to meet Big Daddy's hand.

"Ow! The fuck!" he cried.

Eric shoved him back and opened his mouth. Human teeth cascaded to the floor, revealing sharp, spiny, barbed things.

Big Daddy screamed in terror, even while clutching his hand that had already begun to swell and purple.

"His name was Andy, not gook, you fuck."

Eric walked out the door, stately as if in a procession, even as he felt the cold, familiar prickling of scales sprout up his right arm. He ignored Big Daddy's howls of fury as he turned back towards Sloan Lake, trailing the tatters of his red dress behind him.

The skin between his fingers itched and tightened as they fused into fins. Once clear of the Impala, he broke into a run, not out of fear, not in fury, but for the sheer joy of it, even as the skin beneath his jaw opened up and feathery gills sprouted.

He returned to Sloan Lake, gasping for breath from a mouth twisting sideways, fell into the water with a resounding splash and disappeared beneath the surface, leaving only a ribbon of taffeta red as blood behind him.

Some Kind of Wonderland

Richard Bowes

ON A SUNDAY AFTERNOON GILDA DARNELL AND I ARE IN her living room, phoning in one last conference call. I tell the host, "We two have been buddies since we were both in Scott Holman's Alice film *Some Kind Of Wonderland*, back in 1965. She was the Duchess. I was the Cheshire Cat."

With the show's fiftieth anniversary/resurrection scheduled for Monday evening, we've chased down every promotional opportunity we could find.

Gilda says, "*Some Kind of Wonderland* came out early in 1966. The *Village Voice* had us on the front page. 'Hippy Alice Hits The Big Apple!' was how they put it. We got lots of downtown Manhattan attention but *so* many underground films got released around then. And Scott Holman our producer/director had passed away. But I never forgot about it. A few years ago I managed to buy the rights from the Holman family and got The Film Annex interested in restoring it."

She nods to me and I say, "Scott Holman had this off-kilter perspective—like the Alice books themselves. He caught New York at a certain moment. And he created the cast out of people he found. His Alice was a young model he saw on a fashion shoot."

Gilda says, "I'd been in a couple of Off-Off Broadway shows but I came to his attention because I was the mouthiest waitress in all the West Village."

"And what were you, Justin?" the host asks me.

"A street boy who got very lucky," I hear myself say as the interview ends.

Gilda gets a call from a publicist she hired. This one actually works on Sunday. "The approach is: 'It Was Worth The Wait,'" she says.

Things I learned working on *Wonderland* led to my nice gig as a location scout and fixer for movies and TV shows shooting in New York. But Gilda has managed to learn the ways of Manhattan real estate and politics. She's my hero.

While she talks strategy, I look down at the world from her twentieth story windows in Tribeca. Below is the intense green of Washington Market Park. Late afternoon sunlight bounces off the Hudson.

I love the way she doesn't forget the actual past. Prominent in her living room are framed black and white photos from fifty years back and more. They show a stark, corroded highway, a junk-riddled Hudson riverbank, and the wrecked warehouses where this building and other high-rises now stand.

This had been the thriving, sprawling Washington Produce Market. The neighborhood that fed New York until the city abandoned it in the 1960s. Bringing those ruins to Scott's attention was my proudest contribution to the film.

Gilda has a photo of Scott Holman displayed prominently. The writer/director/producer wears black-rimmed glasses and a Borsalino hat like a European auteur. But underneath that you can see a young guy staring intently at something off camera. I want to believe he's watching me.

The editor of an online entertainment site calls Gilda. At the same moment Lucinda Gold comes out of her room and floats through the apartment in dark glasses and a lovely green kimono. Gilda is Lucinda's partner and care giver. Lucinda was Alice in the film. She's gone a few rounds with addictions and had a stroke a decade or two back. The glasses hide a dead eye and she speaks a bit haltingly.

We go out on the balcony and watch the sun set. I sit on her good side and catch a hint of the lovely kid for whom I once was a body double.

She's kind of excited by the revival and tells me, "Gilda tries to appear so cool and professional. Actually, she's gaga. I hope you invited all the freaks and monsters?"

I start to run down the list of invitees. Then I recall a recent confrontation that I'm not sure wasn't a nightmare and blurt out, "I got asked about Bonibo and how I killed Scott."

"Oh Justin, I'm sorry." She looks like she's ready to cry. "Everyone who matters knows how much you loved him." I feel bad about having stupidly upset her and try to lighten things.

"He may have loved me but he wanted to *be* you!" I say and somehow we laugh. With an early spring night falling on the city, I kiss her and wave goodbye to Gilda.

At ground level, the gathering darkness and the absence of pedestrians could give a minor chill. But this is Tribeca, now the safest of Manhattan neighborhoods, not the bombed-out wreckage where we filmed much of *Some Kind of Wonderland*.

On a cobblestoned side street leading away from the river I pass the eighteenth century two-story townhouse we once used as the White Rabbit's home.

Fifty years back it was on a different street, with faded tradesman signs over the door and shingles falling off. Now it's been moved and refurbished. A light is on in a second floor window and a figure stands talking on a cellphone. He turns slightly and reveals rabbit's ears.

Someone walking her dog stops and stares. A male couple snap cell phone shots. The light goes out, and I wonder if this is something Gilda's created as publicity for the revival.

I also remember Scott telling me, "It's a kind of leakage. A story spreads out into the world around it. Even someone who's never read the Alice books remembers a song or once saw a drawing."

As I walk uptown through Soho and into the Village, I remember thumbing my way to Manhattan from South Jersey when I was seventeen. People back home said I talked and walked funny. Everyone knew my mother drank and did drugs and that my father was nowhere to be found.

On my way to the city, I dumped that prior life.

When the last lonely driver let me out of his car on Bleecker Street, I took one look around and knew this was my place. I wasn't the hottest boy but I wasn't stupid. I used whatever charms I had. And I learned to talk to everyone, forget nothing, and smile a lot. I could be trusted to run errands, keep my eyes open, and be discrete.

One night, I was filling in for the busboy at the Village Gate and caught the eye of a young man in glasses sitting with some other guys When I paid an unnecessary visit to their table, he said, "You've got a smile like the Cheshire Cat.'

Because I'd gotten a really lousy education, I had no idea what he was talking about. The night after that he came alone and met me at closing time.

We went out drinking. Scott was his name. He'd just graduated from Yale and moved into the city. Scott took me to his apartment on the first floor of an old brownstone on a quiet old street.

My trip from Gilda and Lucinda's leads me down that street and into the apartment where I've lived ever since.

Yes, I'm lucky and, yes, it's haunted. There's a mirror over the unusable fireplace. When I flick on the light it catches my favorite Scott photo on the opposite wall. My lover sits twirling his horn rim glasses, smiling at me. I walk closer, kiss his reflection on its lips then wipe it clean.

ON MONDAY EVENING AT THE FILM ANNEX WE'VE turned out a crowd. The theater seats about two hundred, and there are standees. A curator tells the audience how editors managed to reconstruct our nearly lost Manhattan Alice film. She describes the mid-sixties explosion of New York's underground cinema, cites stuff like Anger's *Scorpio Rising*, *Chafed Elbows* by Robert Downey Junior's father, and the rise of Warhol's publicity machine. "It seems *Some Kind of Wonderland* got lost in the melee," she says.

Then it's my turn to stand before the screen in my best suit and talk about Scott Holman. The world has changed for certain when an aged former rent boy is called on to explain a director's work.

The first thing I say is, "When we first met, Scott called me *The Cheshire Cat*. All I knew was that he was magic.

"For me it was magic that he was able to devote every minute to what obsessed him. And his obsession was a movie about Wonderland, but with New York grit.

"He was shocked that I'd never heard of Alice. He read the first part of *Alice in Wonderland* aloud to me. I read the rest—first book I ever finished. Within a few weeks I found myself immersed in that story.

"Not my first lover or my last," I say, "But the only one who woke me in the middle of the night to wonder how gay the Frog Footman was."

I don't describe Scott's telling me how trust funds worked and my awe at such things' existence.

At the Annex I don't dwell on his downfall. "Maybe Scott Holman wasn't meant for the long haul. He gave everything he had to one dream and you'll see it wasn't in vain."

There is some applause as the lights go down and I step aside. Just before the opening credits, the curators have inserted a tiny clip from the film. The Cheshire Cat (me in mask and costume) all lunatic smiles, pounces upon an invisible mouse.

This gets laughs but I hear a woman murmur in the dark, "The cat must have been on Bonibo." And I freeze. Right about the time the movie was made, an anonymous chemist achieved the dark marriage of junk and speed. Bonibo was the street name.

SCOTT HOLMAN INTERSPERSED THE OPENING CREDITS between shots of Alice waking from a nap on a wicker couch in the living room of our apartment.

He told me early on what caught him about Lucinda. "She was at the center of this chaos of models, photographers, art directors on a fashion shoot. She wasn't twenty but had this expression of amused disbelief. Just the way a modern Alice should react.

Scott came from a well-to-do family that didn't know what to make of a boy who read and reread *Wonderland* and *Looking Glass*. In his heart of hearts, this thin guy with thick glasses wanted to be Alice. Instead he tried to live through Lucinda.

At moments early in the shooting, with her long blond hair and wide-open eyes, Lucinda combined Tenniel's drawings of a self-assured Alice with her persona as a bright young woman in New York almost one hundred years later.

On screen, Alice arose and parted the curtains. The first thing that caught her eye was a human sized rabbit played by an elegant kid in a waiter's outfit with a white rabbit's tail on the seat of his pants. He murmured to himself about being late.

Alice took one look and slipped on her sandals. She wore a dancer's cream-colored leotard and a long, flowing, embroidered blouse over it. Lucinda had designed what would be her costume throughout the film.

The audience saw Alice go out the door, then saw her on the street. She followed the rabbit along that old block, hurried to keep up with him.

Watching this on screen, I remember being across the street with Scott and Jackstone, his cameraman. They caught some good footage of the Rabbit and Alice. But gawkers and passers-by did double takes and ruined a lot of shots. This was street photography without red tape or licenses.

What the viewer saw next was the rabbit running down a flight of stairs and through a door with *Down the Rabbit Hole* painted above it.

Jackstone rarely spoke and never smiled. But he caught Alice following the rabbit through the door really nicely.

Scott had been told about a legendary bar in the Village called *Down the Rabbit Hole*. Rich kids are used to getting what they want, but nobody could find him such a place.

Over my last couple of years in the city I had learned more than he could imagine about how the Village worked. I knew, for instance, of a beat-to-hell bar located in a cellar on a back street. The owner was always broke.

When I told Scott what I was going to do, he didn't have total confidence in me. But I did get the hundred dollars I said it would take. With that I bribed the owner into painting *Down the Rabbit Hole* over his door. Scott was impressed.

A bit later he said, "The Cheshire Cat's a small part. Alex quit today and I'm giving it to you." I was terrified. "All you need is that wild smile. I'll coach you."

He then rented the place, which was a dark semi-hellhole with low lights and old, scarred furniture, for a shoot. Much of the newly assembled cast and extras of *Some Kind of Wonderland* were there in costume. Human-size birds and turtles, Mad Hatters and

Dodos leaned on the bar. Men dressed as playing cards and women in crowns sat at tables. There's no scene like it in the book. The camera caught me in my Cheshire cat suit. Gilda as the Duchess had a small guy in bonnet and gown who played her child, sitting on her knee.

On screen the rabbit passed through the room and out a rear door with Alice following. Next we saw them go down a long, dimly lit corridor where she found a small table with a bottle and the note. "Drink me." After debating the idea for a moment she popped the cork and took a belt.

Back when I stood next to Scott watching her do this, I found it amusing. The bottle was full of tea.

The next scene was shot from the floor up. Alice didn't get giraffe-necked or anything. But Scott had Jackstone somehow make it seem that her head was floating on the ceiling like a helium balloon.

Further down the hall she found a cake on another table. "Eat Me," was written in frosting. Alice was a sensible but daring girl: so she did. Watching her on screen in The Film Annex fifty years later, knowing how fond of strange potions she became, I shivered.

On screen, Alice started to cry. Mice and rats and birds, all human sized, watched a puddle of tears form.

The next moment the audience saw a pool of tears with Alice swimming in it. This was shot a few nights later without too much light in the swimming pool at an old health club. To get us in after hours I'd bribed the night watchman.

That night Scott was drinking and smoking weed. This evoked my mother and my home and showed me a part of him I didn't want to see.

Scott told Lucinda a couple of times; "Alice swam fully dressed in the pool of her tears." Like this somehow meant she should be able to do that. Scott wanted to film her in semi-darkness swimming in tears. Lucinda couldn't do much more than hang onto the pool's ledge and kick her feet

I saw him have trouble distinguishing the imaginary Alice from Lucinda in the real world.

Jackstone was uninterested in anything not involving lenses. So I was the only one who actually worried about her drowning in the dark. One way sissy boys fulfilled their high-school gym requirement was the swim team. I stripped to my briefs and played lifeguard. When Lucinda had trouble staying afloat, I jumped in and helped her out of the water.

Scott wasn't pleased. But she and I weren't that different in height and my hair in those days was long and blondish. I wore the Alice outfit and the scene was dimly lighted enough that the viewer saw what could well be Alice swimming in tears with her clothes plastered to her.

That night I saw Scott divide people into those who could help fulfill his fantasies and those couldn't. He relied on me and I was in awe of him. But I remembered that night.

As I thought about it, the audience in the Annex watched the White Rabbit scamper by, talking to himself about his impending execution by the queen. He threw open a door and outside there was sunshine.

Then he noticed Alice all dry and dressed somehow and said, "Mary Ann, quick now fetch me a pair of gloves and a fan," before he stepped into the light.

———

ON SCREEN, ALICE IN HER LEOTARD AND BLOUSE, BUT looking a bit wary followed the Rabbit out the door and onto a street paved with broken cobblestones.

Scott and Jackstone had complained about their trouble shooting in noisy, crowded Greenwich Village. So I'd taken them on a tour of the lost Washington Market neighborhood that I knew about. He was fascinated, and from then on much of the film was set in a world stranger than anything in the book.

Empty brick hulks with faded wooden signs like: *Collin Brothers: Egg Brokers* and *Josephson: Grain Wholesaler* lined the streets. The windows were full of jagged glass and seemed to stare down on Alice or any trespasser, with expressions of shock and horror. At the end of the street was a rusty elevated highway and beyond that the murky Hudson River.

In this neighborhood nothing moved and there was little noise. Most of the abandoned buildings had rusted loading docks.

On screen, Alice and the audience saw something blue move on one of those docks. It was a large caterpillar smoking a hookah.

He stared at her and asked disdainfully, "*Who are you?*"

And she answered, "I hardly know, sir, just at present," and told him she had been several different people since that morning.

Watching her on screen, I felt exactly as I had when I saw her perform this scene on that wrecked street fifty years before. She had her lines down and delivered them. But her Alice seemed a bit remote and withdrawn—changed by the world into which she'd wandered.

When Scott whispered to me, "The city's making our Alice tough," I got that when he talked about Alice he was talking about himself.

"*Explain yourself,*" said the Caterpillar and took another hit from the hookah.

"I can't explain myself, I'm afraid sir, because I'm not myself, you see." When Lucinda delivered that line, it sounded like the truth.

But the contemptuous insect again spoke with disdain, "*I don't see.*"

All this was in the script and the Caterpillar is a satiric creation. But I'd heard the actor playing the part express his contempt for people like Lucinda and me, because he was a professional and we weren't.

Scott let the scene play out. The viewer saw Alice appear to break off and eat a piece of the mushroom on which the caterpillar sat.

Then he muttered, "The scene doesn't go anywhere," and looked at me like he expected a solution. I was in the next scene and was already in the Cheshire mask and costume. Before the second take I said, "I can jazz it."

Scott nodded. When he said "Action" I was moving toward the loading dock. The other thing sissy boys did in high school was gymnastics.

Late in life a sudden glimpse of yourself when young can be like a flash of sunlight in a dark woods.

Before the Caterpillar even spoke, my Cheshire Cat with his mad grin, grabbed the pipe from the hookah and drew deeply.

On screen I imitated a cat doing a long, fond inhalation. My eyes crossed and my mad smile seemed to spread all the way to my ears. Later I found out this was called improvisation. On my own inspiration, I crouched down, hissed at something only I could see and pounced on an invisible mouse.

My shenanigans ended up in the film. Watching in The Annex I was impressed at how catlike and off script I'd managed to be.

The Caterpillar stared at me, affronted, and I was pleased to see how pissed off I'd made him. He was just an actor with a couple of off-Broadway credits. I was the director's boyfriend.

After shooting stopped that day, Scott turned to me and said, "We should drop by *Down the Rabbit Hole*. The crowd there is amazing."

I smiled and reminded him that he had hired that entire crowd. He seemed startled, but I knew he had a lot of things on his mind.

———————————

IN THE FRONT ROW OF THE FILM ANNEX, GILDA SITTING beside me says, "Now my big moment is here."

On screen the Duchess went into her act. Gilda in the movie wore an enormous, misshapen hat. Flaming ringlets of red hair clashed with a chartreuse lipstick shade never seen before or since. Her dress looked like an orange tablecloth tied around her waist.

During the filming I'd heard about a tired, old restaurant on the waterfront that had suddenly gone out of business and left everything behind. For a price we shot the Duchess's house scene in the kitchen.

On screen a shrill-voiced midget played the cook. She and the Duchess tossed plates and cutlery at each other.

Then Gilda held "the baby" who actually was the very short actor she'd held in her lap at the Rabbit Hole.

Gilda smacked his ass while he pretended to sneeze. On the first take Gilda had felt too softhearted to lay into him.

But when he complained that he wasn't given enough screen time, she got way more aggressive.

Scott had paid someone to come up with a raucous tune for the famous song that she sang far off key:

> *Speak roughly to your little boy*
> *And beat him when he sneezes*
> *He only does it to annoy,*
> *Because he knows it teases*

The cook, the Duchess, even the "little boy" sang it. Then the Duchess's Frog Footman and The Queen's Fish Footmen, the White Rabbit and a lizard, a dodo, a lobster and finally Alice and the Cheshire Cat and a dozen others appeared behind them and we all sang. I think it was the White Rabbit who began doing the Twist. That stupid dance was several years old by then. But we all knew it and did our own versions of it. Lucinda was smiling.

Scott too was wide-eyed. I never saw such joy on his face before or after. The next day, he had us dancing on a wrecked street in Washington Market. Everyone who saw the movie in its first incarnation agreed this was a great chaotic moment.

Fifty years later the Annex audience applauds. I turn and watch Lucinda stare up at herself on screen. Gilda whispers something to her and she cracks a tiny smile.

WITH ALMOST NO PRELIMINARIES, THE RED QUEEN (A tall, mad-eyed drag) strode on screen. And she and Gilda as the Duchess had a short but vicious croquet game on a patch of dying grass. They glared at each other with genuine hate and used pink lawn-ornament flamingos to whack balls across the lawn.

THEN I WATCH LUCINDA IN HER ALICE OUTFIT AND ringlets walk down a Washington Market alley that looked like Berlin after the bombing. This was from the period in the shooting when she wanted me on screen with her all the time.

Unless it involved swimming or somersaults I never was much of a performer. I got reminded of this as I watched myself on screen standing in the shadow of a building. Alice walked by and I was supposed to ask her, "What happened to the Duchess's baby?" Rather than expose the New Jersey accent I was trying desperately to lose, Scott had an actor overdub my lines.

"It turned into a pig," Alice said and shrugged.

"I thought it would," the actor's voice replied. But his dubbed voice and my lips didn't coordinate. The Annex audience notices and titters.

Then a Jackstone shot silenced them. Scott had him catch me in evening light and the camera made me fade until only the mask and my phony smile were there: a nice effect.

"Well, I've often seen a cat without a grin," Alice said. This was said in the voice of an Alice who had seen quite a bit. "But a grin without a cat! It's the most curious thing."

Just after I'd read the book Scott told me, "Alice, behind her nice upper-class manners, is kind of a remote, survivor." I'd never met people like Alice or like him. I took in what he said but didn't much understand.

Only later did I realize how a kid who never quite fit into his well-to-do family could worship Alice's independent spirit. In Lucinda he created an Alice with the beauty and confidence he could only dream about.

Back then I mostly managed not to think of home. And I tried not to notice how Lucinda at times acted secretively like my mother did when she got hold of a new pain killer prescription.

The morning we were about to shoot the Mad Tea Party scene it was obvious to me. I asked Lucinda what she was on. She just gave me her coldest Alice look ever, turned her back and walked away. I wasn't in the tea party scene probably at the request of Johnny Breen.

On the Annex screen, the March Hare and Mad Hatter are at a long table on a cobblestone street. They were played by Breen and Ted Libber, a duo who billed themselves as a "Neo-Vaudeville act."

Libber, as I recall, was okay. But Breen had spotted Scott, new to the city and just down from Yale. He'd attached himself to Scott as if they were an item. Johnny Breen was there the night Scott found me at the Village Gate.

On screen the duo start crying "No room. No room," as soon as Alice appears. They run through their routine and yank the dormouse out of the teapot with eye rolls and shtick that was older than *Alice in Wonderland* itself.

They could carry a tune. The Annex audience, in a friendly mood, applauds their singing:

> *"Twinkle, twinkle, little bat!*
> *How I wonder what you're at!*
> *Up above the world you fly,*
> *Like a tea tray in the sky."*

I rise and walk to the back of the house. Breen was full of resentment the moment he saw me on the set with Scott. Fifty years after I'd forgotten him, I discovered he hated me still.

One of my tasks for the revival of *Some Kind of Wonderland* had been contacting as many surviving veterans of the film as possible. Gilda had lists of everyone who appeared on or off camera. Certain names were crossed off because of death. Libber was deceased. There were question marks next to those whose status and/or location was unknown.

Tommy Breen was one of the potentially missing and I'll admit, even after all these years, to not having put a lot of effort into finding him.

So encountering him in the evening dusk a few days before the *Wonderland* showing was uncanny and unpleasant. Breen came around a corner near my place as I walked by. Like he'd planned an ambush, he stood in front of me on the sidewalk as ethereal as a puff of smoke and smiling a tight smile. Two old men stared at each other.

"No room, no room," he said in a hoarse whisper. Then he said, "I introduced Scott Holman to avant-garde theater in New York. I guided him when he babbled about doing *Alice* in dirty old New York. Next thing I knew a certain gutter rat was sleeping with him, appearing in Scott's movie even though he had never acted.

"Libber and I got a few days work out of that film and nothing more. We'd hoped for a sequel. But the movie flopped. Then Scott was dead. Everyone knew you'd given him an overdose but somehow you didn't get touched. We wondered who you bribed, how much you stole."

I made myself smile and said, "No one killed Scott. He still lives. Come to his show and see for yourself. I stepped around him. Breen tried to block me and it seemed like I walked right through him.

Standing at the back of the theater, I'm still not sure if that meeting was real or a dream. Breen couldn't imagine any motives on my part but theft and murder. That was his stupidity. But I think about Scott and how lost and innocent he was. I could have saved him if I hadn't been so young and in awe.

WHEN I TURN MY ATTENTION BACK TO THE FILM, ALICE with a fixed smile wanders with the Cheshire Cat under a corroded highway and down to a junk-filled beach. A tugboat pulls a bunch of barges up the Hudson and sunlight comes through layers of good, old-fashioned New York smog.

On the shore the Griffin and the Mock Turtle, in full costume, dance a pavane and sing "Beautiful Soup," while Alice and the Cat watch.

As that scene ends, a voice that's somehow familiar whispers in my ear, "Remember when we were shooting on that stinking beach infested with truck tires and rats. The only way to get there was by walking under that expressway, hoping all the time it didn't collapse as you did."

I turn and recognize the face. Carson is the name. She was the Griffin. Her girlfriend, Shep, was the Mock Turtle.

Today they wear modified versions of their movie costumes. I recognize Gilda's hand in this. Carson says, "For that four minute scene, I had to stand under the sun flapping my wings and wearing a bird mask. Shep had it worse. I think her shell started out as a bathtub.

"Scott began okay as a director—a sweet guy. But when he did our scene he was less than half present. By the time he and that Golem cameraman found a take they liked we were dying for a drink.

"There was nothing open in that hellhole. But you led us out of the neighborhood and trekked across Canal Street. There was actual life there, including a little deli that sold beer and wine.

"I'm wearing this bird head and wings and Shep's got the turtle shell on her back and they don't let us in. But you're a smiling pussycat and they welcome you, tickle your phony ears and sell you six packs and cold bottles of cheap wine. I love you for that still!"

The two of them are headed out the Annex doors when Shep looks my way and finally speaks. "Watch us on the news!"

THE GRAND FINALE IS THE KNAVE OF HEARTS TRIAL. It was shot amid the mirrors and red velvet of an old-fashioned strip club that I'd found for Scott. Wonderland lizards, rabbits, lobsters, pigs sit in the jury box. The Red Queen and the Duchess glare at each other before a backdrop of a couple of dozen extras dressed as playing cards.

On screen Jackstone made it look like the human playing cards are being shuffled, riffled and fanned. Viewing it I saw how, when the film got released, Jackstone was on his way to Hollywood.

Scott assembled this whole scene, acquired the costumes, supervised the lighting, assigned lines to the performers, and arranged them around the location. When the last take was shot, Scott slumped against me and whispered, "It's over."

What I remember about the end of shooting is getting Scott home after the wrap party. On his desk (the one I still use) I noticed a bill for costumes. It involved the kinds of numbers I'd never even thought about. Scott grabbed it. "This is an investment," he said.

———————

IN THE ANNEX, THE CREDITS ROLL AND MY NAME POPS up on the screen as Alice walks up the stairs of *Down the Rabbit Hole* with a slight smile that says she knows whatever is worth knowing about this town.

There's nice applause and the lights come up. A woman in a devastating suit whispers in my ear that she's from the Tribeca Film Festival, a prestigious event run by Robert De Niro.

———————

THAT EVENING GILDA GIVES WHAT SHE CALLS "A SURVIVORS Party" for those connected with the movie who have made it to old age.

She lets me announce that the Tribeca Film Festival is very interested in showing *Some Kind of Wonderland*. It's ironic that it was filmed in Tribeca before that's what this neighborhood was called.

Gilda knows how to garner publicity. We watch social media display photos of actors she dressed as playing cards standing at attention in front of The Film Annex.

New York One interviews Carson and Shep in their personae as the Gryphon and Mock Turtle as they sing while strolling down the Hudson River Park.

Someone on radio calls the film "As surrealistic as *Alice in Wonderland* has always been." It's getting more and better attention than almost anything got fifty years ago.

Gilda says, "We're here to celebrate a young man who came to New York with a dream and died bringing it to life. Holman went for something dark—Carroll's characters in a ruined city and an Alice who gets tough in ways he couldn't.

"That young man's gone but his better half lives on." She points to me and my eyes tear. The party is running down when I kiss everyone and go out the door. As the elevator opens Lucinda slips in beside me.

"I'd like to visit Scott," is all she says and we walk through the lobby and onto the side street. The upstairs light goes off in the rabbit's house as we approach. "Gilda's doing?" I ask.

Lucinda shakes her head. "She was upset because the Rabbit Guy tried to follow her home. Remember Scott saying a great story had a kind of leakage. Bits of it get out and lodge in peoples' heads? There's plenty of that hanging around right now."

The townhouse door opens. The white rabbit, in a jacket and slacks that display a white tail steps out and walks away briskly. Lucinda and I look at each other, nod our heads and follow him uptown along dark Hudson Street. People on a corner smoking outside a club, do double takes as the rabbit passes.

"It's not just us: ordinary people can see him," Lucinda says.

Unable to stop thinking about Scott, I talk to her compulsively, saying stuff she already knows. "After he'd shot the film, when it was being edited, then shown to distributers he kept spending money on booze and grass. But I thought it was from his magic Trust Fund. As a kid, I'd learned not to notice things I didn't want to see.

"Then I discovered checks were bouncing. The rent was way overdue and his family didn't want to know him. He mainly just lay there smashed out of his mind. Even I knew he was doing narcotics, but I somehow couldn't talk to him about it."

The White Rabbit has led us into the West Village. He turns a corner and facing us is *Down the Rabbit Hole*. "Oh, my," Lucinda says. Without the slightest hesitation, we follow him down the stairs. The bar has, like everything in the Village, been gentrified almost beyond recognition. The rabbit walks past the yuppie clientele, opens the door he opened in the movie and disappears.

On occasion nostalgia has led me here over the decades. I know the door leads, not to a tunnel and a pool of tears, but to a closet full of cleaning equipment. Still, I open it to make sure. The bartender says, "Guy, the restroom's the other way."

Lucinda takes my arm as we exit. Suddenly, on one wall of the bar, we see the whole crew: life size playing cards, birds, beasts, Duchess and Queens. She and I, Alice and The Cheshire Cat, are there. It's not a photo but a kind of living mosaic all alive and nodding to us. We do a double take and they're gone. The bartender and a couple of patrons who were looking our way are blinking and rubbing their eyes.

"Talk about leakage," Lucinda says when we get outside.

"Scott created all that," I say. "I feel like he created me. I even learned to talk like him. To support us when he was down, I ran dirty errands, worked late shifts at clubs, anything short of peddling my ass.

"Around then, Jackstone came by. He was showing New York producers this reel of his camera sequences from our film. This was just before the studios brought him out to Hollywood. He saw Scott and just shook his head. But he connected me with a couple of guys about to film a cop TV movie, told them what I could do.

"I gave them a tour of the waterfront; they gave me a few hundred bucks. Not a lot but it would pay the rent. So, I gave the money to this guy who'd changed my life. The clients wanted me the next day too. So I compounded my stupidity and left him alone in the apartment. When I came home and found him on the floor, I called for help but it was too late."

Because it was drugs, cops were called. Because I was a gay kid I got arrested.

Lucinda knows this story but we need to tell it again no matter how it hurts. Tears come out of her good eye. "I'll never forgive my addiction," she says. "After *Wonderland*, the Warhol crowd and a couple of shock fashion photographers got interested in me. Bonibo was speed to keep you going and then junk to knock you out. I looked like the goddess of death, as you must remember.

"Scott was doing Bonibo, she says. He told me he needed more, said he had to travel. So I furnished his suicide."

We reach my place and she's patting my back and I'm patting hers as we go inside. She calls Uber on her phone. I turn on the light and there's Scott watching us from the photo.

"Justin, you knew I'd dealt him the drugs. You could have told them and you didn't. I still owe you."

"I used my one call to phone Gilda," I said. "Even back then she was connected. Knew a crusading lawyer who got me released. He even found out Scott had put my name on the lease. Made it possible for me to survive."

A horn beeps. I see Lucinda's car in front of the house. She goes to the glass and says, "Oh, Scottso, with you, there was never a regular day. Thank you." She kisses the reflection and me before leaving.

Then I kiss him as always and tell him, *"Some Kind of Wonderland* had a great day. I know you can feel it."

———————

Pan and Hook

Adam McOmber

DO NOT IMAGINE ME NYMPH, NOR FEY, NOR RAGGED spirit of the air. I am a stranger body still. Once, I walked on burnished hooves through the leafy shade of unspoiled Arcadia. Shadows of lush fir spilled over me. I carried a flute of tethered reeds. And there was always music. Or at least the memory of it. I tripped from stone to stone, sometimes pausing to pick lice from the fur of my hindquarters. My mind was quiet, stilled by trees and streams. But in my heart, there hung a kind of longing: a heavy, dripping nest. It was difficult to name all the creatures that inhabited the nest. I could only say that I knew they would never leave me. And I, in turn, would never be permitted to take my leave of them.

How many a handsome soldier did I frighten on those long-ago forest paths? Men, in the dusky light, grew startled at the sound of my music. They claimed they glimpsed a pair of lamp-lit eyes. They heard a violent rustling. There were stories told about me around the campfire. The Beast of Parnon stalks us, they said, the goat-god of the wilderness. And yet, I meant those young Romans no harm. In truth, I longed to hold them, to comfort them. I wanted kiss their full Roman lips and stroke the hard white scars on their shoulder blades.

I remember one dark haired boy, a youth whose name I never learned. I chased him into a copse of Alder trees. He trembled. And then he prayed.

"What have I done?" he said. "The gods—the gods are angry."

I attempted a gentle expression. "I am not angry," I said.

The boy fell to his knees. He shook and wept. Later, I learned he drowned himself in the Tiber.

THERE WAS AN EARLIER AGE, OF COURSE, MORE RUSTIC and more faith-filled. I was worshipped then. Priests made sacrifices in my name. Pindar writes that the virgins sang of me. They called me Ba'al and Tammuz. They wailed and struck their breasts. In truth, the songs of virgins did not interest me. Instead of listening to their paeans, I would climb the barren mountainsides. And in the darkness there, I'd teach handsome shepherds to touch themselves in nighttime fields. I instructed those men how to soothe one another. How to kiss and be kind. I remember the scent of the herdsmen, flesh and sweat and leather. They lay together amongst the broken pillars of long-dead civilizations, wrapped in one other's arms. They were satisfied, clear of eye. And that, to me, was worship. That was praise.

BUT THERE ARE NO LONGER ANY SHEPHERDS ON THE hill or Roman soldiers in the wood. Man is a fool for time. And always, he abandons his gods. Here is how I too was abandoned: One morning, a sailor called Thamus—not a particularly beautiful or interesting boy—was on his way to Florence. Near the coast, he heard what he believed to be a divine voice coming over the water. The voice, in haunted tones, said: *Pan is dead. Proclaim it. The Great God Pan is dead.* I was in the forest when I heard the echo of those words. I listened all day and into evening, hoping for some refute. But the wood remained silent. And I knew the incantation that the voice had spoken was somehow true. The boy, Thamus, repeated it in village and city: *Pan is dead. Pan is dead.* The dreadful words, over and again. And Pan *was* dead. As was Ba'al and Tammuz and even the Beast of Parnon. I was left a nameless thing. Forsaken.

I RETREATED TO AN ISLAND THEN, A BLEAK OUTCROP-
ping in the sea. It was a small enough rock to have no name. White
lilies grew from its crags, and great storms sometimes welled. I
took no interest such things. I did not play my pipe or gambol
along the shores. I hoped only that this place, this empty Never-
Was, might be a vessel strong enough to hold my grief. I told
myself I must learn to feel at home on the cold island. For I too
would "never be" again. I found a grotto. I slept in a cave near a
pool of black water. And there I did not dream. For what would
be the point of that?

And then one day, many years after my arrival on the island, I
heard a clamor upon the sea. There was shouting, and there was
canon fire. I scuttled from my cave and perched upon a stone to
watch two great ships do battle in the island's narrow cove. I saw
fire. The ocean itself turned dark with soot. And after a long while,
when one ship had sunk and the other had sailed victorious, I
slunk back to my cave, wondering whom the dying men might
have prayed to in their last moments.

It was then, on the rocky rim of my home, that I saw a smear
of blood. The blood smelled human. It smelled male. My heart
quickened. I peered into the darkness of my cave and discerned
there a shape: a man, hunched and shivering. I realized he must
have been one of the sailors from the sunken ship. He'd somehow dragged himself here from the sea. The man was handsome,
dark, wearing a red coat with buttons made of gold. His black
hair dripped with brine. The pale fingers of one hand trembled
on his knee.

I crawled toward him in the darkness, hoping not to frighten
him. The sailor, perhaps the captain of the sunken ship according
to his regalia, bled. He'd been wounded in the battle. There was a
deep cut on his cheek. And his left hand, I realized, was entirely
missing. It had been hacked away. Yellow bone, hook-like in its
shape, protruded from the meat of his wrist.

The sailor opened his eyes when he heard my approach. It had
been so long since I was close to a man, since I'd smelled a man's
scent and felt a man's breath. I realized, in that moment, how
badly I wanted this sailor. If he would not worship me, at least
he might know me, make me feel as though I continued to exist.
To my amazement, he did not recoil at my approach. Instead, he

smiled wanly. "Peter—" he whispered there in the darkness of the cave. His lips were bloodless, nearly white. "You're covered in dirt. You've been playing—the river."

I said nothing. For I was not, nor had I ever been, called "Peter." And I did not know what river he spoke of.

"I'm sorry," the sailor said. "I'm so sorry." He winced in pain. "I've wanted to tell you—so many years—I sailed—"

I leaned forward, imagining, for a brief moment, that this bleeding sailor in his red jacket might be the ghost of the other sailor, Thamus, who had long ago proclaimed my death. Thamus had finally come to apologize to me.

Then the sailor spoke again: "You called me *James*," he said. "You tried to hold my hand there by the river. To kiss me. I said you were mad, a strange little nymph. The river Eton, the place we used to go—remember how bright the sun was on those afternoons, Peter?"

I looked into the sailor's eyes.

He did not see me, but instead appeared to recall some long-ago moment.

"I pretend from time to time—" he said. "I pretend that—" He reached for me. "Come closer, Peter."

I crouched.

"Will you stroke my cheek," he said, "as you used to do?"

I touched him, ever so gently, with the sharp claw of my hand.

He raised his own bleeding stump. It appeared as though he thought he was stroking me as well.

"The ship came upon us swiftly," he whispered. "Pirates. Just off the coast of the island. What is the name of this island, Peter?"

Never-Was, I thought.

He sighed. "And my hand—my poor hand."

I gazed at the yellow shard of bone emerging from his wrist.

The sailor spread his lips. There was blood on his teeth. "So strange—" he said. "I dreamed of you just last night, Peter. We were together on board the ship, the Roger. Only, in my dream, it did not sail upon the waters. It *flew*. We traveled together through the clouds. I held you, and we watched a flock of gulls move around us like a school of silvery porpoises. When night fell, we did not land but glided still amongst the bright lamps of the stars."

I touched the sailor's cheek again. His flesh had turned cold.

"I wish that you would kiss me now," James said. "As once you wished to do."

I leaned forward. But before my lips touched his, I paused. Why I did, I cannot say. For wasn't this what I'd longed for? Wasn't this what I'd most desired? Yet to have it now, with a dying man—

It was in that pause that the sailor's eyelids fluttered. His eyes flashed bright. His gaze grew focused. And his expression changed. Fear passed over his dark features. He saw me for what I was. Not Peter. But the Goat. Not the boy he loved. But something he could not even imagine. Something that lived hidden away on an island. Something awful and sad.

The sailor's phantom hand fell away. His breath grew still.

Somewhere in the distance, I heard the divine voice speaking once again. *Pan is dead. And Peter is dead. And now so too, the captain.*

I lay down next to the dead man. I put my arms around him. We remained like that as the sun set on the island, and the night birds began to sing.

———————————

The Summer Mask

Karin Lowachee

I MET YOU IN THE SUMMER WHEN THE BUTTERFLIES began to dance.

You were missing your nose, your right eye, and the top of your lips. Some of your teeth. It made conversation a sort of whistle.

The war had taken half of your face. It had burned your skull into spotted pink and black, like the underbelly of some amphibious creature.

Before the war you were classically beautiful, with classic emerald eyes and a classic strong jaw and classic full lips, but none of these descriptions do you justice. I want to say you were perfect, but it was the imperfections that made you so. Maybe your profile wasn't classically sharp enough. Maybe your smile was a little bit crooked. But who needs perfect symmetry when there is personality? You were perfect enough, so perfectly enough that you brought the beauty with you into rooms and elevated them. You are still a classic beauty.

When I say classic now, I mean the classical sculpture with the nose lobbed off, and the sheared ears, and the missing hands.

When I say classic, I mean the marble you can't touch in museums.

When I say classic, I mean the alabaster hardness of your sorrow.

I FIRST SAW YOU WITH YOUR OPEN FACE TURNED UP TO the sun, the edges of your skull exposed, the emptiness where an eye should have been. The mottled black space stared right at the sun in defiance or entreaty. Your other eye was the color and opacity of smoke trapped in a glass.

God looked back at you but you couldn't see Him.

It was the only reason you didn't burn up. Because you had no seeing eye and all the glory was in the heat. The eye that remained relatively intact saw merely shadows. Maybe that's the only way we can ever see God.

It was the first time you'd felt the sun on your skin, since before.

It was the first time nobody gasped in horror. The nurses, the doctors, the brick manor and the grand fields where lords and their vassals and their hounds used to hunt. All welcomed you and others like you, maskless in the summer. We were there to make you feel at home.

And me, an artist with an artist's eye. Hunting you.

Something about how you stood apart even from your brethren. This platoon of damaged bodies wandering the lawn like the undead, glorying in the simple touch of a summer's breeze. Exclaiming to one another or, like you, moving away from contact as though this shared experience could infect you. You sat by yourself with both hands on the rich green grass, as if it were the only thing holding you to the Earth. I saw your fingers curl into fists and begin to rip it up. You tore the grass from the earth and I wanted to be near you. There was no logic to it but that didn't matter, it was something about the way you destroyed your surroundings, the way your shoulders looked carved out of the day.

They made this place for you. Like I make this mask for you. And other artists make their masks for the other ones who can look in God's eye and not burn.

The ones God had blinded.

But the others aren't quite like you.

I fell in love with your blindness because you couldn't see me. I fell in love with you.

UGLY THINGS NEED TO BE NEEDED. THEY NEED TO have a function to be worthy of their existence. We must justify the spider, not the swan. Beauty can stand on its own.

Beauty is its own kind of magic, you know.

Nobody ever looked at me, but you looked because you couldn't see the bluntness of my features. If God had chiseled man with the precision of focus, He had yawned when he fashioned me. A face that never caught the eyes, never warranted anyone to look twice. Mine was not a face that could ever manipulate, much less lift a room.

So I used my hands.

"MY NAME IS MATTHEW," HE SAID.

We were indoors; the room used to be someone's study. Remnants of bookcases now held carving instruments: blades of different shapes and sizes. Wire. Hammers. A brown globe, its surface like varnished parchment, sat on a corner table. Sometimes I spun it just to hear its joints creak. Through the leaded glass, out in the sun and over Matthew's shoulder, other veterans like him walked around the field. Some played lawn bowling. Others simply lay on their backs on the grass. A few wandered near the garden. They reached to touch the colorful pathways of flowers and turned their faces to the warmth in exultation.

I said, "I'm David. I'm going to remove your mask now, all right?"

"All right," Matthew said, oblivious to what activity he could not see. Maybe he heard them, faintly, like echoes.

His mask was crude, a stitched leather hood like an executioner's, with eyeholes rimmed by tin. Clearly not created for him specifically, for what need had he for eyeholes when he was blind? The metal rings gave the appearance of a machine man locked inside a scarecrow.

"There we are." I gently set the hood on the crafting table beside us.

Matthew blinked his one intact eye, the milky round of it glistening as though some vision moved him. He must have felt me staring. "I know it's hideous," he murmured.

"Not at all."

"Don't lie." There was an edge to his voice. Like a remnant of the war. Or maybe this kind of sharpness only came after all the battles. "I may not be able to see, but I can sense very well."

"I'm not lying. I am your mask maker. I'm seeing your face as it once was and as it will be again."

His partial mouth curled, but it wasn't mirth. "If you're that good, you must be a magician."

He could not see me smile, so I did. "Did you bring your pictures?"

His gaze moved as if he were searching for something, but it was his hands that did the looking. Remnants of white dust coated the lines of his fingers, as though he'd been playing in beach pebbles. An old man's hands, even if he was barely twenty-one. He dipped into the chest pocket of his simple work shirt and withdrew five photographs, all of them burnt a little at the edges. He held them out and I took them. On their sepia surfaces, the man he once was, all of that dark beauty and eyes whose color could still be discerned even in a two tone image. A couple of the photographs faced forward. Two others were profiles. And the last, a three-quarter angle. They were the sorts of portraits one took to hang in a home, framed by gilt. Pictures that would be looked upon by descendants, with static backgrounds and a posed formality.

He didn't say anything and neither did I. He must have known I inspected each one.

Eventually he said, "So what do you think?" The sharpness carved every word, made the soft whistle sound of his speech lilt upward. Like a challenge.

"You remind me of a film star." It was fatuous, too facile a comparison, but I did not care.

"Too bad," he said, with enunciation.

"It will take time," I told him. "But you will see…you will see."

He thought it a turn of phrase. He reached for his blind man's cane where it hooked to the arm of his chair, and pushed himself to his feet. He was already turning away, as if to spare me the sight of him. Or perhaps to spare himself. "I've got all the time in the world, David."

IN THE TWO MONTHS OF OUR SUMMER, I CARVED THE brown clay. From a slab I made angles, and from the angles the vague suggestion of features. I didn't work solely from the photographs. Often I went out to the gardens where he sat and looked at his ravaged profile, no longer something you would see in moving pictures unless it was a horror show. He could be that emaciated vampire now, that ghoul risen from the crypt. But when I looked at him, I saw him whole. My vision reordered itself and wove a glamor. Then I blinked and it dissipated, pulled apart by sunlight.

"How's it going?" he asked, and meant specifically the mask making.

I rubbed at the brown residue on the palm of my hand. "Slowly. I am a perfectionist."

"Don't be." He turned to me, a lopsided regard. The stare of a cyclops. "Anything would be an improvement on this." He didn't speak for pity, but as a matter of fact.

"Would you like to walk in the garden? The flowers smell like Eden."

So we went. He held my arm and tapped his cane in steady rhythm on the flagstones. I wanted to touch his fingers where they curled at my sleeve. We meandered with battalions of flowers at our flanks, such a parade of beauty that the scent of them almost seemed to color the air in rainbows. Without his nose, could he truly smell them? But I didn't ask.

He stopped walking. "What kinds are they?"

"Hydrangeas, marigolds, azaleas…roses. If you squint they look like a Seurat painting."

His grip tightened and he turned as if he could see them. The willows nearby blocked the angle of the sun just enough that I didn't have to blink. His one eye remained round and wide.

"Sometimes," he said, "I see variation in shadow and light. Like… like fish swimming beneath a pond."

"But no color?"

He shook his head.

"But you remember color."

"Yes, of course."

"The imagination," I said, "can feel as real as reality. Think of all the things you could never see, even when you had sight, but you knew them to be true."

"What do you mean?" His breathing was becoming labored, so I guided him toward an iron bench along the path, where we sat.

I turned to his damaged face. "Like emotions. Like love."

I could not tell from the movement of what remained of his mouth if the expression was derision or skepticism, or simply an acknowledgment of understanding.

"We live in a scientific age." I looked at his hands, how they had returned to himself, holding the cane across his lap. "But there is yet so much that science cannot see."

"It's not the same, David. Love and the color of flowers."

"Maybe we blind ourselves," I said. "Maybe they are exactly the same."

———

IF HIS OTHER SENSES WERE HONED, LIKE HE CLAIMED, could he feel what I was feeling when I looked at him? Not disgust or hesitation, not pity or clinical assessment. Even if he didn't believe that I could see the parts of him that were no longer there, could he still discern my longing?

I was never likeminded. Head in the clouds, my parents said. I became mesmerized by the spots on the backs of ladybugs. I spent whole afternoons as a child trying to find four leaf clovers in wild fields. I gazed at clouds. Maybe all children did these things, accompanied by questions like how was it possible that I only saw out of my own eyes? Why was I always inside my own body? Would the Sun ever die? Until those questions became almost incidental considerations when my sight, all of my staring, began to form a second layer.

What I could see, what I could fashion…what I could imagine into being. That became my reality.

His features made of clay had to be perfect. First I was going to mold them with my hands. Then came everything after.

———

BY THE END OF THE SUMMER I CONJURED THE COURAGE to ask him how it had happened. His face. Maybe this was like asking a convict why he was imprisoned and the answer would be a lie or at least some polished version of the truth. But for some reason I knew he would not lie to me. We had spent the weeks nearly exclusively in each other's company. He didn't talk much to the other artists, nurses, or veterans. He isolated himself in more than just his blindness. But for me, his mask maker, he walked along the flower paths. He sat beneath willows and napped by the maples, a black scarf across his eyes like a bandit. He asked me to read him books, especially when I told him I could pronounce Chaucer in the Old English manner.

It was a warm night without being oppressive. The manor house was lit inside, just enough to throw out a glow to meet what the moon made on the Earth. Darkness started at the garden, though, and shrouded even the trees. It was peaceful as we sat on the veranda. Someone played the old harpsichord in the drawing room behind us, a trickle of music.

"I don't remember many details," Matthew said. "The doctors told me that is probably a blessing." He made a sound like a bird rustling beneath newspaper; it was his laughter. "If that word could be applied to my condition at all. Wouldn't you rather be dead?"

No, I thought. But it was a selfish answer. I would not want him to be dead either.

"The last thing I recall is walking through a field. We had just left a village. There was a treeline. It was such a quiet day, like a day here. The sky was so blue, and there was some kind of hawk circling above us. I remember looking up at it and wishing I could be that hawk. Then they opened fire on us and there must have been some sort of explosion..." He gestured to his face but he wasn't facing me. He looked instead toward the dark. "After that, I woke up in the hospital with my whole head wrapped up like King Tut. A miracle, they kept saying. A miracle. Because they were too afraid to say it was a curse."

I knew he had never said these words to anyone else. I thought of what it must have been like in the city, where he had to walk the streets with a crude mask on. Where people stared regardless, children pointed. Where, maybe, he didn't even go out except at night. I didn't work up the nerve to ask him those details yet. But I knew that here, in this place, it was the first time the sunlight and the breeze touched what was left of his face.

"I am not even the same inside," he continued. "My family says, oh Matthew, you're the same person no matter what is on the outside. But I'm not. How can I be?"

"You are not the same person, but that's not wrong." Here I flailed to say something of meaning, something he would hear. But he wasn't listening to my voice.

"I can hear what people think now. It's quite a gift." He laughed again, that paper rustling sound. "I am a creature in the world."

"This world is just as much yours. It will be again." He didn't say anything to that. Affirmations had a way of always sounding like lies. "Where will you go when you leave here?" Stay here, I wanted to say. Even if it wouldn't be possible. This was not a permanent boarding house.

"I live with my aunt. Maybe…maybe you can visit?"

I was surprised. Maybe he had been listening after all.

But the winter was when I had to do the most difficult part of the work. Still, I could not say no to him.

"I would love that."

ON THE LAST DAY OF OUR SUMMER HE ASKED TO SEE ME. We were in my work room. His unfinished mask of clay sat on the table. It resembled him, but like a distant relative, not a twin. "I'm sorry I couldn't finish it for you, but it will be ready for next summer."

He held the executioner's hood in his hands, sitting across from me. "You know what I look like. I want to know what you look like."

So I let him. He used his hands, rough fingers that pressed the edges of my face, found every dry riverbed that creased my skin beyond its years. I had spent long hours in the sun in my youth. He mapped my narrow jaw, the bare growth of stubble, the ax of my nose. The sloping forehead and thick wiry hair. All the while I stared into the black emptiness of his eye and saw his future visage. The remade mouth that would smile without pain. The full arch of his dark brows. Reflected light in jade jewel irises.

"What color is your hair?" he asked.

"Like mouse fur."

He pinched the ends of the locks, then withdrew. Like ritual, he slipped the executioner's hood over his head and pushed himself to his feet, cane in hand. Like so, he was emotionless. Faceless. Anonymous.

Except I saw it in his walk out the door. The cadence of his step and the cane sounded like sadness.

IN THE WINTER IS WHEN YOU BECOME WHOLE, MY golem, the way you imagine yourself to be, the way I know you still wish you were. In the winter I sweep my hands over your clay cheekbones to make them sharper, I carve above your eyes to create eyelids, I readjust your hairline when it reaches too high. Your brows arch easily into a strong forehead. Each crease is a memory, a worry, or the result of a past sun. You must be perfect, and I dig for it like a dog. I find you beneath my fingernails, and no matter how much I peel and scrub, there are parts of you still there, embedded in my fingerprints, staining my cuticles, setting the love and life lines on my palms into relief. You have become a part of my future.

Through the dark months I see your face looking back up at me, smoothed by water and hours and my hands. It is a photograph come alive, but in sleep. Eyes are not open yet, lips do not speak. It is still a death mask.

In my attic room I read your letters, your musings of what you hear from the windows—the dramas of sidewalk life and street traffic; the stray dogs and serpentine strides of men and women about their business, light and wind on their faces (you imagine it)—masks of a different kind. So many thoughts and intentions and worries barricaded behind eyes you cannot see. In your letters there is the absence of admitting you don't like to go out, most days you can't shoulder the scrutiny unless it is so cold you can wrap yourself in wool like everybody else, and become hidden in falling snow. I collect the invitations to come visit you at your aunt's, but I wait until the last minute.

The last minute when there is nothing more left to do with your mask but the final act for the summer and the trees have begun to awaken from their winter slumber.

The last minute where I can look on you with clear eyes, before the blindness takes me.

HIS AUNT'S STUDY WAS UNLIKE THE ONE AT THE MANOR. Here, dusty books piled one upon the other in cascades of leather and paper. The walls were faded red velvet with ivory wainscoting, the drapery full of gray lace and curlicue patterns. The room looked a little like an aged wedding cake. Here, Matthew wore his executioner's hood because he said his aunt was afraid to see his full face in dim hallways.

"What does it look like outside? I put my hand to the glass and it's still a little cold."

It was night. The trees turned into arthritic silhouettes and icy breezes tossed day old newspapers and pamphlets down the street. It was the season of ghosts. But I told him, "It is weather for deep breathing and mittens. You can smell the chimney smoke still."

"Yes," he said, with the eagerness of agreement. Scents, of course, were always present.

"I came to tell you I have finished your mask. But I will give it to you at the summer house."

He straightened his shoulders. He wore a black cable knit sweater that made his body thin. In the photographs he'd seemed broad and strong. "Why didn't you bring it here? Why do you want to wait?"

"There is one last thing to do and it will take some time."

"But you said it was finished."

"Yes…it's difficult to explain."

He looked toward the tall windows, though the drapes were closed. As if he'd heard something outside the gate. "Were you working on other masks?"

"No. I…was supposed to. But yours is the only one I truly cared about."

Was it easier to confess things to the blind? Perhaps. But a voice could be just as revealing as an expression in the eyes. From inside that executioner's mask, he didn't seem to move. One milky eye peered toward me, past me. His hands held his cane as if it were a lifeline on a raft and he was the last survivor of a catastrophic sinking.

"Are you very alone?" he said, though we sat just inches apart.

A question from one creature to another.

"I have been."

It wasn't sadness, but a strange melancholy that beset me when I left his home. He walked me to the door, as if I was some kind of gentleman caller.

"I will see you in the summer," he said. These easy turns of phrases that had now become ironic and impossible.

Nearly, anyway. Nearly impossible.

"You will."

———————

THERE IS BLOOD, OF COURSE. FOR SOMETHING SUCH AS this, there can only be blood and the pain of blood. The Savior bled from every pore and birth is never gentle. Neither rebirth. The incantations of the heart can save or skewer. An eye for an eye.

My eyes for your eyes. The carving blade I set to clay, now to my own skin, my eyes, my face. To carve myself out of myself and to say the words, and taste the blood, that transmogrifies these parts to become yours.

To make them eternal, the Egyptians mummified their royal dead. This is the least I can do. What grander gesture of love and eternity and sacrifice? What better way to say it? Long ago I'd come to realize the absence of my own life. To move through the world unnoticed was more painful than the most lashing mockery. How to justify my own existence when from day to day there was neither joy nor anything as raw as sorrow? There is only a middle place that stretches on, and I can see no end and no beginning, no features on either side, no landmarks and no population; it is only this and I am in the middle of it, turning to all compass points but each way is equally gray. I wake up to count the hours when I can sleep again, seeking oblivion, but my dreams betray me. In them are phantasms of worry and loss, memory mixed with some future I know has happened already because in my dreams I am a child aware of my grown life and all that does not exist anymore. My town, my parents, their harsh judgment and protective love, and all of my resentments and regrets balled up like fists that I beat against each bizarre nightmare that stalks me into the waking world. I am screaming or I am crying, as if the only emotions that can swim to the surface of my living life are born from the dark places, these rooms in which I speak like speech is a covenant made only with devils. The devils linger in the mornings and at the foot of my bed, and I am finished with it.

I need to be done. I need to make meaning and before you there was none.

So now there is the blood and I cry into the bath of it made from the excavation of my own face, each word a scream, each sound a promise, and I touch my wet red hands to the clay mask to make it come alive.

WE ARE AT THE SUMMER HOUSE. ONE OF THE NURSES brings him into the old study, I hear her voice. I hear how she doesn't linger in the room with us and the door shuts. It is late in the afternoon when the sun begins to slant away to shun the moon.

"David?"

"I'm here." My vision is shadow and light, like fish dancing beneath a stream. "I have your mask, but you must sit very still and not say a word."

"I'm not going anywhere." There is the sound of leather set on the floor. His executioner's hood, discarded.

"Don't move and don't say a word. You'll know when it's all right."

"David?" Concern in his tone, because I repeat myself.

But I don't answer. I see just enough of the outline of him. It manifests the way dreams do, where if I stare long enough I can remember when I awaken. I hold his mask in my hands but now edge forward in my seat. I begin to say the words and he doesn't interrupt me, though the sound of the words must perturb or even frighten him. Words that bleed into themselves and begin to sound like nothing at all except discordant keening. There is a stone in my throat, as smooth as something resting in a riverbed, and my words are the tides that glide over it, giving it shape. Changing its shape.

This mask made of me now slips over his skin. He gasps. I speak louder. I touch his cheeks and feel them tighten. I run my fingers over the edges of him, feel muscle and bone, cartilage and tears. His tears. I imagine setting my mouth to them for their salt, I can even see it from within my own shadows, like peering through a keyhole. All the pain was given already, it is splattered and stained in my attic back in the city. The scent of it will never disappear. Maybe it's still on my hands, beneath my fingernails, driven deep into the lines on my palms. Maybe my hands are red when they touch all over his new, perfect face.

He seizes my wrists. "David."
I can't see him. He says, "David."
He doesn't let go of me. He says, "David."
He can see now. He can see me.
He wrenches himself away and runs from the room.

I WAKE UP ONLY TO STAY IN BED. DO YOU KNOW WHAT it's like to sleep when you can't close your eyes? When there are no eyes to shut? Sleep and wakefulness become the same thing, it is only a matter of dreams. And even then.

Of course you came back to me, when the shock wore off. All you kept saying was, "How do I explain? How do I explain?" as if the world had become closed to just that question when in fact it had opened out again. You could see, you were whole, you had your features back, that classical beauty before the ages took you, before any sort of war and walk in the field. You could look up again and see the hawk, the sky was just as blue as you remembered, even bluer, and nothing hurt when you smiled. And you smiled. You smiled like it was the first expression to ever cross your mind, you smiled like a baby does when it wants to understand the world, you smiled like you were in love. Maybe you were in love with yourself and the possibilities and despite what was left of my face you couldn't stop yourself from smiling.

"I don't understand," but it didn't matter because you held my hand in your confusion and you said that I was terrible for doing this to myself but I could hear it in your voice how easy it was to lie. Of course there was guilt but there was also gratitude and that was all that mattered. That and the way you held my hand and you held my mind in the palm of your hand, you were all I thought about and all I had been thinking about since last summer.

Now you read to me, now we took walks in the garden and I held your arm, I tapped a cane, I stared into shadows and the edges of flickering light, like a moving picture that had hit the end of its reel and if I looked very hard, I could rewind to some vision of reality where we are both whole and walking amongst the flowers and we both feel the perfect breeze on our perfect skin and you will let me taste the salt on your cheeks that isn't from tears. This is my dream now.

So we spent the summer and of course I knew it had to end, you kept saying you didn't know how you would ever explain and I said, "Don't explain." What I meant was, Don't say the words. Don't say you're thankful, don't say you'll never forget, don't say you'll write because all I want to hear is *Don't go.* But I'm not the one who's going, after all. I am staying, I will find an attic that doesn't carry the scent and texture of blood because there is no other place in the world for me, we know this. I hear it in the sound of your voice, I feel it in the grip of your hands and it's true, my senses have not diminished, especially not the one that saw you that first afternoon in the first summer when you tore the grass from the earth.

You were tearing my heart out of my chest. You are tearing my heart out of my chest, and I give it to you like I gave you the other parts of me and refashioned them into something beautiful. What was dead has come alive.

You are this beautiful and it doesn't need to be justified. It doesn't need to be explained.

Beauty is its own kind of magic, you know.

The Library of Lost Things

Matthew Bright

THE LIBRARIAN TURNED HIS EYES UPON ME, REVERSED the single sheet of paper once, then neatly back again.

"An excellent candidate," he said.

And:

"Thomas Hardy. An apropos name. We have one of his, you know? No relation, I assume?"

And:

"'Favourite grammatical form: passive voice.'" He looked me up and down, pinprick eyes narrowed, and licked his dry bottom lip. "Marvellous."

"Sir?" I said.

The Librarian's tongue flickered. "So wonderfully *uninterested.* Most boys, well they come here with their nasty adverbs and their present tense, or, God forbid, *second person.*" When he shuddered his spine cracked like an old hardback opened in one swift, cruel motion. "Quite unsuitable. You on the other hand…"

And, after some deliberation:

"Very well. The job is yours, young Thomas."

"Tom," I said and swallowed with relief that he hadn't asked me why I wanted to work for the Library. I'd prepared a response, but I doubted it would impress. The Librarian's eyes were sharp and astute, shadowed in the hollows beneath a foxed brow. He would have picked apart my half-truths, separating non-fiction from fiction and, suspicious, sniffed around the superlative adjectives.

"Come along." He unfolded his eight-foot frame from the armchair. A stick insect stretching. He led me out of his office, down a long hall which echoed our footsteps, and to a set of ornate double doors. "Through here," he said, "is the main hall of the Library. You must always treat this place with the utmost respect. We serve a greater good. Stay long and you will know this."

He guided me through the doors. On the other side, bookshelves reached the horizon.

The Librarian bent close to my ear. He reeked like damp secondhand bookshops, or comic books left to moulder in the bottom of a wardrobe. "How would you describe it, *Tom?*"

I was still being tested. The interview was not truly over. Perhaps it never would be.

I looked from one behemoth shelf to the next: it was a graveyard of spines, leather, paper, string, the wormed carcasses of all those books, buried next to each other one after another into the dark. The feeling of disintegrated sentences hung in the air, a deadness of language, like a word abandoned mid-syllable.

"It's impressive," I said.

"Impressive." The Librarian outstretched his arms to the expectant hall. "It takes you three syllables to encompass all this?"

I had been memorising *Roget's 1911*. "Large," I said.

He chuckled. "Better to be faced with an eternity of literature and render it down to one uttered word, one brief sound. 'Large'— I think you'll be perfect."

From beneath a shelf of peeling grimoires, scratchy muttered sounds could be heard. At first I interpreted them as squeaks, then realised instead that they were voices. Words, I realised. "Stripling! Gangrel! Pilgarlic!" A scurry of grey tiny shapes crossed our path and disappeared among the nearest bookshelf.

"Ignore the rats," the Librarian said. "So bothersome. I try to keep them away from the books, but they over-run the place. They have a particular taste for the folios. I suppose it's only natural they've picked up some words. But such *bothersome* words." He licked a spindly forefinger and thumbed his lapel as if he could turn the page of his suit. "To work then, my unremarkable boy."

He led me through the stacks, past row upon row of books. Some were bound in leather, some gaudy, some decrepit, some little more than stapled paper, and some emanating a faint electric glow. Skittering around in the shadows, the rats could be heard in our wake: "Jackanape! Welkin!"

"*Voilà!*" said the Librarian. "The Index."

Like a still pool in a forest, the library had given way to clear empty space containing a circle of doors, freestanding and unsupported, each unadorned apart from a single round window at head height. Narrow bookcases stood attendant by each, laid out like spokes within the wheel of doors.

"Observe." The Librarian plucked the first volume waiting on one of the bookcase-spokes. It was gently smoking; the Librarian carefully patted out its glowing embers. He inspected both of its covers. "*Sonnenfinsternis* by Arthur Koestler. You do know German? I've been waiting for this one. File this under Wartime Casualties."

And:

A sandy pile of barely bound papers. "*The Visions of Iddo the Seer*—fascinating. File under Myriad Apocrypha."

And:

A sheaf of laser-printed paper. "*Untitled Novel About a Boy with No Hands (Incomplete)* by S. Berman. That's one for the Self-Doubt section—half a novel deleted in a crisis of confidence, if I'm not mistaken." He coughed. No, it was a laugh. "I'm never mistaken."

And:

A threadbare exercise book missing one of its staples. "*The Collected Works of the Poet Jeremiah Blenkinsop, Aged 13-and-Three-Quarters.* Much as I regret that we must collect such ephemeral dross: file under Adolescent Verse. Do I make the task at hand clear? Take the volume, examine its cover, file in the appropriate section."

I nodded.

"Under no circumstances do you *open the book*. Is that clear?"

When I was late in responding, he peered at me. "You are not a curious boy are you? I insist on no aspirations, no predilections. Books are not to be read."

"I haven't read a word since my GCSEs, sir."

He smiled. I suppressed a shudder. His teeth were spotted, like the acid foxing on old paper.

In the round window of the door directly behind the Librarian, a face appeared. It was a wide, flat face, that of a rag doll's, or a scarecrow's—the look emphasised further by thick stitches that shut his eyes. The door opened to admit the lumpish creature. Behind it, I saw a vista: not the Library stretching away but a courtyard at night. A mound of books burned and the silhouettes of men watched from below scarlet flags. At the sound of a bugle, each figure raised their right arm high in salute.

The Librarian noted how I stared. "1943 Common Era," he said in a grave tone. "So many books lost forever. We were understaffed—had been since the Great Pandemic."

The rag-doll creature unloaded an armful of still-smouldering books onto the case before turning back to the door. The Librarian stopped it. "This is a Collector," he said, then added, squinting at the nametag sewed on his chest, "Gadzooks."

"Why are his eyes sewn shut?"

The Librarian scowled. "That's only a metaphor." He squinted at me. "You know…symbolic? *Not real?*" He sighed and bent an arm around my shoulder. "Gadzooks, this is Thomas Hardy. Passive voice, mind you. He's our new Indexer."

Gadzooks bowed his head.

"I trust you'll show him the ropes," said the Librarian, "and then to his chambers at the end of the day." He picked up the next book on the shelf. "Misguided Pornography," he said, then placed it into my hands and shuffled away.

So:

I worked, for an indeterminate number of hours, filing away the books as they were deposited on the stands for my inspection. I saw many more Collectors, barging in and out of their respective doors, carrying armfuls of books; through the frames, I caught glimpses of a multitude of places—a sun-baked Jerusalem, a Scottish highland under water, the underwear-strewn floor of a teenager's bedroom. 1943 remained where it was even as the others changed; clearly there was much work to be done there. Gadzooks lumbered around gloomily beside me, pointing in the right direction for each department: "Censored Tracts? By the fountain. Suicide? Fourth on your left. Hard Drive Failure? Up the ladders by Rejected First Novels." His gentle voice belied his maimed face.

Occasionally on my journeys I would spy the rats. One might dash close and spit out a forgotten word at me—"Nidgery! Borborygmus!"—then skitter away back beneath the stacks. Gadzooks grunted and chased them away. "They seem to like you," he said.

And then:

The day closed, Collectors unloaded their last piles and vanished. All but Gadzooks, who gestured for me to follow him. I did so, because I was a curious boy, and let him lead me into the deep warren of the Library. We arrived at a rickety spiral staircase at the back of Reformation Sermons. The small room at the top was draughty and sparsely furnished, nothing much more than an unmade bed and a little writing table.

"Your room," said Gadzooks.

I thanked him, expecting him to leave. Instead he hovered in the doorway, wringing his massive and scarred hands.

"Yes?" I asked.

"Sometimes at night, we—well, I wondered if you might like to come…to a party?"

And then:

A trio of Collectors recited couplets from *Love's Labour's Won*, regaling each other with smutty double entendres. In another corner, a gaggle of Collectors pored over Byron's diaries, pausing frequently to *ooh* and *ahh*. Another group gathered in armchairs, pouring absinthe over sugar cubes into their glasses, and repeating lines to each other from Rimbaud's *La Chasse Spirituelle*. "Welcome to the Speakeasy." Gadzooks moved with a bit of mirth.

He led me to the bar, introducing me to those we passed on the way, a series of names—Tango, Philtrum, Esperanza, Pushkin—that I immediately failed to correctly attribute to their proper owners. "This is Tom, the new Indexer," he said, and they all earnestly shook my hand and recited couplets for me by way of introduction.

"Whiskey," said Gadzooks at the bar. "You do drink whiskey?"

I felt bold. "Naturally." A glass was pressed into my hand.

Perched on a bar stool atop a table, there was another boy, who looked older than me because of his long silvery hair. He played an elegant tune on the violin. "From the Library of Music across **65** the Silent Canyon." Gadzooks caught me looking, and perhaps mistook the expression on my face. "They sneak across when the Librarian isn't looking. That tune he's playing—Mozart and Salieri's *Per la Ricuperata Salute di Ophelia*. One of their prize possessions." But I wasn't thinking of a boy from the halls of lost music; instead, I was remembering a boy from a place far more ordinary and humdrum, though his fingers were no less nimble on the strings.

Still—he was a long way away, and I was here, in the Library, and that was the price I had paid.

They refilled my glass a second, then a third time, and I gladly accepted.

The door burst open and two Collectors entered, flanking a man covered entirely by a threadbare blanket. The door safely closed behind him, he threw off his covering, and spread his arms; he was greeted with a cheer. At first glance he appeared emaciated, almost consumptive, resembling a child's pipe-cleaner puppet, but he had a flamboyant assertiveness that belied the wispiness of his physical presence. "Ladies and gentlethings, I am *here*! Quite enough of the sad songs, don't you think?"

The musician switched to a guitar and launched into a rendition of David Bowie's "Jean Genie," though this version of the lyrics weren't those Tom remembered; a lost version, he supposed, like everything else here. The song seemed to prompt a sea-change in the party; a Collector with beautiful silver stitching climbed up beside him and swayed her hips, the bartender began acrobatically tossing bottles, the patrons starting to turn around the dancefloor with a newly giddy energy.

"That's more like it," said the man, sauntering to the bar. "And, why *hello* to *you*! Gadzooks, who might this handsome fellow be?"

"Tom—the new Indexer," said Gadzooks.

Although I had known the man was referring to me, I feigned surprised.

"A shame—one must never fall for an Indexer; the lamps are lit, but there's never anyone home." The man seized a glass from the bar, and tapped me on the nose. "Lovely you might be…but I require a tryst to possess a modicum of intelligence. What comes out of a mouth is just as vital as what goes in." He gave me a lingering look and then left for the swell of partiers.

"Who's he?"

Gadzooks looked at me as if I'd spat on his paws. "Jean Genet. We recovered the original *Notre Dame des Fleurs*. The Librarian has no idea."

Genet perched himself atop a suitcase in the centre of the room, thumbing theatrically through a sheaf of papers in his hand. "Shall I *read*?" he called out to the crowd, who cheered and held their drinks aloft. "Very well, very well. *'I wanted to swallow myself by opening my mouth very wide and turning it over my head…'* Oh, this is one of my favourite bits! I remembered it word for word—got this one just right!"

Gadzooks handed me another glass. "That's Hemingway's suitcase that he's standing on," he said, with great import.

When I did not react with awe, he sighed and abandoned me.

I didn't remain alone for long.

Genet plucked at my shirt-sleeve. "Remarkably, I find it easier as the night wears on to ignore your lack of discursive faculties. Animals rut, and *they* cannot reason."

I sipped from my glass, holding it as a meagre barricade between myself and him. I had been with men. I preferred it. But never with a Genet.

He summoned two tall conical glasses from the barman, and placed a slotted spoon across each one, on which he placed a sugar cube. His fingers—contrary to his otherwise louche presence—were long and nimble, executing his actions with quiet delicacy. I found the practised nature of his preparations reassuring.

Absinthe trickled over the cube, dissolving the sugar, and pooling in the bottom of the glass. Genet interlinked his arm through mine, bending it back around to reach his mouth. "Thank goodness you're not Rimbaud," he said before taking a gulp. I sipped and coughed. He laughed. His warm breath traced across my cheek before he kissed me hard. He drank again, and determined, this time, I matched him sip for sip. It lit an emerald fire in my belly.

There were boisterous shouts rippling around the Speakeasy—Genet wheeled around, discarding his empty glass. "What's that? You want me to go on a *night run*?"

I swayed on my stool. "What's a night run?" Was it the longest sentence I had said all day? It felt marvellous.

"Wait and see," said Genet. I caught a glimpse of Gadzooks across the room. He shook his head, and I wondered if the gesture indicated disappointment or a warning. No matter—Genet took my hand and pulled me up. "I'm hearing…'The Ocean to Cynthia' by Walter Raleigh? Any other offers?"

Calls sounded from around the room.

"*The Romance of the Devil's Fart!*" "*Inventio Fortunata!*" "*A Time for George Stavros!*" "*The Poor Man and the Lady!*"

Genet gestured as if he had tasted a bad oyster. "Boring!"

"Plath's *Double Exposure!*"

Genet grinned. "Excellent. Come along, my handsome witling!"

And then:

The overhead gas lamps were extinguished, but a kind of luminescence, much the same lustre as moonlight, emanated from the stitching of the oldest books on the shelves like silvery skeletons. I crouched low.

Genet swaggered ahead of me. I half expected him to burst into song, or start skipping.

At the Index firelight still burned in one door window, casting a lone spot of colour across the flagstones. Genet stood and looked through, waiting for me to catch up. "1943," he said. "I escaped from one hell into another."

He spun on his heel. "Just through that door and a few streets away there is a room above a tavern. And in that room is a bed with springs that sing as you fuck. Would you like to discover conjugating?"

A rat scurried. I jumped, startled, which he mistook for virginal anxieties.

Genet laughed. "Relax. We must forge a path to Plath." He led me away from the ring of doors. He seemed to have a knack for moving without eliciting noise; I did not share it. Each footfall of my own rang back at me from the shelves. I fell behind. Genet had vanished, leaving lazy spirals of disturbed dust in the air, and I was on my own.

I anticipated he would be thumbing through the Suicide section, but I arrived and found it solemn. Rather than being alphabetised, here the shelves were organised by methods of dispatch. Most works were incomplete. I traced my finger along the shelves, moving from gas oven to hanging, then finally to razorblade. I squatted, tilted my head to read the spines.

And there it was:

The Sum of All Our Tales. Barnabus Hardy. A single slim volume, it seemed insignificant in the vastness of the Library. I pulled it carefully from the shelf, and ran my fingers over the plain cover. The type was raised; my skin prickled. To hold the book in my hands had been worth the exhausting pretences of the day.

A tiny voice spoke in the dark, inches from my ear. "Swivet."

I nearly fainted.

I envisioned the Librarian leaning down from the ceiling, his hands armed with a needle and cord with which to sew my eyes shut.

The rat sat bolt upright on the fourth shelf, grooming its snout. "Zamzodden."

I looked around before uttering "Rumblegumption." The sheer delight of multiple syllables, held dammed up inside me all day, burst onto my tongue. I added another for good measure. "Falstaffian."

It paused and cocked its head. Shiny black eyes stared at me. "Anopisthograph."

I thought for a second. "Sardoodledom."

The rat twitched its nose and long whiskers and dashed away, throwing back over its scaly fine tail a disgruntled, "Ninnyhammer." It dislodged a book, which fell with a ponderous thud.

"Well now, my handsome library boy. This is a surprise." Genet was leaning casually against Shotgun/A-G, watching me. He stepped close to me. In the moonlight, it was almost possible to describe his gaunt face as handsome. "I was injurious in my dismissal of your mind. Hiding such an"—he reached out and grabbed at the crotch of my trousers—"impressive vocabulary would be grounds for"—he squeezed and I gasped (truth be told, I was hard, rigid, *tumescent* then, both by the wickedness of the man and my discovery)—"termination."

I stepped back and he released me. His scuffed shoe nudged the fallen book. *Double Exposure*. "Of course," I said. "We should go back."

He tsked. "Say it right."

I sighed. "It would be auspicious for us to return to the Speak-easy before our mischief is discovered by a certain overseer." Somewhere within me a door opened.

———————

THE LIBRARIAN FOUND ME ON THE MORNING OF MY second day's employment hungover and only a few breaths short of whimpering at every book deposited by the Collectors for me to index.

"How's our young man doing?" he said, unfolding his papery frame from between the stacks.

Behind him, Gadzooks mumbled something. He had barely glanced at me beyond the necessary since the night before, when Genet and I had burst into the Speakeasy out of breath and dishevelled and sweaty.

"Fine," I said, enunciating the single syllable with care.

"Tremendous, tremendous," he said, rubbing his endpapers together. "The Index is looking pleasingly sparse. Fine job, fine job." He paused, mid-flow, and looked around, wrinkling his nose. "Hmmm."

And:

"*Hmmmmm.*"

I rubbed my bleary eyes. "What's wrong?"

Gadzooks looked away.

The Librarian took a deep breath which expanded his torso like an accordion. "Something smells amiss," he said. "No. Something smells...*missing.*"

I risked a glance over his shoulder, to where the slim pink spine of *Double Exposure* sat on the shelf.

The Librarian sniffed again. "Most incomprehensible." He departed, dragging his long coat on the ground, which rather than wiping them bare instead lined the flagstones with dust in his wake.

———————

I FRETTED ALL THE DAY. SHELVING VOLUME AFTER volume of lost books, I slipped more than a few times on the cold brass ladders. Behind texts, the rats devoured the deracinated and the archaic. Gadzooks laboured next to me, but he still avoided conversation.

That night he did not invite me back to the Speakeasy. I didn't mind: I had other things to occupy my time. Before he had been smuggled back to 1943, Genet had pressed the worn copy of *Our Lady of the Flowers* into my arms, suggesting that it might make good bedtime reading, and departing with a lascivious wink. (Thinking on it later, his precise words had been, "Take this and think of me in bed," which I supposed wasn't quite the same thing.)

And so it was for a week or so. The Librarian would appear unbidden and unnoticed, sniffing the air before vanishing, leaving me to dreary tasks—filing the assembled works of a seven-volume fantasy epic into Doubt, box after box stuffed into Teenage Diaries, navigating the complex organisation of Pantos/Variations/Peter Pan.

Gadzooks had been correct about the rats' fondness for me; they would appear amongst whatever shelf I was tending. "*Anopisthograph!*" said one in particular. I was convinced it was the very same rodent with which I had exchanged words on the night run. "You've already had that one," I said, and shooed it away.

The next day I saw the Librarian sniffing around the display that featured famous luggage—the Library must have had other workers, still unseen, who tended to the glass-enclosed exhibitions of the detritus of authors—and with that long finger tapped by Hemingway's suitcase. I was thankful that—for tonight at least—Genet's manuscript was not hidden within as it usually was, with such fragrant prose that the Librarian could not have failed to scent its presence.

Yet, for all his strange behaviour, the Librarian didn't seem to suspect I possessed an intellect or a libido.

Eventually Gadzooks thawed, and reappeared at my bedroom door. "Would you like to—y'know…?"

At the Speakeasy, Genet regaled the crowd from atop the suitcase. (I wondered what had Hemingway done to Genet to deserve such roughshod disregard for his possessions, and eventually asked him; he said only "The man is famous for writing about a fish. Not a whale but a fish.") Genet greeted me loudly. "Witling! I don't suppose you have my book on you? I've drunk enough to chase away the memory of what I wrote ages ago. That I can remember my own name is a wonder."

He pirouetted drunkenly, and toppled over. He chuckled. "Perhaps I shall just be Jean tonight and let Genet stay on the shelf."

I helped him to the bar. I arranged two glasses, placed spoons over them, and a sugar cube atop each. Genet watched my hands as I poured the absinthe over it.

"Why do you leave it here?" I said.

"It? Pronouns are the weakest of words. Even an adverb has more panache."

I leaned into him. He thought I meant to kiss him and I moved at the last moment so my lips touched his ear. "Your book," I whispered into it, and felt Genet press vigorously against me; after all, what words could be more seductive to a writer? "They smuggle you in, they smuggle you out—couldn't you take it with you?"

Genet held my face in his hands and blinked a while. "A first draft—a mere masturbatory fantasy. It belongs right here, one more lost book. It's a dirty rag for my spent fantasies, written in the throes. What was published is superior." He frowned. "At least, that's what the Collectors say. I've only sold…" He let go of me and began to count on his fingers but quickly lost his way. "Well, not many, but they tell me that one day—"

I kissed him. Our teeth clicked and thankfully parted. We had yet to even drink the sugared absinthe but I found his mouth so pleasing that I did not notice someone tugging at the cuff of my trousers.

No, not someone. A rising wave of noise broke the familiar chatter. The minstrel faltered in his song; the assembled revellers bloomed into panic. The single rat at my feet let go of the fabric and leapt for my knee, claws digging through my trousers into the skin. "Anopisthograph. Anopisthograph!" and then at the doors the noise crescendoed with a tumult of panicked rats spilling through and across the floor.

Genet cursed. I shouted, "The Librarian!"

And:

"Run!"

And:

We dashed, and it was hard not to laugh with how Genet smiled as we escaped. I pulled him towards the Index; he pulled me towards the staircase; in the tension between the two we spun in each other's arms as if we were dancing. In the end, I did not deny him another night spent in my bed. I shut the door fast, almost crushing the rat that scampered in and took refuge in my writing desk.

"Ow," Genet said as we collapsed onto the mattress. "How can you sleep? What is in this? Horsehair?" He wet my lips. "Have you ever eaten *cheval?*" He groped me. "It's an acquired taste."

Authors were indeed.

––––––––––

I NIBBLED ON THE SWEET ROLLS THEY FED US. I HAD pocketed an extra one for Gadzooks.

"The last Indexer would give me his meals," Gadzooks said as he chewed. "He never came to the Speakeasy. He wasted away in his room."

"Lost in a book?" I said.

"Oh, no. He didn't dare read. I think that's why he faded to nothing. Every time he spoke he lost the words in his head." Gadzooks rapped on his misshapen skull. "If you don't replace that with something…even feelings, then you stop."

I had so many words in my head but I wasn't sure if there would be enough feelings if I lost my vocabulary.

A rat scurried into the middle of the Index.

"Anopisthograph."

And then:

"Thomas Hardy," said the Librarian. His fingers traced down my cheek and neck, and far from the brittle dryness I had imagined, they felt sharp, as if they might leave a trail of papercuts on my skin. "Quite fascinating. Such a faultless résumé should have been enough to make me doubt. Clever boy…I was lulled by the passive voice. I should have checked your references."

The rat turned slowly, almost apologetically, and backed away beneath the stacks. I sighed.

"Indeed," I said. "That would have been prudent of you. Judicious. Shrewd. Discerning, even."

The Librarian winced.

Gadzooks attempted to fade away into the shelves. "Ah-ah-ah," said the Librarian. He beckoned Gadzooks closer with a crooked finger. "Surreptitious sneaking—I'm afraid I cannot allow that."

With one hand the Librarian covered my face. I feared he meant to smother me; his skin against my nose smelt of spilt ink, the   73 emaciated palm against my mouth made me choke with its taste of glue.

Then I heard Gadzooks scream.

The Librarian released me. All that remained of my Collector friend was a large hessian sack and some old wooden toys. A yo-yo stopped spinning, its thread a last umbilical cord.

"Don't think of it as murder," said the Librarian. "Think of it as a *metaphor* for murder."

I swallowed.

"The old beak warned me. Something missing. Boys before you sneaked into Unwarranted Adventures or Illegal Pornography. But you went *there*." He gestured at the door. Neither of us needed to say aloud the section.

"What am I to do with you?" He plucked from his coat pocket a book that made my heart sink. "And more importantly, what am I to do with *this*, found in your mattress." He inspected the spine. "*The Sum of All Our Tales*, by Barnabus Hardy. Father? Grandsire? Brother?" He leered. "Lover?"

"Father."

"Pity," the Librarian said. "You must have been so young. The age when you were warned about razorblades in Halloween candy—not the bathtub."

I stiffened.

"No note. Just his final manuscript. Did the literary world mourn his loss?"

"Stop."

The Librarian shut the book hard enough that his clothes rippled. "By all means. But tell me, young Hardy, have you ever heard the word 'deaccession'? Not so common any more, which is a shame." He opened the grate of the nearest gas lamp. I screamed at him to cease, to desist, but still he poked one corner of my father's only book into the flame.

He dropped the papers curling into ash as the fire spread.

"A lesson, a dear lesson in realising what a lost book is," he said.

The Librarian's immense arm pressed me back, anticipating me wrestling free, though I didn't know what I would do even if I could escape his grasp—perhaps throw myself on the fire in hopes of extinguishing it, rescuing the scorched remnants of the manuscript from the ashes? But it would be futile: it does not take long for poetry to burn. Verses are highly flammable—it's because they were dear fuel in someone's imagination.

"Consider that a written warning—obviously it cannot be filed away, but...well, I am a practical man. With the elder Hardy's *esprit* in ashes perhaps you will no longer want to open a book again." The Librarian straightened his bow-tie. "You may take the rest of the day off. If I find you at the Index in the morning, I will know your decision to stay with us. At a reduction in salary."

Perhaps my gaze was too wet with tears to set his retreating backside ablaze.

I trudged to my room. The Librarian's search had torn apart bed and desk. I sat down on the floor and wrapped my arms around my knees.

Something climbed up my back and to my ear. "Empressement."

I stroked the rat with two fingers. It chirped and then nipped gently at my earlobe. "Frantling." It leapt to the ground and ran towards the door, stopped and looked over its shoulder at me and squeaked. "Usative."

I followed it through the maze of the Library. The lighting where we tread was dimmer. I had not been everywhere. Some subjects were unknown to me. Down one path I saw a familiar figure reclining on the penultimate shelf devoid of books. The rat scampered away as Genet peered up at me.

"Sometimes I do not go back," he said, looking chagrinned. He handed me the book his head had been resting on. *A Scheme for a New Alphabet and a Reformed Mode of Spelling* by Benjamin Franklin. "How he loved whores. Once they brought him to the Speakeasy and all he wanted to do was steal a boy's glasses and find the door leading to ancient Lesbos."

Genet stretched, a gesture that was part exercise and part pretence to embrace me suddenly. "I doubt more than a handful of authors end up in Wasted Graphemes so it is safe here." He touched my face, my cheeks. "Ahh, but you recently had a terrible encounter with the wicked regent, I see."

I told him of my father, of his poetry. It had been years since I spoke of being away at school when they found his body, of life at the homes of distant relatives who could not look at me without seeing a debt to family they wanted little part of. My last name was all I had of my father's until I learned of the Library.

"You must feel his loss keenly."

I shrugged. "My father is a long-closed chapter."

"Ah, I see. The book, then—you mourn the loss of the book."

"Something like that."

"We shall toast to both the man and his book at the Speakeasy tonight," Genet said, laying a hand on my shoulder.

I rested my cheek against Genet's fingers. "Actually—I had another thought. If you don't mind."

And finally:

1943 smelt of fire and paper. Feet stamped in unison, close by; voices intoned, "Heil Hitler!"; the books of Germany burnt in the courtyard, a gout of gluttonous smoke bearing their words into a sky already thick with many volumes. I backed away from the bonfire as fast as I could, pushing through the crowds that railed against the soldiers, shouldering my way through and away. Away from the crowd, away from the noise. Ducking into an alleyway, I paused to breathe, heaving against the damp wall.

One hand was in Genet's as I pulled him along behind me; the other clutched tight to the worn leather handle of Hemingway's suitcase. Several street corners away, I pulled Genet into an alleyway. "You said you had a room near here—the room above the tavern, where the bed-springs sing?"

He pressed against me, mouth close to my ear. "How forward of you—I like it."

He led me a few streets further, arriving at a narrow doorway in the shadow of rotting tenements, the tavern windows the only warm thing in sight. He fumbled with a key, whilst I wrapped my arms tight around myself and shivered. Away from the book-burning, the city was freezing. Eventually, Genet persuaded the door to open, and he led me up rickety stairs to a room reminiscent of my chambers at the Library: sparse, furnished with a bed and a writing table. The greying sheets were balled on a threadbare mattress, and the table was strewn with papers. The floorboards creaked and wobbled beneath our feet.

There was a murine flicker by the doorway, and a scaly tail darted between my feet. A whispered word floated back in its wake.

"Anopisthograph!"

I sat on the bed, still shivering. Genet watched the rat depart and closed the door. The sound of the key in the lock released me; the tension of weeks in the Library, fumbling around under the Librarian's watchful eye, drained away. I sank back.

Genet lay down beside me, his skin warm against mine. He smelt of absinthe and book dust; I had the urge to bury my face in his chest, but my bone-weary limbs wouldn't co-operate.

"Will you read to me?" I said.

He arched an eyebrow, and nuzzled against my shoulder. "My handsome witling—foreplay, is it?"

"This isn't foreplay."

"I have nothing to—"

"The suitcase."

The bed-springs sang as he arose; I heard the grate of the lock opening, and the rustle of papers, then Genet returned to me with the contents of the suitcase in his hands: the first manuscript of *Our Lady of the Flowers*, where I had returned it when I had finished.

Genet smiled faintly. "My slack-handed first draft—but if you insist…" He cleared his throat, and raised the first page to his eyes. "'*Wiedmann appeared before you in the five o'clock edition,*'" he began.

"No," I said. "Turn it over."

He did as I asked, squinting at the fresh scrawl that coated the reverse of his pages.

"Sorry about my handwriting," I said. There had not been light in my Library chambers, or much space with which to work. My letters had been shrunk to the smallest I could manage to cram in everything I needed to write on the pale underside of Genet's own pages.

Genet sat up on the bed, crossed his legs, looked from the page, to me, and to the page again. He cleared his throat theatrically. "'*The Sum of All Our Tales*, by Barnabus Hardy'," he began.

———————————

Making the Magic Lightning Strike Me

John Chu

THE CLIENT LIES SLUMPED ACROSS MY SHOULDERS. I
have an arm around his thigh, another around his upper arm. His
immaculately tailored silk pajamas are soft against my hand. They
must feel amazing on his body. Right now, the client may as well
be a loaded barbell, except his body gives and his weight shifts
more as I walk toward the bed. The company seems to assign me
only the heaviest clients. Not only do the ultra-rich not appreciate
being bruised, though, once they're conscious again, they have
the means to make sure you don't appreciate it either. There's a
conversation drifting past on the side of the door, but the room is
dark and silent. Slowly, I lower him then tuck him into the bed.

I do one final sweep of the hotel room to make sure everything
is in order. His wallet, phone, and fountain pen are in the nightstand drawer. Check. His clothes have been unpacked and stowed
in the dresser drawers or hanging in the closet. Check. His briefcase and business documents are sitting on the desk. Check. The
hotel room is surprisingly small, but functional and tasteful. The
wall art is abstract and modern. The furniture is all clean lines
and rounded corners. The most garish thing in the room is the
basket of champagne and caviar on the desk next to the briefcase.
Whoever this client is, he came to work.

79

My job is to make sure that once he falls asleep in his bed in New York, he wakes up the next morning in this bed in Zurich. No airport security. No border security. No trace of travel at all. At no point does anyone produce a passport or have anything inspected. Whether bypassing all those layers of security is a necessity—say, he no longer has a passport and no other way to leave the country—or just a convenience is none of my business. Someone else in the company gets to make sure he wakes up in his own bed in New York after he falls asleep here in Zurich however many days from now. There are no short cuts here, just private jets and a lot of impeccably trained teammates doing the impossible. The company doesn't really have a name. Internally, we've always called ourselves BedEx. I'm sure someone found that funny once and it stuck.

I peel the patches off his temple then tuck them into my pants pocket. They've been keeping him in REM sleep and adjusting his circadian rhythms. He'll wake up in the morning—a few hours from now—already adjusted to UTC+1. I tap my earpiece and indicate the client has been installed. While I wait for the all-clear, I collapse the luggage bags—can't expect the ultra-rich to pack for themselves—for ease of carry. The room's key card slides under the door into the room. The process is more efficient if my teammates rectify the hotel's records while I'm installing the client and I've been trained to break into places way tougher to crack than hotel rooms. The process is also more efficient if we hack into the hotel's computers. So much faster than waiting for a hotel employee. Besides, our clients don't always stay under their own names and, this way, not only do they not need a passport, they don't need any ID at all. I place the key in the nightstand drawer next to the wallet, phone, and fountain pen. The all-clear arrives a matter of moments later and I dissolve into the night.

No one notices me sneaking out of the hotel and into a van in the parking lot. My two teammates nod at me as I enter then slide the door shut. Like me, they're dressed in work blacks. There's no substitute for actual physical access to computer systems when possible and we pride ourselves on making the impossible possible.

Our van speeds away. Of the three of us, one of us is going back to base for some sleep before her Zurich-Dublin job tonight. One of us has a few days off and he's taking it in Zurich. I have re-arranged my work schedule so that I can be in Boston tonight to catch Ayckbourn's *Intimate Exchanges* with Thom. Our first stop is the airport.

We do not wear our gear off-site off-duty. That violates our NDA. I need to be in normal clothes before they drop me off at the airport. Stripping out of my work blacks and changing into a pair of jeans and a T-shirt in the van is always a special experience. There's not a whole lot of room. It's a lot of twisting and writhing to wrestle the work blacks off me. All things considered, I'd rather not be naked in front my co-workers so it's sweater off, shirt off, T-shirt on, pants off, jeans on as quickly as possible. Nevertheless, the instant I pull off shirt or a pair of pants, someone always wolf whistles or cat calls.

Tonight, I get plenty of both from both of them. Since I'm going to Boston through Brussels then Toronto, there's even the predictable unfunny rhyme about "hauling Charlie's muscles to Brussels." That said, I never get anything like say, "sending Charlie back to Chinatown" even though my name is Charlie—Tsai, not Chan, my parents were strict, not intentionally evil—and, in this case, Toronto actually has a Chinatown. A vaguely racist joke is always right there but no one ever goes for it.

If one of my teammates on a job is a big, muscular guy—and the male teammates tend to be—he'll quip about my arms. Tonight's no exception. The guy staying in Zurich goes on about how he'd like to build a set like mine and asks me about what I do in the gym. Since the guys who do this are invariably the sleeve-busting sort—more so than I am as far as I can tell—it took me months before I realized they were complimenting me, not mocking me. Their questions are genuine not sarcastic. Now, I just squirm and mutter something about curling with a full range of motion.

My body apparently deserves this sort of reaction now. I'm still not used to it. It's not an exaggeration to say that I literally grew into this job. But the magic lightning that will change me into who I want to be hasn't struck me yet. I'm still waiting. Maybe after, some guy can compliment me on my body and I won't want to dissolve into the earth.

The only nice thing about the airport first thing in the morning is the lines are short. I always request the pat-down. Ironically, **81** considering what I do for a living, what the company has done to my body means I will never make it through a body scan. The company does helpfully supply a note from a doctor should airport security somehow detect the pumps and other nanomachinery implanted in my body. Having some airport security guy get all handsy with me is annoying, but they do ask before they touch anything and none of them have ever prevented me from getting on a plane.

After that, my tiny backpack and I wait then sit in a plane whose seat is a little too narrow and has no leg room. I used to be the right size for airplane seats. It's only when I have to sit in one again that I remember that I'm not anymore. Still, I never put the seat back. It doesn't help me as much as it annoys whoever is behind me. Lather. Rinse. Repeat. Some fourteen hours or so later, I'm at Logan and still waiting. This time for the Silver Line, then the Red Line.

It'd all be easier if I could fall asleep in Zurich and wake up in my bed in Boston. No lines, no waiting, and no convincing US Customs that I'm a US citizen even as the Customs official has my US passport in hand. Magically, I'd cross international boundaries without Customs even noticing. Someone ought to come up with a service that does that. The rich, of course, play by different rules than you and me.

Thom is waiting for me just outside the theater. I see him as I sprint down Mass Ave., past the fish place, ducking and weaving around the sidewalk crowd. The flight arrived in Boston with just enough time for me to get home, pound down thirty-two ounces of protein shake, change into a belted pair of chinos and the dress shirt that fits, then get back onto the T to Central Square. The sophisticated technology inside me is playing all sorts of interesting games to keep me awake and alert. It'll be fine as long as I get some rest after the play.

He waves when he spots me. We met in grad school. In the university weight room, actually. I was the guy trapped between a loaded bar and the bench. He was the guy who set the bar on the rack then, rather than laughing, quoted Kander and Ebb at me. We may have bonded over the distinction between a cast album and a soundtrack. He showed me how to lift properly. We saw shows together. Sometimes, his boyfriend of the moment joined us. We kept in touch through texts after graduation. He moved here about a year ago for a residency at Mass General. Since I'm not in town a lot, we still text each other all the time.

Thom is this walking shard of sunshine, all warm and golden even on this winter night. He's rocking the grizzled face, cargo pants, and broken-in leather work boots. Even the bulky winter coat looks good on him. It's hard not to despair a little when I look at him. It's hard to remember the rest of the world exists when he smiles. All of that company training must be good for something because even as I see nothing but him, I don't crash into anyone. It's only when I reach him that I realize he's waiting by himself.

He hugs me. It's still weird be able to look at him eye-to-eye. He's never pointed out that I do that now. Maybe a few years apart are enough for him to forget that I used to be shorter than him.

"Where's Andy?" I ask. Thom doesn't have a type, as far as I can tell, except male. Short, tall, hulking, gaunt, light, dark, I've seen him date them all.

"Oh, we broke up. Turns out he smokes." He shrugs. Thom is still built like an All-American wrestler and he's impossibly charming when he wants to be. A steady supply of boyfriends has never been a problem for him. "Come on. The play's about to start."

The theater is a flight of stairs up from the entrance. The usher at the door scans our tickets.

"Do you want to go somewhere after the play?" I sit down and pull my arms in as Thom takes the seat next to mine. "I can run interference against the throng of guys you aren't interested in."

"Charlie," Thom looks at me oddly for a moment. "You know that you scare people, right? You look dangerous. You'd also run interference against the guys I am interested in. But put you in a tight T-shirt and in the right bar—"

"You don't think I'm dangerous, do you?" If anything, I think of myself as more cuddly than dangerous.

"I remember when you still had a neck."

The lights go down and the play starts. Alan Ayckbourn's *Intimate Exchanges* doesn't get produced much. It's a cycle of eight plays, each of which have two endings, or one play with four junctures where a character's choice causes the play to go in one of two directions. Doing all eight plays in repertory would take up an entire theater season. In this production, five seconds into the play, **83**

Celia always decides to smoke the cigarette. Whether Lionel goes on a date with Sylvie depends on which performance you catch. The production makes the next choice itself then polls the audience to decide which of the two possible endings they perform. Not even the actors know which ending they're heading towards until the end of the penultimate scene when dialogue from the ending they're about to perform plays over the sound system. It's not what Ayckbourn intended but this production has only a two-week run. Rehearsing and performing all the possibilities is impractical. As the audience applauds, I wonder about the choices we could have made and the choices we never had a chance to make.

We don't hit any bars after the play. Thom hugs me and we go our separate ways. It's weird how easily my arms reach around him now. Still not used to it.

On my days off, I eat, rest, work out, text Thom, and not much else. The three workouts and nine meals a day it takes to maintain my current shape doesn't leave much time for anything else. And I want to be fitter than I am now. Stronger. Tougher. More muscular. When I'm not in Boston, I inevitably spend the whole day on base. Eating, resting, working out, and texting fills the days until the company needs me again.

I've been lifting since college, but it didn't change my body the way the company did. It's not that I didn't get stronger in college. It's just that I lifted believing it would transform me into someone else. The truth, of course, is that if you are short and slight and you don't want to be, lifting doesn't actually help. It may fill out your frame, but your frame is still short and slight. The company recruited me in part because I worked out so hard at the gym, but not Thom, even though he worked just as hard and was literally standing right over there making me look all of twelve years old in comparison. Then again, Thom wouldn't have found the offer the company made to me appealing. He has probably never wanted to make his body anything other than what it already is.

They rebuilt me from the inside out. Molecular biologists rewrote my DNA. Surgeons cracked then extended most of my bones. They pulled out my shoulders, expanded my rib cage, stretched out my limbs to build me a taller, broader frame. I spent months of agony enduring metal frames jutting out of me, holding cracked halves of bone apart so they could knit together millimeter by millimeter. I looked like some sort of high tech porcupine. The nanomachinery implanted in me constructed and distributed chemicals through my body that sped my recovery and packed on mass. Over time, a flat chest began to bulge. Stick-like limbs thickened with sharp curves.

While the body was healing, they attached my mind to a virtual reality and taught me to fight. With my skeleton being stretched out, I could barely move in the real world, but, in the virtual world, my body was fluid, agile, and strong. Or it became that. At first, as in actual reality some months later, I spent a lot of time falling on my face. Time in the virtual world patterned my responses. They trained me in hand-to-hand combat and I lost count of how many weapons. I'm not the greatest fighter but I'm good enough. Or at least I hold my own sparring my workmates. I've never had to fight or use a weapon on a job yet, but I'm so prepared to do so.

I joined the company with the body I was born with but work for the company with the impossible body I was promised. As it turns out, this is not quite the body I want. Despite all the changes, I still feel like me, the scrawny grad student trapped under the bar. And the changes were drastic. Nothing the company did to build my body was approved for use on humans or even published as research. Laws, even the ones on what they can do to other people, don't really apply to the rich.

It's a few weeks later when, as Thom and I are texting each other, he asks when I'm free for coffee. There's nothing he can't say to me in a text, but I'll always rearrange my work schedule to see him in person. I'm in Hong Kong but, of course, he doesn't know that. A quick search of flights says I can fly home, have coffee with Thom, then fly back in time for my next job. Of course, if I could afford that, I wouldn't need this job. I managed Zurich to Boston only because I arranged for my following job to start there. The company covered part of the flight cost. Anyone with a lifestyle where they can fly from Hong Kong to Boston just for the afternoon can afford and can pull the strings to have his body reconstructed.

Asking around on the base, I work out some job trades that get me to Boston in a couple days. We just need our supervisors' approval. Mine agrees with a cryptic "Sure. You're ready for those sorts of jobs now," before she breaks the encrypted connection.   85

The first job in the sequence that will take me back to Boston is innocuous. It's the one I was already assigned to. I go into the briefing during the flight out for the next one wondering what I've gotten myself into.

This extraction is like all the other ones I've done, except the client doesn't know we're coming. And the site isn't some expensive hotel or other piece of overpriced real estate. It's a camp site in the middle of nowhere. And it turns out we're not extracting the client. She's a worried and, apparently, fabulously wealthy mother in California. She's paid for a large crew of us to extract her teenage son. By the time the briefing is over, this extraction is nothing like any of the others I've done. Change a few of the details and we could be the kidnappers rather than the rescuers. Depending on the details of custody that we, the crew, aren't privy to, we may still be the kidnappers.

We unlock and drive through the camp's gate. I recognize the sign overhead and the buildings on the grounds. Conversion camps stay around as long as there are parents who want to make their son a Real Man, I guess.

The barracks are cold and dark. It stinks of sweat and urine. The kid is chained to his bed. Welts cover his body. The camp's techniques haven't changed and he's apparently as bad at being a Real Man as I am. It's hard to look at the rows of sleeping teenagers without being reminded that they are me when I was their age. A teammate hands me a set of keys and I snap to.

The patches that will keep him in REM sleep fit snugly against his temples. The manacles unlock with a soft click. I move the chains out of the way slowly to avoid making any more noise than I have to. He is too light. His body is a tree in winter, all thin and angular. I barely feel it across my shoulders. Several more of him wouldn't weigh me down and there are a couple dozen here. I don't free any more of them, though. It's not in the plan. I tell myself that maybe they all have one rich parent who can steal them away from the machinations of the other rich parent. I know it's not true.

His bedroom in his mother's house is ostentatiously comfortable. The air is thick and warm. An overstuffed bed sits against one wall. Shelves of books line another. Dance gear litters the floor. It's going to be a while before his body is tough enough and strong enough to dance again. He should be in a hospital, but I'm sure we advised against it when we booked the job. Her house has more layers of security should anyone want to steal her son back.

The next job is much more typical. High Powered Executive is extracted from her elegant high-rise condo. High Powered Executive is installed in her discreet but absurdly tasteful hotel suite. The hotel's bottled water is thawing ice from a hundred thousand year old glacier. When you open the bottle, trapped air from a distant age attacks your senses. Or so I gather.

Several more flights and I'm headed to a coffee shop in Davis Square running on too little sleep. When the plane lands it's such that I can hit Davis Square within a few minutes of when Thom says he's free for lunch. This is either perfect or perfectly awful. I don't get to choose how well flight schedules and Thom's schedule play with each other or, rather, don't play with each other. The nanomachinery inside me manufactures chemicals that force me awake. I've barely rested since the briefing for the conversion camp job. To line up jobs to get you where you need to be when you need to be there, something generally has to give. It'll be all right as long as I rest eventually.

Thom hugs me when we meet. Somehow, I always manage to let go when he lets go. He orders some drink that takes a minute to describe. The clerk repeats it back to him perfectly. I stare at the drinks board for what feels like a millennium before I give up and order the gigantic herbal ice tea. There are already enough stimulants racing inside me. We get our drinks and go to a table next to the shop's giant street side window. He seems to grow as he takes off his denim jacket. It obscured the way his chest and arms bulge, depriving the world of his perfection.

"How's Jamal?" I sit across from him and clutch my iced tea like a giant sippy cup.

"It's Aaron now." Thom looks down before he meets my gaze again. "Charlie, what do you do for a living?"

"I've told you." My brow furrows. "I'm a courier. Why?"

"How do you have a job and still be that broad and carry that much muscle." He sips his drink. "It takes too much time and effort. No one is built like you unless they need to be. Like professionally or something."

"So I've spent time picking up heavy things and setting them back down again." I gesture at his arms and chest. "Nothing you're not still doing."

"I'd say that you're also taking some of the more effective drugs—which I never have—except you're also taller now. You used to be shorter than me. What are you doing to yourself? It can't be healthy."

The question punches the air out of my lungs. Thom won't believe the truth. He's not rich enough to have heard of the secretive company that specializes in extracting and installing people. Half of what they did to me are things no one outside the company know are even possible.

"You have a problem because I'm as big as you now?"

His eyebrows rise. His face writhes trying to stifle a laugh.

"As big as?" His gaze sweeps up and down my torso. He gets up and steps around to check out my legs. "You have maybe forty pounds of lean muscle on me. And, you know, if that's the body you want, that's great—"

He tries to put me into a joint lock. I slip out of it before I've even thought about what I'm doing. We're not really sparring. There's no follow through and I just manage to keep myself still rather than fight back. He's just hugging me now, his grip like a drowning man on water-soaked shard of deadwood. Eventually, he pulls back, his hands still around my shoulders. His gaze narrows. We both know my reactions aren't what they would have been when I was in grad school.

"What have you done to yourself, Charlie?" He goes back to his chair and he sits so far back I can't tell if he's trying to get comfortable or out of striking distance. "It's not bad. It's just... sooner or later, either it'll kill you or your job will. Is whatever it is you really do for a living that important?"

"Look." I set down the iced tea. "We're not all you. Practically nobody is you. The rest of us need a little help."

The idea of lying to him makes me sick so I violate my NDA for him and risk some of the truth. I don't tell him about the gene resequencing but I do tell him about the surgery to stretch out my skeleton. Distraction osteogenesis. What they did to me is more involved than that, but close enough. I tell him about the cocktail of drugs rushing through me, but I leave out the implanted nanomachinery and I don't mention my job at all. Throughout all of this, Thom just nods.

"God, Charlie, if you just wanted to be bigger, you got that with the surgery. I can see taking the drugs to help you fill out your expanded frame faster, but you don't need them now. Not anymore."

Thom can't understand. He's wrestled all his life. All-American in college. When I first met him, even now, he's always been on the deadly side of handsome. He doesn't know what it's like to be towered over.

"What's it to you, Thom? Just let me do what I want." I'm still waiting for the magic lightning to strike. I'm still waiting to feel big, brave, and strong.

"Fine." Thom pushes himself away from the table. "I can't stick around and watch you kill yourself, Charlie. I'm sorry."

He puts on his coat. It's like watching a superhero bury himself in his mortal disguise. He nods at me, then leaves.

I text Thom between jobs. He never answers. The man goes through boyfriends like he changes shirts but we've been friends for over a decade so I hoped we'd be different. Guess not. I know what I have to text him to get him to text me back. All I have to do is tell him he's right and that I'll stop with the chemicals and I'll quit this job. My hands freeze, my heart pounds too hard, and I can't breathe whenever I try to text him the lie. I stop texting him instead. Not being able to talk to him tears me to pieces, though, and I can feel my life ebbing out through the wounds.

The next few months grind on. I pick people up. I set them back down. I pick up heavy weights. I set them back down. My body is its usual never not sore. I date a guy from work. Bad idea. I'll never do that again. So little in my life has changed but everything is different. Thom is this palpable lack, a void that nothing can fill. The only thing pushing me from one day to the next is a concert production of *The Golden Apple* in New York City in May. I'm counting down the days. The show is almost never produced and who knows when I'll have another chance to see it.

The company is assigning me to fewer hotels now and more campsites, hole-in-the-walls, and odd shacks in the middle of nowhere. Sometimes, we are chased extracting or installing the client.

Most of the time, we aren't. The job I swap into so that I can be in NYC in time for *The Golden Apple* almost doesn't surprise me.

As with all of our operations, it's the middle of the night. This one will take literally two dozen of us. In addition to mics and earpieces, we are outfitted with combat armor and a wide variety of weapons. It's one thing to know the company has military-grade weaponry. It's another to have it issued to you for a job. The nano-scale chemical factory inside me keeps my mind focused and my heart from pounding through my chest. We go through our obligatory checks then we load into the helicopters.

The helicopters have a stealth mode. They whisper towards the compound. High walls surround a two-story building. One helicopter lands just outside. My workmates stream out to secure the perimeter. The other hovers just inside the walls. Ropes drop. We slide into courtyard. One after another, we rush out of the way of the one above us as we hit the ground.

Unlike most of our operations, there's no sneaking in and out of this one. Explosives blow out a house wall and door. We rush in then fan out through the house, looking for the hostage. Plan A, as always, is to find her and whisk her away before anyone can mount a response.

My partner and I sweep room by room down a hall on the second floor. The first few rooms are empty. The door to the next is blocked by something on the other side. I step back, aim just below the doorknob, then kick as hard as I can. The door splinters off its hinges. Something skids, thuds then crashes. Screams tear through the air. Except for the noise, that worked much better than I expected.

The splintered wreck of a dresser is scattered on the floor. My flashlight sprays the room. Four people huddle on a bed against the far wall. The fear carved into their faces deepens as I step through a mix of wood shards and clothes on the floor. My partner slides past me towards the bed. The glare she shoots me with on the way screams "You dumbass."

We get the signal to leave over our earpieces as we examine the people on the bed. They're neither dangerous at the moment or, obviously, the hostage, not that anyone expected to find the hostage just sitting in a bedroom. On the way back to the helicopter, the hostage is asleep, wrapped in a blanket. She's a string draped over the woman carrying her. We all load into the helicopters with breathless precision. They take off. Dust bursts in silent plumes from the ground.

The client has obtained a bed for the hostage at a military hospital in the States. Again, the rules for the rich are different from the rest of us. You don't even need to change any of the details of this job for us to be the ones taking her hostage rather than the ones rescuing her. We install her then the team breaks up, most of us headed off to the nearest base. In my case, I change my clothes in the van to the usual jeers and compliments then they drop me off at the bus station. It's still the middle of the night and the bus to New York City won't be for a few more hours.

Sleep isn't really something I do any more. Too many drills where someone comes at me with a knife while I'm in bed means I rest but I don't know that I ever really sleep. Right now, though, I can't even rest. Knocking myself out or taking a little something to just to relax me is always an option. After all, there's a complex and sophisticated chemical factory installed in my body essentially at my command. At the bus station, though, the former is a bad idea and I never do the latter. Maybe it's odd considering the chemicals I do pump through my body, but there are lines I don't cross.

While I wait for the bus, I close my eyes and the job replays in my imagination. It's stupid what weighs my mind. Maybe I overestimated how solid the door was. Or maybe assuming I always need to hit as hard as I can is not a good idea anymore. Mostly, though, my imagination is stuck on the faces of those huddled on the bed. Not that they were the epitome of calm before, but a couple shifted to panic and the rest to a flinty stoicism as I stepped into the room. Maybe strangers have been shifting to their "This is how I meet Death" face when they first see me for a while now, but I've only just noticed. There are too many scenarios where we all meet Death together. That is, if the chemicals that make me who I am don't kill me first.

Is it even possible to quit this job? In theory, yes. They've always made it clear that I can hand in my resignation and walk away at any time. But do I want to? The company specializes in stealth extraction and installation. If I quit, I'll wake up one day with a few days unaccounted for and mysterious scars across my body. They don't need to leave scars but they will to make sure I know.

The nano-scale chemical plant that makes me **me** or at least gives me the chance to become who I want to be will be gone.

Who I was in grad school is just a bad memory never to return. They've lengthened my limbs, pulled out my shoulders and expanded my rib cage. None of that will go away. If I survive the sudden, drastic shift removing the nanomachinery will inflict on body chemistry, I won't regress to my old self. My chance to become who I want, though, will be gone. I'll become this tallish, gaunt figure instead. Plenty of amazing people are tall and gaunt but, after years of being whatever I am now, it's not what I want for myself. And I can't make myself want that.

That's why the company recruited me in the first place, I realize. And why they never recruited Thom. They spent who knows how much money on this body certain they'd make their investment back. Because, even if my rational mind understands becoming ever harder and more muscular won't make the magic lightning strike me, I'd still rather die than quit.

I pull my cellphone out of my pant pocket. They are disallowed on-duty which makes me oddly addicted to mine off-duty. Messing with a nanogram app, though, can't possibly fill the Thom shaped void in my life. It's been months since I last texted Thom but I send him one last, possibly ill-advised, message:

"Thom, you're right about everything. How people see me. What I'm doing to myself. What my job is doing to me. I know exactly how I'm going to die. I can see it happening and I can't make myself stop it. I'm sorry."

I stare at my sent message for who knows how long. People start to line up for the bus to New York and I join them.

Every city has its own tempo. New York City's is allegro. It is so easy to become one with the crowds on the sidewalks of Manhattan. In short, swift steps, I dodge and weave around the pedestrians, a Quickstep against the Mambo of the city. I don't know why I'm in such a hurry. When I get to City Center, Thom won't be there. His empty seat next to mine is going to be this visible reminder of the gaping maw in my life. Maybe I'm rushing to that doom because almost no one ever produces *The Golden Apple*, a folk opera re-telling of *The Iliad* and *The Odyssey* re-set to the turn of twentieth-century America. I can easily die before I have another chance to see it.

The usher hands me a program then points me to my seat. It's empty, which is good. A broad, solid, ostentatiously grizzled man is in the seat next to mine, which is not. I recognize him instantly. There's a hard elegance to him that's obvious even when he's seated a dozen feet away. The person behind me in line has to push at my back before I stumble down the aisle. The remaining steps to my seat feel like city blocks. Falling out of helicopter then charging into building to face the unknown was easier.

Thom smiles at me. Not a "well, how awkward is this?" smile but the real thing. If he keeps it up, this concert production won't be able to go on because the house will be too bright. He doesn't offer me a hug and I'm too scared he'll refuse to spread my arms to ask for one. I just take the seat next to his.

"Charlie," He lays his hand over mine on the arm rest. A thick vein arcs down the length of his bulging biceps. "Why can't it be—"

"Are we quoting Sondheim at each other now?" I let out a long breath. "Not a blessèd day—How's…"

I have no idea who he's dating now. It's been months since we last talked. He rolls his eyes.

"It's still Aaron." He shrugs. "I'm tired of relationships measured in hours. I tend to bug out the instant anything doesn't go my way and I should stop doing that. Honestly, I'm even not sure I like Aaron, but I have no good reason to leave. If I have to be in a long-term relationship, it might as well be with him."

"I don't think I'd appreciate that if I were Aaron."

"You're not Aaron." He gaze narrows. "Charlie, have you *grown?*"

The program is now this tightly wound, twisted stick in my hand. I've squeezed it so hard as we were talking, its pages are now crinkled and tattered. Slowly, I force my hand open and the program falls into my lap.

"No. I mean, yes. I mean…" I take deep breath. "It's an optical illusion. More muscle. Less fat. I'm actually three-eighths of a pound lighter—Thom, why are you here? We both know where I'm headed. Did you want to see *The Golden Apple* that badly?"

"Well, that, too. But the world is round, Ulysses." His hand squeezes mine. "You wander far enough away and you'll find yourself coming home instead. Someone needs to yell at you when you get back and to make sure there's still a home to wander back to. Not in that order."

"Oh, I see." Actually, I have no idea what he means, but I wonder at his faith in me.

"Nothing lasts, you know. A handsome face. A muscular body. It all goes away eventually. As they say, even the Rockies'll crumble and Gibraltar'll tumble."

"Yeah, but they're made of clay." My hand pats his implacable upper arm, which gives as easily as marble. "Probably not a face or body, but maybe some things are here to stay."

"That's not how the Gershwin goes."

My hand slides down to cover his on the arm rest. I want to feel a shock, as though his faith that I'll eventually come around is enough to jolt me into strength and bravery. Life isn't that simple though. His hand doesn't turn to clasp mine, but it doesn't pull away either.

"Hey, it's not like you got the quote right either." His hand is tight around the armrest and I lace my fingers between his. The tendons in his fingers give a little. "You know, it'd be easier for both of us you if pretended that I'm already dead."

"Yeah, if I could, it would be." He shrugs and smiles.

The house lights go down. The stage lights and curtain go up. The conductor walks onto the stage to the applause of the crowd. He raises his hands. The applause ends and the overture starts.

———————————

Salamander Six-Guns

Martin Cahill

HE DESCENDED ON THE TOWN LIKE A SAINT SENT FROM Dark Heaven, six-guns shining like twin torches in his hands, down to the border where we had our battle on. Summers are always the worst in Sunblooder's Stand, as the scale-folk grow riled earlier in the bright days.

We'd been fighting the scale-folk off for an hour when the stranger threw himself into the fray. One moment I was shoving a pitchfork into the belly of a croc-man, and next I knew, the flashing of the stranger's salamanders blinded me, sea-foam flame belching hot lead as natural as rainfall. He danced between us sunblooders like a phantom. Not a one of us knew who he was, but when help arrives, you don't ask from whence it came. He helped us drive back the line, the gator-kin and the croc-men screeching, the snake-touched and the iggies squirming; their shattered teeth and scorched scales left behind in the swamp as they dove into the murky water and made for the heart of their Scaled Nation.

Many of the towns inland would have taken to whooping and celebrating, but the thirty or so sunblooders on the swampy shore only sighed with temporary relief; here, at the fringe of civilization, the scale-folk were as consistent as the sunset.

The mystery man made a show of looking over each dead scale-folk at his feet, before turning his spring-green eyes on me. He had scars across his face and throat, pale against his dark skin, but I didn't bat an eye; anyone hugging the coast ended up with a souvenir sooner or later. Holstering his salamanders, which hissed and spat like grease on a skillet, he put his hands on his hips, and said, "Looks like y'all could use some help around here," his voice singing like a rusty six-stringer.

Something sour settled into the back of my throat, and I spat into the mud. Plenty of fancy folk had come through the town of Sunblooder's Stand, hoping to make a name for themselves in the last living border town abutting the Scaled Nation. Plenty of other folks had drawn inland, away from the diseased coast of swampwater where creatures became people and hunted us normals like food, but not us. Some said it was the stubborn nature of those in the South, but I'd like to think it was a certain amount of sick pride, too; when you got good at protecting your home, you didn't give it up easy for the illusion of safer ground.

I wiped my hair out of my eyes, too long again and as red as my name, and fixed him with the look I gave every stranger with boots that shone too much. "We been doing fine without you, stranger. Reckon we'll be just as fine with you."

He smirked, and I knew I disliked him, like a fish knows it hates the sky. "Sugar," he said, "You'll be finer than you ever been with me around."

My hands curled into fists, and I bit down the urge to snarl. "Sugar is for horses, stranger. You call me Copper or you call me nothing."

The volume of my vitriol took him by surprise. After a moment's consideration, he took his hat off, and crinkled his fingers around its edges like all the children do with their songbooks come High Dark. "Begging forgiveness, Copper, sir. A man travels a lonely, dangerous road for a long time, and well, he tends to leave his manners at every crossroad, waystone and mile marker he puts behind him, if it means he lives a little longer. Coming back to society, I've neglected to bring my manners along with me."

I saw the other sunblooders looking for my reaction. Ever since Momma took a claw to the gut and got sent to the bottom of the swamp, they watched for her leadership in me. So I snorted, and stabbed a finger in his direction. "Gather 'em up quick then, stranger, or you're no better than the scale-folk, understand?"

He looked like I'd slapped him. Figured I'd hit him where his pride lived, but after helping us, I supposed he didn't deserve all scorn and no sweet. I scratched the back of my head. "Manners or none, you did us a good service today. If you could help bring back the wounded, might be a bed you could hunker down in for the night, but I can't make any promises."

He smiled, bowed at the waist, called me sir again, and began to gather up the injured. Saw him carry Old Kearney back, singing "Take Me Down To Starry Town," to keep the poor fool's mind from his missing leg; a clean rip was better than a bloody bite. One bite, and you may as well sink into the swamp or blow your brains out.

Walking back, we cleaned our weapons with rags, and began to murmur amongst ourselves. I watched him go, this stranger, watched him smile and laugh in a cluster of shocked, scared people, and found myself even more distrustful of him. What right had he to smile so? Easy enough for a stranger to pick up such habits inland, away from the Scaled Nation and the cancerous holes in the sky that hovered over the coast. But bringing those habits right to the edge of civilization, mocking the people who lived there without a second thought? Made me uneasy.

But I tried, I really did. I tried not to judge too quickly, tried to be the best person I could under the eyes of Shadow Matron, shades keep her. A person is made of nothing but show and bluster, a hurricane wrapped in a shirt and pants, and sooner or later, they'll blow themselves apart, or quiet down. I had to wait and see what this man would do.

Except he walked into my town like he'd lived there all his life, and I felt like the only one who remembered he'd only shown up an hour before. The people of Sunblooder's Stand were fascinated with him, his Northern drawl, his green eyes, the way his black coat seemed to bend the light; he seemed to be a long-lost relative, not a random gun newly arrived. Only thing he didn't seem to show off was the fancy silver chain around his neck, but I figured he was saving that for a rainy day.

He sauntered around town like a rooster, clucking and crowing at every person who fawned over him. Bunch of bright-eyed toad-lickers, to be taken in, to not see him for the threat he was. I fumed to see him chat up every man, woman, and child he happened to walk by. Respect had to be earned, and they were just giving it to him. Looking back, I can see why I fumed so: took me years to gain the same level of respect, and here he was doing it as easy as breathing. Not my proudest moment, no.

Come New Dark, as the sun slipped beneath the world, he smoked scales, the air burning magenta, steel, emerald, depending on the variety stuffed into the pipe. Children gathered around him, asking for stories from the safe world, and he delivered. Four people offered their homes to him, and before I knew it, he was a stranger no longer. The Mayor was here to stay, it seemed, and some furious and hurt part of me settled to the bottom of my heart like a stone in the sea.

Ah, right. His name.

A week or so after his arrival, folks started calling him Mayor. I said to them, "We didn't have a mayor before, why we need one now? Even Momma didn't have such a title and you all looked to her like she was Shadow Matron come High Dark to bless!"

People shrugged with moony eyes, and glanced at him, sitting on the barstool, talking and talking and talking, like words were water and these people hadn't been rained on in quite some time.

So they named him Mayor. What was his name before? Doesn't matter, I don't think; he slid into the role like a knife into a heart. It fit him.

He tricked the town into loving him, and not a one of them could see the strings he was pulling within them. Day after day, he taught them that the scale-folk were nothing to be afraid of. He'd lay his supernatural six-guns into the coals of fires to warm their guts, tell stories over their crackling, stories that gave every sunblooder a sense that there was more to life than survival. There was another world out there, he said, one free of scale-folk, where a body could live a day doing whatever they wanted, not always having to rush into battle come the clarion call of the bell.

He was going to get everyone killed. Every single person who drank in his poisonous stories became a little less cautious, a little more reckless. He was inspiring them at the wrong angle. The truth was, there's no part of the world that's safe anymore; only lands that the swampwater hasn't touched yet.

It finally hit him when Fennel got his throat ripped out by a pyth-person, on account of he was too busy singing "Guts, Gators, and Glory" to notice the alabaster fangs snapping for his throat.

The Mayor had taught him the song the night before, said how it would lull a new baby to sleep in a moment. The young lad had blushed, his wedding band bright and clean, and the Mayor had roared with joy to see his cheeks redden.

It was the Mayor that put a bullet through Fennel's brain. If it was because of the snake poison that swept through his blood, or the scales that had begun to boil down his neck, I never found out. Mayor carried him home, silent like the sea.

No more songs were sung at the border after that day.

But no matter who fell, the Mayor was loved and I found myself alone. They'd trail after him, asking about this song or that, and everywhere they went, in the opposite direction I'd go, dragging along a bottle of whiskey, swallowing shots like bitter medicine. The town didn't ignore me, but they didn't love me like they loved him and it hurt like the oldest wound known to this world.

He tried to include me, invited me to meetings, to drinks at the saloon, but every time I saw that damned smirk of his, I hated him a little more, even if I didn't want to; it had been nearly a whole month of bluster, and it pushed me to an edge I didn't think I'd see again.

And if I said it didn't bother me, would you forgive me for lying? After Momma died and Da ran, taking up the town was the only thing that let me ignore the pain in my gut, made feel important, loved even. Mayor had taken that from me, taken them all from me, and now I couldn't do anything but sit beneath the stars and scratch at that terrible itch in my heart.

I went looking for him one night, and I had been at the bottle a little more than usual when I shoved him. He fell back against the wooden fence atop the only grassy knoll in town; folks said you could see clear to Coaltown from there. His six-guns were sitting in the dying embers of a fire, drinking their fill, some scale-folk magic in their hot hearts lapping up the heat.

He adjusted his coat, and coughed. "Something on your mind, Copper?"

I felt the whiskey in my blood urging me to say something mean, something that'd cut him down. But I was still my Momma's son and I wouldn't let liquor get the best of my decorum. "Just expressing my feelings as to your new position within the Stand, Mr. Mayor." Was there venom in my voice? Aye, a little.

He took it all with grace, though. "Told Duncan to quit it with that damn title, but that boy has a mouth bigger than a full-grown croc, and twice as loud." He looked back at me, must have seen something that made him stoop a little lower, pull the collar of his coat up. "Right sorry, Copper. Didn't mean to take anything away from you. This is your town, and I have no right to be making calls on it."

A wind cut through me, the wet of the swamplands settling into my bones, the night chill making me hold myself, the bottle dangling limp in my hand; relief and paranoia warred within me at his words. "Why are you here anyway, Mayor? What's a body to find in the Stand but death? We don't leave because there's nowhere in this world we can go. Too many of us are poor, and lack in all things but heart; what else is out there in the safe world for us? That's our excuse, weak as it is. So what in the Bright Hell is yours?"

He pulled out his pipe, nestled a fresh ball of tobacco and scales into the end of it, and lit it with a salamander shell, tamping its metallic end down until it caught. "Looking for someone."

The way his voice went frosty, the way his eyes cast down into the swamplands with a searing heat, made me take a step closer to him. He was reeling me in, telling another of his damn stories, and I fought hard to shake off its magic. "If you got business here, let us help so you can be on with it. You've been tearing through scale-folk for a month, but never once ask for anything in return. Let this be it. Let us get you what you need and get you out of this nightmare. You came here by choice, and you can make the choice to leave, too."

He took a long drag. The smoky, flesh-like stench of the scales burning in his pipe filled my nose, made me feel drunker than I was. To smoke of the scale-folk was said to be elixir before it killed you. How long had he been at it?

He huffed out a noxious cloud smoke, red at the edges, and smiled through its dissipation. "Kind offer of you. But what business I got would get a body killed for its doing. And I'm not the kind of man to throw people on the Red Coal Trail, just so I have something cool to walk over on my way to Bright Hell." He smirked with sad eyes. "But as I said, mighty kind of you."

I threw my fist into his side, the cold in my gut making way for the red-hot rage I loved so. "Toads take you! Don't go playing that card, Mayor. I've heard enough dramas on the crank to know a foolish line when I hear it. You've been giving and giving to this town without a single receipt for bullets. You're aiming for something and I want to know what it is!"

I wasn't backing down. I wouldn't let this town become beholden to the stranger in the dark coat with pistols of flame and a past that swallowed him like thorns. This close, he smelled like dying fires and hot lead. His eyes shone through the red smoke like evergreens bowing beneath a volcano's weeping.

And if our lips were only inches apart, wasn't it because I was trying to shout through the scent of him? If I was lonely and a little out of touch with the world, wasn't that to blame on the whiskey in my blood and the scale-smoke in my nose and Momma passing without a goodbye and Da leaving me to die and my lovers packing up in the night, afraid of being singed by the hurt in my heart?

Wasn't it enough to want a man who wasn't afraid of getting burned?

His hand went around my wrist then, his other on my shoulder; he pressed me back down to the earth, quiet as a tomb.

"You afraid of a little fire?" I said, my throat dry and rough, knowing it to sound petty and small. I hated him and I wanted him at the same time.

His voice came out raw; he seemed older than I'd ever thought of him. "It's just not a good idea." Around his neck, the shine of his silver chain blinded me.

I wrenched my arm from him, and walked away right quick; didn't want him to see me with my eyes leaking. Couldn't give a body the idea that fire could be quenched.

THE NEXT WEEK, WE LOST A HALF A MILE TO THE SCALE-folk. The bodies of their family had floated downstream, right to Momma Scales. They came surging out of the swamp, urged on by their mother, voices ululating and screeching with anger.

I was only a boy when the sky opened up. I'll always remember the swath of emerald light I saw on the other side, always remember the screaming wings that fell out of the hole in Dark Heaven. I remember the shaking of the earth, quake upon quake as beasts not of our world crashed, seeding themselves along the coast. From my vantage then, I could see two, maybe three, but as reports came in, more than twenty of the monsters fell from their world into ours.

That's when the scaled things of the swamps and jungles and deserts started up and moving, becoming more man than beast. The wings from beyond the sky were urging them up the food chain with an awful rapidity. But they weren't the worst.

Like any good infection, it started small. A scratch is sometimes all it took, though it could vary. "If the skin starts turning, you better get to burning," is something Da used to say before he left for lands inland, lands unscaled.

I think seeing his brothers rise out of the swamp, reptilian armor flying up their necks, their brown eyes going gold... I think it broke him to see his family become their family.

I'll always forgive him that, at least.

But if you didn't defend what family you had left with all you had, what were you?

I hadn't seen such a number of the scale-folk as I did the day we lost that half mile, surging forward, snapping jaws and stronger claws with a swiftness to make wind balk. Our toes dug into the swampy earth as we battered scaled ribs with plunging knives and pikes. But really, we were a shield for the Mayor, who fought like a man haunted.

White-hot bullets flew with such speed as to shatter skulls, two, three in a row. The air was alive with the screams of his salamanders. He was an artist that made death.

They were gunning for him. Momma Scales urged them on with her grief, and soon enough, we had fallen back. If I looked out of the corner of my eye, I could see the outskirts of town.

But I couldn't look away from the battle for fear I'd die if I did. So I didn't miss the moment when the Mayor went down under a pile of snapping jaws.

For a heart-wrenching moment, I forgot how to breathe.

But in the next, he threw them off, pulling strength from where, only Bright Hell knew. Scale-folk scattered in the air, fell to the ground, and we were there to thrust steel through their bellies.

I turned to smile at the Mayor, glad to see him alive despite any awkwardness that had come of my stupidity a few days before. Despite my hurt, he was a part of this town now; it would kill everyone to see him kiss the bottom of the swamp.

We locked eyes from across the murky water and I lost my breath again.

His green eyes were gone. In their place were thin pupils, vertical, bright as molten sunflowers, and his teeth had taken on a sharper edge than any man I'd ever seen.

Years of combat instinct surged through me and had I a gun in my hand and not a pike, I would've shot a bullet right through him, faster than you can say "Gator-man gonna get ya."

He staggered to his knees in the water, and yowled like a cat whose tail had found the rocker. When he looked up, pale and shaking, he had recovered his green eyes; he looked at me, ashamed and exhausted.

That night, I grabbed his hand after dinner, and steered him to my cabin. Some of the others threw whistles and whoops after us, but I paid them no mind. Upon entering, I threw him into a chair, and kicked him hard back into it when he tried to stand. I didn't know if I was angry or frightened or both.

"Show me."

Mayor stared up at me, grim. "You don't want to see this, Copper."

I stared him down, arms crossed and feet wide, trying to channel my Momma as much as I could. Finally, he began to undo his shirt.

The mossy green and bark brown scales that mottled his chest glistened as they caught the moonlight. They trailed up to his chest from a terribly sewn gash in his side, divots of teeth marks and puncture wounds running around the edges.

I felt my muscles go hot, my throat tight. "How? Most men would be tearing out their lover's throats after a day with a bite that big."

He fixed me with a gaze, hung up on my words. He fingered the necklace he wore, rubbing a silver feather. He winced as he buttoned up his shirt. "Smoking the scale seems to trick a body into **103** thinking you've already turned. Slowed it down somewhat. But a body can't be tricked forever."

"What in the world made you think to do such a reckless thing?"

His eyes went glassy and the moonlight seemed to pass through them and illuminate some memory held in the back of his skull. "A lover, a…companion. Name of Adam. He was bit when we were crossing the Brollins Canal looking for mercenary work. Gator-gal snagged him off the side of the boat, tried to drown him, but we were able to kill her and drag him back on deck. Old healer onboard stuffed the pipe into Adam's mouth, lit the scales, and said it would help. It did for a time. Adam held on, but—" and here's where the glass of his eyes went dark, and he stopped straying down memory's path, "After a few months, Adam couldn't fight anymore. He liked the voice in his head, he said. He liked being a good son to Momma Scales, liked how it made him feel. So he let it happen, and dumb toad I am, I let him live. Thought I could appeal to him, my sandy-locked lover. But all that happened was he took a bite out of me and fled into the water. I been tracking him ever since, and well—"

"He's here. He's come to the heart of the Nation." I finished the thought for him, though by no means did it give me pleasure to deduce his intentions, nor did I feel superior knowing the full measure of his pain. My eyes roved the landscape of his body, its lean curves cutting the night to ribbons. My mouth wanted to taste his, but all I could do was imagine the pain racing through him like a panting hound. "Can you last long enough to find him?"

Mayor had sunk into the high backed chair, refused to meet my gaze. "I'll find him, that's for sure. But living? Well, shit. If I'm as good a liar as I hope, then next year, a year after, if I'm careful. But—" he laughed then, his eyes getting fever-bright, almost yellow in the dark room. "I can…hear her, Copper. When I'm down at the border, pushing back my would-be brothers and sisters, I can hear her, right here." He tapped his temple. "She whispers to me in verses of fire and smoke, seduces me with the promise of family, of living forever, I—" He stopped, put a shaking hand to his eyes. His breath rushed out of him, ragged and low. "She's

a compelling Momma, Copper. Broke my Adam like a piece of

driftwood, and he was a saint compared to me. Whatever she's doing to drive the scale-folk, it's leaking into me, and I don't know when I'll be too full up of her to resist."

It's a hard thing, watching the strong at their weakest moments. Saw it with Da when he wept at his brothers' empty graves, saw it with my own Momma clutching her gut, trying to keep her insides on the inside. How do you build someone back up when they've gone as low as they can go?

In my experience, you either kick 'em in the ass or let 'em work it out. And the Mayor? He needed a kick. "Well, you're just going to have to hang on a little while longer, mister," I said, with as much authority as I could muster, "because you still have work to do, and no lizard bitch momma is going to keep you from doing it. In fact, I say we kill two crocs with one bullet, if you catch my meaning."

When he looked back up, his smirk was wide, his evergreen eyes bright.

———————————

WE RODE OUT THE NEXT DAY, OUR PACKS STUFFED WITH as many knives, bullets, and pikes as we could shove into their confines. Mayor followed the pressure in his mind south and east, and we marched out behind him.

A few bodies from the town had joined us, folk who found the idea of a suicide mission to rid Sunblooder's Stand of the biggest progenitor of scaly bastards appealing. No use in telling them the story of Adam. Mayor would kill me if I revealed his secrets, and so I kept my mouth shut.

Was it a dumb plan? Sure as the sun is bright. But Mayor was dying and I was lost. And if we had a way to find Momma Scales in the tangled heart of the Scaled Nation, well, we were just desperate enough to try to put her to rest.

The mood was light as we crept past the border and through the swamp, with Felbrem and Ko betting on who would win themselves the heart of Momma Scales herself. Jocularity on the road to Bright Hell; who'd have thought it?

Mayor walked in the front, sullen and gaunt. If he was smoking scale, he could have been fine. But every scale-folk in a mile would be drawn us to like gators to guts, and so he couldn't stymie it.

With every step, he fought the infection through sheer will. **105**

And with every step, he lost a little more.

We passed through pools of murk and forests of reeds, keeping our eyes split for any scale-folk that may have been lingering. Mayor said we'd be fine for a few miles more.

When pressed for answers, he tapped his temple with a pained look, turned back to the front, and shaded his eyes. Were they golden just then? Or was that the light being tricky with me?

At night, Mayor and I shared a tent, where he went to the farthest corner, and wouldn't look me in the eye. Did he think I'd hate him, to see those yellow eyes in the night?

I awoke to guttural coughs, hissing whispers. Wrenching myself up, I saw Mayor curled around himself in the corner, shaking like a rattlesnake in the brush. He was covered in a cold sweat, and on his neck I saw scales creeping up behind his ear, brushing the back of his neck.

He was all motion then, sprang at me, hands clamping down on my shoulders. His eyes were a totality of gold and they were never going to change back.

"She was never meant to be here, Copper." His voice was high, and shook like a willow in the wind. "Her, her brothers and sisters, they were thrown from their lands through a rent between spaces, denied any succor, say, or justice. Their enemies threw them through the sky and gifted them to us."

I tried to shake myself from his grip. "Damn it, Mayor, snap out of it!" His fingers dug deeper, the nails longer, his eyes twitching.

"They're changing us, Copper. She's making us family, an army." His gaze snapped up, and it was as though he could see through the tent top, into the sky and beyond. "Someday, they're going to go back, and take back what's theirs. And we're going to go with them."

I slammed my fist into his gut as hard as I could and he let go, fell to the damp earth, lay there, sobbing and sobbing.

Should I have gone close to sit with him, be there to lend him a little humanity, which was dying in his chest like a timid cinder caught in a storm? Should I have put my hand on his hand, and shown him he wasn't alone, not even here, at the end of his life? Should I have kissed his brow, and promised that he still had a chance to live?

Aye, maybe I should have.

But I stayed in the corner, terrified, and watched him sob himself to awful sleep, remembering that iron grip on my shoulders, that piercing golden light in his eyes, the scales that were marching across his skin. To this day, it churns my gut to think of how I failed him in that moment.

It wouldn't have stopped what happened next, but Bright Hell burning, what in all this terrible world do I know?

THE NEXT MORNING, MAYOR WORE A CLOTH AROUND his eyes. When Ko asked him why, all Mayor did was smirk and say, "So those scale-folk see what I really think of them."

The group laughed at that. I shivered.

It was no matter, because everyone forgot about his eyes when we entered the Scaled Nation proper. In the morning light, scattered across the thin reeds and fuzzy bulrushes and angular black trees of the swamp, there were scale-folk of every kind.

They had taken a cue from their ancestors, and lounged along the banks of the swamps, letting the sunlight flood through them like liquor, making them drunk and sleepy. Some of the croc-folk had their mouths open, nestled in the cattails, jaws working against empty air, while pyth-people rubbed and coiled their long necks together, splashing in the muck. Gator-folk lay on their stomachs in the water among pink-flowered lily pads, nostrils just above the surface, while the iggies draped themselves across branches of heavy bald cypress trees.

Mayor put a gloved finger to his lips, motioned for us to get close. When he started walking, I felt a pressure in the air, slight, and wondered if Mayor was keeping us safe, trying to hide us and disguise us with the other scale-folk.

We walked slower than slow; slow enough that time could miss us if it wasn't looking.

Up ahead, through the density of green palm fronds and low-hanging cypress leaves, I spied a mighty crater deep into the earth, and saw something enormous shift in the shadows. I turned to confirm with Mayor it was Momma Scales, only to see he wasn't there.

The whole group stopped dead. I couldn't feel the ripple in the air. The nearest gator-man's nostrils flared. Icicles pierced my heart, eyes searching for the Mayor. I looked back the way we'd come. **107**

Mayor was standing over a gator-man.

He had his gun drawn, aimed at the gator-man's heart. His hand was smoking, he was holding the six-gun so tight. His arm was shaking, fresh tears rolling down his cheeks, staining the bandage around his eyes. His mouth opened, and it looked he was trying to say something, but his mouth would not obey.

I read his lips, best I could: *Adam,* he said, over and over again.

How does a body run as slow as they can? I moved as through spiderwebs, inching my body forward in the water, going to Mayor as slow and as fast as I could.

I stood a foot from him, glanced at the sleeping croc on the ground, Adam, who had a silver chain around his neck, a feather at the end glinting in the light. Around the Mayor's neck hung its twin.

Mayor worked his mouth at me, unable to talk for the grief that blocked his throat. I shook my head at him, lips shut.

Mayor thrust the gun out at the sleeping gator. The Mayor's eyes were pleading with me, bleeding water like a stuck cactus.

I pointed back at the group of frightened sunblooders, to the stirring figures scattered around us, at the viper's nest we had walked into.

I'll never forget that moment, when he ripped the band of cloth from his eyes, turned his golden lights on me and mouthed, *I'm so sorry, Copper.*

His arm went limp.

He dropped the gun into the water.

The sleeping gator-man, Adam, opened his eyes.

As other scale-folk began to wake at the sound, Adam rose and seemed to see the Mayor, really see him.

And then Adam remembered what he'd become, and did the only thing he knew how to do, did to the Mayor what he had tried to do so many years ago when he had first turned.

His jaws clamped around the Mayor and then he dragged him under the water, blood already staining the air.

I swear I saw Mayor smile, a smile as wide and sad and starless as Dark Heaven.

It didn't matter if I screamed at that point or not, because the air had become nothing but sound, nothing but motion and pain and teeth, as the scale-folk sprang from sleeping and saw how we had slipped past them.

We pulled out our pikes and our steel and our guns.

I screamed to move onward, toward the crater.

The scale-folk were still groggy from sleep, but there were so many of them. How do you fight off a world of hate? I sent a pike through the neck of a pyth-person, and sidestepped the swipe of a gator-gal, whose needle teeth were flecked with blood and grime. Her tail sent me flailing, splashing down into the water. I could feel her moving towards me.

I had never contemplated my death, only figured it would come when stupidity got the best of me. Never figured it on someone else's stupidity, but that's life, I guess.

Then I noticed how the water near me was boiling. I plunged my hands into the mud, and found the scorching handle of one of Mayor's salamander six-guns.

I whipped the weapon skyward and fired. A lance of flame blew through the gator-gal in front of me, rocketed across the sky, and exploded over the crater.

The echo of the gun caused the scale-folk to stop their attacks, and quirk their heads as though they heard something far off. Fine, let 'em listen. I searched the mud for the other shooter, found its hot handle and lifted it out of the water, steaming.

In that pause, my heart broke to see Mayor's silver necklace shine up from the muck. I snatched it up and put it in my pocket. Someone had to carry his ghost home.

I turned just in time to see Momma Scales rise.

Her shadow could've shrouded the town proper, and I had to put my arms up against the windstorm her wings whipped up, though I caught glimpses of scales the color of deep fire, a belly as white as fresh sand. She shrieked in a language of a land astride ours, and I didn't have time to think as from her great jaws erupted a hurricane of heat.

The spear of flame made for me and mine like an arrow. With no time, and no place to run to, I thrust the six-guns into the air, remembering how Mayor would nestle them in the coals to charge them, and praying to Shadow Matron, oh, how I prayed it would be enough.

The fire slammed down on us, and arced around the guns in my hands. I could feel the salamanders drinking, deeper and deeper and deeper still, learning that their guts were not meant for so much power.

The salamander in my left hand exploded. The worst pain I've ever known washed through me and took my hand away in a burst of blood and bone. I screamed.

The other six-gun barely held. The wash of flame from above subsided, and in my remaining hand, the salamander glowed as if born from Bright Hell's forge. The scale-folk screeched and roared, cheering on their Momma who'd come to protect them. In the sky, she wheeled, circled back to me, to the sunblooders behind me.

At my feet, Ko and Felbrem were dead and smoking.

I stood, letting my stump of a hand drip blood onto the scorched and glassy swamp. Raising the salamander, so hot I could smell my hand roasting, I leveled it at the great Momma from another world, whose jaws snapped the air, screaming for her fallen babies.

I was ready to die, I suppose.

I mean, the Mayor was dead. Ko and Felbrem were dead. The rest of the sunblooders huddled around me, bloody and scorched and beaten. I wanted to die because it honestly seemed the easiest thing to do.

But if you didn't protect your family with all you had, what were you?

Momma Scales fell like a comet from Dark Heaven. Her jaws opened and I saw behind her teeth a great, bubbling heat. Her and I, our hands were on the triggers.

She approached.

The universe yelled, "Draw!"

We fired.

I was faster.

The bullet ascended like a star from Bright Hell, cutting through the flames of her jaw, and out the back of her mighty skull.

She didn't scream as she fell, but her babies did. They cried and wept as she landed into the swamp behind us, dead as dead as dead.

Last thing I remembered was dropping the six-gun to the water, sizzling, and staring at my lost hand, the bloody stump, and smiling like a fool before I fell with her.

WHAT HAPPENED TO THE SCALE-FOLK AFTER THEIR Momma died? Well, I imagine they did what we all have to do: they learned to live on without her.

There've been raids every so often, but they're few. Without her, they're lost, as lost as the sunblooders without the Mayor. But we all learn to make do with loss; life is just learning how to lose things with grace.

Would the Mayor have been proud of us, to see us fight back so? Did he even care for us? Or was he just a broken body searching for a ghost, before he could let himself die?

He may have been poisoned, and he may have been foolish, but he was right about one thing: The world is larger than the Stand, and to sit still in a world going down in flames without trying to help douse the inferno is just as bad as being the one to start the fire.

So I'm headed out. I've got a horse. I've got his last six-gun, battered and busted as it is. Even got his silver chain around my neck; maybe his ghost can help keep my feet on this earth. Momma Scales is dead by my horrific, scarred hand, and if I can do that to one, I can teach others how to do it to the remaining lizard lords that still dot the coast, biding their time until they bring their war back through the skies. I'll see if we can't drive those bastards back to their world without taking ours with them.

One of these days, I'll die. I'll be dragged under or poisoned or turned to their family. But not before teaching every person I meet that the world can only survive if you help it to, and fear is just a rope holding you back.

I don't know if it's what he would've wanted, but hope is all I've got left to give.

I gave it up, once upon a time and a hand ago. I don't intend to again.

Cracks

Xen

1

ASAD GREGORY JOHNSON COUNTED THE BEAT OF HIS heart in the closing of doors.

That was how he knew it was time to wake: when throughout Boston, one door after another after another slammed shut. Windows closed without so much as a single crack. Blinds shuttered with one last nervous glance. Runners pushed up against the bases of door frames, stopping the gaps beneath. Vents snapped air-tight. Each day the sound swelled like rain, fleeing in advance of sunset in a wave across the city.

Asad sat up in bed, leaned against the headboard, and watched the sun sink across the horizon, a bloody egg yolk punctured and melting across the sky. He reminded himself, as he did each day, that he was one of a small few allowed to see this. One of the few who could look at the sunset with his window unshaded and his eyes wide open, and that should be privilege enough.

It wasn't.

The other bed in the room was empty, the sheets carelessly smoothed. A battered, scarred Sox jacket was draped over the pillow, clean clothes and underwear laid out across the duvet. His brother was up already, but not gone yet. The patter-splat of the shower mixed with the hiss of a sizzling skillet, the smell of frying ham.

"Saad?" Gam called. Her voice creaked querulous as his mattress springs as he rolled over and buried his face in his threadbare pillow with a groan. "Ain't no dawdlin', boy. You know night comes on faster after equinox. I done taught you not to waste the dark."

Asad said nothing.

But he wondered, as he had with many sunsets and many moonrises, what it would be like to lock himself away with the coming of the dark, and sleep through the night without a care in the world.

He let himself roll until he hit the edge of the bed, then fell and caught himself on his legs at the last second. As Asad's feet hit the floor, Tarif knocked the bedroom door open and strutted in with a towel around his waist, his skin steaming dark as volcanic stone and the tight, close-cropped curls of his hair beaded with water droplets like dew on cobwebs. "Shower's yours, baby bro," he announced, decisive as calling a ringside hit; that was how Tarif did everything, in grand proclamations. Half the damn time he sounded like a club promoter in a Steve Harvey suit.

"Didn't even use all the hot water this time."

"You in some kinda hurry?"

Tarif grinned and thumped his broad barrel chest, then the smaller, rounder cask of his belly. "Just get moving. Haul your Black ass or I won't leave you any breakfast, squeak."

"Sure." Asad pulled the closet open and dragged a clean t-shirt and jeans off their hangers—but stopped when Tarif curled a hand on his shoulder.

"Hey. You okay?"

Asad stilled, looking down. The denim draped over his arm was ratty and torn, the knees of even his newest jeans blown out, the seams down the sides worn down to stripes of fibrous thread threatening to rip at the slightest pull. He plucked at one loose scrap, then lifted his head and turned a smile over his shoulder. "Yeah. I'm fine."

"You look tired."

"I am."

Tarif watched him with a knit to his brows, a furrow to his lips making the dip between his broad, smooth nose and upper lip sink into a little almond-shaped canyon. "It gets better, Saad. It really does."

Asad laughed briefly. "Do it?"

"You ain't old enough yet. When you finish school—"

"I'll still be kept in the dark." He turned to face his brother. "Not enough of us, Rifi. You know they'll never let me go dayside. And even if they would, Gam would be ashamed of me."

"Gam's her own person. She gotta let you be your own person, too."

"Can she, though?" Asad bit off. And when Tarif reached for him again, Asad knocked his brother's hand away and backed up until the closet doorknob hit the small of his back. "No point in trying to have a life when that life could get swallowed up."

Tarif stared at him, his eyes wide and liquid and strange. Asad stared back, and wondered for the millionth time if Tarif had chosen this—the darkness, the weight of it all—or if he'd been given no choice but to come back.

When all you knew was the dark, sometimes the light burned too much to stand.

Tarif looked away first. Looked away, and pulled his towel off to scrub his hair dry as he walked stark-ass naked across the room. He picked up his boxers from his bed.

"Happened again last night," drifted over his shoulder, a subdued murmur. "Louisville."

Asad sucked in a gasp. It lodged in his throat like swallowed gum. Last he'd heard, Louisville still had well over two hundred thousand people within the city limits. People who walked the day, and people who kept the night away; people like him, who stopped the dark from splitting open into cracks and canyons that could swallow the world up and seal it off without so much as a burp.

"Nobody talking about it," Tarif continued. "Not on the news, anyway. Total blackout, like the whole place never existed. Only a few people got out—the dark ones—but no one knows what happened to them since then. If they're being blamed."

Asad's heart thumped violently. He stared at his brother. "Where you hear that, if nobody talking?"

"…somewhere. Don't you worry none for it."

"Where's somewhere? Rifi, what you been doing?"

"It's just a thing." Tarif hunched his shoulders and stepped into his boxers, then swiped his phone off the dresser and thumbed the screen. "Links you up to other people like us. Anonymous. Deletes the messages five minutes after. Ain't nothing but underground chatter, but the news telling us less and less."

"You can't be fucking serious."

Tarif hissed under his breath, glaring, clutching his phone harder. "We *dying*, Saad. I can fucking bet you. It's not just the cracks. If a place goes dark, we go dark with it, even the survivors. People who don't get out fast enough, run somewhere else, get snatched up and don't nobody ever hear from them again. If them dayside folk won't tell the truth, we gotta find other ways to say it."

Asad leaned over and stole a glimpse at the screen, before Tarif jerked it away. What he'd seen didn't tell him much: a simple black screen with rapid-scrolling letters, timestamps, strings of numbers instead of user names.

It told him enough.

It told him this was trouble.

"You don't know who's really on the other end," he said. "What if the wrong people watching?"

"They can't do nothing," Tarif retorted sullenly. "We don't give out locations or meet up. No identifying info. Nobody dime out nobody."

"Except IP addresses, cellphone triangulation…"

"All that shit's encrypted."

"Okay. Sure. Who told you that? Santa Claus?" Asad dumped his clothing on his bed and pushed past his brother to the door. "I'm gonna shower. Delete it."

"You don't tell me what to do, baby brother," Tarif snarled after him.

"You want Gam to kill us both?" Asad paused in the doorway, glancing back. "*Delete it.*"

"We ain't doing nothing wrong." Tarif turned his face away, glaring at the window, his mouth twisted up into a knot. "*They* need *us*. They don't get to control us."

"Yeah?" Asad laughed bitterly. "But they do."

2

BREAKFAST WAS QUIET, BUT THEN BREAKFAST WAS always quiet. Felt like church sometimes, and maybe Asad was only imagining an old memory of bursting white flowers and ladies in hats like great netted boat sails and matching jackets and skirts, everybody in pale Easter colors that made their dark, dark skin only shine that much more. Maybe he'd seen it on TV, the choir clapping and the reverend up there swaying back and forth with his glasses gleaming and his thick bristly mustache and his purple sash draped over his black satiny robe, because Gam had never taken them to daytime church. Not that he could remember.

Daytime church was for praying. Nighttime folk was for fixing things, 'cause Gam always said weren't no room for praying when there was time to do.

Still, when Tarif and Asad finished eating—still not looking at each other, still not speaking to each other—and pulled on their jackets, Asad in his threadbare *Fresh Waffles* hoodie, Gam stopped them at the door. She barely came up to his ribs; she used to fill up the world, but he'd hit a growth spurt a few years ago, and Tarif had always been big. She was a tiny thing between them; tiny, but not small. Gam could never be small, for all the wrinkles and the thinness of the bones poking through her wrists. All that power in her had compressed, over the years. Concentrated. And concentrated things just meant it took a lot less to knock you on your ass, one hundred eighty-proof liquid fire and not a bit watered down.

That power brimmed in Gam's hands, as she laid them atop Tarif and Asad's heads. Her palms were dry and neither warm nor cold, as though they weren't flesh at all but paper written with the secrets carried between them. They whispered, a crawling sensation against the skin of his brow, and his own palms tingled in echo.

"Come home," Gam said, as she always did—Gam's prayer, more powerful than begging and pleading and wailing to the sky could ever be, more powerful than Sunday church hats and clapping hands and gospel hymns. This was their church: her hand on their heads, her voice both whisper and resonant command. "You boys stay together, and you come home to me."

"We will, Gam," Asad promised, knowing damned well they might not come home at all.

Pointedly not looking at each other, tension bristling between them, Asad and Tarif clattered down the concrete steps of their narrow brick apartment building, feet scuffing over the faded remnants of children's chalk drawings. Little things—yellow chalk suns with radiating spears of light, pale blue crescent moons, stick figures of mommy and daddy and the dog and cat and little girls' and boys' friends and enemies and make-believe stories. But Asad stopped on the bottom step, and studied a sigil chalked on the corner in white: an eye with a slit pupil and long cats-eye lashes, enclosed in a dashed circle. The dashes weren't right, should be runework, but nobody knew the runes but him and people like him, the after-dark people. Daytime people didn't have the eyes, but they understood.

And some little boy or girl in this building understood enough to ask Asad to watch over them tonight. A little boy or girl who had nightmares, maybe—bad dreams 'bout falling through the cracks, slipping away from all the people in those stick-figure pictures, the little pink chalk version of themselves washed out with the rain and never drawn back in.

Asad closed his eyes. His breaths had thorns, and he didn't like it. This was why he'd never go dayside, even if he had the choice.

Even if he missed the sun on his face, baking into his flesh, searing and shining on black skin that had been made to drink the light into its glow.

Tarif touched his shoulder, his arm, a silent gesture that said, *I know.*

I know.

And just like that they weren't fighting anymore. They drifted close to each other with their hands in their jacket pockets against the early evening chill, elbows bumping together as they stepped out into the night.

The street lights were out again, except one flickering at the end of the block where Floyd turned onto Callender Street. Turned all of Mattapan into shades of blue and gray with little touches of gold where the light seeped between buildings from Stratton across the way. Made the shadows thicker, alive, heavy enough that if Asad looked at them long enough they took on weight and started to crawl, oozing along the spidery chasms in jagged side-walk that hadn't been repaired since the last big split. He'd always thought people who fell through the cracks looked like that. They stopped being human, and turned into awful carbon-paper tatters. Even if he knew better; Gam had told him what happened, how bad it was. Like crossing the event horizon of a black hole, she'd said.

And people who fell through the cracks got torn to pieces, shredded by the gravitational forces holding two worlds both to-gether and apart. Anything that came back out weren't nothing he wanted to meet. Besides—things that came through? Nobody knew what *they* looked like.

Because they swallowed everything up, and didn't leave a single eye left to see.

He tilted his head back, and looked up at the sky. His school books said in places where the city lights had gone, people could see the stars as more than one or two pinpricks here and there. His school books said, too, before the first big split there used to be cars in the streets with their tail lights red and glaring, and airplanes and helicopters up there with their running lights blink-ing, their engines roaring, instead of this dead, empty silence and starless wrongness lit only by a pallid infected mood, seeping its clear pale juices onto the edges of the clouds ringing its light.

"Think they'll ever fix the street lights?" he asked.

"Nah. Keeping us in the dark means they don't have to look at us."

"Do they hate us that much?"

"Ain't us they hate. It's that we can walk where they can't." Tarif ginned and spread his arms. "Nothing like this. This quiet night, when the whole world's made out of silver and blue velvet. They can't never see this. They come out here, they die. But us?" He turned with his arms still flung out wide, spinning a slow full circle. "We own this. It don't own us."

Asad glanced around—at the broken heaps of concrete apart-ment tenements with their hollow eyes, so run-down it was hard to tell which were occupied and which were condemned. At the scrub pushing up through the sidewalks. At the barren desolation of a neighborhood with the abandoned look of a place no one wanted to live, even when they had no choice.

One block over, the brownstones started. Tall and sleek and gentrified, restored and polished and rented out at three times their original value. But right here, right now, on Floyd Street, wasn't a single damned thing anyone wanted to own.

Just what they settled with.

"What the hell do we own?" he asked, and Tarif snorted.

"Nuh-uh. I'm not letting your fucking tired soggy ass bring me down tonight." He elbowed Asad. "Let's split up."

Asad stopped, knees locking, and stared at his brother. "Gam said—"

"You're seventeen. Don't be a baby."

The words came out in a sneer, but Tarif's cheeks burned red, dark and deep, and he hunched his shoulders and kicked at the sidewalk, looking past Asad but never quite making eye contact. Asad sighed.

"You meeting that girl, huh. The one from down south."

Tarif broke into a broad grin, all the stars missing from the night sky right there in his smile. "Her name's Shawna," he said, then laughed and rubbed the back of his neck. "What? Why you looking at me like that?"

"You goddamn well know why."

"I got a weakness, okay?" Tarif ducked his head. "Girl *thick*."

"Sure," Asad said dryly. "You know this how people die in horror movies, right? Split up when we ain't supposed to."

"You scared?"

Asad said nothing. He wasn't supposed to be afraid. He was supposed to keep the fear away for other people, which meant he couldn't give in to the brittleness in his thigh-bones or the way his chest folded in like it would snap right in the middle faster than a greasy wishbone at Thanksgiving.

Tarif clapped both thick, heavy hands to his shoulders, weighing him down, grounding him with a touch and warm brown eyes he'd known his whole damn life, as constant and steady and right as Gam and her electric palms.

"Nothing gonna come through, baby brother," Tarif said. "Nothing ever come through, 'cause we do our jobs. Because all the others do their jobs."

"Louisville. You said it—last night, Louisville went dark."

"Because they didn't do their shit. Because it was too big for them. It's not like that here. I won't let it be. It's gonna be all right. Promise." Tarif squeezed his shoulders, his heat soaking through Asad's jacket, his fingers pinching Asad's collarbones in a way that always hurt but he'd never let go of in a thousand years. "I'm gonna help Shawna check her block, then come back and find you. Okay?"

"Okay." Asad nodded, pressing his lips together and biting back the taste of ash and fear souring in the back of his mouth. "Be careful. Don't fall through."

Tarif stepped back, that broad grin back, blush so deep, and Asad wondered how it must feel, to be so deeply in love he would brave the dark, the unknown, the places where people fell through the cracks in the world and never came back.

"Nothing gonna happen to me, baby brother," Tarif said, with his confidence that filled up his thick barrel chest like a keg that never ran dry. "We the superheroes in the dark, man. We the ones who hold the world together."

Then he was turning away, already half-gone. Wasn't hard to see Tarif was somewhere else, his thoughts on Shawna, on kisses, on thick lush thighs and the way girls had of changing the way the air of a room breathed, like it went down smoother because they were there. Tarif's back grew smaller and farther away, words drifting over the night in laughing, light promise.

"One way or another, baby bro...we gotta pull through."

3

IT WASN'T THE FIRST TIME ASAD HAD WALKED THEIR block alone. Technically seven blocks; the Johnson family owned the world-ways down Floyd from the curve of Callender to Blue Hill, where Callender became Greenrock Street and Floyd became Donald Road and those streets became someone else's responsibility. Asad and Tarif would start at the point where Floyd and Callender met, then follow the curve of Callender around until it ran parallel with Floyd again, stopping to peek in between, down the cross-street of Lucerne before moving on until they hit Blue Hill and circled back around.

They'd kick rocks as they walked and shout *GOOOAAAL!* when they snapped a hunk of asphalt into a sewer grate, then laugh and   **121** hush each other even though no one would be brave enough to open their windows and look outside. They had to be quiet, because they had to listen. Cracks didn't always open outside, and if they caught that *feeling*, if they heard those cries of fear, they had to be ready to bolt in like the fire department, all shoulders and bluster, and break down doors and do what they came to do.

But tonight, Asad kicked rocks down Callender Street alone because Tarif had run off to chase a girl. Last time he'd run off to chase some boys who wanted to form a sundown baseball team, though it had fallen apart when their parents had caught wind and said if they had time to play ball, they had time to work runes. Before, Tarif had been thinking about going dayside, sleeping nights and waking up days to look for a job when not many dayside jobs needed the kind of skills nightsiders learned in school.

But Tarif still tried, while Asad watched and held his tongue because he wasn't gonna be the jackass shitting on the weird hope Tarif held onto, a hope that made him the younger one though he had four years on Asad. Somehow, Asad always ended up playing the older brother. The voice of reason. No *thick* girl was gonna turn his head 'cause girls didn't turn his head at all, and the odds of finding someone like him—someone with the eyes, someone who saw, someone who knew the runewords and closed the cracks and kept the nothing at bay—who was also *someone like him*?

Never gonna happen. Not today, not tomorrow.

So he did his duty, he did his homework, he followed the old ways, and he let Tarif be young and joyful for both of them, optimistic and hopeful and full of things Asad didn't think he'd ever possessed.

That was the way things were. The way things had always been, and always would be.

So why did the silence tonight feel different?

He knew every corner of his blocks, and he traced every square of sidewalk, peering into the chips and crevices in the concrete to make sure they were *just* concrete, and not a rift taking advantage to fit itself into the ready-made shape. He climbed ladders that had become law since the first split—not having one installed was punishable by fines from city inspectors. Couldn't risk it. Couldn't risk that one rooftop passed over might be the one place a crack opened big enough to swallow the whole city.

He crept along rooftops, peered between apartment buildings and weathered brick-fronted houses, inspected beneath dumpsters, scaled street lamps, ran his fingers along awnings, tried not to flinch when motion-sensor lights on porches snapped on. He knew most of them—from the Norfolks' blinding strobe spots to the dim little yellow light that always drew mosquitos and moths to the Hernandez porch—and they knew him, knew the boy creeping silent around their houses weren't trying nothing but to hold them all together.

Yet he still felt like a thief, if only because he didn't want to be seen. He didn't like the way daysiders looked at him, when they recognized what he was. Like they needed something from him.

Like he actually gave them hope.

Sometimes they peered at him through the blinds, but tonight brought no cautious, frightened eyes; nothing but the occasional sound caught through glass and brick and wood, close-held murmurs and television channels flicking and dinner plates clanking. He was alone, unseen, and maybe that was what had him so uneasy.

He wouldn't mind being seen, for once. By someone. Tarif had Shawna, had his baseball team boys, but Asad was the quiet one, the responsible one, and even in school the other nightsiders never much looked at him when Tarif's bright personality took up enough space for both of them.

"You getting yourself all messed in the head," he muttered to himself. "You mad Tarif ain't here, or you mad at the space he take up when he *is* here?"

No one and nothing answered. Not even the dog he heard rummaging in the trash as he drew up on Lucerne; not the wind wobbling the power lines until they made strange, warped, wailing sounds as they bounced and jostled. That wind hit hard for a September evening, and Asad pulled his hoodie up and hunched into it, zipping up the neck until it covered his mouth. Wind in September shouldn't be like this. Wind like this came with summer storms, then left and didn't come back until the winter snows.

The back of his neck prickled. What had Gam always said? *If things ain't right, things ain't right.* The wind was wrong. This whole night was wrong, and that was why Asad was really mad:

'Cause he was afraid he would find something, and he was never afraid when he walked the blocks alone. 'cause Tarif never left him when things felt *off*, but he'd been too fucked in the head to even notice the air tasted like flat stale cola and wet quarters, and he'd left Asad to handle what was supposed to be both their shit when Asad shouldn't be closing seals solo until he was eighteen, maybe twenty.

God damn it.

Just find it. Now that he'd stopped ignoring his screaming instincts, there was no mistaking: it was close. He didn't think he'd passed it yet, but if he didn't find it by the end of the sweep he'd circle back. Crawl under houses if he had to. Use the block key and go sniffing inside. If he followed the direction of the rising hairs on the backs of his arms, he'd at least be able to narrow it down to a few buildings before he had to go door to door, slipping inside and creeping unwanted among people's lives, bringing fear into their homes until he told them it was safe, they were safe, they wouldn't fall between tonight.

He palmed the skeleton key in his pocket, held it close until it printed hot against his palm and he smelled the tinny stink of brass soaking in the sweat of his skin. He kept his eyes keen with every step, listened for the tingle and pull that was as much sound as sensation, a buzz on the back of his scalp, that weird naked crawl like he'd just gotten his edges done and everything felt prickly and too cold. It wasn't on Lucerne. He wasn't being drawn there, and the scent was fainter, buried under dumpster rankness and a little gift that dog had left behind. Had to be close, if the dog had run. Strays didn't run from one boy on the street, but they ran when something shifted in the polarity of the world, when their instincts told them a disaster was on the horizon and they had to seek high ground.

Maybe that was what made people like Asad, like Tarif, like Gam. They hadn't lost their instinct. They'd long ago forgotten being animals and become men, the first men, the men who became all other men...but some men, some women, some *humans* didn't lose what connected them to what they once were.

That connection drew him down Callender, right up on the Blue Hill crossways. He stood on the center median of the deserted street and listened to the howling silence: the lonely keen of the wind coiling serpentine between buildings, caressing the walls, begging to be let in. The trees planted along the median whispered, as if they could tell him what to do, how to do it. He toed out of his Adidas, pulled his socks off, and balled them up before stuffing them into his left sneaker. Feet bare and planted on the dirt, grass tickling between his toes, he closed his eyes and tried to shut everything out and just *feel* where that wrongness, that prickle, pulled stronger.

It was like standing in the ocean and feeling for the changes in current, where once you got out deep, deep enough to drown, the water had layers—some hotter and some colder, making them move past each other at different speeds. Tarif said it was like swimming through the pee-patch in the public pool, but pee in the pool didn't make currents that pushed Asad one way, then the other, then the other again. He stood with his hands at his sides and his fingers spread like bracing them on a table, bracing to keep from coming unmoored when, eyes closed this way—shutting down one sense after the other until he no longer felt the cool itching grass or the ice-biting breeze or the scratchy threads of his hoodie, until he no longer smelled pavement still baking from the sun and stinking of used bubblegum and exhaust, until he no longer heard the trees' curious whisperings—he could easily lose himself, in the black space behind his eyelids. He could easily become nothing, abandon all connection with the world as it was, while he cut himself free from his senses to feel the one place where an electric wound had been cut into the skin of reality.

The currents pushed him to and fro, swaying on his feet with a kind of dreamy vertigo. He stopped trying to keep his balance, stopped trying to focus on his body, and gave into the draw, until he leaned over and over and *over* and almost fell. He caught himself as that lurch started in his gut and everything rushed wrong-ways, eyes snapping open and arms windmilling as he pivoted himself around and rocked forward onto the very tips of his toes until gravity righted itself and he knew up from down. He stood up straight, and looked.

He faced across Blue Hill Avenue, his body an arrow pointing across the street. Next to a three-story pastel blue house with white trim, with an empty lot's space between, stood a long, low, rectangular building: two stories, a storefront painted over with a mural of Black folk dancing and playing music below, tape-marked rectangular windows up top, pale gray cement in the front, red brick in the back. Metal stairs ran up the side to the second floor. Both the wall and the second-floor wooden access door had been painted over with graffiti tags in shades of blue, the letters so fat and stylized it was impossible to tell, at this distance, what they meant to say.

Asad bit his lip. Over on that side of Blue Hill belonged to the Roberts, old Marsha and her cranky nephew Jonas with the gold stud in his nose, and they didn't like people stepping in and doing their job. Technically the Johnson block cornered right there on the bus stop where, by day, people waited for the 28 and 29 and hoped this wouldn't be the one day they got stranded when the buses ran late and took everyone back to the transit center to wait out the night behind shuttered windows and doors.

But he didn't see Marsha and Jonas around. And the Roberts hadn't been in Boston as long as the Johnsons anyway, and when shit hit the fan everyone from all around—the Roberts, the Gurneys over in Dorchester, the Ndiayes from Roxbury, everybody from everywhere—came to Gam to make the hard choices. And Asad was Gam's grandson, and a crack had opened somewhere in or around that building, reaching for him like it had put out feelers and knew how hard to pull to make him twitch.

So he had to be like Gam, and make the hard decision to do something about it whether old Miss Marsha would like it or not.

Right?

He balled his fists up inside his pockets. The skeleton key bit into his knuckles. Gam trusted *him* with the skeleton key, not Tarif. The key that would open every door in Boston. She trusted Asad to have this key and not abuse it, not do stupid shit, not run around fucking everything up just because he was seventeen and he fucking *could*. So she'd trust him to do the right thing now, and the right thing was to cross out of his territory and take care of that fucking crack before it spread large enough to swallow something up.

He rolled his shoulders, again and again and again. He'd learned the trick at school, one of those things they taught the nightsiders and not the daysiders: how to loosen the body to be ready to run, to fight. It worked the tension out of the neck, stopped it from radiating up into a headache that would cloud his thoughts and his perceptions, calmed him with the familiar and the routine. One more time, he rolled and rolled and rolled, until his muscles were putty and his head went light and a soft burn sank in at the base of his skull and nape of his neck, pleasant and deep.

Then he pushed his feet back into his socks and shoes, stepped off the median into the street, and crossed Blue Hill into the vacant lot.

The moment he set shoe rubber to the pavement of the lot, a charge shot up through him, crawling up his legs and pulling in his groin and making his bladder go loose even as his ass clenched up.

"Damn," he gasped, then let out a nervous laugh. "*Damn.*"

Fucking *strong.* He'd never been close to a crack so large he felt the charge of its edges before he even saw it, but he had to be careful. That much potential energy meant the crack might be unstable, its edges fluctuating and malleable, and lowering his guard for even a blink could leave him chewed up and spat back out in particles compacted denser than a neutron star.

He circled the building slowly, casing the entire lot first; the pull came from straight inside the shop, but he did his job and he did it right. He walked every inch of the lot, hissing now and then as another step surged those weird shocks up his legs and left his knees numb and his butt tight and tingling as if he'd been sitting on a hard chair for five straight days.

Nothing in the lot. Nothing when he circled the building, either, unless it was up high where he couldn't see. He ran his fingers around and around the walls, tracing circles, feeling for anything that would sizzle through him like sticking his fingers in an electrical socket, pausing to follow the contours of the painting on the storefront, the rounded limbs and stylized shapes catching people in motion. People in *life.*

He wondered if this had been painted before the split as a promise of what could be, or after—as a memory of what never would be again.

No cracks outside, that he saw. No ladder on the building. Marsha had probably reported it, but he should say something to Gam. Asad fished a pair of folding miniature binoculars from his pocket,   **127** pressed them to his eyes, and circled the building one more time, scanning the high places. Nothing. He'd have to get up on the roof, climb from the staircase maybe, but first he'd check inside.

The skeleton key unlocked the storefront, and the faint jingle of a little brass bell dangling down over the door from a colored ribbon announced his entry. He caught it in his palm, stopped the clapper, then crept inside and locked the door behind him.

"Hello?" he called. In the silent, darkened shop, floating over the silhouetted racks, his voice sounded soft and scared, because *he* was soft and scared. That charge raised every hair on his body and prickled his scalp like a coming storm, and he was scared all he would find were the remnants of the people who should've been here, because he'd come too late.

No one answered. Probably home for the night, unless they lived upstairs. The silence in here was wrong, when the tension of a nearby rift felt so *loud*—like it should come with the crash of rending seas and clouding skies and shaking earth. Asad moved slowly through the racks: magazines and Little Debbie cakes, mini keychain lighters and frizzy ten-dollar sew-ins in plastic bags, lit faintly by standing fridges full of Coke and Sprite and Mountain Dew and box milk. The pale blue of the refrigerator lights glowed the same color as an open crack, and even though he knew he was being paranoid, Asad made himself lean in and check, probing around the cold misty insides with a trembling, outstretched hand, brushing up against nothing but the stinging heat of the rows of bulbs along the top.

He had to go slow. Had to be careful, letting himself into the cashier's safety booth, searching around, his breaths filling his ears in dragging rasps loud as an astronaut on a spacewalk. He paused under the eye of the security camera, held up his skeleton key, and sketched the sign of the eye in the air with his fingertip. Just so the shop owner wouldn't freak out, when they reviewed the security tapes in the morning.

Then he pocketed the key and moved on.

The back storeroom was next. With every room he checked, that crackling sensation grew fainter while his unease grew stronger, like the crack was baiting him with a game of hot and cold. *Colder,* it said as he rummaged among shelves and crates and boxes. *Colder, colder…*

Until he found the door in the back of the storeroom, and that charge shot from his feet right to his scalp, stinging in his nose worse than plucking a hair, burning in his eyes like a handful of grit, wet quarters and blood on his tongue.

Warmer, that jolt mocked. *Getting warmer.*

He tried the doorknob, then jerked back with a hiss. *Hot*—hot as if a fire raged on the other side, but he smelled no smoke. Only ozone, and the tang of his own terrified sweat.

He pulled the sleeve of his hoodie down over his hand, then tried again—gingerly, gingerly. The door swung open on darkened stairs. He fumbled for the light switch on the wall and flicked it on, illuminating narrow, stained stucco walls and pitted concrete steps covered in a fur coat of dirty fuzz. No one had been up here in a while.

"Hello?" he called anyway.

A voice responded.

His stomach lurched up, slammed into the bottoms of his lungs, punched the air out of them, and sank back down. He flattened his damp palms against his thighs, curled them, knotted up furrows in his jeans, made himself let go. *Calm the fuck down.* Might be someone living up here after all. But if there was, they weren't answering; he couldn't make out more than a low mumble. Sounded like *singing,* humming under their breath. He recognized that kind of hum—earbuds in, head down, busy. They didn't even know he was here. Minding their own business, and he was fixing to bust in and fuck up their night.

Better than letting them get swallowed up.

He knocked on the walls as he climbed the steps, rapping firmly and raising his voice loud enough, he hoped, to be heard over headphones. "Hello?" he called again. "If you can hear me, don't be scared." It came out *skeert.* "Just doing inspections. Checking out a vibe."

Still no answer; only that humming and bopping, voice oddly familiar.

"Promise I'll be in and out, sure as shitting," he tried, then winced. Gam would've popped the back of his head for cussing in front of ordinary citizens, when he had a job to do. But he was nervous as fuck. Every step brought him closer to fucking *puking,* the charge was so thick here. So thick even a daysider should've been able to feel it, the kind of premonition even the insensitive got, something warning them away. Why the hell hadn't they booked it the fuck out of here?

"Sorry," he said as he crested the stairs, and leaned around the wall to peek into the second floor. "I cuss when I get nervous, and I think maybe I need to get you gone 'cause I'm picking up some serious bad shit—"

He nearly fell back down the stairs.

The second floor had been bisected down the middle into day and night. The half closest to the stairs was shadow and night and stacked boxes, some taped up and scribbled with illegible Sharpie words, some pried open with old newspaper and random shit popping out, all of it covered in dust. The other half was lamplit, golden, filled with all the warmth in the world—a cozy living room full of plush furniture in beige linen draped over with colorful patterned throws, potted plants in the corners, wooden statues crouching on shelves and watching over the place, a shriveled leaf of cabbage nailed up over an open doorway leading into another hallway.

A boy sat on the couch, wearing a red hoodie with *Fresh Waffles* printed on the chest, earbuds in his ears, the cord trailing into his pockets. A skinny rawboned boy with that look of someone waiting for one more growth spurt to round out his sharp edges; a Black boy with a cut to his lids that made his eyes taper sly, pucker at the corners, angle up at the edges; a compact, self-contained boy with a point to his chin Asad had always hated because it made him look like he was sassing off even when he wasn't. A boy Asad would know anywhere.

Because that boy was him.

Through a shimmering, crackling barrier like a wall of water transfused into rippling film, he was looking at his own fucking *self*.

His throat slammed shut. He couldn't feel his body, but he knew he'd fallen because he was suddenly on eye level with a coffee table that cut off in the middle of a decorative bowl of polished stones, ending where it met the filmed barrier. That wasn't a crack. It was a fucking *hole*, and Asad should be drawing the runes and screaming for Tarif and calling his Gam, but all he did was thud down on his butt and stare at himself like he was looking in a goddamned mirror.

Except in that mirror, he was no longer sunken-eyed and hollow. In that mirror, he no longer had the ashen undertone to his skin from never seeing the sun, his skin so rich and dark a brown he glowed, smooth and suede-soft. His other self's knuckles weren't white with dried, thickened skin. His other self's cheeks weren't concave caverns of exhaustion. His other self's clothing was scuffed and torn from natural wear and tear, instead of years of growing into and growing out of and stretching them thin at the seams until they were ready to burst.

His other self looked *alive*, while Asad was his own ghost, haunting from an unseen otherworld.

He fumbled onto his hands and knees and reached toward the hole in reality, but stopped just short of touching it. Just short of making contact with the prickle and charge and *pull* of a vacuum on the other side, waiting to be filled.

No—the vacuum wasn't on the other side. It was inside. Inside *him*. Empty. Lonely. Hungry. While this other Asad?

Looked like he'd never known a lonely, hungry day in his life.

Asad's mouth filled with wetness, tasting of spit and snot, his nose thick and tacky on every gasping breath, and a hot wet burn came down in a blurry shield over his eyes. What the fuck had he done wrong? What the fuck was he being punished for, to be born on this side of the cracks? Was this purgatory, when he'd never even committed the original sins of a broken world and all his crimes were the small, private misdemeanors of a greedy and wanting soul?

He spilled out a rough sob, letting his hand fall. The other Asad didn't respond, didn't even notice, kept humming and bobbing his head along to whatever played through his earbuds. Those from the other side never saw through. The eyes only went one way, like some kind of fucking *gift* for people from the shadow-side, as if it could ever make up for everything that had gone so catastrophically awry.

He had to close it. He had to close the fucking crack and seal the worlds off from each other, because he couldn't stand to look at this. To see himself, the self he should have been, content and glowing with serenity, bristling with something like eager anticipation. He had all of Asad's little tics, when he was nervous and excited: knotting and unknotting the earbud cord between his fingers, smiling to himself for no reason and then forcibly schooling his face back to neutral calm, sitting all the way forward on the edge of his seat, so fucking familiar that for a heartbeat Asad was *there*, the springy couch cushion under his ass, and he imagined the room smelled like sandalwood and something comforting and sweet, like sugar cookies.

He trembled, and dragged himself to his feet; he had to spread his legs wide to stay upright, and braced his soles flat against the floor. With shaking hands, he brushed off the clumps of fuzzy dust sticking to the legs of his jeans, then spread his arms with his fingers splayed. His palms tingled, his fingertips buzzing. This was the tricky part, the scary part, when he was too small for a crack this big and he would have to draw off some of the energy charging its edges to power the runes. Shadow defined its boundaries—where bright light ended, and past the light spread the darkened room that fit his world. The hole was oblong, cutting a floor-to-ceiling and wall-to-wall diagonal with tapered top and bottom points, a ripped sword-slash in the curtain of reality. He touched the rippling air to one side of the tear, and sucked in a breath as concussive shocks slammed through him, electric fists beating at his chest and trying to crack his ribs.

The stairwell door opened at his back.

He whirled. Those pounding shocks stopped, leaving him gasping. No one there. The door was closed, just as he'd left it—but he'd heard it, echoing up from down the stairs, followed by steps drawing closer and closer. He *still* heard those steps, the sound muted and wrong, coming through cotton.

Coming through the rift.

The steps grew louder. An easy, casual stride, drawing so close he sensed their presence right in front of him, then passing through and leaving behind a chill, a strange impression of displacement. Then another boy stepped into view, in the room through the rift. He was tall, taller than Asad, with shoulders so broad and a waist and body so narrow he didn't fit together quite right, but his grace and loping stride made it work. He wore braids down his back in black ropy tangles, and the lamplight made his deep brown skin glow like he'd rolled in gold dust and come up shining. He wore a shirt with the sleeves ripped off and paint splatters slashed across ripped black fabric, and carried a backpack over his shoulder.

A backpack he tossed on the couch as he crossed the room to the other Asad, gripped his hands, pulled him to his feet, and kissed him.

Asad's heart tried to beat as he watched the other boy's lips press against lips that were his own but weren't; as he watched full thick plush mouths meld together with a sighing sweetness that said they'd done this again and again and it never got old, only familiar and breathless and perfect. His other self twined his arms around the tall, braided boy's neck, and Asad shivered, his mouth pulsing in strange ways. He touched his lips, pressed down on them until they gave as they must be giving underneath the strange boy's kiss, and felt something he'd never known before curling in the pit of his stomach and sinking its hooks into him from the inside.

The boys on the other side of the rift pulled apart with a faint sound, the dampness of a seal breaking, and Asad's other self smiled—a smile made of lazy things and wonder and bright breathlessness.

"Avondre," he said. "Hey. Thought you'd never get back."

Avondre. Asad mouthed the name; it became a flower, blooming on his tongue.

Avondre laughed and settled his hands on the other Asad's hips. He had a kind of slow drawl, not quite southern but still as if molasses had a sound, dripping and sugary. "Moms let you up here?"

"I sweet-talked my way through."

"Bullshit. More like she too damn tired to argue with your shit."

The other Asad leaned into Avondre, looking up at him with his eyes glittering with unvoiced laughter. "Think she knows by now, Von."

"Knowing and being okay with us locked up here together ain't the same thing."

"We ain't locked up together." The other Asad brushed his lips to Avondre's. "We just together. That's all."

Together.

Asad sucked in an awful, braying cry, drowning and choking on wet runny salt. *Together.* Life had fucking traded *that*, that being, that togetherness, for the eyes, for the sight, for a duty to set right something he'd never fucking set wrong in the first place, but now he knew the gift for what it was.

A goddamned curse.

A curse to have to sit here and watch this, and know it could never be his.

His other self and Avondre kissed once more, lingering, slow, as innocent as if they'd never touched original sin, never had to atone.

Asad scrambled to his feet, clambered away from the crack in the universe, and threw himself down the stairs on clumsy steps. Out into the night. Away from *that*.

Where he wouldn't have to see the wordless thing he'd always craved given form, and locked worlds away.

Forever out of his reach.

4

HE'D STOPPED SOBBING BY THE TIME HE HIT THE BUS stop on the corner of Callender and Blue Hill, but what followed wasn't much better: this hollow husked-out rawness, as if he'd been opened like a pumpkin and had all his good soft parts scooped out. He sank down on the bus stop bench and buried his face in his hands.

He'd left the crack. Left it open.

But he couldn't go back there. Not right now.

Maybe not ever.

Twenty minutes later he was still there, staring at his feet, when Tarif came strolling up Callender, kicking pebbles and flapping his jacket with his hands in his pockets and whistling fit to whistle down Dixie. He had a shit-eating grin on, his mouth red like he'd been doing something, and Asad kind of wanted to hate him because everyone had someone, while Asad only got to watch.

But he scrubbed at his face and sniffled back hard, and tried not to look like he'd been crying for half an hour, curled over his thighs and pressing his face into his knees. Tarif came swinging in, a big black bird touching down for a landing, arms flapping, voice large and loud and brassy as joyous screeching music.

"You ain't gonna believe my night," Tarif said. "How'd it go, squeak? You finish the bl—" Then he stopped, his smile vanishing.

134 He stared at Asad. "God damn. You look like shit. You okay?"

"No," Asad answered without thinking, and immediately regretted it.

Tarif plunked down on the bench next to him. "Fuck. Something happen? You hurt?"

Not where you can see.

He stared down at his hands—at his old man's hands, weathered and worn, and tried to remember he was only seventeen. Then he shook his head, swallowing back the bitterness sitting on his tongue like cough medicine.

"Nothing happened," he said. "Nothing came through. I'm okay. Just…just saw some bad shit on the other side. That's all."

Tarif whistled through his teeth. "That fucking sucks. I once saw this dog get hit by a car, and I couldn't stop it."

"I remember. You cried for a week."

"Man, I don't cry." Tarif hunched his shoulders, then snorted. "…yeah. I cried." He bumped his elbow to Asad's. "Was it something like that?"

"Yeah. Something like that." But Asad said nothing else. It was his secret, his longing, his ache curled up in a little knotted kernel inside him. He scrubbed at his nose one more time, then stood. "I'll be okay. We gonna be late for school. Block's not done. We can check it on the way."

He stepped off briskly, before Tarif could protest. And he put up with his brother's babbling, his whispers about *Shawna, Shawna* as if worshipping with words and tonguing her name, as they cut down Blue Hill and circled back up Floyd, stopping to fetch their backpacks where they'd left them inside the foyer of the apartment building. The whole time Tarif didn't notice that crackling, that pull, that surge. Maybe because it wasn't meant for him. Maybe because it was meant for Asad, and only Asad.

It was his other life, his problem to fix, and he'd failed.

He'd come back after school. After homework, before sunup, when Gam and Tarif were in bed. He'd fix everything. He'd close the crack.

He would.

But he wondered if, when Boston was swallowed up, he'd even have a second left to realize, *This was all my fault.*

5

IN SCHOOL THEY LEARNED ABOUT TIME AS A FUNCTION of gravity, about singularities, about how sometimes a rift was similar to a singularity and had the same effects on its local environment, on a smaller scale. Asad tried to pay attention, but couldn't stop thinking about the crack. So big it could easily spread; they did that, once they fixed in place. They fed on themselves and opened wider and wider, greedily eating more and more of the world until they hit some break point and entire chunks of reality popped out of existence.

Soon. He'd fix it soon. Just a few hours. He didn't have to hold out long. A little while longer, and he would shut the door on that liar's hope. That liar's hope that someone like Avondre would ever look at him with golden lamplight in his eyes and his lips a full sweet smile, just for Asad.

He was in the wrong world. The wrong universe. The wrong timeline.

Shadow-siders didn't get to have things like that.

Gam was in love once, he thought. *I wonder if Mom loved my Dad, 'fore having folks with the eyes got too weird and he took off.*

During gym class he checked Twitter for Louisville, a quick general search across the entire network of accumulated tweets.

The search returned zero results, as if the city hadn't even had a name, vanished as if it never existed at all.

6

SCHOOL LET OUT LATE. TOO LATE, AND THE MOMENT his sixth period teacher let them go, Asad shoved his books into his bag and hauled ass to the door, not even slowing down when Tarif shouted his name from across the quad as he emerged from the building where the college-level students took vo-tech classes and university entrance prep courses.

"Hey! Hey, squeak, slow the fuck down! Where you going?"

"Home," Asad said, and doubled his stride.

Tarif trailed him, huffing and panting and interrogating him with every step, but Asad kept his mouth mutinously shut. He couldn't waste breath on talking. He had to *move.* He was tempted to skip home, but Tarif would follow, and Gam would want to know why, so he veered off on their street and clattered up the steps into their building.

He barely made it to their floor and to their door. Gam was waiting. Like she *knew*, Gam was waiting just past the door, watching them both with shrewd eyes. Asad kept his head down and brushed past her with a mumble—but she shot a hand out, barring the way. Asad drew up short, staring at his feet.

"Tarif," Gam said firmly, "Go to your room."

"But—"

"I said go to your room, boy." Gam snapped Tarif a look fit to freeze lava and boil glaciers. "Me and your brother, we gonna have a sit-down."

Asad flinched. Tarif stared at him with wide *you-gonna-get-it-now* eyes, then scurried past and disappeared into their room. Gam let her arm drop and studied Asad in that way she had, as if the eyes let her see not just the rifts, but all the broken places and lies and wrongdoings inside a boy. Then she folded her arms over her narrow, twig-boned chest and tossed her head toward the kitchen. "You come on, now."

"Yes, ma'am."

Gam stalked into the kitchen. Asad shuffled after her; in his peripheral vision he caught her bony finger pointing, her pink and white lacquered press-on gleaming.

"You sit," she commanded. "You sit and you tell me what happened."

Asad dropped into the chair immediately. When Gam ordered, anyone with the sense God gave little green apples obeyed. Yet his tongue didn't want to move; no use lying to Gam, and he was gonna have to tell her, but she'd be disappointed in him and he couldn't stand that. Not when all he wanted, right now, was to bury his face in her plaid muslin apron and sob while she petted his head like she had when he was a little 'un and didn't have to carry all this weight.

"I saw…" His mouth was dry ash, words sticking to his tongue. "I saw me. The me through the cracks."

She clucked her tongue. "And he had something you want, that it?"

He stared at her. "How did you…?"

"Because that's how it goes. Ignorance makes life easier." She let out a heavy sigh and levered herself into the chair opposite his. She might have shrunk with age, but she carried herself as if her bones were densest lead, her every motion a weighted thing of momentum and kinetics. "And if you ain't seen something you wanted out there, you'd have done your duty instead of sittin' here trembling. You didn't close it, did you?"

Asad's stomach rolled over hot with shame. He bowed his head again. "I'm sorry."

"We all got moments of weakness. You marked it?"

"I touched it. It touched me. It's good as marked."

"Then I'll go do it. You best get on to bed. I'll close it."

"Can't you leave it?" He scrunched his hands against his thighs and squeezed his eyes shut. "Just until tomorrow night. Please. Let me watch for a little while. I—I'll close it after."

"Boy, I ain't never raised my hand to you once. Don't make me start." She trailed off, swearing under her breath. "I will refuse and rebuke you if you forget what the goddamn hell we here for."

"I'm sorry, I—"

"If the you on the other side got something you want, if he happy, you want to risk that happiness? Longer the cracks stay open near him, more likely he gonna fall through. Or something come through, split the worlds a little more. You leave that crack open, you put him in danger. Bet he got a grandma just like you. Brother. Maybe even still got parents. You don't wanna take that away from him, or him away from them."

Asad squirmed his shoulders. "No...no, I don't."

"Then we do what we gotta do. We close them ways. We don't, sooner or later they gonna learn how to see, too. Mirror can't go both ways."

"Would it be so bad? They never hurt us."

"They would." She folded her hands. Her knuckles were massive, the knuckles of a man three times her size, but her finger-bones were thin and tiny as the bones left over after chicken dinner. "They might not mean to, but they would. See, people got wanting in their hearts. And it's wanting that makes the dark. It's wanting that made our time the way it is." Her lips had gone loose in the way the old ones always did, soft half-full sacks without enough flesh inside them, and they pursed pillows around her words.

"Maybe they see something they want over here. Maybe we see something we want over there. Maybe people get scared, and it becomes about take them before they take us, but no matter who do what it just gonna break both sides till ain't nothing left."

She paused, considered, then stood. Her slippers shuffled as she crossed to the sink and fished two glasses out of the dish rack, then turned the water on in the sink. She filled both glasses so full they nearly brimmed over, making curved tops barely held by a thin skin of surface tension. That skin quivered as she brought the glasses back to the table with her arthritic fingers, never quite spilling over.

"There gotta be a balance to all things, Saad," she said. "Now I want you to listen. The books in your school, they only teach you a little of this. They don't know nothing. They don't know nothing but you don't go out after dark, or you might slip through the cracks and fall away." She set one glass down delicately. "We got a finite amount of matter and energy in the universe, and there gotta *stay* a finite amount. Just the right amount on both sides. Say their universe and our universe these two glasses, filled right up to the brim." She tilted the glass in her hand. Surface tension broke, and the water spilled over, trickling down into the glass on the table. It splashed and overflowed, rivulets spilling down the sides, cutting lines in condensation, pooling across the table, but still she didn't stop. "You pour water from the first glass into the second, the second gonna overflow. What overflows don't go back in the first glass. It's gonna fall out, get lost in between."

"Is that what happened to Mom?" Asad stared at the trickle of water, caught by the tinkling sound. "She get lost in between?"

Gam cut him a stern look. "Your mother ain't talk for a day like today, boy. You listen. I'm teaching."

"Sorry, ma'am."

Gam turned that penetrating witch-eye on him, then hmphed, set the half-empty glass down on the table, and dropped back into her seat. "So when you tip from one glass to the other, you got one glass full, but it done lost some of what belongs to it. And you got one glass that much closer to being empty. And what happens when a universe get empty, boy?"

"Entropy," he recited dutifully from his lessons. "Everything dies that much faster."

"Damn right it do. But see, that law of finite matter, that law of conservation, it's got this idea of balance. So what's gonna happen is some of what went into the second glass gonna come back to the first. Until they got the same amount of water in them. 'cause both universes gotta have an equal balance of matter and energy." She tilted the full glass over the half-empty one, pouring carefully until both were roughly three-quarters full. "So maybe the first glass a little more full, but now the second one a little more empty, too. So now they both closer to dying; they just split that debt up in between." She set the glass back down and left them both sitting there in those puddles of spilled water, of wasted energy. "You know the main difference between them and us?"

"No, ma'am."

"They don't have people like us. People who can see the cracks." She tore a swath of paper towels off the roll on the table and thrust them at him. "So we not just protecting us. We protecting them. We do this to protect that goodness long before we do it for them daysiders' wills and whims. Remember that, and don't go wanting for what's on the other side."

Asad took the paper towels and, chagrined, bowed over the table to wipe up the puddles, soaking the paper towel in big wet spots. "Yes, ma'am."

"Where was it?"

"Blue Hill. On the Roberts side. Right over. Second floor of the store with the painted front, no ladder."

"That explains it, then. Marsha's laid up with a bad hip, and that Jonas boy always been sloppy." With a wheezing groan, Gam hefted to her feet again. "You go on an' forget about it. Go to bed. I'll close up."

"But Gam, it's almost morning—"

"I'm old. I ain't slow." She grinned fiercely, her yellowed teeth and high gums showing. "I got this. You fucked up tonight, Saad. Not gonna pretend you didn't. You gotta learn to put yourself away when things like this happen, and do what you gotta do." Her hand rested to the top of his head: her skin crinkly as crepe myrtle, the warmth of her living soul shining through to soak into him. "But I love you. I love you and it don't take a third eye to see this hurts you. I ain't gonna make you do a thing that hurts you, boy. So you stay here and let Gam take care of things for you.

When I get back, you be good and do your homework, and then we can go to the night market. Got to cash that government check, and then I'll make them Crispy treats. Good?"

"Yeah," Asad said, and leaned into her touch, and told himself this love and this life were enough. "Good."

7

WHEN HE WENT BACK THE NEXT NIGHT, DUCKING TARIF for half a second to sneak onto the Roberts side, the crack was gone.

He was gone, and Avondre with him.

Nothing remained but empty boxes, Gam's mark chalked onto the wall, and the smell of old dust and ashes and burning bone.

8

THE NEXT SUNDOWN, HE STOLE TARIF'S PHONE WHILE his brother was in the shower.

Quick, furtive, he scrolled through his apps, looking for that chat room he'd told him about. He tabbed past Candy Crush and Bejeweled and some hentai thing he didn't want to know about but couldn't unsee, but nothing that said *sundowners* or *nightsiders* or any of the things they called themselves when the dayside world didn't have an official name for them but *them*. The only thing he found that didn't make sense, that could be a *thing*, was a black square icon with a string of numbers underneath, four sets separated by three periods. No name, nothing he could look up in the app store.

Those numbers looked like an IP address.

Asad scrambled for his backpack, tore a sheet of paper from his history notebook, and scribbled the numbers down. The water shut off in the bathroom; he crumpled the piece of paper, stuffed it in his pocket, dumped Tarif's phone back on the nightstand, and skittered back to his side of the room. He needed to know something.

Something he could never ask Gam, or anyone who would call and curse his name for his blasphemy.

9

HE DIDN'T TRY THE IP ADDRESS UNTIL HE AND TAR-
IF had come back from that night's rounds—kicking cans and
kicking stones, but Asad kept drifting off and missing—and done
their homework. Tarif made a mound in his bed, faint edges of
daylight creeping around the blinds to make him shine gold and
red, while he groaned and drowsily rubbed a belly full of Gam's
turkey drumsticks and peas. Wasn't long until those groans turned
to quiet whistling snores, and Asad leaned over to peer at him,
then pulled his covers over his head to mask the glow of his own
phone.

He opened the web browser and put the numbers in the address
bar. It took a long time loading, like it was traveling a long long
way to get from somewhere to him, and he was starting to think
he was wrong and it wasn't an IP at all. But then a page loaded:
black, all black, with a beveled silver button.

INSTALL

Asad's thumb hovered over the button. His heart beat hard,
rough. What he was about to do wasn't smart. He was inviting
mess, and if Gam found out she'd kill him.

He closed his eyes and pressed the button.

He half thought his phone was gonna explode in his hand. But
it only blipped, and he opened his eyes and watched the progress
loader inch across the status bar, downloading *25%, 37%, 52%, 79%,
100%*, and then it was done and installing and his screen went
black except for a white blinking cursor.

ENTER>NAME?_

He bit the inside of his cheek. No way he'd use his real name,
get pinched up by the daysiders for talking about things nobody
was supposed to say, put away for saying words about the world
that existed instead of the world the dayside pretended to be. He
hesitated, then typed in *S-A-Y-I-D* and hit the Enter key.

USERNAME>ASSIGNED S3982

USERNAME>S3982 WELCOME

The message held for a hot second, then disappeared, replaced by a screen full of scrolling lines.

> **N3329:** Ok but maybe not
> **D274:** why not
> **D274:** its not like they can tell
> **I8804:** iz it really that hard to play dayside.
> **I8804:** all you gotta do is play ignorant.
> **K001 (Admin, God):** Hold up
> **K001 (Admin, God):** Wait
> **K001 (Admin, God):** Who is S

Asad swallowed, his mouth dry. The whole chat had stopped. Even as he watched, the lines disappeared, first N3329, then D274, until nothing remained but that damning question:

Who is S

If he answered, he was in this. He pressed his tongue to the roof of his mouth, breathing deep, and tapped his thumbs to the on-screen keyboard.

> **S3982:** I'm new
> **S3982:** My brother been here
> **I8804:** dont tell us that.
> **I8804:** no iding details.
> **I8804:** i dont want to fucking know you even have a brother.
> **N3329:** U don't answer questions nobody asked
> **I8804:** cause then if someone asks they can force us to answer.
> **S3982:** Sorry
> **S3982:** Sorry. I know better
> **S3982:** I'm kinda nervous
> **D274:** errybody nervous there first time
> **S3982:** Yeah
> **S3982:** Thought this was a bad idea
> **S3982:** Still do
> **N3329:** Then why u here
> **S3982:** I want to know about Louisville
> **S3982:** I want to know what happened
> **K001 (Admin, God):** Look for yourself.

A photo flashed into the chat, breaking the lines of text. The chatter stopped, leaving only that picture standing silent and still and accusatory. Hard to see at first; at first it only looked black with a few traces of lighter shadow, like a piece of black construction paper crumpled into a ball, its corners catching the light. But slowly he picked out edges of terrain, the lines of roads, a few stubbornly clinging buildings, his eyes accustomed to finding details in the dark even when the dark was the blur of a night-locked snapshot taken at a distance. And he realized: the few buildings scattered around the outer edges of the photo cut off as if they'd been shorn, their insides exposed like dollhouses. The roads converged toward the center of the image and then disappeared into a blackness so thick it reflected nothing, as thick as the shadows he imagined on lonely nights. A blackness with *substance*.

A sea. A sea of the dark, so deep it couldn't even be called a hole, swallowing everything into it.

The only way to find its edges was to find the light: a subtle crackling blue-white glow following the contours of the land, jagged at the edges as lightning, ringing the perimeter of that dark space. The edges of the crack. The edges of a hole in the universe, ripped open and swallowing an entire city into the void.

Asad's throat clenched, knotting painfully.

Was this what happened when people got sloppy with wanting, and left the cracks open too long?

> **S3982:** Where this from? Where you get this picture
> **K001 (Admin, God):** Military surveillance drone
> **K001 (Admin, God):** Fished it from the data feed before the drone went dark
> **K001 (Admin, God):** Swallowed up
> **K001 (Admin, God):** Fell through
> **S3982:** So this is real
> **K001 (Admin, God):** Real as a hole in the head
> **S3982:** Does it have a bottom?
> **K001 (Admin, God):** Don't know.
> **K001 (Admin, God):** If the military's gotten close again I haven't seen it
> **K001 (Admin, God):** But they upped their sniffers hardcore after this and it's harder to get in
> **K001 (Admin, God):** As soon as i crack the network encryption I get maybe 20 ms of data capture

K001 (Admin, God): and then it locks down
K001 (Admin, God): changes the algorithm.
N3329: Culd b other cities like Louisville
N3329: & we don't even know
N3329: everyone just stops talking about them one day
N3329: And u don't say a thing when ur people down there stop answering the phone
S3982: We didn't hear any reports about Louisville being unstable where I'm from
I8804: not for me either but it happened.
D274: heard it wasn't unstable
D274: heard it was fine
D274: and then errythin just went fuckin sideways and shit
D274: just overnight
D274: no time to fix it
D274: no time to run

No time to run.

Asad closed the chat window without answering, clutched his phone to his chest, and tried not to think about Boston swallowed into darkness, nothing but roads sheared off into nothing and Tarif and Gam gone.

Because Asad had wanted too much.

10

BUT HE WENT BACK THE NEXT NIGHT.

He had the icon on his phone's home screen now, like Tarif's, but he hid it several side screens away so it wasn't visible at first. He told himself it was in case someone got hold of his phone or glanced at it sidelong, but truth was he didn't want the temptation.

But that question still ate at him, tearing him to bits. Like he was in goddamned mourning, and he wouldn't stop grieving until he got some closure.

He tapped the black square, and let the darkness fill his screen.

D274: man fuuuuuuuck my bio teacher
D274: made me stay after today
N3329: Haha yeah but you probably dserved it
I8804: hey its s.
K001 (Admin, God): Hey S

S3982: Hey
K001 (Admin, God): You left kinda weird lst night
K001 (Admin, God): You okay?
S3982: Yeah
S3982: Just got a little freaked out
S3982: Got a question
K001 (Admin, God): Shoot.
S3982: You ever see yourself on the other side?
D274: don't go lookin for yerself
S3982: I didn't look
S3982: But I found me
N3329: don't look again
S3982: Why?
N3329: my sister looked
N3329: and then she killed herself

Asad sucked in a sharp, hurting breath, his stomach tight.

S3982: I'm so sorry
D274: i think it makez the cracks wider
D274: can feel the other me sumtims
D274: like were connected
D274: maybe were all connected
I8804: maybe if we get too close to our other selves we make a crack.
I8804: a crack big enough to fit through.

Breaths wet in the back of his throat, Asad closed the app, clutching at his phone.

Then he uninstalled it, wiped the address from his browser history, and pressed his face into his pillow until the cool wet cotton stuck to his cheeks and he couldn't breathe for the soaked cloth filming his mouth.

11

ANOTHER WEEK PASSED BEFORE HE SAW HIMSELF again.

The raw, aching pain of it had faded somewhat. The loneliness. The loathing, when he looked in the mirror and saw not plump, smiling cheeks but haggard hollows above his jawline. He could deal. He was like the water in that glass, and water always found an equilibrium.

He'd read once in class that the human brain was wired for unhappiness. That unhappiness made humans try so hard to make bigger and better things; every time they found a peak that felt like happiness, the brain reset where *happy* was so *happy* became *normal*, and normal wasn't enough. The goalposts always kept moving, because an unhappy person was a hungry person, and a hungry person fought to claw higher and higher just to be able to eat.

He thought sadness might be like that, too.

He thought sometimes you got so used to the sadness it became normal, and then not so bad at all.

He was kicking an old dented Pepsi can toward that corner bus stop at Blue Hill, going long for a gutter shot to beat Tarif and make a final goal, when they came on it. That prickling, and this time it came so sharp and full of static fire that Tarif and Asad stopped at the same time. *That feeling,* Gam had told them when she was first in the teaching, *that's what they mean when they say it's like someone walked over your grave. It's like you shiverin' with the cold, but it's all heat. All the heat at the heart of a star.*

The crack split open right in the wall of the bus stop. Walk around the stop and it was empty except the stink of hobo piss and a crushed juice box some kid left on the bench. But look through the wall, look through the crack, look inside, and *he* was *there.*

Right fucking there.

Sitting with Avondre, hand in hand, leaning on each other and talking in low murmurs. Through the wavering-shimmer breach Asad couldn't tell what they said, nothing but quiet distorted sounds, but it translated into a hard, trembling language of heartbreak, striking him with every word.

He stared, his hands clenching in his pockets. Tarif stood next to him, then leaned over, pressing the solid warmth of his arm against Asad's, reminding him what was real.

"This what you saw, ain't it," Tarif said. "This why you cried when you thought I was asleep."

Asad nodded, gulping in thick breaths. "Yeah."

"I'm sorry."

"It ain't *fair.*"

"What ain't?"

"Everything went right for them," Asad whispered, as his other self leaned in and nuzzled Avondre's shoulder. "They made all the right choices, and they got the good life. They get to be happy, and safe. But us…" His chest constricted. He wanted to look away, but couldn't. "Too many wrong turns. I know we the ones who broke everything, but…"

"…but if we could just…turn back." His brother's voice cracked.

"Yeah. That. Do you think it'll ever get better for us?"

"Maybe. Not in our lifetime, though. Just like the worlds didn't first break in our lifetime. Universe don't count in human lifespans." Tarif nudged Asad's arm until one hand fell from his hoodie's pocket, and then Tarif's thick, soft fingers curled in his, gripping tight and hot and steady. "It counts in the lifespans of stars."

"It still ain't *fair*."

"You want his life?"

"Maybe not his life." Asad lingered on Avondre's laughing eyes, the way he kept his arm around the other Asad as if he wanted to *protect* him. "But I want one thing he has."

Tarif sucked his tongue against his teeth, making a sympathetic sound. "No good looking at things that way. Everything's different over there. The lines that led him to what he found only happened 'cause of different choices they all made in the past." Tarif squeezed his fingers. "We so far off their path…it's a damned miracle we even see ourselves in them at all."

"…at least he's happy."

"Yeah. There's that." Tarif sighed, and his hand slipped free from Asad's, leaving a chill where it had been. "We gotta seal it up, Saad."

His heart dropped down to his knees, threatened to fall out and slip through the cracks in the sidewalk. "But—"

"We gotta. I'm sorry."

Asad told himself he wouldn't cry again, but that wetness was in his nose, making it hard to breathe. "Can I…can I have one more look?"

"Sure."

"Alone."

Tarif gave him a long, thoughtful look. "Don't do anything stupid, baby brother."

"I won't," he promised.

But when Tarif disappeared around the corner, giving him one last moment, one last look, one last chance when the odds were nil of this crack ever opening at this right place, at this right time...

Asad pressed his palm to the bus kiosk over Avondre's cheek, and imagined he could soak in the radiant warmth of his skin.

12

ANOTHER NIGHT. ANOTHER WALK AROUND THE BLOCK. Another long evening in class, and when he sketched Avondre's face in the margins of his notebook, he tried to capture the shape of his lips with every precise scratch of the pencil's tip.

And when Tarif ran off to be with Shawna again, Asad managed to smile for his brother while Asad walked their blocks alone.

Yet he wasn't alone, tonight. Tonight, new shadows drifted out from once-empty apartment buildings, and turned their faces up to the moon. They haunted the streets like ghosts, people Asad didn't know but recognized like family. The nightkin knew each other, and this moment, this ritual of moonlight and the whispering black, was communion, rooting them into the earth of a new place, a new city.

Asad wondered what city had gone dark now, and left these drifters washed up ashore.

At the corner of Blue Hill, he sank down on the bus bench and watched the dark ones stroll past, taking in their new streets with their new eyes, now and then nodding to him in passing with something too close to deference for his comfort, even if this was his post and his place and that honor was rightfully his.

He still didn't know how to feel. And he was relieved to recognize, among the drifters, a familiar shuffling gait: Miss Marsha Roberts, with her big gray church curls and little pillbox hat and an old housecoat that was half dress, half disco-era upholstery. She was made of the same stuff as Gam; every family had one, bowed and stoop-shouldered matriarchs who smelled of sweet pecan pralines but turned into steel when you tried to make their sugared edges crumble.

She had her cane, with its four-pronged rubberized tip, and she limped and leaned and rolled toward him until he stood and took her elbow and eased her to a seat.

"Miss Marsha," he murmured.

She hooted and sighed and grinned; her two front teeth were missing, and her words whistled through the gap. "See you mindin' your manners and staying on your side now, eh?"

He bowed his head. "I'm sorry."

"Don't be apologizing for doing what's necessary." She sat with her knees spread wide, her tan diabetic socks rolled at the top. Her freckled brown face shone in the moonlight as she watched the streets. "Crowded out here tonight."

"Who are they?"

"New folk. Refugees. More'f 'em coming up now." She leaned back against the kiosk. "Hear Tuscaloosa gone dark. All dark."

Asad sat down next to her. She had that warmth like Gam, too, thin skin made of burning paper. "What happened?"

"People got scared. Left. Not enough to hold it together, so the cracks stayed open." She clapped her hands on her knees. "Saw it happen once myself in Biloxi, back where your Gam came from. They'd run people like you and me out, after dark. Call 'em sundown towns. No negroes allowed in the city limits." Her laugh was a cough both merry and cynical, a knowing thing rattling in her throat like tin cans. "Learned the foolishness in that real fast, after a few of them pretty white women they so hot to protect fell through into the dark places. Suddenly we all that stands between them and the dark. Suddenly they got time for us. They call us welfare queens and lazy gov'ment freeloaders, but they quick to pay that due when the world turn strange and they get scared."

Why? Asad wondered. *Why did it fall on us to clean up a mess they made?*

Why we gotta fix they trouble?

But all he asked was, "Why us?" Then, "Why we the only ones who see it?"

"It ain't all of us. Not by a long shot." She turned her strange-colored eyes on him. Cataracts had turned them odd and rough and milky, brown clouded through with blue. "It's those of us who still got hope left. Who still got something good in us. That something good can feel what's right, feel what's on the other side. Like it's reaching for it."

"You think I still got hope in me?"

Miss Marsha smiled, and poked him with her bony elbow. "Boy," she said, "you too young not to."

13

HE COULDN'T HELP HIMSELF. HE CAME BACK TO THE bus stop, night after night, searching. Waiting for that prickle that should be warning, but to him only meant a breathless promise, something to hold on to, something to long for.

He wanted to cross the street, to step onto Roberts land, but Tarif caught his hand and held him back and shook his head.

"They got pains too, you know," Tarif said. "They got pains and hardships and losses. It ain't a perfect life. No such thing as a perfect life."

"Maybe not," Asad answered, and turned away from the building with its painted-on pictures of something sweeter, something brighter. "But they got different rules."

"Rules still rules."

"Yeah, but you ever wonder what it's like when the rules actually fair?"

"I try not to," Tarif murmured, and pulled Asad away. "Wondering that makes it hard to live with the rules we got."

"Maybe we shouldn't," Asad said, staring up at his brother, pleading. "Maybe we shouldn't live with the rules we got, Rifi."

But his brother said nothing at all.

14

SCHOOL WAS MORE CROWDED, NOW, MOSTLY IN THE younger classes. Spent less time learning, more time talking about zoning, figuring out what to do with the new ones, how to train the babies. Some talked of sending them dayside. Giving them a different life, letting them leave the darkling world.

Nobody said a thing about giving Boston's first ones some relief, letting them walk away.

"What's ours is ours," Gam said. "And ours it'll stay."

What was *his* felt like his alone, tonight, as Asad kicked his soles against the sidewalk until they made rasping sounds to fill the silence of the night. Tarif was gone *again*, sneaking off with Shawna, and Asad thought Gam might know but that boy was damn fool in love, and nobody was gonna steal his joy. If Gam didn't trust

Asad to do things alone, she'd have said something. But she let him go, let him handle things.

It was something, that he had Gam's trust.

But still he lingered on the corner of Blue Hill and Callender, looking at the building where a hole had opened in the world and shown him what might have, could have, should have been.

No sign of Miss Marsha, or her dumbfool son.

Asad looked to the left and then the right, saw no one, and crossed the street to climb those outside stairs, grip the edge of the roof, and hoist himself up.

He watched moonset from the rooftop, sitting on the edge and counting the stars as they winked out. Somewhere, in another universe, those same stars were winking out for the other Asad, and maybe Avondre was tucked in next to him, their limbs tangled up all smooth and brown and their sleeping breaths mingled. It wasn't his…but it was someone's, and he liked the slow way his blood moved when he thought about that world, that life, that belonged to someone who had his face.

Footfalls rattled on the stairs below, and he sighed. Tarif had found him. He closed his eyes, held that little bit of sparking rebellion against his chest, and waited for the scolding.

Those steps scuffed up behind him, then fell still. No scolding. Just quiet. He waited, and then a low, drawling voice spoke, gravel at the edges, molasses crumbled into sugar when it dried.

"Almost sunup," someone said. Not Tarif. "Should be heading in, yeah? Or they do things different up here?"

Asad snapped his eyes open, staring across the Boston skyline. He'd only heard that voice in murmurs and in dreams. Couldn't be. Couldn't damned well be. He tried to talk but his words were sticks in his throat, and he barely rasped out, "Depends where *down there* is."

"Tuscaloosa," the other boy said. "And in Tuscaloosa, we go in before the sun comes up."

"Why, though?" Something fierce burned in Asad's chest, something ignited by that voice, and he was so fucking scared to look but he wanted to, *needed* to, but he held himself back because he couldn't stand to lose his hope, his fire. "Just because they afraid of the night, why we gotta hide from the sun? That ain't in the rulebook. Never was. I wanna watch the sun rise, and I'm gonna."

"Reckon as I'll watch it with you, then."

The other boy sat down next to Asad, body heat and, in his peripheral vision, long thin legs in battered jeans covered with Magic Marker designs. Asad risked a glance, and that burn in his chest burst into a supernova.

High cheekbones. Long, twisting braids. Angular fingers, a strong jaw, broad shoulders and dark eyes and maybe he was a little thinner on this side, maybe a little more raw about the edges, maybe a jagged thin pink scar cut from the corner of his eye down to his neck, and maybe his skin didn't shine with gold dust, but luminous bronze glowed underneath rich brown nonetheless.

And maybe he wasn't the one Asad had seen, but he was just the right one for this place, this now, this quiet and aching need.

"Hi," the other boy said, his thoughtful, heavy-lidded eyes scrunching at the corners with his smile. "I'm—"

"Avondre," Asad breathed. "Von. I know."

Avondre blinked, cocking his head. "How you know my name?"

"I just do." And Asad smiled: a silly smile, a goofy smile, a smile so big it could seal every crack in the world and every crack in his heart. "Think I saw you at school. Wanna go for a burger after sunup?"

"Sure," Avondre said, and smiled back—so shy, so wonderful, all brightness and softness. "Sure. I'd really like that. But I'd like it even more if you told me your name."

"Can't do that."

"Why not?"

Asad grinned wider. "Because I'm a superhero, and we never tell anyone our real names."

"I'll find out." Avondre laughed, eyes glittering slyly. "If you're a superhero, I'm gonna be Lois Lane."

Asad leaned closer. He didn't know what he was doing, but he *did*, and every day should be like this, every night, with a smile on his lips and a wondering, a wishing, a hoping *what if*. "Lois was in love with Superman," he mock-whispered, and Avondre smirked.

"Don't get too big with yourself."

Asad laughed. "Asad." He offered his hand. "Saad. My family calls me Saad."

Avondre slipped his hand into Asad's. Squeezed, his palm dry and hot and smooth. A prickle sparked through Asad, a prickle like the sensation of a rift opening close by, yet it was within him. A crack opening inside him, spilling out all the awful, all the pain, until he was Pandora's box with nothing left inside but the pure bright fire of *hope*.

Gam had warned him against wanting, against the sin of covetousness, of greed.

But she hadn't said a damned thing about hope.

"Nice to meet you, Saad," Avondre said.

"Yeah," Asad replied, and didn't let go of Avondre's hand. "Yeah, it really is."

———————————

The Future of Hunger in the Age of Programmable Matter

Sam J. Miller

VASHTI'S POLYMER WAS PURPLE-FLECKED, FIST-SIZED at normal density, and we all watched dutifully while she tapped at her phone and cycled through the rather stale parlor tricks of turning the lump of soft pseudo-styrene into a tiny dinosaur, a sword, a little stripper who shrank to the size of a quarter and then ballooned to Labrador-Retriever proportions. The roast was taking too long and Trevor was in the living room being charming instead of mixing up the salad dressing—*and why did I have to have such a charming boyfriend?*— and the doorbell was ringing and no one was answering it and I huffed my way to the door and forced a smile onto my face as I wrenched it open.

As soon as I saw him, I knew I was doomed.

"Hi," he said, "I'm Aarav."

"Vashti's brother," I said, seeing his bear-beard and wolf-smile and feeling my stomach plummet, "of course."

His hand was hot in mine.

I'd been doing so well. I'd fought temptation at every turn. I'd never cheated on Trevor, not once, never mind how every stroll down a Chelsea block flashed a couple dozen lean-and-hungry golden-boy-or-silver-fox grins at me, and surely just *once* wouldn't hurt—except that I knew, from the still-raw psychic wounds of my momentarily-vanquished crystal meth addiction, that once was all it took to bring your life crashing down into the gutter. Not because one snort would wake you up covered in blood at Central Booking or Lincoln Hospital, but precisely because it would not, because you'd get away with it, and remember how magnificent it was, and forget every awful consequence, and keep doing it, until you'd lost everything.

And now Once had walked into my living room, his ass perfect and his eyes alive with the knowledge of what a weak creature I was. And I was doomed.

I led him into the living room.

"Your polymer is impressive," Fennis was saying to Vashti in a superlatively unimpressed voice—but then again he'd never liked her, and *why had we invited him again?*—and produced his own polymer, a jagged solid jelly in a glass jar, marbled and muddied with a mix of clear first-generation inert polymer and the darker second-gen stuff that could change color, cast light, play videos, and he opened the app on his phone and we watched it come to life, writhing and thrashing and then elongating, sharpening, shattering the glass with a single explosive motion. It penetrated Vashti's polymer, which denatured and was assimilated into Fennis's. Before her cry of protest was completed his polymer spat hers back out and both stood there as though the whole thing had never happened. His finger swirled on his phone screen and the thing took a wobbly bow. Everyone applauded.

"Field control assertion like that must have cost you a pretty penny," she said sourly.

"Not really. Some boys on my block are battlers, they love sharing their new tricks."

"Otto is working on a story about polymers," said Trevor, patting my thigh proudly when I came to hover over him and silently command him to return to the kitchen. He was using That Tone, the one that said *Be chatty, be witty, be handsome, perform.* "About the dangers. Aren't you, honey?"

"I am," I said, doing my best to simultaneously smile at our guests and glare at him.

"Vastly exaggerated, those dangers," said Aarav, who I'd been doing a damn good job of not looking at since he walked in the door, except now he was talking so I had to look, and, yes, damn, there it was, those broad chunky shoulders, that ample bottom he was surely standing in three-quarters profile precisely to best display, and I hated Vashti so much in that moment, for calling that morning to plead with us to make space for him at our annual vernal equinox supper—"He just moved to New York, he hardly knows any other gay guys, I feel so bad for him." I gave him the most withering smile I could find. He continued, "No more dangerous than cell phones or networked microwaves, and no one's writing articles about *that*." His face was warm, almost sad, and the multiplex of my mind stuttered to life with a dozen different pornographic scenes starring only us.

"You should interview Aarav for your story," Vashti said. "He works on polymers!"

"Not exactly," he said. "I do communications for Verizon. My unit does focus a lot on polymer-related promotions. The kaiju battle community is a very important demographic."

"You two talk," Trevor said. "I'll go make the dressing."

And what could I do, but be seated, beside Aarav, and curse the smallness of our couch, because I could feel the heat of his leg where it pressed against mine, and surely everyone in the room would know, at once, how badly I wanted him, what a disgusting pervert I was? And, of course, matters were made immeasurably worse by his wisdom and sense of humor—he had everyone giggling, which meant I had to giggle too, lest someone wonder why I wasn't.

"I heard that hammer sales are plummeting," someone said.

"Screwdrivers too," said someone else.

Ten people at our party, and suddenly everyone had something to say about nanopolymers. I didn't care one way or another about the damn things. They assigned me the story because I'd cultivated relevant contacts on previous articles. I drank my gin and tonic in one long gulp and switched to wine.

Aarav would not let me stay silent. When I failed to weigh in on whatever theory or fact or opinion was passing around the room, he touched my arm and said, "What do you think, Otto?" Was that because he was a kind and generous person? Or did he know the game I was playing—the game of hunger, of lust, of trying to be good—and could play it just as well as me? The problem with returning to the smiling happy world of dinner parties and office jobs and responsible adults after a long addiction is that you've seen people at their worst, especially yourself, and it's hard to assume the best about anyone.

"When my old broom wore out, I didn't buy a new one," someone said. "So much easier to just download broom instructions and beam them into your polymer."

"Dinner!" Trevor called, and I sprang from the couch. He frowned at the glass in my hand, made stern eye contact.

"We never buy new toys for Tripp anymore," said Fennis, leading the troupe into the dining room. The oven had heated the whole place up so high that we'd had to open a window, and an undercurrent of cold city winter wind tugged at our sleeves. "Whatever he wants, we can just make it on the spot. Now the problem is, he keeps on begging us for more and more putty! Quite the status marker at school, how big your total polymerload is."

"Kids are so insufferable with it," someone else said. "I made the mistake of calling it 'magic clay' the other day and my seven-year-old said 'It's not clay, it's a plastic-based gel. And it's not magic, it's got millions of tiny machines inside of it that respond to commands from wireless devices.' Can you imagine?"

We could all imagine.

"So is your article about the death of the manufacturing sector?" Aarav asked, sitting down beside me, and his eyes were immense, so light they looked like gold. "They say we're less than five years from polymer automobiles. Imagine being able to upgrade to the latest car model with just a software update!"

"That's ridiculous," someone said. "Toys and simple tools are one thing, but shape-memory polymers are a long way from being able to emulate complex machinery. Nanite stereolithography doesn't even do batteries very well—the storage capacity is shit, they overheat…"

"I don't know," someone else said. "I spun mine into a laptop, on a business trip last month. Wasn't winning any beauty contests—battery was like a weird bloated tumor on the back, and it kept, I don't know, writhing—but it got the job done."

"They let you take programmable matter on a plane?"

"No, of course not," she said. "But Virgin is doing this thing now where you can give them your polymer at the gate and get a bar code voucher, and then when you get off at your destination they give you the exact same amount back. They even get the blend of first-gen and second-gen stuff precisely right."

"Delta, too," someone said.

I prayed for them to stop. I drank a third cup of wine praying it, practically chanting it out loud. I wanted them to be quiet and I wanted them all to get the fuck out. Especially Aarav.

Of course it was silly. No one could see the filthy thoughts I was thinking, how precarious this lavish scene of domestic virtuosity truly was. No one suspected how unhappy I was, how hungry. No one but Trevor, who put his hand out to stop me when I picked up the bottle of wine.

Trevor was older, wiser. He'd picked me up out of the gutter—or, more accurately, picked me up off the floor of a dark room at a particularly nasty sex party. It was his apartment we were in; his job that bought the roast and the good wine and the cheeses on the platter. And I loved him. I truly did. But he was good and I was bad and his smile said he knew I was a fraud, and loved me anyway.

"So?" Aarav asked. "Your article. You haven't said what dangers you're covering."

"Hacking," I said, passing the rolls, pleased with how perfect they'd come out, how brown. The roast, on the other hand, lying in a dish of its own blood, was a different story. Our oven heated unevenly. One corner was blackened and burnt. Absolutely everything in the world was wrong.

"What, like that whole thing about how terrorists might make your polymer bracelet turn into a razor blade and slit your wrist open? I thought people gave up on that kind of hysterical scaremongering two years ag—"

"Not that, so much," I said. "There's this whole new wave of what they're calling aggregative malware, which could in theory cause polymers to compulsively link up. Predictives anticipate some pretty destructive scenarios as a result. Especially once the third-gen stuff comes out…"

"Interesting," he said, his sturdy forearm innocuous on the table beside mine. Against mine.

"Not sure I buy it, myself," I said. "Though lots of smart people do."

"Thinkpieces will be the death of us all," Fennis said. "Every other day people are trying to tell you we're sowing the seeds of our own destruction with some stupid thing. No offense, Otto."

"None taken. Anyway, I'm with you. Even if it's true, what are we supposed to do about it?"

Everyone agreed that we were helpless, guiltless.

Trevor turned his head in a slow circle, his smile immense, proud, blissful at what we'd built, what a life we had, what wonderful friends, what a stable glorious home he'd made for me. For us. I tried my best to smile back.

I loved him. So, what was I hungry for? What did I still want, why couldn't I keep from imagining ravaging Aarav in the wreckage of our living room?

"It *is* inherently less secure," someone said. "You can't encrypt them in the same way. Your shaping app can lock the nanites, but only until something with a stronger field comes along. It's fundamental to how the distributed CPU functions."

"I went to a kaiju battle last week," Vashti said. "That's the whole point of them, that struggle for control. Some pretty big mother fuckers."

"I've only ever seen the web videos. And that awful reality competition show."

"It's so much fun," she said. "Grimy, and a little bit scary. Some of these creatures look like something from a nightmare. Most fights, there's this part at the end, what they call the death roll, where it's essentially one big Silly Putty blob wrestling with itself to see which one has the stronger field control. People sitting in the front rows say they can feel their polymers moving in their pockets."

"Did you read that article, *The Future of Hunger in the Age of…*"

Everyone had read that article.

"Good lord," Trevor said, finally. "This is worse than lunch with the straight guys from work, hearing them talk about football!"

"Have you guys seen *I Can See Right Through You* yet?" I asked, because Trevor had me well-trained, and nothing derailed a boring conversation better than a controversial art/horror film. "That guy they got to play the demon lover was *hot*."

The night went on like that. Everyone happy but me—or everyone doing just as good a job as me of faking it. Snow and wind hammering at our windows. People peeling off, departing with regrets as the night got longer and the storm got worse. Me doing my damnedest not to make eye contact with Aarav, not to notice how smart he was, how once he'd voiced an opinion on something it just felt right, like my own, like it had always been my own. I tried, too, not to notice how nice it was to hang out with another gay guy who wasn't Trevor, Trevor whose prim paranoia about my inherent weakness kept us from all but the most unfuckable friends.

"Shit," Aarav said, past two, the last guest, long after his sister had left, seeing the snow of an early-spring surprise storm stacked against our glass. "It's piled up so much!"

"Subways run all night," I said, cheering inside as I went to get his coat. "Best part of New York City life, newbie."

"I have my car," he said. "I know it's not practical for the city, but I just can't bring myself to get rid of it."

"That sucks," Trevor said. "It isn't safe to drive in this. Should be all plowed and cleaned-up by morning." His eyes flitted to mine, made the smallest frown, a fraction of a second, long enough for me to read whole oral epics into it—he could see my weakness, knew what I ached to do to Aarav, saw how unwise it would be to have him in our house for a single unnecessary extra second. But he could see, too, with his exquisite WASP etiquette, that there was no other option than to say to him: "You can crash here for the night, if you want."

"You sure?" Aarav asked, looking to me, and I was conveniently taking a long sip of wine at that point, screaming inside, *No don't do this,* but eventually the sip had to end, and I nodded as enthusiastically as I could.

He did the dishes. We made up the guest bedroom. We all watched polymer videos online, saw the terrifying monsters and fancy clothes and seawalls and emergency shelters that people had built from nanopolymer, watched trailers for three or four new polymer-based reality competition shows. We placed our polymers and our phones in a heap by the charging hub. I was furious with Trevor for extending the invitation, with myself for getting so drunk, for enjoying the husky sound of Aarav's laughter so much.

"You shouldn't drink so much," Trevor said, once the bedroom door was shut behind us.

"What?" I stammered, all false innocence, because, of course I shouldn't. "Why?"

"You embarrassed yourself. Practically drooling over Aarav."

"I was not!" I said, reddening, from alcohol and guilt, shame and defensive anger.

Trevor shrugged and undressed, like it was all too obvious and inconsequential to argue over. I'd been surprised, when we first started dating, when we had The Talk about our sexual parameters, that he insisted on monogamy. "Addicts never stop with just a little," he'd said, and what could I say to that? What could I say whenever he brought that up, which was often—whenever he wanted to end an argument? And what could I say now? Because any argument I offered would be a lie. He was right and I was wrong, he was perfect and I was wretched. I slid into bed beside him, felt the whisper of the wind from where we'd left the window open, heard the clanking of our radiators trying too hard. I touched his hip with one hand, which he seized, and held.

He had been right, too, about my having had too much to drink. I slept poorly, in and out of hungry dreams—burnt meat and hairy barrel chests—too dizzy to lay still, until I sat up with my head spinning and my stomach doing its best to expel the charred corner of the roast that I'd taken for myself so none of our guests would eat it and think less of us.

Dawn, almost. The sky just starting to brighten past the normal city luster of snowy winter nights. Everything else a blur. Was I home? Was I back in the hallway of that filthy apartment building where a john had kicked me out and I'd fallen asleep outside his door? I staggered towards the bathroom, imagining myself projectile vomiting absolutely everything absolutely everywhere.

I had to puke. This much was true. But was that why I was out of bed? I walked slowly, silently, suspecting in my groggy fuddled state that this was all an elaborate ruse to watch Aarav sleep, taunt myself with his tantalizing profile and hope for a glimpse of a furry bare arm or the sheet-hidden outline of an erection. But would I be able to stop myself there, in the doorway, watching?

Is this me? I wondered, peering into the dark. *Am I capable of this?*

What I saw was so much better than mere sleeping nudity. And

so much worse.

His ass. Bare, damp with sweat in the overheated apartment, moving, a dire implacable rhythm. The chubby, perfect, naked bulk of him. My boyfriend beneath him. Trevor's groans of pleasure. Aarav's hand, clamping over Trevor's mouth to quiet him.

They didn't hear me. I'd never seen Trevor eyes look like that. I didn't move. I watched helplessly, wanting to, not wanting to want to. Memorizing what I saw, for the long lonely nights to come. Bracing myself for the apocalypse that was on its way, almost here, that would arrive the moment I opened my mouth to shout hate and rage at them. Wondering why I couldn't open my mouth.

COFFEE IN THE CAMPS WAS ALWAYS A CRAP SHOOT, MOST mornings merely warm brown water the color of iced tea when half the ice has melted, but once in a while they'd get a donation of decent stuff, several bins of Folgers sent by fundie jocks or soccer moms in some idyllic safe small town who did a Kickstarter or bake sale to send toiletries or pleasantries to the poor benighted New York refugees, and that's what kept us coming back, every morning, the hope that we'd get something other than shit—Upper West Side dowagers and Brooklyn graffiti virtuosi waited in line together, sweaters held tight against the wind, and then we drank the coffee we were given, and shivered together in the long windy tents, beside the stripped-bare orchard, and tried not to think about what lay behind us, or what lay ahead…and it was there, in the Canajoharie resettlement area, in a forest two hundred miles north of the crater where my city used to be, cradling a cup of so-called coffee, that I saw Aarav for the second time.

As soon as I saw him, I knew he was doomed.

Six months had passed, since the last time I saw him—the night he spent in at our apartment. Six months, since polymer kaiju stomped New York City into rubble. He'd lost weight, wore dark sunglasses now. The rest of him was unmistakable.

I won't lie: my first emotion was happiness. To see someone I knew, a memory of my vanished world. My mouth opened, eager to call out his name. But happiness faded fast, replaced by lust, which triggered rage.

"And to think," someone was saying, "we used to think it'd be rising ocean levels that would wipe us out!"

"Stop being melodramatic," said someone else, because everyone was an expert when it came to the polymer kaiju uprising, and these breakfast-table conversations were interminable, "We're not wiped out. All those attacks barely made a dent in the total human population of the planet. Rising ocean levels still have plenty of time to destroy us."

"All our fault, either way."

"Is it?"

"You don't think so?"

"What else could we have done?"

"That's exactly the problem. Keep telling yourself you're helpless, pretty soon you'll start to act like it."

"They're still out there," Aarav said, and his voice was just as wise, just as insightful—except now I could hear his wisdom for what it was, what all of us were doing when we tried to sound like we understood what was going on around us. Cave men at the campfire trying to feel less afraid. "Just because we can't see them, doesn't mean they're not coming."

Rage lit me up inside. Revenge plots percolated. Bloody murder tingled in my fingertips, aching to be let out.

And it felt…familiar. Murder wasn't meth, not exactly, but it brought back the old buried joy, the bliss when I'd scored enough to last me through the whole weekend, the ecstasy before the first hit, when my head was still full of perfect scenarios, the thousands of sexual partners and the endless dance floor hours and the loud howling down late-night residential streets. I looked at Aarav and I felt alive in a way I'd spent years trying not to feel. Except that now there was no reason not to. No Trevor telling me to stop. No police waiting to arrest me for possession or prostitution.

Because what else did I have? After all I'd lost, here, at last, was something I could do. Something I could control.

What are the odds, I thought, but I knew the odds, could do them in my head, math had always been my strong suit, back when math mattered—two thirds of the city's population made it out alive, half of them ended up in a camp, and there were four possible camps. So, approximately an 8.33% chance that we'd both survive, both have nowhere else to go because our nearest relatives lived too far away for the perilous land trek, and he would end up in the same camp as me.

Shouts, from a corner of the tent. Kids fighting over the radio. Music came and went, replaced by a tired-sounding woman reading bad news. Beside me, a bandaged man read a newspaper whose front page sported a particularly gnarly spider woman kaiju.

I thought of hiding from Aarav. Keep my distance, bide my time while I concocted some spectacular revenge.

But why should I hide? He didn't know that I knew. That I'd seen. The next morning, over coffee and complaints of hangovers, he and Trevor certainly hadn't said anything about it.

And neither had I. Not that day, and not the next. I waited. Heart and mind breaking from the stress of wondering when it would happen, when Trevor would tell me it was over, he'd found someone new, he was tired of my weakness and my damage.

Five days later, when it was clear that he wouldn't be bringing it up, I resolved to bring it up myself. My nerve failed at dinner, that night, but the next day, surely—

The next day Trevor died in the ring of radioactive fire that took out a third of us.

So: I would not hide. I moved closer. Aarav's arms, like mine, were taut and muscular from running the hand-cranked generators that powered the radio, the medical equipment, batteries for approved non-networkable electronic devices.

Somebody ate the bacon off his plate, and I saw that Aarav was blind.

The first kaiju assault was an accident. A faulty German software update rolled out in select markets; conflicting code in a bloated proprietary phone manufacturer operating system; aggregative commands accidentally exploiting field-control backdoors to cause polymer to seek out polymer. No shape, no animating intelligence, just an ever-increasing plasticine blob of horror that bored through walls, crushed buildings, leveled streets until it had assimilated every shred of shape-memory polymer animated by the same operating system and come to a sated stop. At which point forty German cities were mostly gone.

After that, everything happened so fast. Four hundred million tons of styrene polymers in active use worldwide. The software update in question was easy to copy, change, twist.

"Aarav!" I said, standing over him, enjoying several milliseconds of him smiling and looking confused and ashamed.

"I'm so sorry," he said, gesturing to his sunglasses. "I'm—"

"Otto!" I said, and took his hand. "Otto Trask? You stayed—"

"Otto!" He cried, his mouth a trembling crooked rhombus of happiness, his face darkening like he was about to cry. No flicker of shame, no hint of guilt. He stood and hugged me, hard. "Is Trevor…"

"No," I said. "Probably the same blast that took your eyesight."

Aarav hugged me harder. He smelled good. I hated him worse for it.

"And Vashti?"

It took him so long to answer me. "Gone too. Where were you, when it happened?"

"Home. Writing." *In the room where you fucked my boyfriend.*

Leaves had piled up at our feet. The forest smelled sharp and smoky. I smiled for what felt like the first time. When Trevor died, all my anger at him turned on myself. I'd been such a bad boyfriend. I'd been so hungry. He'd been smart enough to see it. My fault, that he'd fucked Aarav. My hunger.

One week after Germany, Ukrainian resistance fighters gave six hundred thousand dollars to the nineteen-year-old kid who came in third on the second season of *Polymer Kaiju Prime*, a crowd favorite with a twelve-foot-tall version of a certain famous Japanese movie monster. He gave them a flash drive with his monster's schematics on it. Then they pegged it to a more aggressive form of the aggregative software and added in a remote control. The next day the residents of Russia's two largest cities found that something was compelling their polymers to move on their own, heading straight for the nearest storm drain or toilet. Breaking through whatever they used to try to contain them. That evening, two four-hundred-foot-tall clear Godzillas rose out of the Moskva and Neva Rivers. They couldn't breathe fire, back then, but they didn't really need to. Helicopters dropped bombs on one of them, and they did almost as much damage as the monster did. The monster's polymer fragments re-assembled and she continued on her merry way.

"What's your plan?" Aarav asked, his hand holding mine, with no lust or lewdness this time, just fear and hunger and loneliness and need, and I smiled, at it, at his weakness, at the knowledge of how I could use it to destroy him.

"Watch my money dwindle. Pick up odd jobs where I can."

"Yeah," he said. "Me, too."

Dogs barked. So many people in the camp had dogs. A gunshot in the distance: upstate boys hunting deer, like this was any other autumn, which for them it pretty much was. Girls in leather and camouflage swapped packages. Black marketeers, officially tolerated because they filled in the gaps that the under-resourced camp administration couldn't.

Corporations, governments, out-of-power political parties, local militias—everybody started building their own monsters. People stockpiled polymer. Nations took steps to ban or destroy it. When the mayor of Quezon City ordered wholesale surrender from his own citizens, the subsequent stockpile was stolen by—or possibly sold to—a street gang, who made a handful of mid-sized monsters and used them to break their members out of several prisons.

Old hierarchies of power were inverted. Mighty nations were powerless to stop the rogue kaiju of terror cells and coder collectives. But we *were* being melodramatic, when we called it an apocalypse. Only a few big cities had been hit. Most kaiju dust-ups took place in geopolitical hot spots, contested spaces where conventional violence had been powerless to rupture the status quo: Kashmir, Tibet, Chiapas, the Northwest Passage, the Diaoyu Islands, Jerusalem. The North Cali/South Cali border. Easy to see them as monsters, to look in their eyes and see a malevolent intelligence, but they were still just machines, masterpieces of programming, doing what humans had programmed them to do.

"You have people who know you're here?"

He shrugged. "Supposedly they keep people informed. But most of my people are in big cities, and who the fuck knows what's really going on there?"

Every day now was chillier than the one before. New York fell in late March, and we'd been blessed with warm weather ever since. Almost October, now, and I felt it in my tightening testicles: the fear of winter, the stripped-down human animal whimpering in the wind.

I shut my eyes and I could see it, as it had been in the thousands of photos that people had taken and shared in the instants before they died. A three-headed white wolf, forty stories tall. Flames spiraling in the ruins at its feet. Stomach aglow in the dusk, burning brighter as its auto-generated nuclear reactor went critical.

"You know what I miss most?" he said. "About New York?"

"Getting stuck behind slow people on the subway escalator?"

He chuckled. "No. Worse."

"The thoroughly-reasonable rents?"

"Shake Shack."

"Fucking tourist."

"I know!" he said, and laughed. "I'm sorry, I love a milkshake. It was my guilty pleasure. I'd only go late at night, when I was by myself, so no one would know."

"It's a damn shame," I said. "You became a New Yorker just in time to lose the city forever."

His laughing lowered, and wobbled, and somewhere along the way it became crying.

"I'm sorry," he said. "I've just been so lonely. You can't imagine."

"I think I can," I said.

"It's so good to find you again."

"Likewise," I said, and meant it, my smile sincere, because here, finally, was something I could do, even if that something was murder.

I hugged him. He hugged me back, hard, grateful; blind, as Trevor had never been, to the wickedness inside my head.

I took in the scene around us, assessing my options. Looking for ways to make it look like an accident. Forest brightening with fall. The high cliffs above the Mohawk River.

Those. Those would do.

"Now you wouldn't happen to have a stash of real coffee squirreled away somewhere, would you?"

I laughed. "I wish."

I didn't do it just then. I could have. If I asked him, "Wanna go for a stroll," promised him a blowjob or a cask of Amontillado, he'd have taken my hand and followed me anywhere. But I wasn't ready. Had to plan. Write my lines. Rehearse.

And besides. We were in the crowded dining tent. People had seen us. Security in the camps was minimal, practically non-existent, but in the remote chance that his water-logged body turned up not far from here, was traced back to the camp, and someone came looking, I didn't want to be the last person seen with him.

That's what I told myself, anyway. That I was being smart. Not weak. Not hesitant. Not waiting for a way to talk myself out of it.

Not wrestling with myself over how badly I still wanted him.

"I gotta go," I said. "It's my shift at the hand-cranks."

"Okay," he said, looking crestfallen.

"Shift ends when the sun sets," I said, squeezing his shoulder.

"I'm in Tent 57!" he called, and I heard him, and I did not respond.

I didn't have a hand-crank shift. I scouted the location, the bluff where I'd bring him. I practiced what I would say.

I didn't think about Trevor.

Every day, I thought about Trevor. Too-good-for-me Trevor. Comforting myself with the knowledge that I never did a single one of the awful things he'd always been expecting me to do.

I found the spot. I mapped out our steps. I waited until everyone had gone to dinner, and Aarav remained, alone in Tent 57, waiting for my return, like I knew he'd be.

"Wanna go for a stroll?" I asked, and watched him brighten.

Is this me? I wondered, while we strolled. *Am I capable of this?*

We walked between the trees. Leaves fell all around. None struck us. He was not as sexy as he'd been that night. He'd lost heft, and confidence. But I could feel his heat when we walked together. Smell his body. Feel myself stiffen.

And why shouldn't I have him? Before I murdered him? I had denied myself this pleasure, before, for love, for stability, for the sake of my happy home, and look where that had gotten me. I had been so good.

When we got to the cliff, when we stood at its edge and only I could see how close he was to doom, I grabbed him by the shoulders and pulled him into a kiss.

It lasted a long time. But it didn't last long enough. Because when it was over he said, "Why didn't you say anything?"—and I knew, from the tremble in his voice, exactly what he was talking about, but of course I had to say:

"Say anything about what?"

"About what you saw. That night. Me and Trevor."

"You *knew*?" I said, and the rage was back, grown to kaiju proportions, and my grip tightened on his shoulders, slid down to take hold of his biceps and squeezed to stop my arms from shaking. River wind roared up hungrily from far below.

"Trevor heard you. Behind us. He told me later."

"Trevor? He...?"

"He knew. Of course he knew."

He knew. Of course he knew.

"I'm sorry," Aarav said. "I can't believe I did that. There's no excuse. I'd had a lot to drink that night, and I woke up to him kissing me, and—"

"Don't," I whispered. The wind stood still. The river went silent.

"Shit," he said. "Sorry. I'm sorry."

We were so close to the edge. The most effortless pivot of my hips was all it would take. So why couldn't I move?

"I called you," he said. "The next day."

I said "Liar," but wasn't sure if any sound came out at all.

"I did. On your cell. Trevor answered. That's how I know he knew you knew."

It wouldn't have been the first time Trevor had taken a call meant for me and told them to go to hell, and purged the call from my cell phone log. Dealers, usually, but sometimes exes who he feared would pull me back into the life. And sometimes friends. "Aren't you the chivalrous adulterer, making the gallant gesture of rubbing my nose in how you'd fucked—"

"Otto, no," he said, and there was a realness in his voice, a gravity, and I knew that he was going to tell me the truth, a truth I didn't want to hear but could not escape. "I called to tell you that you deserved better. Better than Trevor."

"Stop," I said, again. The wind was back, strong, screaming. My grip relaxed. Tears gathered.

"What you two had, that wasn't healthy. He was awf—"

I dropped to my knees because it was the only thing I could think of. To stop him talking, to silence the wailing inside my head. I expertly unbuckled his belt. Because he was right, about Trevor, and I'd always known it, and I'd told myself I was wrong, that it was my weakness talking, my wickedness.

"Up," Aarav said, gruff and tender, pulling me off my knees. "Stand up."

Moments later I was up against a tree, arms embracing it, the bark rough and good against my face, his hips grinding against my backside. I felt him fatten, expand, and I had a ridiculous and irrational flashback: Vashti's purple-flecked polymer. The little dance it did. How harmless it seemed. How small. How secure we all felt, in that too-warm living room.

They add up, the tiny harmless things we harbor, the little guilts and baby sins, the crimes we think we only commit against ourselves. The indignities we suffer. The stories we tell ourselves about how wicked we are. Or how helpless. They can crush cities, raise seas.

"You want it?" he asked, poised to enter.

"I want it," I said, because I did, I wanted, because all I *was* was wanting, was hunger. But hunger is no crime. And I was no monster.

A low rumble shook the air. I turned my head, looked up. The moon was full, illuminating the winter cloud cover. But something was up there: silent, immense, jet black, like a wound in the bright sky. Something flew. High; so high. Far to the west of us. A manta ray kaiju; a flying polymer as big as the George Washington Bridge. Massive fin-wings propelled it through the sky with slow majestic strokes.

"What is it?" Aarav asked, his breath hot in my ear.

"Nothing," I said, staring into the sky. The monster flew, free as any animal could ever be, and my heart soared with it. What was it doing? Where was it going? I watched it diminish into the distance, moving leisurely for all its speed, like a lifted burden leaving me behind.

———————————————

Uncanny Valley

Greg Egan

1

IN A PAUSE IN THE FLOW OF IMAGES, IT CAME TO HIM that he'd been dreaming for a fathomless time and that he wished to stop. But when he tried to picture the scene that would greet him upon waking, his mind grabbed the question and ran with it, not so much changing the subject as summoning out of the darkness answers that he was sure had long ago ceased to be correct. He remembered the bunk beds he and his brother had slept in until he was nine, with pieces of broken springs hanging down above him like tiny gray stalactites. The shade of his bedside reading lamp had been ringed with small, diamond-shaped holes; he would place his fingers over them and stare at the red light emerging through his flesh, until the heat from the globe became too much to bear.

Later, in a room of his own, his bed had come with hollow metal posts whose plastic caps were easily removed, allowing him to toss in chewed pencil stubs, pins that had held newly bought school shirts elaborately folded around cardboard packaging, tacks that he'd bent out of shape with misaligned hammer blows while trying to form pictures in zinc on lumps of firewood, pieces of gravel that had made their way into his shoes, dried snot scraped from his handkerchief, and tiny, balled-up scraps of paper, each bearing a four- or five-word account of whatever seemed important at the time, building up a record of his life like a core sample slicing through geological strata, a find for future archaeologists far more exciting than any diary.

But he could also recall a bleary-eyed, low-angle view of clothes strewn on the floor, in a bedsit apartment with no bed as such, just a foldout couch. That felt as remote as his childhood, but something pushed him to keep fleshing out the details of the room. There was a typewriter on a table. He could smell the ribbon, and he saw the box in which it had come, sitting on a shelf in a corner of a stationers, with white letters on a blue background, but the words they spelled out eluded him. He'd always hunted down the fully black ribbons, though most stores had only stocked black-and-red. Who could possibly need to type anything in red?

Wiping his ink-stained fingers on a discarded page after a ribbon change, he knew the whole scene was an anachronism, and he tried to follow that insight up to the surface, like a diver pursuing a glimpse of the distant sun. But something weighed him down, anchoring him to the cold wooden chair in that unheated room, with a stack of blank paper to his right, a pile of finished sheets to his left, a wastebasket under the table. He urgently needed to think about the way the loop in the "e" became solid black sometimes, prompting him to clean all the typebars with an old T-shirt dampened with methylated spirits. If he didn't think about it now, he was afraid that he might never have the chance to think of it again.

2

ADAM DECIDED TO GO AGAINST ALL THE ADVICE HE'D received, and attend the old man's funeral.

The old man himself had warned him off. "Why make trouble?" he'd asked, peering at Adam from the hospital bed with that disconcerting vampiric longing that had grown more intense toward the end. "The more you rub their faces in it, the more likely they'll be to come after you."

"I thought you said they couldn't do that."

"All I said was that I'd done my best to stop them. Do you want to keep the inheritance, or do you want to squander it on lawyers? Don't make yourself more of a target than you need to be."

But standing in the shower, reveling in the sensation of the hot water pelting his skin, Adam only grew more resolute. Why shouldn't he dare to show his face? He had nothing to be ashamed of.

The old man had bought a few suits for him a while ago, and left them hanging beside his own clothes. Adam picked one out and placed it on the bed, then paused to run a hand along the worn sleeve of an old, olive-green shirt. He was sure it would fit him, and for a moment he considered wearing it, but then the thought made him uneasy and he chose one of the new ones that had come with the suits.

As he dressed, he gazed at the undisturbed bed, trying to think of a good reason why he still hadn't left the guest room. No one else was coming to claim this one. But he shouldn't get too comfortable here; he might need to sell the house and move into something far more modest.

Adam started booking a car, then realized that he had no idea where the ceremony was being held. He finally found the details at the bottom of the old man's obit, which described it as open to the public. While he stood outside the front door waiting for the car, he tried for the third or fourth time to read the obituary itself, but his eyes kept glazing over. "Morris blah blah blah... Morris blah blah, Morris blah..."

His phone beeped, then the gate opened and the car pulled into the driveway. He sat in the passenger seat and watched the steering wheel doing its poltergeist act as it negotiated the U-turn. He suspected that whatever victories the lawyers could achieve, he was going to have to pay the "unsupervised driving" surcharge for a while yet.

As the car turned into Sepulveda Boulevard, the view looked strange to him—half familiar, half wrong—but perhaps there'd been some recent reconstruction. He dialed down the tinting, hoping to puncture a lingering sense of being at a remove from everything. The glare from the pavement beneath the cloudless blue sky was merciless, but he kept the windows undimmed.

The venue was some kind of chapel-esque building that probably served as seven different kinds of meeting hall, and in any case was free of conspicuous religious or la-la-land inspirational signage. The old man had left his remains to a medical school, so at least they'd all been spared a trip to Forest Lawn. As Adam stepped away from the car, he spotted one of the nephews, Ryan, walking toward the entrance, accompanied by his wife and adult children. The old man hadn't spent much time with any of them, but he'd gotten hold of recent pictures and showed them to Adam so he wouldn't be caught unaware.

Adam hung back and waited for them to go inside before crossing the forecourt. As he approached the door and caught sight of a large portrait of a decidedly pre-cancerous version of the old man on a stand beside the podium, his courage began to waver. But he steeled himself and continued.

He kept his gaze low as he entered the hall, and chose a spot on the frontmost unoccupied bench, far enough in from the aisle that nobody would have to squeeze past him. After a minute or so, an elderly man took the aisle seat; Adam snuck a quick glance at his neighbor, but he did not look familiar. His timing had turned out to be perfect: any later and his entrance might have drawn attention, any earlier and there would have been people milling outside. Whatever happened, no one could accuse him of going out of his way to make a scene.

Ryan mounted the steps to the podium. Adam stared at the back of the bench in front of him; he felt like a child trapped in church, though no one had forced him to be here.

"The last time I saw my uncle," Ryan began, "was almost ten years ago, at the funeral of his husband Carlos. Until then, I always thought it would be Carlos standing up here, delivering this speech, far more aptly and eloquently than I, or anyone else, ever could."

Adam felt a freight train tearing through his chest, but he kept his eyes fixed on a discolored patch of varnish. This had been a bad idea, but he couldn't walk out now.

"My uncle was the youngest child of Robert and Sophie Morris," Ryan continued. "He outlived his brother Steven, his sister Joan, and my mother, Sarah. Though I was never close to him, I'm heartened to see so many of his friends and colleagues here to pay their respects. I watched his shows, of course, but then, didn't everyone? I was wondering if we ought to screen some kind of highlights reel, but then the people in the know told me that there was going to be a tribute at the Emmys, and I decided not to compete with the professional edit-bots."

That line brought some quiet laughter, and Adam felt obliged to look up and smile. No one in this family was any kind of monster, whatever they aspired to do to him. They just had their own particular views of his relationship with the old man—sharpened by the lure of a few million dollars, but they probably would have felt the same regardless.

Ryan kept his contribution short, but when Cynthia Navarro took his place Adam had to turn his face to the pew again. He doubted that she'd recognize him—she'd worked with the old man in the wrong era for that—but the warmth, and grief, in her voice made her anecdotes far harder to shut out than the automated mash-up of database entries and viral misquotes that had formed the obituary. She finished with the time they'd spent all night searching for a way to rescue a location shoot with six hundred extras after Gemma Freeman broke her leg and had to be stretchered out in a chopper. As she spoke, Adam closed his eyes and pictured the wildly annotated pages of the script strewn across the table, and Cynthia gawping with incredulity at her friend's increasingly desperate remedies.

"But it all worked out well enough," she concluded. "The plot twist that *no viewer saw coming*, that lifted the third season to *a whole new level*, owed its existence to an oil slick from a generator that just happened to be situated between Ms. Freeman's trailer and…"

Laughter rose up, cutting her off, and Adam felt compelled once more to raise his eyes. But before the sounds of mirth had faded, his neighbor moved closer and asked in a whisper, "Do you remember me?"

Adam turned, not quite facing the man. "Should I?" He spoke with an east-coast accent that was hard to place, and if it induced a certain sense of déjà vu, so did advertising voice-overs, and random conversations overheard in elevators.

"I don't know," the man replied. His tone was more amused than sarcastic; he meant the words literally. Adam hunted for some-   177 thing polite and noncommittal to say, but the audience was too quiet now for him to speak without being noticed and hushed, and his neighbor was already turning back toward the podium.

Cynthia was followed by a representative of the old man's agents, though everyone who'd known him in the golden age was long gone. There were suits from Warner Bros., Netflix, and HBO, whose stories of the old man were clearly scripted by the same bots that wrote their new shows. As the proceedings became ever more wooden, Adam began suffering from a panic-inducing premonition that Ryan would invite anyone in the hall who wished to speak to step up, and in the awkward silence that followed everyone's eyes would sweep the room and alight on him.

But when Ryan returned to the podium, he just thanked them for coming and wished them safe journeys home.

"No music?" Adam's neighbor asked. "No poetry? I seem to recall something by Dylan Thomas that might have raised a laugh under the circumstances."

"I think he stipulated no music," Adam replied.

"Fair enough. Since *The Big Chill*, anything you could pick with a trace of wit to it would seem like a bad in-joke."

"Excuse me, I have to…" People were starting to leave, and Adam wanted to get away before anyone else noticed him.

As he stood, his neighbor took out his phone and flicked his thumb across its surface. Adam's phone pinged softly in acknowledgment. "In case you want to catch up sometime," the man explained cheerfully.

"Thanks," Adam replied, nodding an awkward goodbye, grateful that he didn't seem to be expected to reciprocate.

There was already a small crowd lingering just inside the door, slowing his exit. When he made it out onto the forecourt, he walked straight to the roadside and summoned a car.

"Hey, you! Mr. Sixty Percent!"

Adam turned. A man in his thirties was marching toward him, scowling with such intense displeasure that his pillowy cheeks had turned red. "Can I help you with something?" Adam asked mildly. For all that he'd been dreading a confrontation, now that it was imminent he felt more invigorated than intimidated.

"What the fuck were you doing in there?"

"It was open to the public."

"You're not part of the public!"

Adam finally placed him: He was one of Ryan's sons. He'd seen him from behind as he'd been entering the hall. "Unhappy with the will are you, Gerald?"

Gerald came closer. He was trembling slightly, but Adam couldn't tell if it was from rage or from fear. "Live it up while you can, Sixty. You're going to be out with the trash in no time."

"What's with this 'sixty'?" As far as Adam knew, he'd been bequeathed a hundred percent of the estate, unless Gerald was already accounting for all the legal fees.

"Sixty percent: how much you resemble him."

"Now that's just cruel. I'm assured that by some metrics, it's at least seventy."

Gerald snickered triumphantly, as if that made his case. "I guess he was used to setting the bar low. If you grew up believing that Facebook could give you 'news' and Google could give you 'information,' your expectations for quality control would already be nonexistent."

"I think you're conflating his generation with your father's." Adam was quite sure that the old man had held the Bilge Barons in as much contempt as his great-nephew did. "And seventy percent of something real isn't so bad. Getting a side-load that close to complete is orders of magnitude harder than anything those charlatans ever did."

"Well, give your own scam artists a Nobel Prize, but you'd still need to be senile to think that was good enough."

"He wasn't senile. We spoke together at least a dozen times in the month before he died, and he must have thought he was getting what he'd paid for, because he never chose to pull the plug on me." Adam hadn't even known at the time that that was possible, but in retrospect he was glad no one had told him. It might have made those bedside chats a little tense.

"Because…?" Gerald demanded. When Adam didn't reply immediately, Gerald laughed. "Or is the reason he decided you were worth the trouble part of the thirty percent of his mind that you don't have?"

"It could well be," Adam conceded, trying to make that sound like a perfectly satisfactory outcome. A joke about the studios' bots only achieving ten percent of the same goal and still earning   **179** a tidy income got censored halfway to his lips; the last thing he wanted to do was invite the old man's relatives to view him in the same light as that cynical act of shallow mimicry.

"So you don't know *why* he didn't care that you don't know whatever it is that you don't know? Very fucking Kafka."

"I think he would have preferred 'very fucking Heller'…but who am I to say?"

"Next week's trash, that's what you are." Gerald stepped back, looking pleased with himself. "Next week's fodder for the wrecking yard."

The car pulled up beside Adam and the door slid open. "Is that your grandma come to take you home?" Gerald taunted him. "Or maybe your retarded cousin?"

"Enjoy the wake," Adam replied. He tapped his skull. "I promise, the old man will be thinking of you."

3

ADAM HAD A CONFERENCE CALL WITH THE LAWYERS. "How do we stand?" he asked.

"The family's going to contest the will," Gina replied.

"On what grounds?"

"That the trustees, and the beneficiaries of the trust, misled and defrauded Mr. Morris."

"They're saying I misled him somehow?"

"No," Corbin interjected. "US law doesn't recognize you as a person. *You* can't be sued, as such, but other entities you depend on certainly can be."

"Right." Adam had known as much, but in his mind he kept glossing over the elaborate legal constructs that sustained his delusions of autonomy. On a purely practical level, there was money in three accounts that he had no trouble accessing—but then, the same was probably true of any number of stock-trading algorithms, and that didn't make them the masters of their own fate. "So who exactly is accused of fraud?"

"Our firm," Gina replied. "Various officers of the corporations we created to fulfill Mr. Morris's instructions. Loadstone, for making false claims that led to the original purchase of their technology, and for ongoing fraud in relation to the services promised in their maintenance contract."

"I'm very happy with the maintenance contract!" When Adam had complained that one of his earlobes had gone numb, Sandra had come to his home and fixed the problem on the same day he called.

"That's not the point," Corbin said impatiently. Adam was forgetting his place again: Jurisprudentially, his happiness cut no ice.

"So what happens next?"

"The first hearings are still seven months away," Gina explained. "We were expecting this, and we'll have plenty of time to prepare. We'll aim for an early dismissal, of course, but we can't promise anything."

"No." Adam hesitated. "But it's not just the house they could take? The Estonian accounts...?"

Gina said, "Opening those accounts under your digital residency makes some things easier, but it doesn't put the money out of reach of the courts."

"Right."

When they hung up, Adam paced the office. Could it really be so hard to defend the old man's will? He wasn't even sure what disincentives were in place to stop the lawyers from drawing out proceedings like this for as long as they wished. Maybe a director of one of the entities he depended on was both empowered and duty bound to rein them in if they were behaving with conspicuous profligacy? But Adam himself couldn't sack them, or compel them to follow his instructions, just because Estonia had been nice enough to classify him as a person for certain limited purposes.

The old man had believed he was setting him up in style, but all the machinery that was meant to support him just made him feel trapped. What if he gave up the house and walked away? If he cashed in his dollar and euro accounts for some mixture of blockchain currencies before the courts swept in and froze his funds, that might be easier to protect and enjoy without the benefits of a Social Security number, a birth certificate, or a passport. But those currencies were all insanely volatile, and trying to hedge them against each other was like trying to save yourself in a skydiving accident by clutching your own feet.

He couldn't leave the country by any lawful means without deactivating his body so it could be sent as freight. Loadstone had promised to facilitate any trips he wished to make to any of the

181

thirty-nine jurisdictions where he could walk the streets unchaper-oned, as proud and free as the pizza bots that had blazed the trail, but the idea of returning to the company's servers, or even being halted and left in limbo for the duration of the flight, filled him with dread.

For now, it seemed that he was stuck in the Valley. All he could do was find a way to make the best of it.

4

SITTING ON TWO UPTURNED WOODEN CRATES IN AN ALley behind the nightclub, they could still hear the pounding bass line of the music escaping through the walls, but at least it was possible to hold a conversation here.

Carlos sounded like the loneliest person Adam had ever met. Did he tell everyone so much, so soon? Adam wanted to believe that he didn't, and that something in his own demeanor had in-spired this beautiful man to confide in him.

Carlos had been in the country for twelve years, but he was still struggling to support his sister in El Salvador. She'd raised him af-ter their parents died—his father when he was six months old, his mother when he was five. But now his sister had three children of her own, and the man who'd fathered them was no good to her.

"I love her," he said. "I love her like my own life, I don't want to be rid of her. But the kids are always sick, or something's broken that needs fixing. It never fucking stops."

Adam had no one relying on him, no one expecting him to do anything. His own finances waxed and waned, but at least when the money was scarce no one else suffered, or made him feel that he was letting them down.

"So what do you do to relieve the stress?" he asked.

Carlos smiled sadly. "It used to be smoking, but that got too expensive."

"So you quit?"

"Only the smoking."

As Adam turned toward him, his mind went roaming down the darkness of the alley, impatiently following the glistening thread, unable to shake off the sense of urgency that told him: *Take hold of this now, or it will be lost forever.* He didn't need to linger in their beds for long; just a few samples of that annihilating euphoria were enough to stand in for all the rest. Maybe that was the engine powering everything that followed, but what it dragged along behind it was like a newlyweds' car decorated by a thousand exuberant well-wishers.

He tried grabbing the rattling cans of their fights, running his fingers over the rough texture of all the small annoyances and slights, mutually wounded pride, frustrated good intentions. Then he felt the jagged edge of a lacerating eruption of doubt.

But something had happened that blunted the edge, then folded it in on itself again and again, leaving a seam, a ridge, a scar. Afterward, however hard things became, there was no questioning the foundations. They'd earned each other's trust, and it was unshakeable.

He pushed on into the darkness, trying to understand. Wherever he walked, light would follow, and his task was to make his way down as many side streets as possible before he woke.

This time, though, the darkness remained unbroken. He groped his way forward, unnerved. They'd ended up closer than ever—he knew that with as much certainty as he knew anything. So why did he feel as if he was stumbling blindly through the rooms of Bluebeard's castle, and the last thing he should want to summon was a lamp?

5

ADAM SPENT THREE WEEKS IN THE OLD MAN'S HOME theater, watching every one of the old man's shows, and an episode or two from each of the biggest hits of the last ten years. There could only be one thing more embarrassing than pitching an idea to a studio and discovering that he was offering them a story that they'd already produced for six seasons, and that would be attempting to recycle, not just any old show, but an actual Adam Morris script.

Most of the old man's work felt as familiar as if he'd viewed it a hundred times in the editing suite, but sometimes a whole side plot appeared that seemed to have dropped from the sky. Could the studios have fucked with things afterward, when the old man was too sick and distracted to notice? Adam checked online, but the fan sites that would have trumpeted any such tampering were silent. The only re-cuts had taken place in another medium entirely.

He desperately needed to write a new show. Money aside, how else was he going to pass the time? The old man's few surviving friends had all made it clear before he died that they wanted nothing to do with his side-load. He could try to make the most of his cybernetic rejuvenation; his skin felt exactly like skin, from inside and out, and his ridiculously plausible dildo of a cock wouldn't disappoint anyone if he went looking for ways to use it—but the truth was, he'd inherited the old man's feelings for Carlos far too deeply to brush them aside and pretend that he was twenty again, with no attachments and no baggage. He didn't even know yet if he wanted to forge an identity entirely his own, or to take the other path and seek to become the old man more fully. He couldn't "betray" a lover ten years dead who was, in the end, nothing more to him than a character in someone else's story—whatever he'd felt as he'd dragged the old man's memories into his own virtual skull. But he wasn't going to sell himself that version of things before he was absolutely sure it was the right one.

The only way to know who he was would be to create something new. It didn't even need to be a story that the old man wouldn't have written himself, had he lived a few years longer…just so long as it didn't turn out that he'd already written it, pitched it unsuccessfully, and stuck it in a drawer. Adam pictured himself holding a page from each version up to the light together, bringing the words into alignment, trying to decide if the differences were too many, or too few.

6

"SIXTY THOUSAND DOLLARS *IN ONE WEEK*?" ADAM WAS incredulous.

Gina replied calmly, "The billables are all itemized. I can assure you, what we're charging is really quite modest for a case of this complexity."

"The money was his, he could do what he liked with it. End of story."

"That's not what the case law says." Gina was beginning to exhibit micro-fidgets, as if she'd found herself trapped at a family occasion being forced to play a childish video game just to humor a nephew she didn't really like. Whether or not she'd granted Adam personhood in her own mind, he certainly wasn't anyone in a position to give her instructions, and the only reason she'd taken his call must have been some sop to Adam's comfort that the old man had managed to get written into his contract with the firm.

"All right. I'm sorry to have troubled you."

In the silence after he'd hung up, Adam recalled something that Carlos had said to the old man, back in New York one sweltering July, taking him aside in the middle of the haggling over a second-hand air-conditioner they were attempting to buy. "You're a good person, *cariño*, so you don't see it when people are trying to cheat you." Maybe he'd been sincere, or maybe "good" had just been a tactful euphemism for "unworldly," though if the old man really had been so trusting, how had Adam ended up with the opposite trait? Was cynicism some kind of default, wired into the template from which the whole side-loading process had started?

Adam found an auditor with no connections to the old man's lawyers, picking a city at random and then choosing the person with the highest reputation score with whom he could afford a ten-minute consultation. Her name was Lillian Adjani.

"Because these companies have no shareholders," she explained, "there's not that much that needs to be disclosed in their public filings. And I can't just go to them myself and demand to see their financial records. A court could do that, in principle, and you might be able to find a lawyer who'd take your money to try to make that happen. But who would their client be?"

Adam had to admire the way she could meet his gaze with an expression of sympathy, while reminding him that—shorn of the very constructs he was trying to scrutinize—for administrative purposes he didn't actually exist.

"So there's nothing I can do?" Maybe he was starting to confuse his secondhand memories of the real world with all the shows he'd been watching, where people just *followed the money trail*. The police never seemed to need to get the courts involved, and even civilians usually had some supernaturally gifted hacker at their disposal. "We couldn't…hire an investigator…who could persuade someone to leak…?" Mike Ehrmantraut would have found a way to make it happen in three days flat.

Ms. Adjani regarded him censoriously. "I'm not getting involved in anything illegal. But maybe you have something yourself, already in your possession, that could help you more than you realize."

"Like what?"

"How computer-savvy was your…predecessor?"

"He could use a word processor and a web browser. And Skype."

"Do you still have any of his devices?"

Adam laughed. "I don't know what happened to his phone, but I'm talking to you from his laptop right now."

"Okay. Don't get your hopes too high, but if there were files containing financial records or legal documents that he received and then deleted, then unless he went out of his way to erase them securely, they might still be recoverable."

Ms. Adjani sent him a link for a piece of software she trusted to do the job. Adam installed it, then stared numbly at the catalog of eighty-three thousand "intelligible fragments" that had shown up on the drive.

He started playing with the filtering options. When he chose "text," portions of scripts began emerging from the fog—some instantly recognizable, some probably abandoned dead-ends. Adam averted his gaze, afraid of absorbing them into his subconscious if they weren't already buried there. He had to draw a line somewhere.

He found an option called "financial," and when that yielded a blizzard of utility bills, he added all the relevant keywords he could think of.

There were bills from the lawyers, and bills from Loadstone. If Gina was screwing him, she'd been screwing the old man as well, because the hourly rate hadn't changed. Adam was beginning to feel foolish; he was right to be vigilant about his precarious situation, but if he let that devolve into full-blown paranoia he'd just end up kicking all the support structures out from beneath his feet.

Loadstone hadn't been shy with their fees either. Adam hadn't known before just how much his body had cost, but given the generally excellent engineering it was difficult to begrudge the expense. There was an item for the purchase of the template, and then one for every side-loading session, broken down into various components. "Squid operator?" he muttered, bemused. "What the fuck?" But he wasn't going to start convincing himself that they'd blinded the old man with technobabble. He'd paid what he'd paid, and in the hospital he'd given Adam every indication that he'd been happy with the result.

"Targeted occlusions?" Meaning blood clots in the brain? The old man had left him login details allowing him postmortem access to all his medical records; Adam checked, and there had been no clots.

He searched the web for the phrase in the context of side-loading. The pithiest translation he found was: "The selective non-transferral of a prescribed class of memories or traits."

Which meant that the old man had held something back, deliberately. Adam was an imperfect copy of him, not just because the technology was imperfect, but because he'd wanted it that way.

"You lying piece of shit." Toward the end, the old man had rambled on about his hope that Adam would outdo his own achievements, but judging from his efforts so far he wasn't even going to come close. Three attempts at new scripts had ended up dead in the water. It wasn't Ryan and his family who'd robbed him of the most valuable part of the inheritance.

Adam sat staring at his hands, contemplating the possibilities for a life worth living without the only skill the old man had ever possessed. He remembered joking to Carlos once that they should both train as doctors and go open a free clinic in San Salvador. "When we're rich." But Adam doubted that his original, let alone the diminished version, was smart enough to learn to do much more than empty bedpans.

He switched off the laptop and walked into the master bedroom. All of the old man's clothes were still there, as if he'd fully expected them to be used again. Adam took off his own clothes and began trying on each item in turn, counting the ones he was sure he recognized. Was he Gerald's Mr. Sixty Percent, or was it more like forty, or thirty? Maybe the pep talks had been a kind of sarcastic joke, with the old man secretly hoping that the final verdict would be that there was only one Adam Morris, and like the studios' laughable "deep-learning" bots, even the best technology in the world couldn't capture his true spark.

He sat on the bed, naked, wondering what it would be like to go out in some wild bacchanalia with a few dozen robot fetishists, fucking his brains out and then dismembering him to take the pieces home as souvenirs. It wouldn't be hard to organize, and he doubted that any part of his corporate infrastructure would be obliged to have him resurrected from Loadstone's daily backups. The old man might have been using him to make some dementedly pretentious artistic point, but he would never have been cruel enough to render suicide impossible.

Adam caught sight of a picture of the two men posing hammily beneath the Hollywood sign, and found himself sobbing dryly with, of all things, grief. What he wanted was Carlos beside him—making this bearable, putting it right. He loved the dead man's dead lover more than he was ever going to love anyone else, but he still couldn't do anything worthwhile that the dead man could have done.

He pictured Carlos with his arms around him. "Shh, it's not as bad as you think—it never is, *cariño*. We start with what we've got, and just fill in the pieces as we go."

You're really not helping, Adam replied. *Just shut up and fuck me, that's all I've got left.* He lay down on the bed and took his penis in his hand. It had seemed wrong before, but he didn't care now: He didn't owe either of them anything. And Carlos, at least, would probably have taken pity on him, and not begrudged him the unpaid guest appearance.

He closed his eyes and tried to remember the feel of stubble against his thighs, but he wasn't even capable of scripting his own fantasy: Carlos just wanted to talk.

"You've got friends," he insisted. "You've got people looking out for you."

Adam had no idea if he was confabulating freely, or if this was a fragment of a real conversation long past, but context was everything. "Not any more, *cariño*. Either they're dead, or I'm dead to them."

Carlos just stared back at him skeptically, as if he'd made a ludicrously hyperbolic claim.

But that skepticism did have some merit. If he knocked on Cynthia's door she'd probably try to stab him through the heart with a wooden stake, but the amiable stranger who'd sat beside him at the funeral had been far keener to talk than Adam. The fact that he still couldn't place the man no longer seemed like a good reason to avoid him; if he came from the gaps, he must know something about them.

Carlos was gone. Adam sat up, still feeling gutted, but no amount of self-pity was going to improve his situation.

He found his phone, and checked under "Introductions"; he hadn't erased the contact details. The man was named Patrick Auster. Adam called the number.

7

"YOU GO FIRST," ADAM SAID. "ASK ME ANYTHING. That's the only fair trade." They were sitting in a booth in an old-style diner named Caesar's, where Auster had suggested they meet. The place wasn't busy, and the adjacent booths were empty, so there was no need to censor themselves or talk in code.

Auster gestured at the generous serving of chocolate cream pie that Adam had begun demolishing. "Can you really taste that?"

"Absolutely."

"And it's the same as before?"

Adam wasn't going to start hedging his answers with quibbles about the ultimate incomparability of qualia and memories. "Exactly the same." He pointed a thumb toward the diners three booths behind him. "I can tell you without peeking that someone's eating bacon. And I think it's apparent that there's nothing wrong with my hearing or vision, even if my memory for faces isn't so good."

"Which leaves…"

"Every hair on the bearskin rug," Adam assured him.

Auster hesitated. Adam said, "There's no three-question limit. We can keep going all day if you want to."

"Do you have much to do with the others?" Auster asked.

"The other side-loads? No. I never knew any of them before, so there's no reason for them to be in touch with me now."

Auster was surprised. "I'd have thought you'd all be making common cause. Trying to improve the legal situation."

"We probably should be. But if there's some secret cabal of immortals trying to get re-enfranchised, they haven't invited me into their inner circle yet."

Adam waited as Auster stirred his coffee meditatively. "That's it," he decided.

"Okay. You know, I'm sorry if I was brusque at the funeral," Adam said. "I was trying to keep a low profile; I was worried about how people would react."

"Forget it."

"So you knew me in New York?" Adam wasn't going to use the third person; it would make the conversation far too awkward. Besides, if he'd come here to claim the missing memories as his own, the last thing he wanted to do was distance himself from them.

"Yes."

"Was it business, or were we friends?" All he'd been able to find out online was that Auster had written a couple of independent movies. There was no record of the two of them ever working on the same project; their official Bacon number was three, which put Adam no closer to Auster than he was to Angelina Jolie.

"Both, I hope." Auster hesitated, then angrily recanted the last part. "No, we were friends. Sorry, it's hard not to resent being blanked, even if it's not deliberate."

Adam tried to judge just how deeply the insult had cut him. "Were we lovers?"

Auster almost choked on his coffee. "God, no! I've always been straight, and you were already with Carlos when I met you." He frowned suddenly. "You didn't cheat on him, did you?" He sounded more incredulous than reproving.

"Not as far as I know." During the drive down to Gardena, Adam had wondered if the old man might have been trying to airbrush out his infidelities. That would have been a bizarre form of vanity, or hypocrisy, or some other sin the world didn't have a name for yet, but it would still have been easier to forgive than a deliberate attempt to sabotage his successor.

"We met around two thousand and ten," Auster continued. "When I first approached you about adapting *Sadlands*."

"Okay."

"You do remember *Sadlands*, don't you?"

"My second novel," Adam replied. For a moment nothing more came to him, then he said, "There's an epidemic of suicides spreading across the country, apparently at random, affecting people equally regardless of demographics."

"That sounds like the version a reviewer would write," Auster teased him. "I spent six years, on and off, trying to make it happen."

Adam dredged his mind for any trace of these events that might have merely been submerged for lack of currency, but he found nothing. "So should I be thanking you, or apologizing? Did I give you a hard time about the script?"

"Not at all. I showed you drafts now and then, and if you had a strong opinion you let me know, but you didn't cross any lines."

"The book itself didn't do that well," Adam recalled.

Auster didn't argue. "Even the publishers stopped using the phrase 'slow-burning cult hit,' though I'm sure the studio would have put that in the press release, if it had ever gone ahead."

Adam hesitated. "So, what else was going on?" The old man hadn't published much in that decade; just a few pieces in magazines. His book sales had dried up, and he'd been working odd jobs to make ends meet. But at least back then there'd still been golden opportunities like valet parking. "Did we socialize much? Did I talk about things?"

Auster scrutinized him. "This isn't just smoothing over the business at the funeral, is it? You've lost something that you think might be important, and now you're going all Dashiell Hammett on yourself."

"Yes," Adam admitted.

Auster shrugged. "Okay, why not? That worked out so well in *Angel Heart*." He thought for a while. "When we weren't discussing *Sadlands*, you talked about your money problems, and you talked about Carlos."

"What about Carlos?"

"His money problems."

Adam laughed. "Sorry. I must have been fucking awful company."

Auster said, "I think Carlos was working three or four jobs, all for minimum wage, and you were working two, with a few hours a week set aside for writing. I remember you sold a story to the *New Yorker*, but the celebration was pretty muted, because the whole fee was gone, instantly, to pay off debts."

"*Debts?*" Adam had no memory of it ever being that bad. "Did I try to borrow money from you?"

"You wouldn't have been so stupid; you knew I was almost as skint. Just before we gave up, I got twenty grand in development **191** money to spend a year trying to whip *Sadlands* into something that Sundance or AMC might buy—and believe me, it all went on rent and food."

"So what did I get out of that?" Adam asked, mock-jealously.

"Two grand, for the option. If it had gone to a pilot, I think you would have gotten twenty, and double that if the series was picked up." Auster smiled. "That must sound like small change to you now, but at the time it would have been the difference between night and day—especially for Carlos's sister."

"Yeah, she could be a real hard-ass," Adam sighed. Auster's face drained, as if Adam had just maligned a woman that everyone else had judged worthy of beatification. "What did I say?"

"You don't even remember *that?*"

"Remember what?"

"She was dying of cancer! Where did you think the money was going? You and Carlos weren't living in the Ritz, or shooting it up."

"Okay." Adam recalled none of this. He'd known that Adelina had died long before Carlos, but he'd never even tried to summon up the details. "So Carlos and I were working eighty-hour weeks to pay her medical bills…and I was bitching and moaning to you about it, as if that might make the magic Hollywood money fall into my lap a little faster?"

"That's putting it harshly," Auster replied. "You needed someone to vent to, and I had enough distance from it that it didn't weigh me down. I could commiserate and walk away."

Adam thought for a while. "Do you know if I ever took it out on Carlos?"

"Not that you told me. Would you have stayed together if you had?"

"I don't know," Adam said numbly. Could this be the whole point of the occlusions? When their relationship was tested, the old man had buckled, and he was so ashamed of himself that he'd tried to erase every trace of the event? Whatever he'd done, Carlos must have forgiven him in the end, but maybe that just made his own weakness more painful to contemplate.

"So I never pulled the pin?" he asked. "I didn't wash my hands of Adelina, and tell Carlos to fuck off and pay for it all himself?"

Auster said, "Not unless you were lying to me to save face. The version I heard was that every spare dollar you had was going to her, up until the day she died. Which is where forty grand might have made all the difference—bought her more time, or even a cure. I never got the medico-logistic details, but both of you took it hard when the Colman thing happened."

Adam moved his half-empty plate aside and asked wearily, "So what was 'the Colman thing'?"

Auster nodded apologetically. "I was getting to that. Sundance had shown a lot of interest in *Sadlands*, but then they heard that some Brit called Nathan Colman had sold a story to Netflix about, well…an epidemic of suicides spreading across the country, apparently at random, affecting people equally regardless of demographics."

"And we didn't sue the brazen fuck into penury?"

Auster snorted. "Who's this 'we' with money for lawyers? The production company that held the option did a cost-benefit analysis and decided to cut their losses; twenty-two grand down the toilet, but it wasn't as if they'd been cheated out of the next *Game of Thrones*. All you and I could do was suck it up, and take a few moments of solace whenever a *Sadlands* fan posted an acerbic comment in some obscure chat room."

Adam's visceral sense of outrage was undiminished, but on any sober assessment this outcome was pretty much what he would have expected.

"Of course, my faith in karma was restored, eventually," Auster added enigmatically.

"You've lost me again." The old man's success, once he cut out all the middlemen and plagiarists, must have been balm to his wounds—but Auster's online footprint suggested that his own third act had been less lucrative.

"Before they'd finished shooting the second season, a burglar broke into Colman's house and cracked open his skull with a statuette."

"An Emmy?"

"No, just a BAFTA."

Adam tried hard not to smile. "And once *Sadlands* fell through, did we stay in touch?"

"Not really," Auster replied. "I moved here a long time after you did; I wasted five years trying to get something up on Broadway before I swallowed my pride and settled for playing script doctor. And by then you'd done so well that I was embarrassed to turn up asking you for work."

Adam was genuinely ashamed now. "You should have. I owed it to you."

Auster shook his head. "I wasn't living on the streets. I've done all right here. I can't afford what you've got…" He gestured at Adam's imperishable chassis. "But then, I'm not sure I could handle the lacunae."

Adam called for a car. Auster insisted on splitting the bill.

The service cart rattled over and began clearing the table. Auster said, "I'm glad I could help you fill in the blanks, but maybe those answers should have come with a warning."

"*Now* a warning?"

"The Colman thing. Don't let it get to you."

Adam was baffled. "Why would I? I'm not going to sue his family for whatever pittance is still trickling down to them." In fact, he couldn't sue anyone for anything, but it was the thought that counted.

"Okay." Auster was ready to drop it, but now Adam needed to be clear.

"How badly did I take it the first time?"

Auster gestured with one finger, drilling into his temple. "Like a fucking parasitic worm in your brain. He'd stolen your precious novel and murdered your lover's sister. He'd kicked you to the ground when you had nothing, and taken your only hope away."

Adam could understand now why they hadn't stayed in touch. Solidarity in hard times was one thing, but an obsessive grievance like that would soon get old. Auster had taken his own kicks and decided to move on.

"That was more than thirty years ago," Adam replied. "I'm a different person now."

"Aren't we all?"

Auster's ride came first. Adam stood outside the diner and watched him depart: sitting confidently behind the wheel, even if he didn't need to lay a finger on it.

8

ADAM CHANGED HIS CAR'S DESTINATION TO DOWNTOWN Gardena. He disembarked beside a row of fast-food outlets and went looking for a public web kiosk. He'd been fretting about the best way of paying without leaving too obvious a trail, but then he discovered that in this municipality the things were as free as public water fountains.

There was no speck of entertainment industry trivia that the net had failed to immortalize. Colman had moved from London to Los Angeles to shoot the series, and he'd been living just a few miles south of Adam's current home when the break-in happened. But the old man had still been in New York at the time; he hadn't even set foot in California until the following year, as far as Adam recalled. The laptop that he'd started excavating had files on it dating back to the '90s, but they would have been copied from machine to machine; there was no chance that the computer itself was old enough to be carrying deleted emails for flights booked three decades ago, even if the old man had been foolish enough to make his journey so easy to trace.

Adam turned away from the kiosk's chipped projection screen, wondering if any passers-by had been staring over his shoulder. He was losing his grip on reality. The occlusions might easily have been targeted at nothing more than the old man's lingering resentment: If he couldn't let go of what had happened—even after Colman's death, even after his own career had blossomed—he might have wished to spare Adam all that pointless, fermented rage.

That was the simplest explanation. Unless Auster had been holding back, the thought of the old man murdering Colman didn't seem to have crossed his mind, and if the police had come knocking he would surely have mentioned that. If nobody else thought the old man was guilty, who was Adam to start accusing him—on the basis of nothing but the shape and location of one dark pit of missing memories, among the thirty percent of everything that he didn't recall?

He turned to the screen again, trying to think of a more discriminating test of his hypothesis. Though the flow into the sideload itself would have been protected by a massive firewall of privacy laws, Adam doubted that any instructions to the technicians at Loadstone were subject to privilege. Which meant that, even if he found them on the laptop, they were unlikely to be incriminatory. The only way the old man could have phrased a request to forget that he'd bashed Colman's brains out would have been to excise all of the more innocent events that were connected to it in any way, like a cancer surgeon choosing the widest possible sacrificial margin. But he might also have issued the same instructions merely in order to forget as much as possible of that whole bleak decade—when Hollywood had fucked him over, Carlos had been grieving for the woman who raised him, and he'd somehow, just barely, kept it together, long enough to make a new start in the '20s.

Adam logged off the kiosk. Auster had warned him not to become obsessed—and the man was the closest thing to a friend that he had right now. If everyone in the industry really staved in the skulls of everyone who'd crossed them, there'd be no one left to run the place.

He called a car and headed home.

9

UNDER PROTEST, AT ADAM'S REQUEST, SANDRA SPREAD the three sturdy boxes out on the floor, and opened them up to reveal the foam, straps, and recesses within. They reminded Adam of the utility trunks that the old man's crews had used for stowing their gear.

"Don't freak out on me," she pleaded.

"I won't," Adam promised. "I just want a clear picture in my mind of what's about to happen."

"Really? I don't even let my dentist show me his planning videos."

"I trust you to do a better job than any dentist."

"You're too kind." She gestured at the trunks like a proud magician, bowing her head for applause.

Adam said, "Now you have no choice, El Dissecto: You've got to take a picture for me once it's done."

"I hope your Spanish is better than you're making it sound."

"I was aiming for vaudevillian, not voseo." Adam had some memories of the old man being prepared for surgery, but he wasn't sure that it was possible to rid them of survivor's hindsight and understand exactly how afraid he'd been that he might never wake up.

Sandra glanced at her watch. "No more clowning around. You need to undress and lie down on the bed, then repeat the code phrase aloud, four times. I'll wait outside."

Adam didn't care if she saw him naked while he was still conscious, but it might have made her uncomfortable. "Okay." Once she left, he stopped stalling; he removed his clothes quickly, and began the chant.

"Red lentils, yellow lentils. Red lentils, yellow lentils. Red lentils, yellow lentils." He glanced past the row of cases to Sandra's toolbox; he'd seen inside it before, and there were no cleavers, machetes, or chainsaws. Just magnetic screwdrivers that could loosen bolts within him without even penetrating his skin. He lay back and stared at the ceiling. "Red lentils, yellow lentils."

The ceiling stayed white but sprouted new shadows, a ventilation grille, and a light fitting, while the texture of the bedspread beneath his skin went from silken to beaded. Adam turned his head; the same clothes he'd removed were folded neatly beside him. He dressed quickly, walked over to the connecting door between the suites, and knocked.

Sandra opened the door. She'd changed her clothes since he'd last seen her, and she looked exhausted. His watch showed 11:20 p.m. local time, 9:20 back home.

"I just wanted to let you know that I'm still in here," he said, pointing to his skull.

She smiled. "Okay, Adam."

"Thank you for doing this," he added.

"Are you kidding? They're paying me all kinds of allowances and overtime, and it's not even that long a flight. Feel free to come back here as often as you like."

He hesitated. "You didn't take the photo, did you?"

Sandra was unapologetic. "No. It could have gotten me sacked, and not all of the company's rules are stupid."

"Okay. I'll let you sleep. See you in the morning."

"Yeah."

Adam lay awake for an hour before he could bring himself to mutter his code word for the milder form of sleep. If he'd wished, Loadstone could have given him a passable simulation of the whole journey—albeit with a lot of cheating to mask the time it took to shuffle him back and forth between their servers and his body. But the airlines didn't recognize any kind of safe "flight mode" for his kind of machine, even when he was in pieces and locked inside three separate boxes. The way he'd experienced it was the most honest choice: a jump-cut, and thirteen hours lost to the gaps.

IN THE MORNING, SANDRA HAD ARRANGED TO JOIN AN organized tour of the sights of San Salvador. Her employer's insurance company was more concerned about her safety than Adam's, and in any case it would have been awkward for both of them to have her following him around with her toolbox.

"Just keep the license on you," she warned him before she left. "I had to fill out more forms to get it than I would to clear a drone's flight path twice around the world, so if you lose it I'm not coming to rescue you from the scrapyard."

"Who's going to put me there?" Adam spread his arms and stared down at his body. "Are you calling me a Ken doll?" He raised one forearm to his face and examined it critically, but the skin around his elbow wrinkled with perfect verisimilitude.

"No, but you talk like a foreigner, and you don't have a passport. So just…stay out of trouble."

"Yes, ma'am."

The old man had only visited the city once, and with Carlos leading him from nightspot to childhood haunt to some cousin's apartment like a ricocheting bullet, he'd made no attempt to navigate for himself. But Adam had been disappointed when he'd learned that Beatriz was now living in an entirely different part of town; there'd be no cues along the way, no hooks to bring back other memories of the time.

Colonia Layco was half an hour's drive from the hotel. There were more autonomous cars on the street than Adam remembered, but enough electric scooters interspersed among them to keep the traffic from mimicking L.A.'s spookily synchronized throbbing.

The car dropped him off outside a newish apartment block. Adam entered the antechamber in the lobby and found the intercom.

"Beatriz, this is Adam."

"Welcome! Come on up!"

He pushed through the swing doors and took the stairs, ascending four flights; it wouldn't make him any fitter, but old habits died hard. When Beatriz opened the door of her apartment he was prepared for her to flinch, but she just stepped out and embraced him. Maybe the sight of wealthy Californians looking younger than their age had lost its power to shock anyone before she'd even been born.

She ushered him in, tongue-tied for a moment, perhaps from the need to suppress an urge to ask about his flight, or inquire about his health. She settled, finally, on "How have things been?"

Her English was infinitely better than his Spanish, so Adam didn't even try. "Good," he replied. "I've been taking a break from work, so I thought I owed you a visit." The last time they'd met had been at Carlos's funeral.

She led him into the living room and gestured toward a chair, then fetched a tray of pastries and a pot of coffee. Carlos had never found the courage to come out to Adelina, but Beatriz had known his secret long before her mother died. Adam had no idea what details of the old man's life Carlos might have confided in her, but he'd exhausted all the willing informants who'd known the old man firsthand, and she'd responded so warmly to his emails that he'd had no qualms about attempting to revive their relationship for its own sake.

"How are the kids?" he asked.

Beatriz turned and gestured proudly toward a row of photographs on a bookcase behind her. "That's Pilar at her graduation last year; she started at the hospital six months ago. Rodrigo's in his final year of engineering."

Adam smiled. "Carlos would have been over the moon."

"Of course," Beatriz agreed. "We teased him a lot once he started with the acting, but his heart was always with us. With you, and with us."

Adam scanned the photographs and spotted a thirty-something Carlos in a suit, beside a much younger woman in a wedding dress.

"That's you, isn't it?" He pointed at the picture.

"Yes."

"I'm sorry I didn't make it." He had no memory of Carlos leaving for the wedding, but it must have taken place a year or two before they'd moved to L.A.

Beatriz tutted. "You would have been welcome, Adam, but I knew how tight things were for you back then. We all knew what you'd done for my mother."

Not enough to keep her alive, Adam thought, but that would be a cruel and pointless thing to say. And he hoped that Carlos had spared his sister's children any of the old man's poisonous talk of the windfall they'd missed out on.

Beatriz had her own idea of the wrongs that needed putting right. "Of course, she didn't know, herself. She knew he had a friend who helped him out, but Carlos had to make it sound like you were rich, that you were loaning him the money and it was nothing to you. He should have told her the truth. If she'd thought of you as family, she wouldn't have refused your help."

Adam nodded uncomfortably, unsure just how graciously or otherwise the old man had handed over paycheck after paycheck for a woman who had no idea who he was. "That was a long time ago. I just want to meet your children and hear all your news."

"Ah." Beatriz grimaced apologetically. "I should warn you that Rodrigo's bringing his boyfriend to lunch."

"That's no problem at all." What twenty-year-old engineer wouldn't want to show off the animatronic version of Great Uncle Movie Star's lover to as many people as possible?

WHEN ADAM GOT BACK TO THE HOTEL IT WAS LATE IN the afternoon. He messaged Sandra, who replied that she was in a bar downtown having a great time and he was welcome to join her. Adam declined and lay down on the bed. The meal he'd just shared had been the most normal thing he'd experienced since his embodiment. He'd come within a hair's breadth of convincing himself that there was a place for him here: That he could some-how insert himself into this family and survive on their affection alone, as if this one day's hospitality and good-natured curiosity could be milked forever.

As the glow of borrowed domesticity faded, the tug of the past reasserted itself. He had to keep trying to assemble the pieces, as and when he found them. He took out his laptop and searched through archived social media posts, seeing if he could date Beatriz's wedding. Pictures had a way of getting wildly mislabeled, or grabbed by bots and repurposed at random, so even when he had what looked like independent confirmation from four different guests, he didn't quite trust the result, and he paid a small fee for access to the Salvadorian government's records.

Beatriz had been married on March 4, 2018. Adam didn't need to open the spreadsheet he was using to assemble his timeline for the gaps to know that the surrounding period would be sparsely annotated, save for one entry. Nathan Colman had been bludgeoned to death by an intruder on March 10 of the same year.

Carlos would hardly have flown in for the wedding and left the next day; the family would have expected him to stay for at least a couple of weeks. The old man would have been alone in New York, with no one to observe his comings and goings. He might even have had time to cross the country and return by bus, paying with cash, breaking the trip down into small stages, hitchhiking here and there, obfuscating the bigger picture as much as possible.

The dates proved nothing, of course. If Adam had been a juror in a trial with a case this flimsy, he would have laughed the prosecution out of court. He owed the old man the same standard of evidence.

Then again, in a trial the old man could have stood in the witness box and explained exactly what it was that he'd gone to so much trouble to hide.

THE FLIGHT TO L.A. WASN'T UNTIL SIX IN THE EVENING, but Sandra was too hungover to leave the hotel, and Adam had made no plans. So they sat in his room watching movies and ordering snacks from the kitchen, while Adam worked up the courage to ask her the question that had kept him awake all night.

"Is there any way you could get me the specifications for my targeted occlusions?" Adam waited for her response before daring to raise the possibility of payment. If the request was insulting in itself, offering a bribe would only compound the offense.

"No," she replied, as unfazed as if he'd wondered aloud whether room service might stretch to shiatsu. "That shit is locked down tight. After last night, it would take me all day to explain homomorphic encryption to you, so you'll just have to take my word for it: Nobody alive can answer that, even if they wanted to."

"But I've recovered bills from his laptop that mention it," Adam protested. "So much for Fort fucking Knox!"

Sandra shook her head. "That means that he was careless—and I should probably get someone in account generation to rethink their line items—but Loadstone would have held his hand very, very tightly when it came to spelling out the details. Unless he wrote it down in his personal diary, the information doesn't exist anymore."

Adam didn't think that she was lying to him. "There are things I need to know," he said simply. "He must have honestly believed that I'd be better off without them—but if he'd lived long enough for me to ask him face to face, I know I could have changed his mind."

Sandra paused the movie. "Very little software is perfect, least of all when it's for something as complex as this. If we fail to collect everything we aim to collect…"

"Then you also fail to block everything you aim to block," Adam concluded. "Which was probably mentioned somewhere in the fine print of his contract, but I've been racking my brain for months without finding a single stone that punched a hole in the sieve."

"What if the stones only got through in fragments, but they can still be put together?"

Adam struggled to interpret this. "Are you telling me to take up repressed memory therapy?"

"No, but I could get you a beta copy of Stitcher on the quiet."

"Stitcher?"

"It's a new layer they'll eventually be offering to every client," Sandra explained. "It's in the nature of things, with the current methods, that the side-load will end up with a certain amount of implicit information that's not in an easily accessible form: thousands of tiny glimpses of memories that were never brought across whole, but which could still be described in detail if you pieced together every partial sighting."

"So this software could reassemble the shredded page of a notebook that still holds an impression of what was written on the missing page above?"

Sandra said, "For someone with a digital brain, you're about as last-century as they come."

Adam gave up trying to harmonize their metaphors. "Will it tell me what I want to know?"

"I have no idea," Sandra said bluntly. "Among the fragments bearing implicit information—and there will certainly be thousands of them—it will recognize some unpredictable fraction of their associations, and let you follow the new threads that arise. But I don't know if that will be enough to tell you anything more than the color of the sweater your mother was wearing on your first day of school."

"Okay."

Sandra started the movie again. "You really should have joined me in the bar last night," she said. "I told them I had a friend who could drink any Salvadorian under the table, and they were begging for a chance to bet against you."

"You're a sick woman," Adam chided her. "Maybe next time."

10

REASSEMBLED BACK IN CALIFORNIA, ADAM TOOK HIS time deciding whether to make one last, algorithmic attempt to push through the veil. If the truth was that the old man had been a murderer, what good would come of knowing it? Adam had no intention of "confessing" the crime to the authorities, and taking his chances with whatever legal outcome the courts might eventually disgorge. He was not a person; he could not be prosecuted or sued, but Loadstone could be ordered to erase every copy of his software, and municipal authorities instructed to place his body in a hydraulic compactor beside unroadworthy cars and unskyworthy drones.

But even if he faced no risk of punishment, he doubted that Colman's relatives would be better off knowing that what they'd always imagined was a burglary gone wrong had actually been a premeditated ambush. It should not be for him to judge their best interests, of course, but the fact remained that he'd be the one making the decision, and for all the horror he felt about the act itself and the harm that had been done, his empathy for the survivors pushed him entirely in the direction of silence.

So if he did this, it would be for his benefit alone. For the relief of knowing that the old man had simply been a vain, neurotic self-mythologizer who'd tried to leave behind the director's cut of his life…or for the impetus to disown him completely, to torch his legacy in every way he could and set out on a life of his own.

ADAM ASKED SANDRA TO MEET HIM AT CAESAR'S DINER. He slid a small parcel of cash onto her seat, and she slipped a memory stick into his hand.

"What do I do with this?" he asked.

"Just because you can't see all your ports in the bathroom mirror doesn't mean they're not there." She wrote a sequence of words on a napkin and passed it to Adam; it read like "Jabberwocky" mistranscribed by someone on very bad drugs. "Four times, and that will take the side of your neck off without putting you to sleep."

"Why is that even possible?"

"You have no idea how many Easter eggs you're carrying."

"And then what?"

"Plug it in, and it will do the rest. You won't be paralyzed, you won't lose consciousness. But it will work best if you lie down in the dark and close your eyes. When you're done, just pull it out. Working the skin panel back into place might take a minute or two, but once it clicks it will be a waterproof seal again." She hesitated. "If you can't get it to click, try wiping the edges of both the panel and the aperture with a clean chamois. Please don't put machine oil on anything; it won't help."

"I'll bear that in mind."

ADAM STOOD IN THE BATHROOM AND RECITED THE incantation from the napkin, half expecting to see some leering apparition take his place in the mirror as the last syllable escaped his lips. But there was just a gentle pop as the panel on his neck flexed and came loose. He caught it before it fell to the floor and placed it on a clean square of paper towel.

It was hard to see inside the opening he'd made, and he wasn't sure he wanted to, but he found the port easily by touch alone. He walked into the bedroom, took the memory stick from the side table, then lay down and dimmed the lights. A part of him felt like an ungrateful son, trespassing on the old man's privacy, but if he'd wanted to take his secrets to the grave then he should have taken all of his other shit with them.

Adam pushed the memory stick into place.

Nothing seemed to have happened, but when he closed his eyes he saw himself kneeling at the edge of the bed in the room down the hall, weeping inconsolably, holding the bedspread to his face. Adam shuddered; it was like being back in the servers, back in the interminable side-loading dream. He followed the thread out into the darkness, for a long time finding nothing but grief, but then he turned and stumbled upon Carlos's funeral, riotous in its celebration, packed with gray-haired friends from New York and a dozen of Carlos's relatives, raucously drowning out the studio executives and sync-flashing the paparazzi.

Adam walked over to the casket and found himself standing beside a hospital bed, clasping just one of those rough, familiar hands in both of his own.

"It's all right," Carlos insisted. There wasn't a trace of fear in his eyes. "All I need is for you to stay strong."

"I'll try."

Adam backed away into the darkness and landed on set. He'd thought it was a risky indulgence to put an amateur in even this tiny part, but Carlos had sworn that he wouldn't take offense if his one and only performance ended up on the cutting room floor. He just wanted a chance to know if it was possible, one way or the other.

Detective Number Two said, "You'll need to come with us, ma'am," then took Gemma Freeman's trembling arm in his hand as he led her away.

In the editing suite, Adam addressed Cynthia bluntly. "Tell me if I'm making a fool of myself."

"You're not," she said. "He's got a real presence. He's not going to do Lear, but if he can hit his marks and learn his lines…"

Adam felt a twinge of disquiet, as if they were tempting fate by asking too much. But maybe it was apt. They'd propelled themselves into this orbit together; neither could have gotten here alone.

On the day they arrived, they'd talked a total stranger into breaking through a fence and hiking up Mount Lee with them so they could take each other's photographs beneath the Hollywood sign.

Adam could smell the sap from broken foliage on his scratched forearms.

"Remember this guy," Carlos told their accomplice proudly. "He's going to be the next big thing. They already bought his script."

"For a pilot," Adam clarified. "Only for a pilot."

He rose up over the hills, watching day turn to night, waiting for an incriminating flicker of déjà vu to prove that he'd been in this city before. But the memories that came to him were all from the movies: *L.A. Confidential, Mulholland Drive.*

He flew east, soaring over city lights and blackened deserts, alighting back in their New York apartment, hunched over his computer, pungent with sweat, trying to block out the sound of Carlos haggling with the woman who'd come to buy their air conditioner. He stared at the screen unhappily, and started removing dialogue, shifting as much as he could into stage directions instead.

She takes his bloodied fist in both hands, shocked and sickened by what he's done, but she understands—

The screen went blank. The laptop should have kept working in the blackout, but the battery had been useless for months. Adam picked up a pen and started writing on a sheet of paper: *She understands that she pushed him into it—unwittingly, but she still shares the blame.*

He stopped and crumpled the sheet into a ball. Flecks of red light streamed across his vision; he felt as if he'd caught himself trying to leap onto a moving train. But what choice did he have? There was no stopping it, no turning it back, no setting it right. He had to find a way to ride it, or it would destroy them.

Carlos called out to Adam to come and help carry the air conditioner down the stairs. Every time they stopped to rest on a darkened landing, the three of them burst out laughing.

When the woman drove away they stood on the street, waiting for a breeze to shift the humid air. Carlos placed a hand on the back of Adam's neck. "Are you going to be all right?"

"We don't need that heap of junk," Adam replied.

Carlos was silent for a while, then he said, "I just wanted to give you some peace."

WHEN HE'D TAKEN OUT THE MEMORY STICK AND closed his wound, Adam went into the old man's room and lay on his bed in the dark. The mattress beneath him felt utterly familiar, and the gray outlines of the room seemed exactly as they ought to be, as if he'd lain here a thousand times. This was the bed he'd been struggling to wake in from the start.

What they'd done, they'd done for each other. He didn't have to excuse it to acknowledge that. To turn Carlos in, to offer him up to death row, would have been unthinkable—and the fact that the law would have found the old man blameless if he'd done so only left Adam less willing to condemn him. At least he'd shown enough courage to put himself at risk if the truth ever came out.

He gazed into the shadows of the room, unable to decide if he was merely an empathetic onlooker, judging the old man with compassion—or the old man himself, repeating his own long-rehearsed defense.

How close was he to crossing the line?

Maybe he had enough, now, to write from the same dark place as the old man—and in time to outdo him, making all his fanciful ambitions come true.

But only by becoming what the old man had never wanted him to be. Only by rolling the same boulder to the giddy peak of impunity, then watching it slide down into the depths of remorse, over and over again, with no hope of ever breaking free.

11

ADAM WAITED FOR THE CREW FROM THE THRIFT STORE to come and collect the boxes in which he'd packed the old man's belongings. When they'd gone, he locked up the house, and left the key in the combination safe attached to the door.

Gina had been livid when he'd talked to Ryan directly and shamed him into taking the deal: The family could have the house, but the bulk of the old man's money would go to a hospital in San Salvador. What remained would be just enough to keep Adam viable: paying his maintenance contract, renewing his license to walk in public, and stuffing unearned stipends into the pockets of the figureheads of the shell companies whose sole reason to exist was to own him.

He strode toward the gate, wheeling a single suitcase. Away from the shelter of the old man's tomb, he'd have no identity of his own to protect him, but he'd hardly be the first undocumented person who'd tried to make it in this country.

When the old man's life had disintegrated, he'd found a way to turn the shards into stories that meant something to people like him. But Adam's life was broken in a different way, and the world would take time to catch up. Maybe in twenty years, maybe in a hundred, when enough of them had joined him in the Valley, he'd have something to say that they'd be ready to hear.

———————————————

Love Pressed in Vinyl

Devon Wong

MALIK HAD NEVER TOLD ANYONE BEFORE JOSH, BUT sometime in his acne-speckled youth, he had arrived at the conclusion that a person was a lot like a raindrop. Embarrassed at how silly it sounded when spoken out loud, Malik had gone on to elaborate something along these lines: "You fall with a few billion other raindrops in a storm; then you stop falling."

"I don't know," Josh had said. "It just seems a tad fatalistic is all. Besides, if I'm just a raindrop, and if you're just a raindrop—which still makes no sense, by the way—then what are *we*? I mean us. Together."

"Falling side by side?"

"Oh. How romantic."

As it turned out, Josh had been falling so much faster—just passing Malik on his way down, really. It had taken Malik some time to catch up.

But he was getting close now. He could feel the momentum building as he took the six-gun out of the car's glove box. It looked like a cheap film prop; only the weight assured him it was real. Malik couldn't remember where he'd gotten the thing or how he had known it would be there, just as he couldn't say for certain how he had wound up in this car, with the exhaust clicking away as it cooled in the dry autumn air. It sure wasn't his car. He didn't even own a car. There were no barcode stickers on the windows, so it likely wasn't a rental, but regardless of how he'd come by it, there he sat, and there was no doubt in his mind that someone was about to get shot.

He couldn't really say who that someone was, and after a moment's reflection, he realized that he couldn't even sort out if killing was something *he* had decided to do or if it was the *gun* that had made up its mind. His confusion only grew as he stepped out of the car to discover that he could no longer tell where he ended and the gun began, and that the feeling extended to encompass the cracked pavement beneath his feet, and the car, and the splintering telephone poles, and the boarded-up storefronts, and a nearby oak tree, and a finch perched on the branch of that oak tree where it watched a strange man standing in the street with a gun. The finch quirked its head and Malik fell out of the trance with a gasp. He had to brace himself against the side of the car so that he wouldn't keel right over.

He took a minute to breathe and realized he didn't even know where in the world he was. It could have been any small town anywhere in the English-speaking world, judging by the faded signage. His plates said California, and there were hills in the distance, but that didn't mean anything definite. There was only one other car in sight, and it was just a shell, with the engine and tires missing and the windows broken. The plates had also been jacked, so no clues there. He decided he had to be in California.

Malik had parked out front of an old theater building on the town's main street. The ticket booth and the right-hand set of doors were boarded up like everything else, but the left-hand doors opened easily.

Malik found the lobby empty, though not abandoned. He noted the clean floors, the sharp smell of ammonia, and the sun streaming in through gaps where boards had been removed strategically from the windows. His attention shifted to what must have once been a gift shop, now empty. A door to one of its back rooms swung open on squeaking hinges. Malik raised the gun.

A woman stepped into his sights, considering him and the gun without concern. She was tall, nearly six feet, her hair tied back into a decidedly utilitarian ponytail, and she wore crisply pressed, professional attire. The woman didn't speak as she crossed the lobby toward Malik, her stride quick with what seemed to be impatience.

"Stop!" he shouted, the gun trembling. "You hear me? I said, stop!"

She finally did stop, just a few feet shy of the barrel. Malik almost pulled the trigger when she reached into one of her pockets, but all she pulled out was a pad of paper and a pencil. The scratching of her writing and Malik's heavy breathing echoed in the lobby. She turned the pad toward him.

It read, "Are you here for the performance?"

Malik stepped forward, pressing the gun to her forehead. "Do I look like I'm here for a goddamn performance?"

The woman didn't flinch, and as Malik stared into her calm gray eyes, he wondered why he felt so angry; and then, inexplicably, he didn't feel angry at all. The gun sagged until it pointed to the floor, and he was the gun and the floor, just as he was the woman who wrote something else on the pad, and he was the pad and the pencil.

"You've heard the recording," he wrote with himself upon himself. "You're here for the performance."

Malik nodded slowly. "Yeah," he said. "Yeah, I'm here for the performance. I want to meet him. The performer."

"You can," the pencil wrote on the pad. "You will."

Then the woman took one of his hands in one of hers, and both hands were theirs, because there was no woman and there was no Malik—there was only a pair of bodies—and between them there was a grip, gentle and warm. One body tucked the gun into the waist of its pants as they walked to the inner theater doors. One body held a door open for the other body, and with a grateful nod to the one body, the other body stepped through.

———

SOME TIME AGO—EXACTLY HOW LONG, IT'S HARD TO say—Malik had found the slightly warped record in Josh's living room on the turntable, while Josh sat dead on the couch next to his boyfriend, a nice enough fellow whose name Malik could never remember. The boyfriend was dead, too. The two of them seemed to have just sat down and decided never to get up again. Dark stains had formed in the fabric of the couch around the 211 bodies, which were bloated almost beyond recognition. As much as Malik had once loved Josh, or perhaps because of it, he couldn't bring himself to go near the corpse. He couldn't even bear to look at it.

Malik hadn't seen or spoken to Josh in almost a year. It had taken a week-long flurry of concerned texts, emails, and all-hour calls from mutual friends to convince him to dig up the spare key that he still hadn't thrown away. He was going to hand it off to their friend L'il Lee, but for whatever reason, he wound up taking the bus straight to Josh's place instead. There, he found the front door of the house unlocked. No one had bothered to try it.

As soon as he opened the door, the smell shoved itself down Malik's throat so hard he threw up all over the front stoop. He'd never had a good gag reflex, much to his embarrassment with the occasional lover; though Josh had only ever smiled and stroked his cheek and told him to take his time. He would always be grateful to Josh for that.

After he'd cleaned himself up a bit, he entered the house and found what he found. He wasn't sure afterward why he decided to take the record from Josh's turntable, and he didn't see any need to tell the police about it.

The record's sleeve was a blank grayish thing, the same exact shade as a northern city's late-winter slush that you'd stomp off a boot. There wasn't a single letter of type on it.

Malik didn't own a turntable, so he couldn't play the thing. It just sat there on his desk where he left it, soon buried under unread magazines, outdated to-do lists, and bank statements.

———

MALIK DIDN'T ATTEND THE FUNERAL. NOT MANY OF Josh's friends did. They couldn't bring themselves to stand quietly by while Josh's so-called family pretended to have loved him. Instead, Josh's friends held their own memorial sometime after.

L'il Lee arranged the affair, and she hosted the after-party in her damp armpit of an apartment. Nearly fifty bodies managed to pack themselves in. Malik found himself stranded too far from the sangria pitchers with a chattering straight girl who claimed to have worked with Josh at the bank in his final year of life. Josh had always suffered from a weakness for fruit flies. A veritable swarm of them had been present at the ceremony. This particular midge was deliriously drunk, to the point that she'd lost all ability to discern his team colors, and all of Malik's subtle attempts to clear up matters merely had the effect of encouraging the poor creature.

Just when Malik had resigned himself to causing a scene, a man built like a Brutalist high-rise pressed up next to them. Malik didn't recognize the man, but then he didn't recognize half the faces at the party. The man wore his size like a badge of office, as if it gave him permission to do anything. The stranger winked at Malik before tossing a casual compliment in the girl's direction. She turned her attention to the newcomer, providing Malik with the opportunity to slip away.

He decided to step out for some fresh air and shoved free of the party, finding himself on an empty landing at the top of a steep, narrow set of stairs. The apartment was a walk-up from a busy downtown street. Even sober, it seemed a long and treacherous way down, and it didn't help that the single bare bulb that normally lit the staircase had burnt out at some point in the night. The only illumination came from the headlights of the passing cars strobing through the frosted safety glass door at the foot of the stairs.

Malik felt along the wall for the railing and began to descend slowly. He lowered both feet to a single step at a time, realizing that maybe he wasn't as sober as he'd thought. He was about halfway down and in the midst of lowering his lead foot when a car passed. Someone stood backlit at the bottom of the stairs, looking up at Malik. Their silhouette struck Malik as somehow familiar. Then the hallway went dark again. Malik felt himself tipping too far forward, his foot sinking lower than it should have, as if the stairs had given way to a deep chasm in the Earth, and from the bottom of the chasm he swore he could hear a distant roar that he would have thought was rushing water except for the strange crackling quality to the sound, which made Malik think more of static than water just before he caught himself on the railing with both hands and hauled himself back up. He took in a sharp breath and squinted to peer through the darkness.

"Hello?" he called out.

No reply came, and he felt like a complete idiot when another car passed, revealing that no one stood there, and there was certainly no chasm, and the only roar came from the passing car.

Safely outside, Malik laughed it off, though his hands trembled as he lit a cigarette. He blamed the cold. It was the beginning of winter, and his fingers and ears had already gone numb after only a minute of smoking and watching the gaggles of clubbers pass him by. His nerves had quieted down by the time he'd finished the first cigarette, and as he lit a second, the massive stranger from the party appeared next to him. The man asked for a light and they smoked together in silence for a while, more awkward than companionable. The stranger watched Malik as if waiting to see whether he'd speak first.

When it became clear the man wasn't going to leave him be, Malik gave in. "So are you another one of Josh's work friends? I don't think we've met."

"I work at a record store," said the man. "Joshua used to come by."

Malik shrugged as if this didn't mean anything to him.

"You know what Joshua was into?" asked the stranger. "I mean, just before he died?"

Malik shook his head.

"You ever hear of The Love Song?"

"Hell, I've heard a lot of love songs," said Malik. "You'll have to be more specific."

"Not any old love song. This is *The* Love Song." The stranger raised his eyebrows at Malik's blank stare. "Don't worry," he said. "It's hard to keep up with this kind of hipster shit. Well, anyway, it's a song."

"I guessed that."

"No need to get cute. You wanna hear this or not?"

"I'm listening."

"All right, then. You at least know the album *L'Amour*, by Lewis?"

"Nope."

"Well, Lewis—not his real name, of course—he appears in California in the early nineteen-eighties. Drives a white sports car and only ever wears white suits. He shows up at all the big Hollywood parties, and everyone who's anyone pretends to know him. Anyway, he records this one album, pays fucking Edward Colver to take pictures for the sleeve. You know, the guy who took all the pictures of the American hardcore scene back in the day? Then, just like he appeared, Lewis vanishes. Colver tries to cash his cheque and it bounces. The album, no one knows what to do with it, so they chuck the whole lot in the trash. But a copy, this one copy, somehow winds up surviving, and it makes its way to a flea market in Edmonton. Some fellow from Seattle discovers it in twenty-fourteen, realizes it's brilliant, and it becomes a surprise hit with the critics. I'm pretty sure people started calling The Love Song 'The Love Song' as a nod to that Lewis album. The Love Song is like *L'Amour* but even more of a mystery. See, they tracked down Lewis in the end. Turns out he was just some Canadian stockbroker named Randall Wulff. He took a vacation to California. No big mystery there, really.

"Long story short, a rip got leaked on the internet. Those Soho Clubbers were shitting lavender-scented bricks. There was a real witch hunt for the bootlegger, but I don't think they ever found the culprit. And rumor has it, all of the copies of the twelve-inch went missing soon after. You couldn't even find it on the black market."

The stranger chuckled behind a cloud of smoke.

"Out of the hands of the elite, into the hands of the masses," he said. "The torrents dry up pretty fast, though. No explanation. Seeders just drop off all of a sudden and you have to wait for someone to put up a new torrent. Someone always does, of course, but it's hard to know when, and it's never up for long. You want another?"

Malik looked down at his cigarette and realized with some surprise that it had burnt down to a stub already. Malik declined and the stranger continued.

"Anyway, Joshua was obsessed with the song. Said he'd listened to it a thousand times. You know how he was."

Yeah, Malik knew. Josh had always fancied himself something of a modern Gnostic, and Malik had always liked that about him. Maybe that was just because Josh—he of such discerning tastes—had chosen Malik for a time, and that scratched Malik's entirely unspecial itch to feel special.

"Joshua was convinced that there was more than just one song, though," the stranger went on. "See, rumor has it that the twelve-inches weren't the only vinyls out there. Some people say there's a full LP."

"So you're saying Josh was looking for his own *L'Amour*?"

"Oh, I think he found it."

"What makes you say that?"

"Well, one day, he comes into the store all excited. He didn't come out and say it, but I could tell. He didn't buy anything. Just came in to talk about the weather."

"The weather?"

"The metaphorical weather. The winds of sonic fashion. That was the last time I ever saw him. He found it. I know he found it. He really never told you about it?"

The stranger looked a little too expectant, as if Malik had just been playing dumb this whole time and now was the moment to come clean.

"We weren't really on speaking terms," he said.

"That's a real shame." The stranger handed him a card. "Well, if you do hear anything—you know, while the family's sorting out the will and all—you'll give me a call? I just want to know that he found it before … Well, before."

"I thought you knew he'd found it."

The man just shrugged.

Malik didn't get home until well into the morning, but when he did, he immediately booted up his computer and ran a search for "The Love Song." There were whole message boards devoted to it, plenty of folks lost in the echo chambers of obsession, but all of the links provided to the song itself were dead.

––––––––––––

MALIK CALLED IN SICK TO THE OFFICE AND PICKED UP a used turntable, receiver, and speakers the next day. He suddenly had to hear it: the soundtrack of Josh's death.

He sat on the squeaking leather sofa and listened. The record was warped and the needle didn't have the weight to resist its rise and fall, bobbing like a buoy on choppy waters. It began with the hiss and crackle and occasional pop of static, drawn out for such a long time that Malik couldn't help but fidget, wondering if the record was just that, if he'd somehow been duped. But then, gradually, the static seemed to coalesce into a muffled roar, and out of the roar emerged a faint pulse that one might call a rhythm; maybe brushes on a high hat, but maybe just a trick of the mind. Malik missed the exact moment that the piano joined, hesitant at first, but soon more forceful, though washed out and in some unrecognizable key. Finally came the voice, moaning breathy sounds that weren't words but rather seemed to dance just beyond meaning.

Malik couldn't move, couldn't even—

He startled awake on the couch, hearing only the sound of his heart battering itself against his aching chest. The record had ended. He checked the clock on his phone. Hours had passed, and it was nearly midnight. He must have dozed off and missed it, perhaps not realizing how much he'd really needed that time off work to catch up on his sleep debt.

He should try to listen again, he thought, but the idea brought on a bout of intense nausea that didn't begin to subside until he'd finally stuffed the vinyl back into its sleeve and stumbled out into the night. As he walked the familiar streets, though he no longer felt the urge to puke, he noticed that the air felt strange on his skin, as if it had begun to bleed into him, seeping not just through his pores but through the gaps between the very atoms that comprised his cells. What's more, every now and then, when his mind drifted and he lost hold of himself for a moment, he'd catch the occasional scrap of a ragged melody trying to take shape between the oscillations of his vocal chords. As soon as he became aware of it, the tune would vanish, and all he'd be left with was a frightening feeling that he was far from anyone, that the streets and buildings of the city around him had long been abandoned.

"YOU LOOK OFF TODAY," MALIK'S MANAGER TOLD HIM.

"I'm fine."

"Are you getting enough vitamin D? I used to feel like shit all the time. Like shit that's been walked on and smeared all over the sidewalk, you know? I wasn't sleeping. I was working all hours. My wife nearly divorced me. Then I started taking vitamin D, and, well, look at me now."

Malik nodded slowly. He had opted not to take another sick day, though he regretted it now. "Vitamin D did that?"

His manager nodded vigorously. "Oh, yeah. Vitamin D. Think about it." He rapped his knuckles on Malik's desk and sauntered off, leaving Malik to stare into the glare of his screen with little motivation to work. There was a backlog of design projects, and the marketing department was short-staffed, so Malik couldn't afford distraction, but all he could think about was rushing back home to try listening to that damned record again. That morning, the same idea had driven him to his knees at the toilet, but now the idea of having to wait was driving him mad.

After an hour, in which time he'd managed to open a blank document and save it somewhere on his hard drive, he decided to take a break. He dug the record store clerk's business card out of his wallet and ducked into a washroom stall. The phone had barely rung once when the man answered.

"You found it?" he asked, not even bothering to say hello.

"I have it."

"That's great, man. That's great. Bring me the album and I'll tell you what you want to know."

"I don't even know what I want to know."

There was a pause, and Malik imagined the man shrugging on the other end of the line. "Then figure it out."

Malik thought for a moment. "I want to know where it comes from."

The man laughed. "I figured you were one of those."

"One of what?"

"In my experience, there are two kinds. The first kind is happy to listen, so that's what they do. They listen. The second kind, though, they aren't so easily satisfied. You're the second kind. Bring me the album and I'll put you on the path. How's that sound?"

"I…can't."

"You can't? Sure you can."

"I can't."

The man sighed. "You will. You'll see. Give me another call when you've come to your senses."

And with that, the man hung up. Malik called him back immediately, but all he got was a busy signal. He swore and nearly dropped his cell in the toilet. He stumbled out of the washroom and back to his desk. He knew he should bring the record to the stranger, if only to be rid of it, but the idea made him feel ashamed, as if Josh would have disapproved.

He would bring the album to the stranger after, he decided. He had to listen to the entire thing first. He had to hear it out. He owed Josh that much.

SOME NIGHTS, MALIK COULD MAKE THREE, MAYBE FOUR attempts before sunrise, drifting off then waking in a daze, then spinning the record again. Other nights he could only bring himself to try once, and then the nausea would chase him outdoors. The struggle wasn't unlike a drop of rain hitting the surface of a body of water. If you watch it happen in slow motion, the drop doesn't meld instantly. There's a moment after it hits when the water's surface buckles under the force of its impact, a moment when it's still a discrete object with its own boundaries. That in itself is curious, but an even more curious thing happens next. The drop breaks in two. One half joins the water beneath while the other half bounces back up, as if it's trying to escape having to become a part of that vastness. When that half of the original drop falls, the same thing happens again. An even smaller drop bounces up and falls back down. And so it goes, on and on, and maybe if the energy of the system never runs down, this goes on forever as the drop becomes a smaller and smaller fragment of what it once was; but always trying to free itself from gravity, not out of any desire to be whole again—if separateness can even be considered the same as wholeness—but only as a mechanical reflex.

Sometimes, at the point of splitting from himself, Malik dreamed of Josh—always of Josh. The roar of static panned to the edges of his hearing as he met Josh for the first time at a liquor store checkout. Technically, they'd seen one another before and even exchanged pleasantries, but Malik liked to think of this particular conversation as their first meeting.

"ID, please," Josh would say after barely a glance at Malik.

"Ouch. Really?" Malik would catch Josh's gaze, and Josh would look bored and unimpressed.

"No plastic, no fun times. That's how it works, buddy."

"Oh, I have ID. I was just hoping you'd remember me by now. I'm here every week."

"I guess you don't make much of an impression."

"Guess not. Unless you're just asking to see my ID again because you don't want to *seem* like you remember me."

"You got me. You're all I think about every day I get to work. Will that cute guy with the mini-fro be in today? Please, God, let him stand in my queue."

"So you think I'm cute?"

At last, Josh would let slip a hint of a smile. "That'll be forty-seven twenty-five, if you have ID."

"All right, all right. Here you go."

"Uh huh. Looks like you're older than you look…Malik."

"I'll pay with debit."

"You want it bagged?"

"Please." Then, "Thanks. See you around."

"What, you're not going to ask what I'm doing after work?"

"Naw, I figure you get asked that all the time. But if I keep coming back, one day, you'll ask *me* out."

"And if I don't remember you next time?"

"You'd be lying."

"You think no one's ever tried this?"

"Not like me."

"Well, I guess we'll see then."

"Challenge accepted. Same time next week?"

"I'll be here."

Malik would lean in to read Josh's name tag, as if he had never taken note of it before. "Well, it was a pleasure to meet you, Josh. A pleasure to meet you, Josh. A pleasure to meet you, Josh. A pleasure to meet you, Josh. A pleasure to meet you, Josh. A pleasure to meet you—"

Perhaps because of the warp in the vinyl, on some plays the needle would skip and the music would catch in a brief loop. Malik would emerge from the static wash in those moments to see a familiar figure. The figure sat on a chair far back in the shadows of the room, and the voice that moaned its tortured melody seemed to come from it, not the speakers. Then the needle would catch the groove once more, and the loop would break, and upon waking the next morning, Malik would have no memory of the dark figure or the music.

ON ONE SUCH MORNING, MALIK WOKE TO THE SOUND of curtains screaming as they opened on plastic rollers, letting sunlight spill into a room that Malik didn't recognize. Malik groaned and the woman who'd opened the window frowned at him. She wore a nurse's gown. He tried to speak but could only manage an incomprehensible whisper. Even the slightest movement sent shooting pains up from his abdomen, and he noticed an IV plugged into his arm.

The nurse welcomed him back. L'il Lee was there as well, in a chair next to the bed. She clutched one of his hands in both of hers. He had nearly died of malnutrition. He hadn't shown up to work in weeks, hadn't left the apartment. They thought he'd tried to starve himself out of grief. All of their friends had been by to see him. He'd been in a coma for two weeks.

"What about the record?" he asked as soon as he could speak again.

L'il Lee shook her head in disbelief. "I'm sure it's right where you left it."

MALIK ARRIVED AT THE RECORD STORE AT THE AP-pointed time, and the man from the party ushered him down into the basement, alone. In the basement, amongst the towering stacks of dusty crates, waited a frail and somewhat sickly man in a three-piece suit. He had the look of a Wall Street shark who'd seen better days.

"Did you bring it?" he asked Malik.

"Why the hell do you think I'm carrying this ridiculous tote bag around?"

Malik handed the bag to the man, though as soon as he'd done so, he felt the urge to snatch it back. He might have tried if not for a sudden wave of dizziness. He nearly collapsed, but the man in the suit caught him by the elbow. Frail as the man seemed, Malik was in far worse shape.

Something like recognition passed between the pair in that brief moment of contact. For an instant, Malik swore that he saw himself through the man's eyes. Then the man let go of his elbow.

"I know the feeling," said the man, as if he could hear Malik's thoughts, as if he'd also been Malik in that moment. "It was scary at first. Freedom is always scary at first. But there's really nothing to be afraid of, because that's what you are. You're nothing. You aren't. You shouldn't fear yourself if there's no self to fear."

Malik bristled, though he knew the man didn't mean it as an insult. If anything, the man was all too sincere. "If I'm nothing, then who are you talking to?"

"I'm talking to myself. Except I'm nothing, too, so I guess I'm not talking to anyone. I guess I'm not talking at all. There's no me making words, understand? There's just words. Words, words, words. The only thing holding me together is a pronoun. A pronoun's a prison, you see."

"Just tell me how to find him."

The man looked Malik up and down. "For a while, when I first heard The Love Song, I thought I was like you. I thought that I had to find whoever had made this … thing. I can tell you what I found, and maybe you can follow those leads, and let's say you track down the source of all this. What will you do then?"

"I'm going to kill him," Malik said without hesitation. He glanced nervously around the basement, as if just in case someone was eavesdropping from the shadows. He dropped his voice to a whisper and repeated the same words. "I'm going to kill him."

The man nodded soberly. "There was this one time," he said, "when I was doing my taxes of all things. I had to call for help because I'd lost my pin number. I found myself lost in this maze of recorded messages. Dial one for service in English, dial two for questions about filing your taxes, dial five for information about accounts, until I finally reached a recorded message telling me the exact same thing as the online FAQ, which I'd already consulted, and it didn't tell me how to get a new pin number, I'll tell you that. I think that's when I realized there were no real people working the phones. There was no route through all the bullshit to an actual human being."

"Speak Goddamn English."

The man smiled. There was patience in that smile—a shark's patience—and he spoke as if to a child, or as if explaining to an uncomprehending animal that it was about to be slaughtered for someone's next meal. "You're dialing one. Got it. How's this? When I listen to the song, it's like looking into myself to discover that there's just a bunch of automated messages. Just like when you listen, you look inside yourself and all you see is clear, clear water. You think you're going to kill a man, but the thing you're hoping to kill, it's not a man. You're like a raindrop thinking it can stop gravity."

Malik recoiled at the man's words. He felt a strong urge to bolt. Maybe he should forget about the record, forget about it all. But then the man beckoned him closer.

"Come," he said. "I could tell you what you want to know, but why waste the time? It'll feel like when I held your elbow, but more." His lips trembled just shy of Malik's lips. Malik's lips also trembled. Breath tangled up between them, belonging to neither of them. "Kiss me and you can see the things I've seen; you can know everything I know."

When Malik emerged from the basement a few minutes later, the clerk asked if he'd found what he'd been looking for. The man was grinning when he asked, so smug Malik wanted to punch him in the face. Instead, he pretended to ignore the man on his way out.

MALIK DID EVENTUALLY FIND WHAT HE'D BEEN LOOKING for. He found it in a theater in an abandoned town, somewhere in what was probably California. Time had passed; enough time that his body felt healthy again, strong even. Except that, strong as it felt, the body wasn't sure anymore if it was or wasn't Malik.

It stood in the aisle and noted that the seats for the audience were all empty, while another male body busied itself setting up equipment on the stage. The female body walked past the male body in the aisle to speak to the male body on the stage. The male body on the stage nodded, looked at the other male body, then nodded some more. It approached the other male body and spoke.

"Hi," it said. "I'm Mikey. I'm the sound technician. We're all set up for you. I won't be able to, you know, stay for the performance, for obvious reasons, but Claire here will take good care of you. She'll be up in the recording booth. She's deaf, so you know, she's immune, so to speak. Anyway, you're in fine hands. He's in fine hands, right, Claire?"

The male body that called itself Mikey didn't wait for a reply. It clapped its hands together and left the theater in a hurry, and the male body once called Malik took the stage. It sat at the piano and touched the keys gingerly. The man called Malik had never played an instrument in his life, but Malik was almost free of himself as he watched his body from the recording booth while it straight- **223** ened its back and placed its hands on the keys with conviction this time. The body remembered what to do by doing it, because it was just like all the other bodies that had come before it to sit on this bench a hundred, a thousand, a hundred thousand times. They were the bench and the piano, and they were all the bodies playing their selves, and they played, and as the music took shape, the last vestige of whatever still remembered separateness also remembered a word—just one word—and maybe it was a name.

Josh. Yes, the body remembered Josh. The body was Josh, just as Josh was the song, and they were the air that vibrated with their own notes set in time to their own rhythms, and they were the mics that recorded those vibrations, and they were the vinyl into which the song would soon be pressed. They were everything and they were nothing. They were the river that flowed into the ocean, and they were the ocean, and they were heated and pulled apart by the sun's light, and they were the sun's light carrying themselves upward into the heavens so that one day—side by side for a second—they would fall.

———————————

There Used to Be Olive Trees

Rich Larson

VALENTIN CREPT THROUGH THE DARKNESS TOWARD THE high stone wall of the Town, heart thumping hard against his ribs. His nanoshadow, wrapped around his chest under his shirt, sensed his anxiety and gave a comforting pulse, gritty and warm against his skin. It helped a little. Valentin had never gone over the wall before. He had never left the Town before.

But anything was better than what awaited him in the morning: the *prueba*. His fourth *prueba*, to be precise. Valentin ran a finger over caked scar tissue until it contacted the gleaming black implant poking from the crest of his shaved head. It was the implant that let him control his nanoshadow—for anyone else, it would have been an inert black puddle. It was the implant that let him communicate with some of the simpler machines inside the Town.

The implant didn't make him a true prophet, though. Not until he passed the *prueba*, until the Town's machine god spoke to him. No prophet had ever failed the test more than twice. Valentin was on three and counting.

So he was leaving. Valentin breathed deep, staring up the weathered stone face of the wall that had kept him safe for all his sixteen years. He knew the world outside was a dangerous one. There were wilders and mudslides and scuttling scorpions. Valentin hated scorpions and he had a healthy fear of wilders from growing up with scarestories.

But so long as he had his nanoshadow, he could do things no barbarian could even dream of. He reached out with his implant and summoned the gleaming black motes, coaxing the shadow down his arms, gloving his hands. He steadied his nerves, looked around once more for anyone who might stop him, then took a flying leap at the wall.

Valentin was normally clumsy, but with the nanoshadow strengthening his arms like corded black muscle and coating his hands with clinging tendrils, he went up the sheer wall easily as a gecko. He felt a grin splitting his face as he topped it. Poised there on the edge with his nanoshadow balancing him, Valentin could see the empty campo stretching far and away. Rolling hills of dead gray soil, dotted ruins, crumbling road. It looked like freedom.

With only the slightest guilt thinking of Javier, who would wake up in the morning to find his apprentice gone, Valentin slid down the other side of the wall and started to walk. It wasn't long before he heard a familiar rumble of gods on the move. Valentin kept low but still felt a swirl of static inside his skull, the customary sting of his implant, as the pod of biomechanical gods thundered through the dark sky overhead.

He could sense them, but their thoughts were walled off from him, inscrutable as those of the god who controlled the Town, and a moment later their ghostly yellow lights disappeared into the distance.

Leaving him in the dark again.

"WAKE UP, LITTLE TOWNIE."

Still half in a dream, Valentin thought it was Javier's voice, waking him for the *prueba*. Then he remembered scaling the wall, walking and walking, finding a crevice to sleep in cocooned by his nanoshadow.

His nanoshadow that he could no longer feel against his skin. Valentin wrenched his eyes open, jolted by adrenaline, and found himself face to face with what could only be a monster with beetle-black eyes and an impossibly wide mouth.

Valentin jerked backward, probing desperately for his shadow, and the bag clutched in the monster's pale hand writhed.

"None of that," the monster said sourly, shaking the rucksack where Valentin's nanoshadow was trapped. "None of your Townie tricks. All right?"

It wasn't a monster. It was a boy, maybe his age, maybe a bit younger. His mouth was the normal size, but a raw-looking scar gashed upward from one corner of it, splitting his cheek. He had shaggy black hair and coarse skin and wore a black coat that was different fabrics all patched together, nothing like the identical gray garments made by the Town's autofab.

The boy turned his head, and Valentin realized the other half of his face was beautiful, fine-cut with long black lashes. He had never thought wilders might be beautiful. It didn't do much to help the cold panic numbing his limbs.

"A live shadow," the wilder said, shaking his head. His accent was thick and nasal and dropped the endings off familiar words. "Thought they were only in tales. Are you a prophet, then?"

Valentin tried to clear his head. The wilder had found him while he was sleeping and peeled his shadow off him. Normally he'd still be able to control it, make it leap out of the bag, but he'd used it all through the night to keep warm and now, still without sunshine, it didn't have enough strength to escape.

"I'm a prophet," Valentin said. "Yeah. I am. So if you don't give me my nanoshadow now, I'll have the gods blast you to ashes and a little heap of bone."

Alarm flashed over the wilder's split face for a split second, then he tipped back his head and gave a warbling laugh. "Once you do something for me, Prophet," he said, thumbing an eyelash off his cheek, "you can ask the gods to punish me however you like." He hefted the rucksack onto his shoulders and strapped it tight.

Valentin's heart pounded. Maybe he could run for it, but the cold, hard look of the wilder's eyes and the long knife in his belt made him think otherwise. And no way was he returning to the Town as not only the first prophet to fail three *pruebas* in a row, but the first to lose his nanoshadow to a wilder.

"What do you want?" he asked, trying to sound brave, bored, maybe a little mysterious. The tremor in his voice gave him dead away.

"I'm Pepe," the wilder said. "Who're you?"

"What do you want?" Valentin repeated, and this time with no quaver.

The wilder shrugged. "To do what prophets do, Prophet," he said. "Get a stubborn fucking god to care about us for a change. You help me, I won't cut your toes off." He patted his rucksack. "And maybe I'll even let you have your shadow back," he added.

———

THE CAMPO DIDN'T LOOK LIKE FREEDOM ANYMORE. Pepe set the pace and set it fast, leaving Valentin to stumble along behind him, watching for the telltale skitter of scorpions in the cracked mud. His skin ached for his nanoshadow. A few times he probed hard for it and managed to elicit a sluggish twitch from inside Pepe's rucksack, which in turn made Pepe shoot him a suspicious look from under his eyelids. But without sunshine or Valentin's bioelectricity, the inert nanoshadow was nothing but a lump of gritty black gelatin.

They walked and walked and only paused to eat—a slab of cold *tortilla* comfortingly similar to what they had in the Town—before they walked again. Valentin spent the time trying to think of a way to escape. The wilder had them heading west, toward his tribe's derelict autofab, farther and farther away from the Town. Pepe thought Valentin was going to interface with whatever god was controlling it and set it working again. As if it was that simple.

And when Pepe found out that Valentin couldn't do it, he figured the wilder would use his sawtoothed knife to cut out his implant as a keepsake, then let him bleed out in the dust. He shivered, half from the thought and half from the Andalusian winter, as they walked in silence across another barren field. The soil underfoot was pallid gray.

Another god, this one alone, hummed through the sky overhead, moving like the whales Valentin had seen clips of, the ones that used to inhabit the oceans. Pepe stopped where he was, pulled down his scarf, and craned his neck to watch its passage. The yellow lights bathing his face made the scar glisten wetly.

"Can you talk to them, then?" Pepe asked.

"When they want to talk," Valentin lied, feeling Pepe's dark eyes go to the crest of his head, where he had scar tissue of his own.

Valentin pulled up his hood and glowered. He didn't like people staring at the implant.

"Should tell them to give us a lift," Pepe said, with his macabre grin, and started to walk again. They passed the husk of an old harvester stripped for parts. "There used to be olive trees here," he said. "Far as the unaugmented eye could see, my grandfather says his grandfather said. The harvesters rolled up and down the campo all day long. Back when more things grew. Back when machines listened to anybody, not just prophets."

Valentin probed the harvester as they passed by, wishing he could swing its clawed arm and knock Pepe to the ground, grind him into the dirt, but the farm equipment was long-dead. He didn't feel so much as a flicker from his implant.

Before long the moon was rising overhead, fat and yellow, and the air was turning cold enough to bite. Valentin missed the slick warmth of his nanoshadow again, pulling his scarf snug against the chill. He could see Pepe's exposed hands turning purple in the night air, and after a few more minutes his captor pointed to a crumbling stone derelict up ahead.

"We'll hunker down in there for night," he said, tongue flicking distractedly against his scar. "Start early in the morning, get to the autofab by noon. Make sure you have enough daylight to work."

Valentin gave the ruins a dubious once-over. The sagging stone and twists of old rebar looked like something out of a scarestory. As they approached, Pepe found a torch and thumped it to life with the heel of his hand. The lance of harsh white light strobed damp ground and what was left of the walls. Following Pepe inside, Valentin felt immensely far from the gated pueblo he'd called home only a day ago.

"Wait here, Prophet," Pepe said. "I'll make a sweep for lobos."

"Funny," Valentin muttered. The spidery machines that once hunted down the survivors of satbombed Seville and the other ruined cities had been recycled decades since. Humans knew better than to make war with the gods now, and the gods were otherwise occupied.

His captor bounced off into the dark, and Valentin considered running yet again. The same counterweight held him fast: Pepe had his nanoshadow, and even if Valentin could make it back to the Town without being overtaken—not likely—he couldn't return without his shadow. At that point, he was better off bleeding out in the dust.

A beetle scuttled past Valentin's toe; he stomped it dead and when he looked up he found himself face to face with empty eye sockets and a ghoulish grin. He flinched.

"Boo," Pepe said, waggling the dog skull on its jagged spinal column. He tossed it away. "Found us a nice corner. *Venga.*"

Valentin helped Pepe clear away a few ancient syringes and typically inscrutable bits of plastic, things from the old days. There was space for the blankets and the portable *estufa* that Pepe said had enough solar charge to keep them warm for at least a couple hours. Valentin had to admit that Pepe was far better equipped to wander the campo than he was. But then, Valentin had been counting on his nanoshadow.

"Could keep the heat longer if we use my shadow," he said, watching Pepe strip down to sleep, uncovering the swathes of lean muscle Valentin had yet to develop—if he ever would. He spent his days sitting in the shade, learning his implant from Javier instead of boxing or playing in brutal games of barefooted football. Suddenly he remembered how Pepe must have touched him to take his nanoshadow in the first place. Suddenly he couldn't help but imagine what the wilder's sinewy body might feel like wrapping around his.

"Right, right," Pepe said, sliding on his stomach under the blankets, clamping his arm over the rucksack with knife held loosely in hand. "So it can smother me in my sleep and then whisk you back home."

"Something like that."

Pepe shifted, showing the unscarred side of his face, blinking soot-black lashes. "What were you doing over the wall, anyway?" the wilder asked.

"What were you doing skulking around outside it?" Valentin parried.

The wilder looked at him full-on, exposing his scar. "Was looking for a way to set things right," he said. His black eyes bored hard into Valentin's, then he blinked, and what might have been a smirk tugged at the scarred side of his mouth. "Your ears are red."

"I'm getting fucking frostbite," Valentin said.

"Soft little Townie." Pepe squinted at him. "Did it hurt when they put the godchip in you?"

Valentin's hand went reflexively to his implant. The truth was that he barely remembered his seventh birthday, the scraping caul and needle, the incense-smothered fire. But he wanted an answer Pepe would respect. "They give you something to chew," he said. "But yeah. It hurt." He paused. "It's only successful half the time, you know. There can be bad infection, or they can bore too deep. The two tries before me, one ended up dead, the other one damaged."

Pepe nodded, spinning his knife idly in one hand, not as impressed as Valentin had hoped.

"How about that?" Valentin dragged a finger along the curve of his mouth. "Did that hurt?" Pepe clenched the knife hard and Valentin froze, realizing with a sick drop in his stomach that he'd overstepped, that the wilder was about to stab him in a fit of anger.

Then Pepe's ruined smile returned and he pressed the gleaming flat of his blade against it. "He gave me something to chew."

Valentin turned away to hide his shudder. Everything about Pepe unbalanced him. Even as he'd calculated escapes all day, he also catalogued the looks held too long, the brief moments when the space between them seemed to simmer, trying to decide if it was his imagination or not. Deciding what Pepe would do if he knew. Prophets were meant to be different and the Town didn't care one way or another. But wilders were another breed entirely. Superstitious, hard. Dangerous.

As soon as Pepe was asleep or faking it well, Valentin tugged off as quietly as he could to an anonymous body, trying not to put deep, dark eyes on the face. He didn't think he would be able to sleep tonight.

———————————

IN THE MORNING, WHEN VALENTIN CRAWLED OUT OF his blankets massaging night-numbed fingers, he could smell oil and electricity in the air. Pepe was pulling food out of the rucksack. He handed Valentin a piece of *tortilla* smaller than yesterday's.

"The gods were working in the night," he said, tapping his nostril.

"They do that."

"You ever ask them why?"

"It's colder at night," Valentin said, cobbling an answer from half-remembered lessons. "Machines think faster in the cold." It was flimsy, even to his own ears, but Pepe nodded solemnly and went back to chewing with the unscarred side of his mouth.

When they stepped outside, a thick winter fog prickled Valentin's eyes. Pepe took a moment to get his bearings then set off into it, not even bothering to check his captive was following. Valentin was, of course. The nanoshadow puddled in the bottom of Pepe's rucksack was effective as any tether.

The gradient sloped upward, and gradually the dead soil turned to slippery shale under their feet. Pepe picked his way among the rocks as nimble as a lizard while Valentin labored behind, trying to hide his heavy breathing. The rucksack always bobbed just ahead of him, mockingly, he thought. With his shadow, he could scale a slope like this as easily as he'd slithered up and over the outer wall of the Town.

"Who'll they send to look for you?" Pepe asked over his shoulder. "Will they have a shadow, too?"

Valentin thought of Javier setting out to find him, easing his creaking bones through the Town's gate. No. Javier was sitting in his quickfabbed *piso* at the edge of housing, sipping anise and staring at the blacked window, murmuring to the gods in the dark. As far as he was concerned, whether Valentin came back or not was up to them.

"Nobody," he admitted. "Nobody goes over the wall."

"Your family, though."

Valentin stiffened instinctively at the word, at the reminder of his mother, who caught the last kick of the bleeding virus when he was six, and of the fact no father ever claimed him.

"Don't have one," Valentin said. "That's why I'm a prophet."

"Ah. You came out an autofab full-formed." Pepe gave another solemn nod. "That's why your skin is all…" His hand looped in the air for the missing word.

"All what?" Valentin asked, trying not to sound too curious.

"Smooth." Pepe shrugged. "I was joking," he said. "You didn't come out an autofab."

"No," Valentin said. "I didn't."

By the time they reached the crest, the sun was rising red and smeary like someone had rubbed their thumb across it. Pepe offered a hand for the last lift, and Valentin was tempted but struggled up without it. Pepe didn't appear to notice the slight. He was peering down the other side with an unreadable expression. Valentin clambered up beside him, heart still thudding hard, and wiped the grime of the climb off on his knees. He took a deep breath and smelled overturned earth, and the machine fumes again, sooty and sharp.

"Look," Pepe said.

Valentin looked. Down below, the barren field was no longer empty. Thrusting out from the mist, glistening the biomechanical black of godwork, were rows and rows of man-high carved shapes.

"Heads." Pepe turned to Valentin with an almost pleading look. "A field of giant fucking heads. Why?"

"I don't know," Valentin said. "They might not, either. The gods don't think how we do."

"Straight through is still quickest to the autofab," Pepe said, more to himself, tongue flicking at his scar. "Come on, Prophet. Maybe they'll talk to you."

Valentin imagined the mouths opening wide to swallow him and shuddered. But then he saw the rucksack strap had loosened on Pepe's shoulder, saw how the wilder's eyes were glued to the sculptures. When Pepe started down the slope, Valentin followed.

The fog thickened again as they descended, and at the bottom they found the field had been smoothed and leveled, with uncanny precision, into a flat, gray plane veined by darker streaks of clay. It looked unreal, and Valentin was almost surprised Pepe's boots left prints. Pale vapor roiled back and forth in waves as they approached the heads.

They were taller than they'd looked from above, each at least twice Valentin's height, looming out of the fog. Their enormous faces were cut symmetrical but the features themselves were crude, disproportionate, and with the mist creeping up past their wide mouths they looked like drowning men. Valentin probed. He felt a faint drone of machinery at work, but no god was inside. He couldn't begin to guess the heads' purpose.

"Is there a god here?" Pepe asked.

Valentin turned and realized the wilder had rooted to the spot, his dark eyes roving from one head to the next. "No," he said. "They're just sculptures. You coming, or what?"

Pepe shook himself, then stalked past to lead the way. Silence swallowed up their footsteps as they walked the row. The heads were coated in a glistening, raw black material that sometimes looked as if it was moving—the same material that the autofab in the center of the Town used to make tools and cables and brick molds. As always, Valentin wondered if it was somehow alive.

The strap on Pepe's shoulder slid a bit.

"Tell me about your autofab," Valentin said. "If I'm going to get it running, I need to know details. How old it is. Last it was used. All that."

Pepe shot a shrewd look backward. "Old," he said. "And it stopped working back when my grandfather was young. A few years after our last prophet died. The gods drove him insane, so he pushed his forehead into a spinning drill to get them out."

"He wasn't calibrating enough," Valentin said, to hide the sudden lurch in his stomach. "He was careless."

Pepe shrugged. The strap slipped lower.

"And the implant?" Valentin asked. "The godchip? Nobody else had the surgery?"

"*Hombre.*" Pepe stopped walking and stared at him with something like revulsion. "It was buried with the rest of him. Our band, we respect the dead."

Valentin was equally perturbed. "You have any idea how valuable that implant was?" he demanded. "No autofab will make them anymore. Ever." He frowned. "I mean, if he'd already shattered his skull on a drill bit, how hard would it have been to—"

"I thought everyone in the Town had a godchip," Pepe cut across, starting to walk again. "In the stories you've all got a godchip."

"No. We only have two." Valentin wished he hadn't said it. He felt the crushing weight again, the knowledge that had driven him over the wall. Two godchips in all of the Town—one in Javier's graying head, and one in his own, and if he couldn't learn to interface they would be better off prying it out of his skull and trying again with someone else.

"Guess I'm lucky I found you, Prophet." Pepe flashed his warped grin. "The gods must have wanted—" He froze, head cocked. Valentin stopped, watching the sway of the rucksack. "D'you hear that?" Pepe asked.

Valentin pretended to listen, but he was coiling his legs, running his tongue around his dry mouth. As Pepe lifted the strap of the rucksack to readjust it, still peering into the mist, Valentin lunged. He ripped the bag free and hurtled past. Down the row, a dead sprint, clutching the rucksack to his chest and fumbling for the clasp as he gasped hot air. His pulse foamed in his ears. He could feel Pepe behind him, not bothering to curse or shout, just running him down like a hunting dog. Valentin's cold, stiff fingers bounced off the clasp.

He hooked left at the next head, veering into the fog. He had a grip on the clasp now, thought he could feel his nanoshadow writhing under the fabric. He tore the rucksack open and plunged his hand inside at the very instant Pepe slammed him to the damp ground. Valentin scrabbled desperately for the slippery grit of his shadow, and for the barest slice of a second his fingers brushed against it with an electric tingle.

Then Pepe seized his wrist and pried his hand slowly, almost tenderly, out of the rucksack. Valentin probed hard, trying to make the nanoshadow leap, make it stream up his arm and turn into corded black muscle, make it wrap around the wilder's neck like a noose. There was nothing but a weak ripple in response.

Pepe's dead weight pressed him into the earth, and it was not as comfortable as he'd fantasized it. Valentin could feel his bony knee, his chest, his hot breath at the nape of his neck. He wanted to sink into the mud. His best chance, maybe the only one he would get, gone and wasted.

Pepe refastened the clasp of his rucksack and stood up. "Fucking Townies," he said, breathing harder from the chase than Valentin would have expected. "I was getting to like you, Prophet."

Valentin didn't reply. He rolled over onto his back, getting his lungs back, then slowly sat up. The wilder was sitting cross-legged in front of the head closest to him, tightening the straps of the rucksack across his shoulders. His dark eyes looked almost hurt.

"My brother told me you Townies were snakes," Pepe said. "Said I was going to give you it back, didn't I? Said after you get the autofab working." He spat a glob of saliva. "I should fucking stick you for that."

"Sorry," Valentin said dully. In the moment, he felt like he already had a knife in the gut and one more wouldn't make much difference. They sat across from each other in silence, tendrils of fog creeping around their waists. Scowling, the wilder's scar seemed to distort his whole face, making his mouth one wide gash. Almost as ugly as the sculpture behind him.

Valentin's eyes trailed up the crude face. This head was different. There was a sort of topknot glinting at the peak of its carved skull.

"Did you not hear it, then?" Pepe said.

"Hear what?" Valentin said. His implant gave him a sharp prick of random static. He needed to calibrate again soon.

Then a gnashing metal meteor dropped from the top of the sculpture onto Pepe's back. Valentin hollered, scrambling backward, heaving to his feet. Pepe and the machine creature writhed, rolled, tangling flesh limbs with jet-black running blades. Valentin was frozen. The furious buzz in his implant and every chemical in his body screamed for him to run.

But Pepe still had his shadow. Valentin watched as the wilder flung himself back against the base of the head, smashing the clinging creature free. Its segmented body whirred in midair and it landed on its feet like a cat. Quadrupedal, skeletal black carbon, and where the head might have been, a pair of jagged rotary saws now hummed to life. Scarestories bounced through Valentin's head and he knew the lobos had not all been recycled, not a chance.

Pepe had his knife out now, dropped to a crouch, wrapping his offhand in his scarf. Valentin didn't see what either could do against the lobo's spinning maw. It hurtled at Pepe again; the wilder spun away, slashing low in the same motion. His knife screeched against the lobo's underside to no visible effect. The buzz in Valentin's implant was skull-splitting. He could feel the crude machine mind roaring for function completion, for disable, maim, refuel.

This was not a god. This was an animal.

As Pepe and the lobo broke and collided again, Valentin clenched his teeth and probed inside the buzzing hive. In midstride, the lobo jerked to a stop, shivering in place. Valentin felt a rush of elation. The machine mind was still yammering objectives, but Valentin had it clamped down, iced over. Pepe didn't take his eyes off the lobo, only switching his grip on the knife and circling closer.

"Is that you done that, Prophet?" he panted.

"Yeah," Valentin said, tamping down a grin. "Yeah. So give me my shadow back before I set it on you again."

Pepe was silent for a long moment, maybe trying to suss out if Valentin was bluffing, then he barked an anguished sort of laugh. "All right, Prophet," he said. "Fuck you. But all right." Still watching the lobo, he slid the rucksack off his back and undid the clasp. Valentin's heart laddered up his ribs when he saw the nanoshadow rustle within. He reached out a hand, already imagining the feel of it on his skin.

The buzz in his implant changed pitch. Distracted, Valentin probed. His mouth went dry. The machine mind was trying to squeeze him out. He dug in hard, desperate, but a wave of defenseware carried him away and he felt himself lose his hold all at once. The lobo's formless head swiveled to face him, ignoring Pepe and his knife. The saws began to spin.

Valentin didn't even have time to shout before the lobo pounced, brushing past Pepe and slamming him to the ground. He kicked frantically, but the lobo's black running blades had his arms pinned, and now the grinding, shrieking maw was a millimeter off his face and—

Pepe's scarfed hand drove the knife between the saws. Sparks spat wild; one sizzled through Valentin's shirt. The lobo seized, shuddered, and Pepe dragged Valentin from underneath. He hauled to his feet and spun around just as Pepe's knife shot out of the lobo's mouth and pinged against the side of the sculpture. A ripple clacked through the creature's joints.

"I need my shadow," Valentin panted. "I can kill it with my shadow."

"Do it, then." Pepe shoved the open rucksack into Valentin's chest. As the lobo turned on them again, Valentin plunged both hands into the cold, gritty gelatin. His nanoshadow rippled in response to his touch, his biorhythm, the signal of his implant. The lobo darted forward. The nanoshadow was weak from days without sun, days without electricity. Valentin gripped it hard. As the lobo sprang, the nanoshadow shot away from his hands in a long plume of pitch and met it in the air, streaming into every crack in its carapace with a horrible shredding noise.

The lobo dropped to the dirt as the nanoshadow writhed through its body, leaving it a collapsed husk hemorrhaging sparks. Valentin finally exhaled. Pepe's eyes were wide as the nanoshadow pooled under the lobo's corpse, regaining its shape, then slithered back to its owner.

Valentin's shadow webbed its way up his knee, slipping underneath his shirt to spread cool and gritty and pulsating across his thumping chest. Tendrils wove between his fingers, licked up his neck, wicked sweat from around his nostrils and lips. Valentin closed his eyes as his shadow warmed to skin temperature. With his eyes closed, with his shadow pressing gently against him, he could almost be back home.

"So that's it, then. That's your shadow back."

Valentin opened his eyes. Pepe was unwrapping the scarf from around his left hand. The cloth was stained a dark wine-red, and when it peeled away from his skin he didn't wince but his tongue flicked fast against his scar. The lobo's saw had shorn through the scarf and left gouges on his wrist, his palm. Blood was welling steadily and dripping to the ground.

"Guess you leave now."

Valentin considered it. With his nanoshadow, he could make good time back to the Town with no fear of scorpions or lobos or wilders. Then he would give some catshit story about the gods sending him out into the campo to receive a vision, which Javier would not believe. Then, the *prueba*. Again.

"Yeah," Valentin said. "I go back to the Town with my shadow. You bleed to death in a field of giant heads. I won, you lost." He directed his shadow down his arm in a soft, black ribbon that waved in the space between them. "Here. Let me staunch it."

Pepe looked wary, but also pale and slightly dizzy. He held out his injured hand and watched as the nanoshadow shrouded over his skin, sealing to the wounds. He blinked at the sensation. "How many of these shadow things have you got in the Town?"

"A few," Valentin said. "But you need an implant to work them."

"That's too bad. Wouldn't mind one for the next lobo."

Valentin glanced over at the corpse of the machine and shivered. It looked smaller now, and he could see it was malformed, slightly warped, with one unfinished limb shorter than the others. "I thought they were all gone," he said. "That's what I was taught. That they were all gone. Extinct like the actual animals."

"They were gone for a long time," Pepe said. "Last winter they started to come back." He gave Valentin a considering look. "You don't actually know anything, do you, Prophet? You've never left the Town before."

Valentin bit back his urge to argue. The wilder was right. He'd been right about most things. "So what do you usually do?" he asked instead. "When there's a lobo." He pulled his shadow back up his arm.

Pepe inspected his hand. "Usually you die."

The smaller cuts were beginning to scab shut, but Valentin guessed that the gash along the wilder's wrist would need to be stitched or glued. And disinfected, preferably soon. He still remembered watching the Town's surgeon lop off a woman's two gangrenous fingers. He cast a glance toward the rucksack.

"Have you got anything in there to clean the cut?" he asked.

"Only water," Pepe said. He paused. "The autofab'll make medicine kits. Food for you, too. For your way back."

"Why are you so set on this autofab?" Valentin demanded at last. "If it's so important to your tribe, why's it only you taking me there? And what the hell was your plan if you hadn't found me in the gully? Were you going to knock on the Town gate and ask to borrow a godchip, or what?"

Pepe's face darkened. "What was your plan, heading over the wall?"

Valentin's mouth opened. Closed. "To get away," he finally said. "Just away."

"Yeah," Pepe said. He stumped to his rucksack and pulled it up onto his shoulders, gingerly for his left hand. "I want to help my family," Pepe said. "I want to help the band. If you can't contribute one way, you've got to find another. The autofab would help us. Would make us strong again."

Valentin looked down at the inky black edge of the nanoshadow pressed to his collarbone. He thought of Pepe journeying back to his tribe alone, dragging the same weight Valentin knew so well. Getting muck in his cuts, dying of fever, maybe even running into another lobo.

"What's your name, Prophet?" Pepe asked.

Valentin hesitated. "Valentin."

The wilder's eyes were shiny and desperate. "I can't go back with nothing. Will you help me, Valentin?"

The autofab had to be nearby now. Valentin could try. It would be like a fourth *prueba*, only with a different god, and with nobody watching but Pepe.

"All right," Valentin said. "Fuck you, but all right. To the autofab."

THE AUTOFAB WAS ABOUT HALF THE SIZE OF THE TOWN'S, a featureless black mushroom cap that Valentin knew extended far below the ground. When they stopped in front of it, he felt a familiar twinge of fear, taken right back to his very first *prueba*, his sixteenth birthday. There'd been a procession through the Town's narrow streets, men carrying the plastic mannequins of the saints, women throwing red sand at his feet. He'd sat in front of the hulking black autofab, with Javier behind him and everyone watching, and the god inside had refused to speak to him.

"They used to keep everything clean," Pepe said as they passed the pockmarks of old fire pits and stepped over shattered tent poles. "They used to lay wreaths. But it's been a long time. Nobody comes here anymore."

Valentin probed hard. He could hear a faint, rustling whisper in his implant. The god was communicating, maybe with the pod that had passed over them in the night. Valentin sat, folding his legs, and his nanoshadow slid underneath him to cushion his tailbone. He sucked down a deep breath.

"Should I cant?" Pepe asked. "Don't know any prophet cants. But I could do the one for snakebite."

"Just don't talk," Valentin said, fixing his eyes on the slick surface of the autofab. He could see his own warped reflection in its black mirror. He took another deep breath, reminding himself that nobody was watching, only a wilder, only a stupid wilder with long, lean arms and deep, dark eyes and a careless laugh. Valentin closed his own eyes and willed the whisper in his implant louder. Through the electric cascade of the god's thoughts, Valentin could see, or feel, a fresh stimulus-response that could only be their presence. The autofab knew they were there.

Valentin reached, like he had for the lobo, but this time softly. And he thought: *Help us.* For the briefest instant, he felt the god turn sluggishly toward his probe, felt an interface blink open like a sleeper's eye. Valentin's heart leapt. Then it was gone, walled off behind impenetrable code, and the whisper in his implant receded. He'd failed his fourth. His stomach churned sick with it. Valentin opened his eyes.

Pepe was crouched down in his peripheral, tongue working against his scar. "What did you tell it?" he murmured. "What did it say?"

"It said nothing." Valentin knuckled a bit of sand away from his eye. "Like always."

Pepe's face fell. He stared at the autofab wall with an expression of fury, and for a moment Valentin thought he might try to put his uninjured fist through it. Then his eyes narrowed. "What do you mean, like always?"

"I mean I've never talked to a god," Valentin said. He wasn't scared of Pepe's knife anymore, not with his shadow thrumming against his skin. All he felt was dry and tired.

"The lobo," Pepe said. "You talked to the lobo. You made it stop."

"For five fucking seconds, yeah," Valentin admitted. "But that was a crude mind. Not a god." He tapped his implant. "When you turn sixteen, to be a prophet, you have to take a test. You have to talk to the Town's god, ask it to do some sign. Pulse the electric lights, or print up a plastic bird, or something stupid like that." He swallowed. "The god doesn't speak back to me. I've failed it three times already."

"Three times?" Pepe asked, disbelieving.

"Yeah. And if you count this—"

"Three times is nothing," Pepe said. "Nothing. Listen. I used to footrace my older brother. I wanted so badly to beat him I'd wake up an hour before the sun, go out to the field. Scratch lines in the dirt and run, to train my muscles. Every morning, even if I was sick or if I was up all the night on a scavenging party." His nostrils flared. "It took two years of that before I won. Took a hundred races."

"Running a footrace is nothing like interfacing with a god. If they don't speak to me, there's nothing I can do to change—"

"You said your tribe's got only two godchips," Pepe interjected. "Two in the whole Town. So they must have picked you for a reason."

"Not the one you think."

Pepe leaned close and put his good hand on Valentin's shoulder. "A hundred races, remember?"

Valentin shut his eyes again. He breathed in through his mouth, out through his nose. His nanoshadow pulsed comfortably against his chest, and Pepe's hand resting on his shoulder was comfortable in its own way. Valentin reached out for the autofab. The whisper in his implant rose. A minute passed. Two minutes. More. Valentin's hands were clenched, nails digging crescents in his palms. A blank eternity later, he opened his eyes. He wanted to lie, to keep Pepe's fingers cupped against him.

"Nothing," he admitted.

Pepe's hand squeezed his shoulder, but didn't leave it.

———————

VALENTIN TRIED OFF AND ON AGAIN AS DUSK DROPPED over the campo, with no success. The first probe had at least elicited the autofab's attention, but now he was blocked out entirely. They ate the last of the *tortilla* and a handful of dry dates. Pepe used a bit of water to wash his cuts. He'd stopped bleeding but his face was still drawn and pale. Eventually they camped down at the base of the autofab, Pepe wrapped in a blanket and Valentin using his nanoshadow like a cocoon, exposing only his face. Neither of them had spoken for hours.

As Pepe shifted, finding elevation for his injured hand, Valentin couldn't help but eyetrace the slant of his shoulder blades, his hip, imagining the body underneath the blanket. He felt himself getting hard, and his nanoshadow moved to slide a tendril around his cock. Valentin chewed his lip. Then Pepe gave a ragged groan, and Valentin felt a wave of shame. He yanked his nanoshadow away from his groin and pretended to be asleep.

"You awake still, Prophet?"

Valentin hesitated. "Yeah. I am."

A moment later, Pepe shuffled over, dragging his blanket with him. The nanoshadow stretched membranous to accommodate the both of them, at the same time wrapping Pepe's injured hand. The wilder smelled like sweat and copper. When their arms brushed together, Valentin's heart beat hard. When Pepe touched the back of his head, just below his implant, his breath caught.

"Do you hear them all the time, then?" Pepe whispered.

"Only when they're close," Valentin said, trying to breathe evenly.

Pepe's finger traced the metal edge of the implant. "You can hear them, but they can't hear you."

"Can't. Won't." Valentin squirmed, freeing one arm. "Either." He reached out, hesitantly, heart hammering, and touched Pepe's face.

The wilder stiffened, turning away. His anxious eyes raked across the sky, as if watching gods might be drifting overhead. Then he relaxed and turned back into him with the smirk Valentin recognized from the night before. "Fucking Townies," he said, fitting his good hand around the edge of Valentin's hip.

The kiss was brief and badly angled and went through Valentin like voltage, making his nanoshadow thump against him. When it broke, Valentin leaned forward, unsleeving a grin in the dark, not caring about the autofab or the *prueba* or anything else, only feeling Pepe's lips on his again. He ran his thumb along the wilder's jaw and found the rippled scar tissue.

"Who cut your mouth?" he asked.

A long pause. Valentin remembered when he'd asked in the ruins, wondered again if he had gone too far, but Pepe left his hand where it was. "My brother," he said.

"Right. Because you beat him at the footrace."

Pepe pulled back, staring at him. "No. It was for this." He struggled up onto his elbow, careful with his injured hand. "He caught me with someone. Again. This time he was shitface drunk and angry and he held me down and cut me. Said it was to keep the *maricones* away."

Valentin felt his grin fall off. "I didn't know it was like that. With wilders."

"I'm seventeen now," Pepe said dully. "I have to start fucking who they tell me. I've got good blood. Can't waste it. I have to help make the band strong again." His voice splintered. "I thought if I do something big. Something like this. I thought if I give them the autofab back, maybe it'll be enough." He kneaded his eyes hard. "And then he'll love me again."

Valentin swallowed. "Maybe I'm lucky," he said. "Not having family. That's the real reason they pick you for a prophet. Nobody would have missed me if the surgery went bad. It's not because I was anything special."

Pepe looked at him for a stretched moment. "You are, though. I think." He blinked and turned over.

Valentin stared at the back of his dark head, wishing he could window inside of it and see where he'd been placed. He thought a thousand thoughts as Pepe's breathing slowly steadied. He pictured the pair of them setting off on their own, not back to the Town and not back to Pepe's band and his psychopath brother. Maybe to the wilderness up north in Old France, maybe further south to where the gods were busy reshaping the coastline.

He was half-submerged in a dream when his implant gave him a short, sharp shock. His eyes flicked open. For a moment, Valentin thought he was still dreaming because the glossy black hide of the autofab was now veined with soft orange status lights.

His first instinct was to wake Pepe, but as he sat up the autofab's orange lights wriggled together to form an image. Valentin rubbed his eyes. The autofab had drawn a pixelated face, and as he watched, a pixelated finger rose to its lips. The gesture was unmistakable. Valentin looked down at the sleeping wilder, then back up to the image. The orange ghost stared at him, then slipped around the side of the autofab.

Valentin got quietly to his feet. His nanoshadow came with him, slithering up his body. Pepe shivered. Valentin debated leaving the wilder his shadow, peeling at it half-heartedly with his fingernails. In the end he pulled the dirty blanket overtop of him instead. Sweat was beading along Pepe's hairline. Valentin bit his lip, remembering the fever prediction.

The nanoshadow swathed his limbs as he made his way around to the back of the autofab. The orange ghost had become an orange doorway, pulsing gently in the dark. Valentin stared at it. His implant was no longer humming. The night was dead silent, cold, a sky of tarry black cloud. Then a sibilant whisper entered his head with a feeling like a thousand insects scraping against each other. *Enter.*

Valentin realized, dimly, that he had been waiting sixteen years for the invitation. When the skin of the autofab peeled back, he didn't hesitate. He stepped inside and the autofab sealed shut behind him. He was in absolute dark. A moment passed. Valentin felt a claustrophobic terror stab through him, imagined himself entombed by a malfunct god.

White lights bloomed to life, and he was suddenly a giant, sunk to his ankles in a map of the peninsula. He saw the bone-dry furrow of the Guadalquivir, recognized the mountains around the ruins of Granada, and knew, instantly, that he was seeing what the gods saw when they drifted through the sky in their flying bodies. He found the tiny walled pueblo south of Seville's burnt carcass and felt an ache in his throat.

You are not a scavenger. You are the [organic relay] displaced from [Installation 17].

The god's voice scraped down his neck. The Town swelled on the map. "Yeah," Valentin said. "Yes. That's where I'm from."

The map jumped, and Valentin saw the field of towering heads forming a perfect square.

[Installation 17's patron] requested an early dispatch in [Gestation Field 2944] in order to eliminate the scavenger and ensure your security. Why did you dismantle the [organic disposal module] before it could attain function completion?

Valentin's head was a whirlwind. This was not the voice he'd always imagined. "You watched that?" he demanded. "You've been watching us?"

The map plunged toward the ground, zooming in on the collapsed lobo. Valentin's stomach sloshed with the illusion of falling.

Why did you dismantle the [organic disposal module] before it could attain function completion?

"It attacked me. Both of us." Valentin shook himself. "You mean the Town's god sent that thing?"

You will go back to [Installation 17] now. Supplies have been manufactured.

The map disappeared and Valentin found himself in a small, dark alcove. Facing him, on an illuminated plinth, he saw a slick black carrycase, and beside it a blocky shape he recognized as twin to the printed handgun Javier kept in his house.

If the scavenger attempts to obstruct you, use the weapon.

Valentin stared down at it. "I don't need help," he said shakily. "He does. His tribe, his band or whatever, they need this autofab functional again. Why did it shut down?"

Autofab access was rescinded from all scavengers as the [first act of culling]. [Installation 17] contains sufficient genetic diversity if breeding programs are followed. A larger sample size is unnecessary. Scavengers are extraneous. The [Gestation Fields] are preparing for the [second act of culling].

Valentin thought back to the field, to the rows and rows of heads, and remembered the faint buzz from inside each one. With a sick drop in his stomach, he realized that they were not sculptures. They were wombs. He pictured the carved mouths winching slowly open, the spidery shadows unfolding from inside.

"You're sending more of those things after them?" he demanded. "For what? Stripping parts?"

[Installation 17] will not be affected. You will go back now, before the [second act of culling] begins.

Valentin picked up the case. His nanoshadow clung to it, sticking it to his back like a rucksack. Then he picked up the weapon. "Why didn't the god speak to me in the Town?" he asked shakily. "It speaks to Javier."

[Installation 17's patron] believes it is important that [organic relays] understand the dangers outside its walls. You have completed a [pilgrimage]. Now you understand the [severe mercy of the gods]. Now you will go back.

Behind Valentin, the door peeled open again. Winter air licked his back with ice. "I'll do whatever the fuck I want," he said, sticking the weapon to his hip.

Valentin walked back out into the world. The autofab's status lights had winked off again, but overhead he could make out a shard of moon. Enough light to travel by, if only just. He could start his trek back to the Town. He would have the hard evidence that he'd spoken to a god, and maybe by the time Javier died the god in the Town's autofab would listen to him, too. He could let the wilders find out about the second act of culling when lobos dragged them from their tents and chopped them to pieces.

Valentin went to where Pepe was sleeping, rummaging the medicine kit out of his new case. The wilder was on his side, showing only the perfect side of his face, the faultless bones and dark lashes.

Valentin touched his chin, turning his head. The jagged smile re-appeared and Pepe's eyes flicked open.

"I got disinfectant for your hand," Valentin said.

"From the autofab? The god spoke to you?" His voice was hoarse with sleep.

"I'm a prophet, aren't I?" Valentin shook the tube of disinfectant spray. "This is going to sting a bit."

Valentin helped him wrap his hand and sling it up as he told him, in fragments, about the conversation with the god in the autofab. The whisper in his implant grew louder and louder, and by the time they stole away into the night, heading north to the band's last campsite to give them the warning, it was a chorus of furious voices.

Valentin had his own concerns.

The Secret of Flight

A.C. Wise

***The Secret of Flight* Written by Owen Covington, Directed by Raymond Barrow—Prologue**

ACT I

Scene I

SETTING: The stage is bare except for backdrop screen showing the distant manor house.

The lights should start at 1/8 and rising to 3/4 luminance as the scene progresses.

AT RISE: The corpse of a man lies CENTER STAGE. PO-LICEMAN enters STAGE RIGHT, led by a YOUNG BOY carrying garden shears. The boy's cheek is smeared with dirt. The boy points with the shears and tugs the policeman's hand. POLICE-MAN crosses to CENTER STAGE and kneels beside the corpse. BOY exits STAGE RIGHT.

POLICEMAN puts his ear to the dead man's chest to listen for breath or a pulse. His expression grows puzzled. POLICE-MAN straightens and unbuttons the dead man's shirt. He reaches into the corpse's chest cavity and withdraws his hands, holding a starling (Director's note: use C's, already trained). POLICEMAN holds starling out toward audience, as though asking for help.

Starling appears dead, but after a moment stirs and takes flight, passing over the audience before vanishing. (Director's note: C assures me this is possible. C concealed somewhere to collect the bird?). POLICEMAN startles and falls back. (BLACKOUT)

LEADING LADY VANISHES!
Herald Star—October 21, 1955
Betsy Trimingham, Arts & Culture

LAST NIGHT'S OPENING OF *THE SECRET OF FLIGHT* AT The Victory Theater will surely go down as one of the most memorable and most bizarre in history. Not for the play itself, but for the dramatic disappearance of leading lady Clara Hill during the play's final scene.

As regular readers of this column know, *The Secret of Flight* was already fraught with rumor before the curtain ever rose. Until last night, virtually nothing was known of *The Secret of Flight* save the title, the name of its director, Raymond Barrow, and of course, the name of its playwright, Owen Covington.

Raymond Barrow kept the play shrouded in mystery, refusing to release the names of the cast, their roles, or a hint of the story. He did not even allow the play to run in previews for the press. Speculation ran rampant. Was it a clever tactic to build interest, or was it a simple lack of confidence after the critical and financial failure of Barrow's last two plays?

Whatever Barrow's reasoning, it is now inconsequential. All that is on anyone's lips is the indisputable fact that at the culmination of the play, before the eyes of 743 witnesses, myself included, Clara Hill vanished into thin air.

For those not in attendance, allow me to set the scene. Clara Hill, in the role of Vivian Westwood, was alone on stage. The painted screen behind Hill was lit faintly, so as to suggest a window just before dawn. As the light rose slowly behind the false glass, Hill turned to face the audience. It appeared as though she might deliver a final soliloquy, but instead, she slowly raised her arms. As her arms neared their full extension above her head, she collapsed, folding in upon herself and disappearing.

Her heavy beaded dress was left on the stage. In her place, a column of birds—starlings, I believe—boiled upward. Their numbers seemed endless. They spread across the theater's painted ceiling, then all at once, they pulled together into a tight, black ribbon twisting over the heads of the theater patrons. You can well imagine the chaos that ensued. Women lifted their purses to protect their heads, men ineffectually swatted at the birds with their theater programs. There were screams. Then there was silence. The birds were gone. Vanished like Clara Hill.

Was it all a grand trick, a part of the show? The stage lights snapped off, the curtain fell abruptly, and we were ushered out of the theater, still dazed by what we had seen.

As of the writing of this column, neither Barrow nor any other member of the cast or crew has come forward to offer comment. Dear readers, as you know, I have been covering the theater scene for more years than I care to name. In that time, I have seen every trick in the book: Pepper's Ghost, hidden trap doors, smoke and mirrors, misdirection. I can assure you, none of those were in evidence last night. What we witnessed was a true, I hesitate to use the word miracle, so I will say phenomenon.

Prior to last night, no one save those directly involved with *The Secret of Flight* had ever heard the name Clara Hill. Last night, she vanished. Her name will remain, known for the mystery surrounding it, but I do not think the woman herself will ever be seen again.

Personal Correspondence—Raymond Barrow
December 18, 2012

DEAR WILL,

I know it's absurd, writing you a letter. But a man my age is allowed his eccentricities. Eighty-eight years old, Will. Can you imagine it? I certainly never intended to be this old. The young have a vague notion they will live forever, but have any of them thought about what that really means? To live this long, to outlive family and friends. Well, since I *have* lived this long, I will indulge myself and write to you, even though it's old fashioned, and there's no hope of a response. Forgive an old fool. Lord knows I feel in need of forgiveness sometimes.

It's been fifty-seven years since Clara disappeared. Aside from you, she was my only friend. I wish you could have met her, Will. I think you would have got along—comrades in your infernal secrecy, your refusal to let anyone else in, but somehow always willing to listen to me go on about my problems.

I'm all alone now. The only one left besides the goddamn bird, the one Clara left me. It's still alive. Can you fucking believe it? Starlings are only supposed to live fifteen, twenty years at the most. I looked it up.

Rackham. That's what Clara called him. I didn't want to use him in the play, but Clara insisted, and now I'm stuck with the damn thing. He's not…natural. He's like Clara. I don't think he *can* die.

I'm ashamed to admit it, maybe you'll think less of me, but I've tried to kill him—more than once. He speaks to me in Clara's goddamned voice. Starlings are mimics, everyone knows that, but this is different. I tried to drown him in a glass of brandy. I tried to wring his neck and throw him into the fire. Do you know what he did? He flapped right back out into my face with his wings singed and still smoking.

To add insult to injury, he threw my own goddamn voice back at me, a perfect imitation. He said, "Leading ladies are a disease. You breathe them in without meaning to, and they lie dormant in your system. Years later, you realize you're infected, and there's absolutely nothing you can do about it. You spend the rest of your life dying slowly of them, and there's no such thing as a cure."

Do you remember? I said that to you, years ago. At least it sounds like the kind of pretentious thing I would say, doesn't it? I was probably trying to be clever or impress you. Did it work?

Pretentious or not, it is true. I'm infected, and Clara is my disease. She's here, under my skin, even though she's gone. Everyone's gone, Will. Even you.

Well, goddamn you all to hell then for leaving me here alone.

Yours, ever,
Raymond

Items Displayed in the Lobby of the New Victory Theater

1. Playbill—*The Secret of Flight* (1955)—Good Condition (unsigned)

2. Playbill—*Onward to Victory!* (1950)—Fair Condition (signed—Raymond Barrow, Director; William Hunter, Marion Fairchild, Anna Hammond, cast)

3. Complete Script—*The Secret of Flight* (1955)—Good Condition (signed, Owen Covington)

4. Press Clipping—*Herald Star*—June 17, 1925

"Victory Theater Under New Ownership"

A staged publicity photo shows Richard Covington shaking hands with former theater owner Terrance Dent. Richard's brother, Arthur Covington, stands to the side. The article details plans for the theater's renovation and scheduled reopening. The article provides brief background on the brothers' recent immigration to America from England. A second photograph shows the family posed and preparing to board a ship to America. Arthur Covington stands toward the left of the frame. Richard stands next to his wife, Elizabeth, his arm at her waist. Elizabeth rests both hands on the shoulders of their three-year-old son, Owen, keeping him close. None of the family members are smiling. To the right of the frame, standing with the luggage, is an unidentified young woman with dark hair thought to be Owen Covington's nanny. A shadow near the woman's right shoulder vaguely suggests the shape of a bird.

5. Press Clipping—*Herald Star*—August 7, 1976

"Fire Destroys Historic Victory Theater"

A half-page image shows the burned and partially collapsed walls of the Victory Theater. Dark smudges above the ruins show a sky still heavy with smoke. Certain patches might be mistaken for a densely-packed flock of birds. The article offers scant detail beyond that the fire started early in the morning of August 6, cause unknown. The blaze took several hours to bring under control. No casualties reported.

6. Press Clipping—*Herald Star*—December 1, 2012

"A New Life for the Victory Theater"

The image at the top of the page shows the exterior of the New Victory Theater. A brushed stainless steel sign bears the theater's name, and below it, an LED marquee screen shows the word Welcome. The article discusses the successful fundraising campaign leading to the construction of the New Victory Theater at the site of the original building. Brief mention is made of the architects' intent to incorporate elements salvaged from the old theater into the new design, however all the historic pieces are held by an anonymous collector who was unwilling to donate or sell them. The majority of the page is given over to pictures of the gala opening. The article notes that Raymond Barrow was invited to serve as honorary chair of the event, but he declined.

Incomplete Draft of *Murmuration* by Arthur Covington—typed manuscript with handwritten notes

(CLAIRE glances over her shoulder before hurrying to EDWARD's desk, rifling through the drawers.)

CLAIRE (to herself): Where is it? Where is he keeping it?

(As her search grows more frantic, she fails to notice EDWARD entering the room. EDWARD grabs CLAIRE by the arm.)

EDWARD: Are you trying to steal from me?

CLAIRE: You stole from me first. Where is it?

EDWARD: Stole from you? You live in my house. You eat my food. Everything you *own* is mine.

(CLAIRE tries to strike him. EDWARD catches her hand. He leans close, his jaw clenched in anger.)

EDWARD: Show me how it works, and I might forget about your attempted thievery.

(CLAIRE doesn't answer. EDWARD grips her harder, shaking her.)

EDWARD: There's some trick to it. Look at this.

(EDWARD rolls up his sleeve and shows CLAIRE a long gash on his arm.)

EDWARD: I shouldn't be able to bleed anymore. I shouldn't be able to die.

CLAIRE (her voice hard): It was never going to work for you, Edward. You can't steal a feather from a bird and expect to fly, or steal a scale from a fish and breathe under water. You can't change the nature of a thing just by dressing it up as something else.

EDWARD: Then tell me. Tell me how it works, and I'll let you go.

(ANDREW enters STAGE RIGHT, freezing when he see CLAIRE and EDWARD. Unnoticed, ANDREW hangs back, watching. EDWARD strikes CLAIRE. CLAIRE doesn't react. He knocks her down, pinning her, and puts his hands around her throat.)

God, this is shit. The whole thing is shit. It isn't enough. It doesn't change what happened. It doesn't make up for the fact that "Andrew" just stood there and did nothing. I stood in the hall and listened to them yell, and then when I finally got up the courage to go into the room, I froze instead of helping Clara. Not that she seemed to need my help. Speaking of which, what about the birds? How the hell do I stage the birds? No one would believe it. I don't believe it, and I was there. The room filling up with beaks and feathers and wings. Hundreds of birds coming out of nowhere while Clara lay there, and Richard throttled her, and I did nothing.

What the hell am I doing, writing this thing? Shit.

SUICIDE ATTEMPT THWARTED AT THE VICTORY THEATER!
Herald Star—April 19, 1955
Betsy Trimingham, Arts & Culture

THERE IS A HERO IN OUR MIDST, DEAR READERS. ONE, IT seems, who has been hiding in plain sight at the Victory Theater. For months now, the theater scene has been buzzing with speculation over the Victory's latest production, all of which is being kept strictly under wraps.

Last night, however, one cat escaped the bag. Owen Covington, son of late theater owner Richard Covington, prevented an unknown woman from leaping to her death from the theater's roof. As it so happens, not only is young Mr. Covington a hero, he is the author of Raymond Barrow's mysterious new play.

Although he declined to comment upon his heroic actions, I was able to unearth one piece of information at least. Owen Covington's play, scheduled to open at the Victory later this year, is titled *The Secret of Flight*.

As for the young woman whose life Mr. Covington saved, could she be a member of the cast? Has Raymond Barrow unearthed the next darling of the theater scene? Or is she merely some poor seamstress working behind the scenes? More scandalously, could she be Raymond Barrow's lover? The only clue Mr. Covington provided during my repeated requests for comment was an unwitting one. He said, and I quote: *Clara is none of your business.*

Who is Clara? Rest assured, dear readers, I intend to find out!

Personal Correspondence—Raymond Barrow

December 20, 2012

DEAR WILL,

Here I am, at it again. The old fool with his pen and paper. Did you know they reopened the Victory Theater earlier this month? Not *the* Victory Theater, of course, a new one with the same name where the old one burned. They wanted me to be on their godforsaken Board of Trustees or some bullshit. I almost wish I'd taken the meeting in person just to see the look on their bootlicking, obsequious little faces when I said no.

God, I'm an ass, Will. I was an ass back in the day, and I'm an ass now, just a donkey of a different color, as they say.

Maybe it's the new theater that has me dredging up all these memories. It's like poking an old wound, though there were some good times mixed in with the bad. There was Clara. And of course, there was you. If you could have seen… Well, it doesn't matter. I cocked it all up in the end.

I was so excited when Owen Covington brought me the script of his new play. He was a virtual unknown, this snot-nosed kid who couldn't hold his liquor, but God help me, I thought he would save my career. Old money and all that. I didn't know his family had fallen into ruin. His father murdered, his uncle a suicide. All their lovely money pissed away. I should have done my research, but live and learn.

The whole thing was a disaster from beginning to end. Even before Clara, before… The press was at my throat from the get-go, desperate to see me fail. Then goddamn Owen Covington goes and tries to kill himself. Like nephew like uncle, I suppose.

Clara saved his life. She stopped him from jumping off the Victory's roof, though the newspapers reported it the other way around. Made Covington out to be a hero. What was that horrid woman's name? Betty? Betsy Trimblesomething? She was the one who gave you that absolutely scathing review as my leading man in *Onward to Victory!* God, I hated her.

But there I go, rambling. I was telling you about Owen and Clara. After she saved him, Clara told me how much she wanted to let Owen jump. She showed me her palms. They were all cut up where she dug her nails in trying to stop herself from grabbing him. But she couldn't. She told me she couldn't help saving Owen, no matter how much she hated his family.

That was the closest she ever came to telling me anything about herself. Of course, I knew bits and pieces from Owen, not that I believed half of it. But then here was Clara, someone I trusted, saying the same thing. She said she'd known Owen as a child, that she'd been his nanny, and he was the only good thing to come out of the Covington family.

I asked her what the hell she was talking about, she and Owen looked exactly the same age. I thought maybe she'd finally open up all the way, maybe I'd finally get the truth out of her. Hell, I'd have settled for knowing her real name because I'm sure as shit it wasn't *Clara Hill*.

Instead of answering, Clara pointed out a flock of starlings. We were up on the roof of the theater, smoking, the way you and I used to do after rehearsals. That was the first place you kissed me. Do you remember? I was certain my mouth would taste like ash and whatever rotgut we were drinking and you'd be disgusted, but you weren't.

Are you angry that I spent time with Clara up there? There wasn't anything between us. We were friends. Actually, we became friends because of the roof. We'd both been going up there separately to smoke, and then we banged into each other one day and started taking our cigarette breaks together. It's a lucky thing we never burned the goddamn theater down.

I suppose that's how she found Owen, snuck up for a quick drag on her own and ended up saving his life.

Anyway, the birds. The sun was just starting to rise, and the birds were winging back and forth across the sky like one giant creature instead of hundreds of little ones. Clara watched them for a while; then she said, "Can you imagine what it's like, Raymond? Being part of something larger than yourself, knowing exactly where you fit in the world, then having it all ripped away from you, and finding yourself utterly and completely alone?"

God, Will, it's been years, and I can still hear her asking it. Even when she asked it, it had been two years since you'd been gone. When you died, Will... Well, I knew exactly what Clara was talking about. You were everything, and I couldn't even be with you at the end. I couldn't tell anyone how my heart had been ripped out, or cry at your grave.

Things are different now, but there's no one I want to cry for the way I wanted to for you.

Maybe that's why Clara and I got along so well. We were alike in our loneliness. We both had things we couldn't tell anyone about ourselves. Not all ghosts are about guilt. That's something else Clara told me once, and I understand her now. Some ghosts are about sorrow, and loss. But God, Will, of all the ghosts to have haunt me, why did it have to be hers, and not yours?

Ray

Incomplete Draft of *Murmuration* by Arthur Covington—typed manuscript with handwritten notes

(EDWARD and CLAIRE face each other in EDWARD's office, the same setting as their earlier confrontation. Light flickers through a screen painted to look like a window, suggesting a storm. CLAIRE holds a gun pointed at EDWARD.)

EDWARD: Give me the gun, Claire. We both know you won't shoot me.

CLAIRE: You don't know the first thing about me. You have no idea what I'll do.

EDWARD: Elizabeth is upstairs. She'll hear the shot and call the police. There's nowhere for you to go. You'll be caught, and you'll hang.

CLAIRE (laughing bitterly): It doesn't matter. They can't kill me. It doesn't matter what you took from me, I still can't die. But you can.

(CLAIRE steadies the gun. EDWARD finally shows a hint of fear.)

EDWARD: Claire, be reasonable. I can—

CLAIRE: No, you can't. You can't do anything. You tried to steal from me, but my life can't be stolen, not that way. When you couldn't steal it, you broke it, and now I can't fly away either. I can't leave this place, not while you're alive.

(EDWARD reaches for CLAIRE. OWEN enters STAGE RIGHT, dressed for bed. He looks between CLAIRE and EDWARD, confused, and takes a step toward CLAIRE.)

OWEN: Will you tell my bedtime story?

(CLAIRE fires. EDWARD falls, and OWEN puts his hands over his ears and screams. CLAIRE stands still for a moment, then drops to her knees. Running footsteps can be heard from offstage.)

CLAIRE (barely audible): It didn't work. I'm still here. Oh, God, it didn't work.

This is still shit. That's how it happened, but no one will believe it. The truth is too strange.

Clara shot Richard while Owen watched, and she didn't run away. She let them arrest her. She confessed, but there was never a trial. She vanished out of the cell where they were holding her. The police were mystified.

Shit. I could write my play closer to the truth. No one would know the difference except Elizabeth. Then she'd start asking questions. What's the point? I can never produce this goddamn play, for her sake and for Owen's.

Clara shot Richard with Owen standing right there watching. He doesn't remember, at least not consciously. His young mind couldn't cope, so he shuttered the information away, but something like that doesn't go away completely. It changes a person. It leaves a stain.

I took Owen to see a hypnotist. Elizabeth doesn't know. Dr. Samson put Owen into a trance, and Owen recounted word for word the whole exchange between Clara and Richard. In real life, Owen didn't walk into the room the way I wrote it in the play. He was hiding under Richard's desk, playing a game. He wanted to jump out and scare Clara. He saw the whole thing.

That's not the worst of it though. After describing his father's murder, Owen started laughing. Dr. Samson thought it might be some sort of defense mechanism, his mind, even hypnotized, trying to protect him. He asked Owen about it, and Owen said he was laughing because the bird-lady was making pictures in the sky. She was telling the starlings which way to fly, like she used to on the boat from England.

God help me, he was talking about Clara. I'm more sure now than ever—she isn't human.

TRAGEDY STRIKES THE VICTORY THEATER!
Herald Star—October 10, 1955
Betsy Trimingham, Arts & Culture

OWEN COVINGTON'S LIFE WAS CUT TRAGICALLY SHORT yesterday when he was struck by a subway train. As regular readers of this column know, Mr. Covington was both a playwright, and a hero. I spoke with a police officer who was "unable to comment on an ongoing investigation." He declined to say whether foul play was suspected, but I do wonder how a young man in the prime of his life could simply slip from the subway platform in front of an oncoming train.

Keep your eyes on this column, dear readers. The truth will out eventually, and I will report on it.

Personal Correspondence—Raymond Barrow
December 22, 2012

DEAREST WILL,

Here I am again with my pen and paper. I've been thinking a lot about paper lately, the pages Owen had from his uncle when he first pitched me the idea of his play. He wouldn't let me read them for myself, he just sort of waved them around in front of me and said he was going to use them as the basis for his script. He only had fragments, Arthur Covington killed himself without ever finishing the play.

Of course I read those fragments eventually. It wasn't snooping, just protecting my investment. Besides, it was Owen's fault for passing out drunk on my couch with the damn pages still in his jacket pocket.

It was all there—Owen's father, Richard, his uncle, Arthur, and Clara. Of course in the play they were Edward, Andrew, and Claire, but it's obvious who they were supposed to be. Except it was fiction. Fantasy. Or maybe I was too stubborn to see what was right in front of my face.

This is what I think now: Owen's father did something terrible to Clara a long time ago. Clara murdered him, and Owen witnessed the whole thing. Of course, Owen didn't remember it happening, not consciously. Trauma and all that. But on some primal level he did remember. He was in love with Clara, or he thought he was. It was all tangled up in guilt and her killing his father, like some goddamned soap opera, but real.

Clara loved Owen too, in her own way. Not the way he wanted her to, but like a mother bird that hatches an egg and realizes a cuckoo has snuck its own egg into her nest. Her baby is gone and she's accidentally raised the cuckoo's child, but she defends it and she cares for it because that's her nature, and it's not the baby's fault after all.

It's why Owen tried to kill himself. He thought it would set her free. And it's why Clara couldn't let him.

At first I didn't believe it, any of it, but the more time I spent around them, the more time I spent with Clara... God, Will. You were gone, and I didn't have anyone else. I thought I could help Clara, do one good thing in my life and save her. I started thinking maybe Owen was right. Maybe if no one in his family was left alive, she could finally leave. I didn't...I just bumped him, really. He lost his balance. He was so utterly piss drunk, he probably didn't even feel it when the train hit him.

I never told Clara, but I think she knew. She was the one who insisted the play go on, in Owen's memory. I tried to convince her to leave. I'd just killed a man. I couldn't think straight. I was raving, shouting at her. I think I almost hit her. But Clara just looked at me with this incredible pity in her eyes. She put her hand on my arm, and said, "Grief can change the nature of a person, Ray, when nothing else can. Enough loss, and it weighs you down, you forget how to fly."

She told me everything I needed to know, Will, but I didn't know how to listen.

I didn't know how to listen when you told me you needed help all those years ago. The empty bottles, the needles; I refused to see it because I didn't want it to be true. I should have listened. I miss you, Will.

Yours, always,

Ray

Personal Correspondence—Raymond Barrow

October 20, 1955

DEAR RAY,

This is it, our big night. *The Secret of Flight* opens, and I don't know what will happen after that. There's something I'm going to try, Ray, and if it doesn't work, I might not see you again. So I wanted to say thank you for everything you've done for me, and everything you tried to do. You're a good friend. I don't have many of those, so believe me when I say our time together meant a lot to me even though I couldn't tell you everything about me. Instead, I'm giving you this story. It's the best I can do, Ray. I hope you'll understand.

Love,
Clara

The Starling and the Fox

ONCE UPON A TIME, THERE WAS A FOX, AND THERE WAS a starling. They weren't really a fox and a starling, they only looked that way from the outside, but for the purposes of this story, those names will do. This happened far away, in another country, many years ago.

The starling was flying, minding her own business, when she spotted a tree with lovely branches. She landed on one and discovered a fox lying across the tree's roots, crying piteously.

"Oh, they have killed me," the fox said. "I shall die if you don't aid me."

The starling couldn't see anything wrong with the fox, but she didn't see the harm in helping him either.

"What is it you need, sir fox?" she asked him.

"Only a feather from your beautiful wing, and I will be well again," the fox said.

The starling was doubtful. She looked again and she couldn't see any blood on the fox's fine fur, but he continued moaning as she looked him over, and it certainly sounded as if he might die.

The starling chose one of the small feathers near the top of her wing. She didn't think it would hurt to pull it out, and she didn't think she would miss it either. As she took hold of it in her beak, the fox cried out again.

"Not that feather! Only the long feather at the tip of your wing will do. The straight and glossy one that shines like a still pool at midnight, even when you think there is no light at all."

The starling thought the fox sounded a little foolish with his poetic language and the way he carried on, but the fox rolled on his back, weeping, and put a paw over his eyes. His tongue lolled from his mouth, and surely he would die at any moment if she did not help him.

The starling took hold of her longest and straightest feather with her beak, and pulled. It hurt, worse than anything she had ever felt, like the stars and the moon and the sun going out all at once.

"Good. Now bring it down to me, quickly!" the fox said, jumping to all fours, even though he had been at death's door a moment ago.

Dazed with pain, the starling hopped down to him, half tumbling as she went. She presented the feather to the fox.

"Are you saved now?" she asked him.

"Very much so," the fox replied, and his eyes were bright.

"Then I will take my leave," the starling said.

She spread her wings, but when she tried to take flight, she found she could not. Without her longest, straightest feather, she couldn't fly. She leapt toward the sky again and again, but crashed back to the ground every time.

The fox watched her impassively through all her attempts.

"Help me, sir fox," she said when she had finally exhausted herself.

"Surely I shall," he said, and stepped forward, snapped her up in his jaws, and swallowed her whole.

This is the moral of the story: You should never trust a wild animal. A fox cannot change its nature no matter how it dresses itself up, or what fine words it uses. It will always hunger. If you let your guard down, even for a moment, it will devour you whole.

_____

iPhone Audio and Video Recording—Raymond Barrow

December 26, 2012

[THE IMAGE SWINGS, SHOWING THE FLOOR, A MAN'S feet, and a desk cluttered with papers. A starling perches on a corner of the desk, briefly visible before the camera turns to show the face of Raymond Barrow.]

BARROW: There, you see, Will? I've been dragged kicking and screaming into the twenty-first century after all. My great niece, Sarah's daughter, gave me one of those infernal iPhone things. They were all over for Christmas yesterday, and spent most of the day showing me how to use it. Sarah suggested I might like to record some of my personal recollections of the good old days, something to preserve for generations to come. Ha! If the future is interested in a washed up old has-been who failed at every important thing he ever turned his hand to, then I pity them. But there is something I want to show you, so maybe this thing will be good for something after all.

[The camera turns to face outward again, the image bouncing while Barrow holds the phone in front of him as he walks. The camera catches glimpses of an ornate entryway, a crystal chandelier, a sweeping staircase. Carvings, hangings, sketches, and paintings on the walls depict birds of all kinds. The camera approaches a massive grandfather clock standing next to a door set beneath the curving staircase. The wooden case is chased with mother of pearl, showing a heron standing placidly among a cluster of reeds.]

BARROW: You see, I did all right for myself in the end. Not that I deserved to, but life isn't fair, is it?

[Barrow reaches for the door, holding the phone steady in his other hand. A flight of stairs leads down. There's a rustle from behind the camera, and Rackham, the starling, flies past Barrow's shoulder, disappearing down the stairs. Barrow stumbles, catching himself against the wall, but doesn't fall.]

BARROW: Damn bird will be the death of me.

[The image is dark as Barrow gropes his way to the bottom of the stairs, and flicks on a light. The camera shows rows of red velvet seats on a raked floor, facing a stage. The curtains are open, the set bare save for a painted screen backdrop, meant to look like a window.]

BARROW: It's the Victory Theater. I bought up everything they could salvage after the fire, and had it all restored. What they couldn't restore, I had rebuilt, exact replicas.

[The image wavers again as Barrow moves to a row of seats half-way to the stage. He sits, steadying the camera against the back of the chair in front of him.]

BARROW: I salvaged too much, Will. I was right, all those years ago when I said leading ladies are a disease. I've been carrying Clara in my blood for fifty-seven years, and there isn't any cure. All I ever wanted to do was help her, Will, but I think I know why she chose me. It's what she said about ghosts, and loss, and sorrow. A man can't change his own nature, but the world can change it for him if he lets his guard down. I let my guard down. I fell in love with you. I left myself open, and where did it get me?

[Barrow doesn't move, but the house lights in theater dim, and the lights begin to rise slowly on the stage. As the lights reach full, they reveal a woman with dark hair, wearing a beaded gown, standing center stage.]

BARROW: That's her, Will. It's Clara.

[There's a faint translucence to Clara's form, but the starling flies from behind the camera and lands on Clara's shoulder. She smiles.]

BARROW (softly): That's what all my love earned me, Will. A ghost, but the wrong one.

[Clara turns toward the camera, and the man behind it. Her expression is sad, but fond. She smiles, but it's pained. Clara raises her arms. As they reach their full extension, birds pour forth from the spot where she stands. Her dress falls, crumpled, to the floor. Dozens, hundreds of starlings boil up toward the ceiling like a cloud of smoke. When they reach the ceiling, they spread outward.

Barrow tilts the camera to show the birds as they pull together into a tight formation and fly toward him. He nearly drops the phone, and the view swings to show him in profile as the birds stream around him. Their wings brush his hair, his skin. His cheeks are wet.

The murmuration flows through the theater. The birds make no noise in their flight. Barrow steadies the phone, turning the camera to face him again. The birds are gone. He is alone.]

BARROW: It's the same thing every night. Every goddamn night for fifty-seven years. I tried to set her free, and she came back. She came back, Will, so why the hell didn't you?

[Barrow fumbles with the camera for a moment. The rustle of wings sounds and the starling lands on Barrow's shoulder. The recording ends.]

———————————————

A Bouquet of Wonder and Marvel

Sean Eads

THE LEADVILLE MINERS, THE PAINTED LADIES AT THE bar and even the piano player laughed at Benson, waving the check in the air and begging again for help.

"We're all rich here. *Metal* rich. No one cares about the promises of a slip of paper."

"It's your Christian duty to help a neighbor. Georgetown is in trouble!"

More sneers showed Benson the futility of his efforts—until the check was pinched out of his grip. He turned to find a man looming over him, regarding the check with heavy-lidded eyes.

"The amount is blank."

"I'm authorized to go as high as need be to get help," Benson said, sweating. Who was this stranger? He must have stood six-foot-three and wore a suit of purple velvet under a yellow frock coat lined with thick fur.

"Your accent is charming, and your pleading makes it more so."

"I'm from Mississippi and my need is great. Give me back that check so I can hire someone who'll help me."

"Well, I'm from Ireland and *my* need is also great—for money. I don't share your fellow Americans' prejudice against paper, I assure you. My name is Oscar Wilde, I am a visitor and I will be happy to help."

Benson laughed, looking the man up and down. "*You?*"

If Benson's response annoyed him, the Irishman didn't show it. Instead he gestured at the room. No one paid them any mind, conversation and the piano music resuming just as quickly as Benson's pleadings interrupted them. "You seem to have slim options. But then I find Colorado is a place of immense thinness."

"What?"

"The air—breathless! The clouds—ribbons! The people—wraiths! The wind makes the dust dance in narrow wisps and the plants have spindles for leaves. This check is drawn on the account of a William Bruckner. Who is he?"

"My employer. I am Mr. Bruckner's gardener."

He found Wilde's eyes brightening, a strange contrast to the sorrow in his expression. "I fear for the fate of botanists in this land. But here miners are the true gardeners, aren't they? Their flowers bloom underground. Two days ago I was lowered into darkness to see a cultivation of gold blossoms, each petal glinting by oil lamp. A cold bouquet indeed."

"Mr. Bruckner might agree with you. He is a metallurgist and an engineer. Have you heard of the Bruckner Cylinder Furnace?"

"Should I have?"

"In Georgetown and beyond, the machine has brought Mr. Bruckner high esteem."

"And wealth enough to have a personal gardener in this unpromising climate."

Benson squared his shoulders, prepared to detail the pride he took in his work. Then he realized how he was falling under the Irishman's spell of complacency.

"Come with me then—if you'll truly help. I'll take *anyone* at this point."

He held out his hand for the check, but Wilde only folded it and tucked it into his breast pocket.

They were in a coach less than an hour later—merely the time it took for Wilde to have his trunk loaded. The Irishman seemed to swell to fill the space of the carriage, so that Benson felt he must draw up his knees up to be accommodating. The fur lining

of Wilde's frock coat settled around the back of his neck like a peacock's plumage. A cravat of purple silk was knotted and bowed at his Adam's apple and he wore his hair as long as a woman's.

"Would you be so good as to explain what trouble Georgetown is having? Since no one in Leadville seemed to care one way or the other, I didn't have the opportunity to eavesdrop."

"Leadville!" Benson said. "I only came there because they're the nearest place of any size. I should have known they wouldn't care."

"I take it there's a rivalry?"

Benson shook his head. "They mine gold here. In Georgetown it's silver."

"A schism worthy of Catholics and Protestants. But what is troubling Georgetown that you come seeking help with a blank check?"

"It began when William—"

Wilde leaned forward. "Who is William?"

"I meant Mr. Bruckner."

"Your employer."

"Yes."

"And you call him by his Christian name?"

Benson's fingers curled against his palms. "I don't know why I said that. It's not proper."

"That's what makes it so American. Please continue."

"Men came to see Mr. Bruckner. He is older and reclusive now. But they kept insisting he go with them. I know he'd given them an improved version of his furnace, and it seemed they had questions. He relented and went with them, but returned less than an hour later, badly shaken. He took straight to bed and babbled in German."

"Is that his native tongue? Was William once *Wilhelm*?"

"Yes," Benson said.

"And you don't know German?"

"Very little. Only *mein liebster freund*."

"*My dearest friend*," Wilde said automatically. "I had a German governess as a boy. She taught me her language, and its stories. I'm curious who taught you that phrase."

Benson's cheeks flushed. "There are many Germans in Georgetown. I overheard it."

"Eavesdropping is the thrifty man's college."   **269**

"Well, the next day, in town, I heard people talking about strange problems in the mines. One old shaft suddenly flooded full of water, drowning several men. Another miner said his bore holes ran red and wet, like the rock walls were bleeding."

"Strange occurrences indeed," Wilde said. "But surely not enough to make you flee in search of help."

Benson stared out the coach window and shivered. "When I went back to gardening, I was on my hands and knees, pulling at a weed. The root was excessively long. I pulled and pulled. Then—suddenly—something pulled back. A force yanked so hard I was thrown face down into the dirt. I swear I heard a whisper coming up through the earth, and that made me run inside."

Wilde drew his coat around him. "This is truly wonderful and unexpected. It's been a long time since we lived in an age of wonder. Instead we live in an age of marvels, which is not the same thing at all."

"What's the difference?"

"Marvels are constructed—engineered—while wonders happen naturally. Or perhaps I should say they are engineered by…a different power, one the mind of man at present has little consideration for. Wonders are often very small, I think, like a moment of fidelity in marriage. Marvels are always large. Mr. Bruckner's furnace strikes me as a great marvel. It conjures visions of enormity."

"It is large. A man could sit upon another man's shoulders and still not see over the central chamber."

"And what does it do?"

"Removes sulfur from ore."

"Sulfur?"

"I couldn't tell you how it's done. But with the sulfur removed, the ore becomes far more valuable. His new enhancements have increased the furnace's speed and power. The smell of sulfur is particularly strong when the cylinders stop. That means more has been extracted from the ore."

Wilde sat back, a bemused smiled on his face. He began to laugh.

"What is it?" Benson said.

"I think I've deduced the problem."

Benson leaned forward. "What is it, Wilde?"

"Quite simply, I think the Devil has come to Georgetown."

"ODD THE STATION'S SO EMPTY," WILDE SAID, EMERGING from the coach when they arrived the next day. Benson was already out and looking around, and seeing Wilde squeeze his body from the narrow confines reminded him of a caterpillar emerging from its cocoon as simply a larger caterpillar, no butterfly transformation in evidence.

"It's still in the early morning."

"If the people of Georgetown don't agree with the sunrise, I shall find myself most happy here. Dawn is best experienced at noon."

Benson walked around the coach. They were by the train station, at the edge of town, and even in the early morning one normally found people milling here and there, along with several dogs looking for a handout. He turned his gaze to the mountains whose slopes created the valley where Georgetown nestled. The fresh morning light did nothing to change his first impression from over a year ago. They were piteously ugly from aggressive logging, leaving stumps and sickly underbrush most prominent to observation.

He became aware of an unearthly silence. Normally the mountains hummed with the sound of equipment, the steam engines and oar carts that put the hillsides under siege. Even at night, when the miners turned their attention to drink and the streets echoed with rowdy intrigues, one heard above it all the massive waterwheels cranking as water from the Georgetown reservoir sluiced down through the Guanella Pass over a mile away and dropped down upon them some seven hundred feet.

Even *they* were silent.

Benson returned to find Wilde staring at the blank check. He scowled. "You seem incredibly unconcerned about this. Yesterday you thought we were dealing with nothing short of Satan."

"Merely a *quip*. But the Devil is rather impractical as an explanation for Georgetown's troubles. If the coachman will be so good as to take my trunk down, we'll then go and see your William—excuse me, your Mr. Bruckner."

Benson turned to the coach. The driver wasn't there. He regarded Wilde, who'd noticed the absence too. "He must have gone inside the station manager's office," Benson said, and went over to see. The door was locked. He peered inside the dusty window.   **271**

Empty.

He returned to Wilde with his hands up and open. The Irishman laughed. "Our coach was driverless? Perhaps the Devil deserves more credence."

"We must find Mr. Bruckner right away," Benson said, pivoting to head into town. But Wilde grabbed his shoulder.

"My trunk," he said.

"You can't be serious."

"Not usually, but I'm afraid I insist on my luggage. And as you're the only manual laborer in an area where things seem to disappear rather quickly, I'd like my trunk removed before the carriage itself becomes…immaterial."

Benson cursed in disbelief, but he climbed up and unstrapped the box, lugging it down with a thud. "Here are your damn clothes!"

Wilde bent to unlatch the lid. "It's the accessories that make the outfit." Benson watched him sift through layer upon layer of fabric until, after a minute of digging, Wilde held up a silver pistol for the sunlight's worship.

"That's beautiful," Benson said.

"A Webley Bull Dog. At the moment, the United Kingdom's second most popular export to America—after myself. I received it as a gift in Leadville the day before meeting you. Funny how the best souvenirs of home are those you travel thousands of miles to obtain. Nevertheless, it's fully loaded and I believe in excellent working order. The Devil, dear Benson, doesn't stand a chance."

THEY HAD ONLY TAKEN A FEW STEPS TOWARD TOWN when the station manager's door opened and a horribly aged dwarf stepped out, shrunken and stooped, his shoulders dominated by a hump. The air turned solid in Benson's lungs as he saw the man's shriveled face. A decrepit, clawed finger rose in caution against grinning lips.

This was not a human being.

"Fire, Wilde," Benson managed.

The Irishman raised the gun and but didn't shoot.

"*Finde mich—finde sie—wo meine Blumen wachsen.*"

The thing laughed and raised its hands. The earth trembled at once, throwing Benson and Wilde off their feet. A sinkhole opened up beneath the creature's feet and it slipped out of sight as surely as a ship caught in a whirlpool. Wilde scrambled up, pulling Benson with him and they stared down a perfectly round chasm no wider than a person.

"How far down do you think it goes?"

"Deeper than even the bravest Alice would dare."

"That *thing* spoke to us."

"In German—curiously enough."

"What did it say, Wilde?"

"The creature told us to find it—and *them*—in the place where *its* flowers grow. It seems you're not the only cultivator in the area, Benson. Though I fear for the lover who receives a bouquet from its garden."

"Let's find Mr. Bruckner."

"Indeed," Wilde said. "Let's find *anyone*."

The streets were as empty as the station. Benson rushed up to the door of D.H. Miller's barbershop and barged through. All he found were quantities of hair all over the floor. A queer sensation overtook Benson. He imagined several people simply vanishing out from underneath their scalps, leaving the hair to fall like tufts of feathers in their wake.

Wilde waited for him outside. "I tried the office of your town newspaper. There were no reporters, no editors, not even a telegraph operator."

"This can't be," Benson said. "Where did everyone go? Ten thousand people live here!"

They reached the McClellan Opera House on the corner of 6th and Taos. A placard outside read—

One Night Only
Callender's Minstrels!
A Colossal Congress of Colored Celebrities!
Beautiful Scenery
Life-Like Pictures
Old-Time Songs
The Steamboat Race
The Levee Roustabouts

"One night? This sign looks more weathered than that." **273**

"It went up just before I left for Leadville."

"Then the town must have emptied very quickly thereafter."

Benson reared back and kicked the placard onto its side and stomped it.

"Appropriately theatrical," Wilde said.

A slow, squealing sound drew their attention. The opera house door opened, and three more creatures like the dwarf from the station office stepped out. They looked identical and carried pickaxes. The trio gave a disagreeable sneer and twisted away from the sunlight.

Wilde grabbed Benson's elbow. "They're blinded—seize our chance." They started running with the quietest footfalls they could manage, a tiptoed dash up the block to the corner of the bank. Benson pressed his back flat to the brick and panted. After a year in Georgetown, he thought he'd gotten used to the thin air. Panic had reverted him back to his first day.

Wilde risked a glance. "I see them. They're going in the opposite direction."

Benson looked too and thought back to his childhood. After the war, when he was only five, Union troops were stationed in his town and they made regular harassing patrols in the streets, knocking on doors at all hours of the day and night. They had made his mother cry. Remembering her tears, Benson's loathing rose. The creatures moved from building to building, dragging the heads of their pickaxes behind them, generating small clouds of dirt in their wake.

There was a scream.

"My God," Benson said as a boy came running from one of the buildings. The creatures raised their pickaxes and pursued. Their gait reminded Benson of a goose, but their swiftness was more like geese in flight. They fell upon the boy. Benson felt a burst of heat from Wilde's body and saw his right hand gripping the Webley very tight.

The creatures stepped away, revealing heavy manacles on the child's wrists and ankles. A metal collar seemed to weigh the boy's neck down.

"How?" Benson said.

"It's as if they forged them from the dirt."

They watched one monster pull the boy on the end of a chain. The other two continued their patrol.

"Where are they taking him?"

Wilde did not respond right away. Then, softly, he said, "The mines. And I wager that's where the rest of the populace is, too. Which mine is largest?"

"I have no idea. There must be hundreds of different shafts. Maybe thousands."

"Surely you have some idea of which—"

"I'm a gardener! Don't act like I'm supposed to *know* anything about the mines."

"Of course not," Wilde said, holding out his hands in a placating gesture. "I only wish I'd paid more attention when I made my descent in Leadville. My guides were eager to explain the process and procedures of mining, but I was too enthralled with the poetry of their bodies to care much about the prose of their labor."

Benson clamped his teeth down against a gasp at such frankness. Wilde flashed amusement but graveness soon returned, and Benson stepped back as the Irishman straightened to his full height. His hair was damp and the beads of sweat on his forehead looked unnatural. Sweat belonged on Wilde's broad white brow about as much as sea foam should be found on a cactus.

"I've been puzzling over why the creature should speak in German. It makes me wonder about something, Benson. I said sulfur was the Devil's odor, and that's so. But perhaps it's the scent of other monstrosities as well."

"I don't understand."

"I'm not sure there is anything to understand yet. How far away is Mr. Bruckner's house?"

"Five blocks."

"Then we must hurry. He might be there if he is as reclusive as you say. These patrols are either poorly sighted or not very thorough if a boy could have eluded them this long. They might not expend the energy on a solitary old man."

They again broke into a pace of quick but careful steps that nevertheless rang like alarm bells in Benson's mind. He imagined his tread sending tremors into the earth, identifying their location. Any moment the earth would open up in a personal sinkhole to hell.

They reached the house and stood in astonishment.

"You, sir, *are* a most remarkable gardener."

In any other circumstance, Benson would have cherished the remark. Instead the words chilled him by confirming his eyes weren't playing tricks. The front yard blazed with blooms of yellow, purple, red and blue. The clusters grew so thick it was as if the yard had been seeded with flowers rather than grass.

"This…this is not my doing."

"Are you sure?"

"I think I'd know! My own garden is my own garden," Benson said. "I don't even recognize these plants. Most of my focus was on asters. They seemed to do the best for the soil and climate. But they shouldn't be blooming until months from now."

"I have a small knowledge of flowers, Benson. These *aren't* asters."

"No."

He bent to touch one. Wilde told him to stop, but he ignored the caution. He pinched one golden bloom and received such confusion from his fingertips he jerked his hand away.

"What is it, Benson?"

"It's cold—*icy*. And the texture…"

"Go on."

"The petals felt hard—like metal."

He heard a distinct cry from the upstairs window. Benson's attention riveted upon the front door. "William," he said automatically, and raced onto the porch. Wilde caught him.

"We must be cautious!"

"To hell with caution. William screamed—"

"Or someone impersonated his scream. But we are past such cautions now. The cry came from upstairs. The bedroom, I take it?"

"I know nothing about Mr. Bruckner's bedroom."

"Do you not sleep here as well?"

"I'm Mr. Bruckner's *gardener*."

"Then one wonders at the strange alchemy turning *Mr. Bruckner* into *William* and back again so rapidly in your thoughts."

"You *dare*—"

"Yes, Benson, I dare *many* things. Let Socrates huff away about the unexamined life. Since the invention of neighbors and newspapers, such examinations are easy to come by. But the *unchal-*

lenged life is solely one's own fault—and the true impetus for all my actions."

He took out the blank check, tore it in half and let the separate pieces fall on the ground.

"We must have honesty or our endeavors here will fail. Come—lead me upstairs either to *your* bedroom or to *Mr. Bruckner's*—for I know they are one and the same."

Benson trembled, his heartbeat now so fast it seemed undetectable in his chest. He led Wilde into the house and up the steps. The bedroom door was closed and Wilde drew his Webley.

"Bruckner?" he called.

William's voice answered, feverish and rambling snippets of German he did not comprehend until suddenly—clearly—he perceived a key phrase:

"*—mein liebster freund—*"

He turned the knob, found it locked, and threw his shoulder against the door. Wilde joined him. The heavy wood shook as its frame creaked and splintered. Then it gave way and they stumbled through.

Two figures rested on the bed, apparently oblivious to the assault on the door. One was William—or some approximation of him. Benson's attention focused on the second. Something decrepit clutched William to its bosom. Grinning, gloating, a living sickness caressed William's left cheek with clawed fingers and drew the feverish sweat of his brow to taste in a lipless mouth.

William tried to sound out a word, but made only the same stutter—"*Koh—koh—koh—*"

"Kobold," Wilde said, and as if his voice gave the first indication of their presence, the nasty creature that cradled William snarled as it rose to a stature no less terrifying for its unimpressive height. In the confines of the room, the creature's body odor became stifling, a stench of crushed earthworms in loose, wet, stagnant soil. Its mottled skin reminded Benson of how his hands looked after digging in the garden, the natural paleness stained dark with heavier motes of dirt clinging in his hair like little moles and blisters.

"Kobold," Wilde repeated, stepping forward with the Webley raised. "My suspicions are confirmed. I know exactly what your kind is now."

He shot, and the creature sprang up, taking up a pickaxe Benson had not noticed. In a blur it swung the head around and Wilde's bullet deflected off it in a cascade of white sparks. The brief flare made the creature grimace and gave Benson his best look at William's face.

Only half of it remained human.

My God, what has the thing done to him?

Wilde kept the Webley trained on the monster. "Shall we duel, Kobold—the wonder of your magic versus the marvel of my gun?"

The thing leapt to the challenge. Wilde fired. If the gun hit the creature, the bullet had no effect. Benson dove as the pickaxe swung, narrowly missing his face. He looked up just as Wilde shot point blank into the fiend's head. The impact sent it staggering against the foot of the bed. There it slumped. Benson's experienced a moment of exultation—the thing was *dead*. But reality would not be denied. The creature reached up and pulled the bullet from the wound, holding it up before its eyes. "Köstliches silber."

It popped the bullet into its mouth like a date and chewed.

"My earlier assessment is confirmed, Benson," Wilde said, backing off fast. "Wonders are much superior to marvels."

The creature held its pickaxe up and followed. Wilde raised his hands in a last ditch effort at self-defense as the axe swung at him.

"Hör auf damit!"

William's voice. Benson saw him on his knees, reaching out toward the monster, which had frozen its attack. He went on speaking in German and the foul, misshapen dwarf answered back. Then it grabbed Wilde's right arm and began to drag him.

Wilde shouted and beat against his captor to no avail. Benson moved to help but William squeezed his shoulder with his transformed right hand. The claw-like fingers dug into his muscle.

"He's beyond your reach, Ben."

"He's here to help us!"

"Why are you here? I told you to run. I gave you the check to draw upon all my assets."

"I gave your check to *him*. I just wanted to get back here."

The remaining human half of William's face showed despair. "One person? Even an army won't help Georgetown now."

"What's happening? What was it Wilde said?"

"Kobold."

"That creature knew it."

"It reacted to its name. Kobold is *all* of their names. And it's *my* name."

Benson shook his head. "You're human, no matter what that thing was trying to do to you."

"It wasn't trying to make me wear a mask, Ben. It was trying to rip off the one I've been wearing."

"William, no—"

"I can't expect you to understand. I'm—the last of my kind. Or so I thought. How can I even attempt an explanation? I woke in darkness. I lived in darkness. There were none like me. When I hungered, I chewed rock and ore and was content—but so alone."

"William, you've lived in Georgetown more than twenty years. You're an engineer. You came here from Germany—"

He laughed bitterly. "Deep below it."

Benson's thoughts became a chaos. William worked his way out from under the blanket and sheet, revealing how his transformation extended further down his body. The sight provoked a sharp inhale from Benson, who turned his face to the wall.

"I'll never believe you're one of *them*."

"I deserve your rebuke and your hatred. What's happened is my fault. I did not realize the consequences of my actions."

William got out of bed. His right leg had shriveled up to a stumpy length, essentially leaving him an amputee. He balanced on his left foot, left hand bracing him against the wall. Benson saw this in his peripheral vision and William's struggle goaded him into standing too.

"What *are* your actions? How can you be responsible?"

"I encountered my first human in 1845—a young man adventuring on his own. I did not realize then that I lived deep inside a mine that had been abandoned many years. This man had become lost and I heard his terror and came to investigate. When I stepped into the light of his lantern, he shouted, 'Kobold!' and fled. Not understanding, I gave chase and captured him. He told me what I was. A creature of the dark, a spirit of the mines. I kept him with me despite his pleas, not understanding how his needs differed from mine until he died. Then I knew sorrow—and loss—and bitterness. Above all I had understanding and vowed to quit the **279** darkness. I found I could take his shape, and I walked into the sunlight in his clothes. I have lived the life he might have lived. But the mines pulled at my heart. I had to be near them. I put an ocean between myself and my origins and came here, to this place where the humans seemed so very much like me in their core. I tried to help them. I made my furnace—and it was my undoing."

"The smell of sulfur."

"Yes. Horrible to you. But to me it was like the scent of myself, the whiff of memory. And I knew there was something about the ore these men mined. Some *trace* of my own being—my own people. For many years I fought the urge to investigate. And then I met you."

Benson's lower lip trembled. "What could I have to do with any of this?"

"You gave me love. I thought I could give it back—"

"You did!"

"No, Ben. I tried. But—I was always lonely, but it grew worse in your company. This is not your fault. In a fashion, you and I have both been in a search for our own kind. Your strength convinced me to indulge a suspicion that more like me existed, but incorporeal and trapped within the rocks themselves. I altered my furnace in an attempt to bring them forth physically. And so I have—to this world's peril."

"How many are there?"

"Seven. More than enough to subjugate Georgetown."

"Seven against ten thousand!"

"You saw the effects of your friend's gun. The bullet is meaningless. But these kobolds are not the same as me. They are vengeful and malignant. I tried to plead with them but they wouldn't listen. They say there are thousands more of them awaiting their freedom, and only my furnace can do it. They don't know how to operate it though. That's the only reason my defiance hasn't brought death. They must be stopped."

"But how, if even guns won't work?"

"Help me downstairs. Help me—into the garden."

"THE FLOWERS," WILLIAM SAID, POINTING TO THE DE-ceptive blooms of cold metal. "Those are your weapons."

"How am I supposed to kill your people with *flowers*, no matter how strange they are?"

"They're not mere flowers, as you've already guessed. I forged them from the earth with the help of a power the kobolds don't comprehend—the power of your intention. You have thought your labors pointless and futile, but every bead of sweat you let fall into the soil was a seed of hope, and that hope carries into the blooms. Wield them as a dagger is wielded. Drive the petals into their backs."

Hesitating a moment, Benson knelt and gingerly pulled at a stem. It came free of the soil with a metallic sound, like a sword exiting a scabbard. The flower had almost no heft to it and yet he sensed tremendous power in the blooms.

"Quickly now. Gather your bouquet. Seven at least. No—eight. There must be eight."

"Why eight if there are seven of them?"

William stared at Benson until he understood.

"No," Benson said.

"You must, Ben. I'm not sure I know myself. I'm not sure this remorse I feel will last. I hear the mines calling to me more than ever. I hear the song of my people, and even if I am against them now, they *are* my kind. Take the eighth bloom. *There.* Now put it in the vase of my heart."

The ground began to tremble.

"Hurry, Ben! They're coming for us!"

He stepped forward. As he did, a sinkhole appeared on the spot he'd just occupied. He lunged forward into the embrace of William's human arm. It wrapped around his waist. His clawed hand took Benson's wrist and raised the flower to his chest.

More sinkholes appeared. The house itself shook, the roof starting to buckle.

"Now, Ben!"

Crying, he drove the stem against William's chest, still convinced it would simply bend and break. But William's mouth opened in a silent scream, and blood that was not red poured forth.

Then the sky sank out of sight.

HE PICKED HIMSELF UP AND CLUTCHED THE BOUQUET, as the sound of people crying grew louder. Benson scarcely believed the scene in front of him. A subterranean kingdom was being constructed, and the men, women and children of Georgetown labored in chains to expand its borders. They had no tools other than their fingernails.

A kobold stood glaring at him, its pickaxe raised. The creature charged him, swinging his weapon as he went. Benson drew a yellow flower and held it out, unable to help feeling foolish.

Until the bloom began to glow.

It flashed like the sun, and the kobold groaned and stopped, squeezing its eyes closed. Benson shot forward and plunged the bloom against the kobold's throat. At once the thing howled and the bloom burst into flames. The kobold pulled back, taking the flower out of Benson's grip. He watched the monster tugging on the stem but the flower only sank deeper into its throat.

The kobold fell forward onto its face and lay motionless.

"*Benson!*"

He spun and found Wilde at the entrance to a new shaft, laboring under heavy chains. Several cuts marked his face. He looked so worn and beaten Benson could not believe he'd been enslaved less than thirty minutes ago.

"I feel like I've been digging for days," he said, holding up his fingers. Wilde's nails were splintered and dark. "I think time must be experienced differently in the dominion of the kobold."

"How did you know their name?" Benson said as he tried to break the shackles.

"As I said, my German governess taught me both her language and its stories, particularly fairytales. And as I've learned in my travels in these states and territories, *everything* has an American cousin. Can you free me?"

Benson regarded the bouquet. He separated one flower from the rest and touched it against Wilde's collar. The invincible iron turned to dirt and Wilde's eyes gleamed. His wrists and ankles were freed in minutes.

"If civilization survives the kobolds, I'll have to add a segment to my lecture tour about the power of flowers. May I?"

He took three stems and held them up for inspection. "A wonder *and* a marvel. Let's get to work, Benson. The war of the roses demands a sequel!"

WHEN IT WAS DONE, THEY LED THE PEOPLE OF GEORGE-town out of the mines and into the light. From their condition and reaction, Benson figured Wilde's assessment was right: time must have moved differently in the mines. The men looked grizzled, their hair exceedingly long and filthy. Boys and girls no longer fit into their clothes. Everyone staggered as if not encountering sunlight in a year.

But they were alive.

Wilde said as much as the two of them trekked back to the ruins of William's house. When they arrived, they found the wondrous flowers were gone. There was only William, dead, his human disguise entirely ended.

"It's a shame you must remember him like this."

"I remember the person I loved. Nothing else matters. But no one else must know his identity."

"I shall be happy to help you bury someone so noble."

"No," Benson said, wiping his eyes before bending to take the small body into his arms. "I will do this alone."

He went off to sow a final seed as Mr. Bruckner's gardener.

———————————

Afterword

Yet each man kills the thing he loves
  By each let this be heard,
Some do it with a bitter look,
  Some with a flattering word,
    —OSCAR WILDE "The Ballad of Reading Gaol"

AND SO YOU HAVE COME TO THE END OF THIS BOOK, AND
so we come to the end of this Wildean journey as this is the final
volume of my year's best of gay-themed speculative fiction tales.
For a decade I've sought to gather from sources popular and eso-
teric what I thought best for readers in this field. My efforts have
always been to entertain neither gay readers who happen to enjoy
stories of aliens amongst us, knights challenging dragons, and
men facing ghosts from their past, nor spec-fic aficionados who
are open to stories about a man's passionate desire, if not love, for
another man—I've sadly learned in my more than twenty years
of reading, writing, and editing that the two camps rarely creep
outside these Eulerian Circles or discover the intersection, which
is where my heart and imagination lie.

   To those of you who have enjoyed this series, thank you. I wish I
could continue editing it forever, but practicality, never my strong

suit, demands that it end and I would rather it end well rather than having me utter *odi et amo*.

When I began *Wilde Stories* in 2008, only one story from the book came from one of the major sources of speculative fiction, a piece by Rebecca Ore from *Clarkesworld*. One story came from an anthology published by a major publisher, Lee Thomas's tale from Ellen Datlow's *Inferno*. The rest were small presses' releases, many very small and aimed at a decided gay male audience. If you wanted to find a great gay fantastical or weird story, your pickings were decidedly few.

Since then more and more of the stories I've reprinted for the series have come from the "mainstream" of spec fic publications. Most of the little gay venues with names like *Velvet Mafia*, *Blithe House Quarterly*, and even my own *Icarus*, have folded. When you grow up Jewish, you encounter the word *assimilation* in a different light than when you grow up as a science-fiction fan. I think readers nowadays have greater opportunities to find quality gay spec fic when they go to the bookstore, when they go online.

Another observation is the demographics of gay spec fic have thankfully widened. Ten years ago there was one person of color in the table of contents, Francisco Ibáñez-Carrasco. And while there are four times as many in this volume, it's less than half of the total, yet I'm pleased that I found greater diversity in whose stories were told and by whom.

I must thank the many kind folk who helped me bring this series to life and deserve to be part of the eulogy: Toby Johnson, Alex Jeffers, and Matt Bright provided the pleasing armatures for the stories; ten years of marvelous artists provided welcome façades that attracted the eye; to all the authors who allowed me to share their voice, especially folk like Hal Duncan, Rick Bowes, and the late Joel Lane. I appreciate the efforts of editors like Ellen Datlow, Gordon Van Gelder, John Joseph Adams, and Julia Rios, who alerted me to stories they thought I might want to include. Thanks also to Brit Mandelo who brought attention to queer spec fic at a time when few people did and paved the way for greater coverage of such books.

And lastly, thank you, Mr. Wilde, for allowing me to make a clever play upon your name; your story to me has always been an inspiration, the first decidedly queer man-made monster.

Good night,

Steve Berman

About the Contributors

RICHARD BOWES has over thirty-five years in the genre written six novels, four short story collections and over eighty stories. He has won two World Fantasy Awards, plus the Lambda Literary, Million Writers, and International Horror Guild awards. More of his stories have been reprinted in the pages of Wilde Stories than any other author.

MATTHEW BRIGHT IS a writer, editor and designer who can never decide which order those come in. His fiction has appeared in *Nightmare*, Tor.com, *Steampunk Universe*, *Clockwork Iris*, *A Treasury of Brenda and Effie*, *Glittership*, and others. He is the editor of several anthologies, including *Clockwork Cairo* and *The Myriad Carnival*. He lives in Manchester, England, where he designs books to pay the bills and keep his dog in the lifestyle to which she has become accustomed. Find him at @mbrightwriter on Twitter or Matthew-Bright.com online.

MARTIN CAHILL is a writer, reviewer, and essayist living in Astoria, Queens and working down at the tip of Manhattan, just askance to the Statue of Liberty. He is a Clarion Graduate and is currently a member of the NYC based writing group, Altered

Fluid. He has been published in Nightmare Magazine, *Fireside Fiction*, and *Beneath Ceaseless Skies*. He also writes nonfiction for *Book Riot*, Tor.com, *Strange Horizons*, and most recently, the Barnes and Noble Science Fiction and Fantasy Blog.

CHRISTOPHER CALDWELL is a queer Black American living in Glasgow, Scotland with his partner Alice. He was the 2007 recipient of the Octavia E. Butler Memorial Scholarship to Clarion West. His work has appeared in *Fiyah*, *Luminescent Threads: Connections to Octavia E. Butler*, and *Fantastic Stories of the Imagination*.

JOHN CHU is a microprocessor architect by day, a writer, translator, and podcast narrator by night. His fiction has appeared or is forthcoming at *Boston Review*, *Uncanny*, *Asimov's Science Fiction*, *Clarkesworld*, and Tor.com among other venues. His translations have been published or is forthcoming at *Clarkesworld*, *The Big Book of SF* and other venues. His story "The Water That Falls on You from Nowhere" won the 2014 Hugo Award for Best Short Story.

SEAN EADS is a librarian living in Denver, CO. He has been a finalist for the Shirley Jackson Award, Lambda Literary Award, and the Colorado Book Award. His first short story collection, *Seventeen Stitches*, was published in 2017. He is originally from Kentucky.

GREG EGAN is the author of twelve science fiction novels and more than fifty short stories. He has won the Hugo Award, the John W. Campbell Memorial Award, and the Japanese Seiun Award. He lives in Australia.

Singer, musician, writer and artist JOSEPH KECKLER has garnered acclaim for his rich, versatile voice and sharp wit. He performs widely and has appeared at Lincoln Center, Centre Pompidou, Miami Art Basel, and many other venues internationally. He is the author of numerous songs and short pieces and several evening-length performance pieces and plays; his work has been featured on BBC America and WNYC.

KARIN LOWACHEE was born in South America, grew up in Canada, and worked in the Arctic. Her first novel *Warchild* won the Warner Aspect First Novel Contest. Both *Warchild* and her third novel *Cagebird* were finalists for the Philip K. Dick Award. *Cagebird* won the Prix Aurora Award for Best Long-Form Work in English and the Spectrum Award. Her books have been translated into French, Hebrew, and Japanese, and her short stories have appeared in anthologies edited by Nalo Hopkinson, John Joseph Adams, Jonathan Strahan and Ann VanderMeer. Her fantasy novel, *The Gaslight Dogs*, was published through Orbit Books USA.

ADAM MCOMBER is the author of *My House Gathers Desires: Stories*, *The White Forest: A Novel* and *This New & Poisonous Air*. His work has appeared recently in *Conjunctions*, *Kenyon Review* and *Diagram*. He lives in Los Angeles, CA.

SAM J. MILLER's work has been nominated for the Nebula, World Fantasy, Crawford, Locus, and Theodore Sturgeon Awards, as well as the World Science Fiction Society Award for Best Young Adult Book, was long-listed for the Hugo and James Tiptree Awards, and has won the Shirley Jackson Award. His debut novel, *The Art of Starving*, won the Andre Norton Award for Best Young Adult Novel and was one of NPR's Best Books of 2017. His latest book, *Blackfish City*, was an Entertainment Weekly "Must Read."

A.C. WISE's fiction has appeared in places such as *Clarkesworld*, *Shimmer*, Tor.com, and the *Year's Best Horror* Volume 10, among other places. She has two collections published with Lethe Press, and a novella, *Catfish Lullaby*, forthcoming from Broken Eye Books. Her work has been a finalist for the Lambda Literary Award, and winner of the Sunburst Award for Excellence in Canadian Literature of the Fantastic. In addition to her fiction, she contributes a monthly review column to *Apex Magazine*, and the Women to Read and Non-Binary Authors to Read series to The Book Smugglers. Find her online at acwise.net.

DEVON WONG lives in Toronto, Canada, where he works in research communications and has just begun studying photography. In his spare time, he climbs rocks. His short prose fiction has been published by *Strange Horizons* and Tightrope Books. His comic book work has been published by Top Cow Productions, Outré Press, Comics Experience, and Source Point Press.

XEN is a New Orleans-born Southern boy without the Southern accent, currently residing somewhere in Seattle. He spends his days as a suit-and-tie corporate consultant and business writer, and his nights writing genre-bending science fiction and fantasy tinged with a touch of horror and flavored by the influences of his multiethnic, multicultural, multilingual background—when he's not being tackled by two hyperactive cats. He writes contemporary romance and erotica that flirts with the edge of taboo as Cole McCade. He wavers between calling himself bisexual, calling himself queer, and trying to figure out where "demi" fits into the whole mess—but no matter what word he uses he's a staunch advocate of LGBTQIA and POC representation and visibility in genre fiction. And while he spends more time than is healthy hiding in his writing cave instead of hanging around social media, you can generally find him @thisblackmagic and blackmagicblues.com.

About the Editor

The first gay story STEVE BERMAN remembers reading was Clive Barker's "In the Hills, The Cities" and he remembers the rush of forbidden excitement gripping him as well as the terrible shame that he could not openly share his passion because he was a closeted freshman in college. He no longer has such worries. If you cross paths with him, please tell him what gay stories you adore.

www.ingramcontent.com/pod-product-compliance
Lightning Source LLC
Chambersburg PA
CBHW030647020726
47493CB00006B/1906